JAMES KOCH

THE GLORKIAN WARRIOR
DELIVERS A PIZZA

PIZZA

:01
First Second
New York

For Eli and Oliver

Special thanks to Mark DeNardo, Miles Tilmann, and Rich Grillotti of PixelJam for all their hard work on The Glorkian Warrior and Glorkbot video games.

:01

First Second

Copyright © 2014 by James Kochalka

Published by First Second
First Second is an imprint of Roaring Brook Press,
a division of Holtzbrinck Publishing Holdings Limited Partnership
175 Fifth Avenue, New York, New York 10010

Cataloging-in-Publication Data is on file at the Library of Congress.

Paperback ISBN 978-1-59643-917-7
Hardcover ISBN 978-1-62672-103-6

First Second books are available for special promotions and premiums.
For details, contact: Director of Special Markets, Holtzbrinck Publishers.

First edition 2014
Book design by Colleen AF Venable

Printed in China by Macmillan
Production (Asia) Ltd., Kowloon,
Hong Kong (supplier code 10)

Paperback: 10 9 8 7 6 5 4 3 2 1
Hardcover: 10 9 8 7 6 5 4 3 2 1

BY ART
WE LIVE

CHAPTER ONE

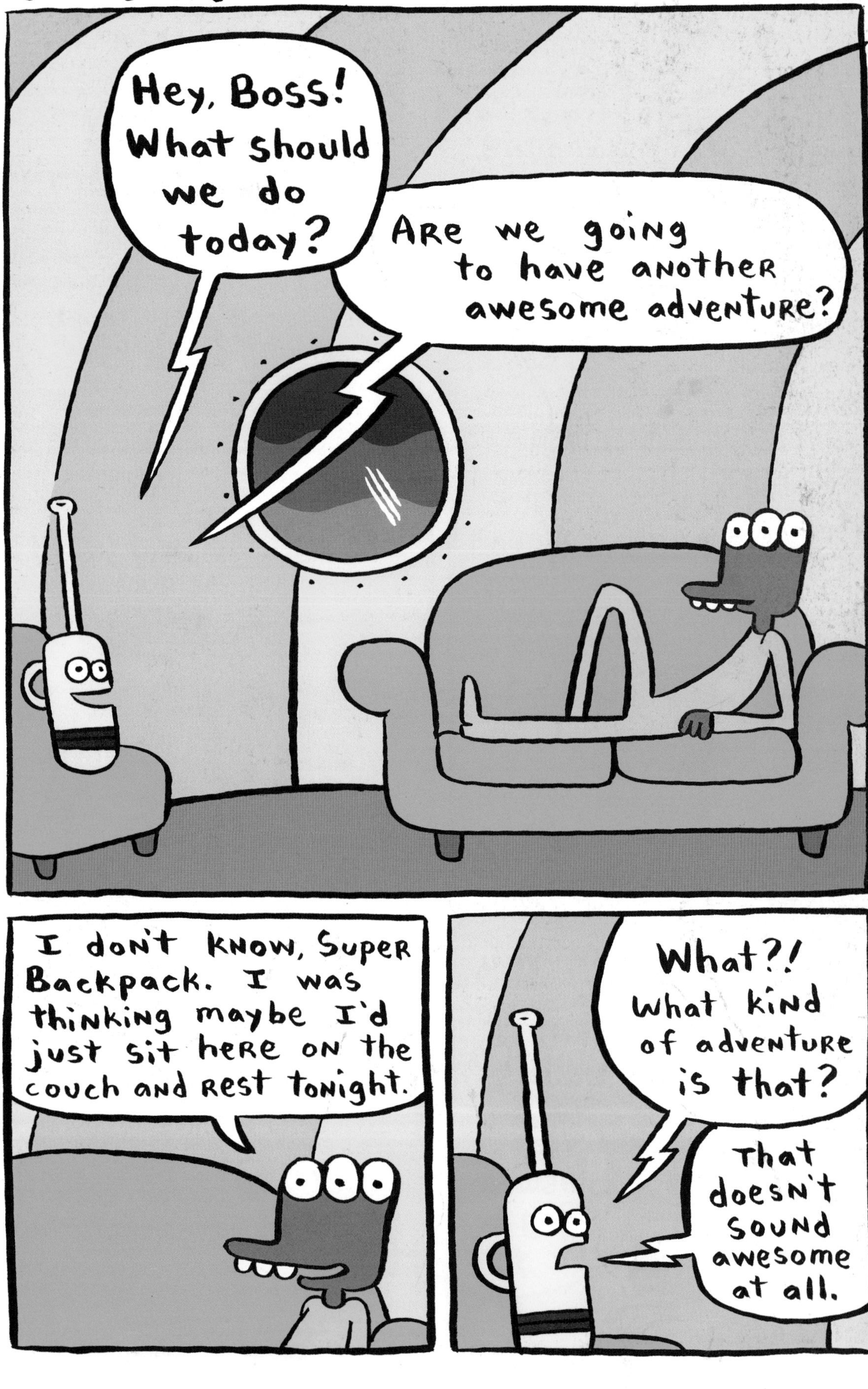
Hey, Boss! What should we do today?
Are we going to have another awesome adventure?
I don't know, Super Backpack. I was thinking maybe I'd just sit here on the couch and rest tonight.
What?! What kind of adventure is that?
That doesn't sound awesome at all.

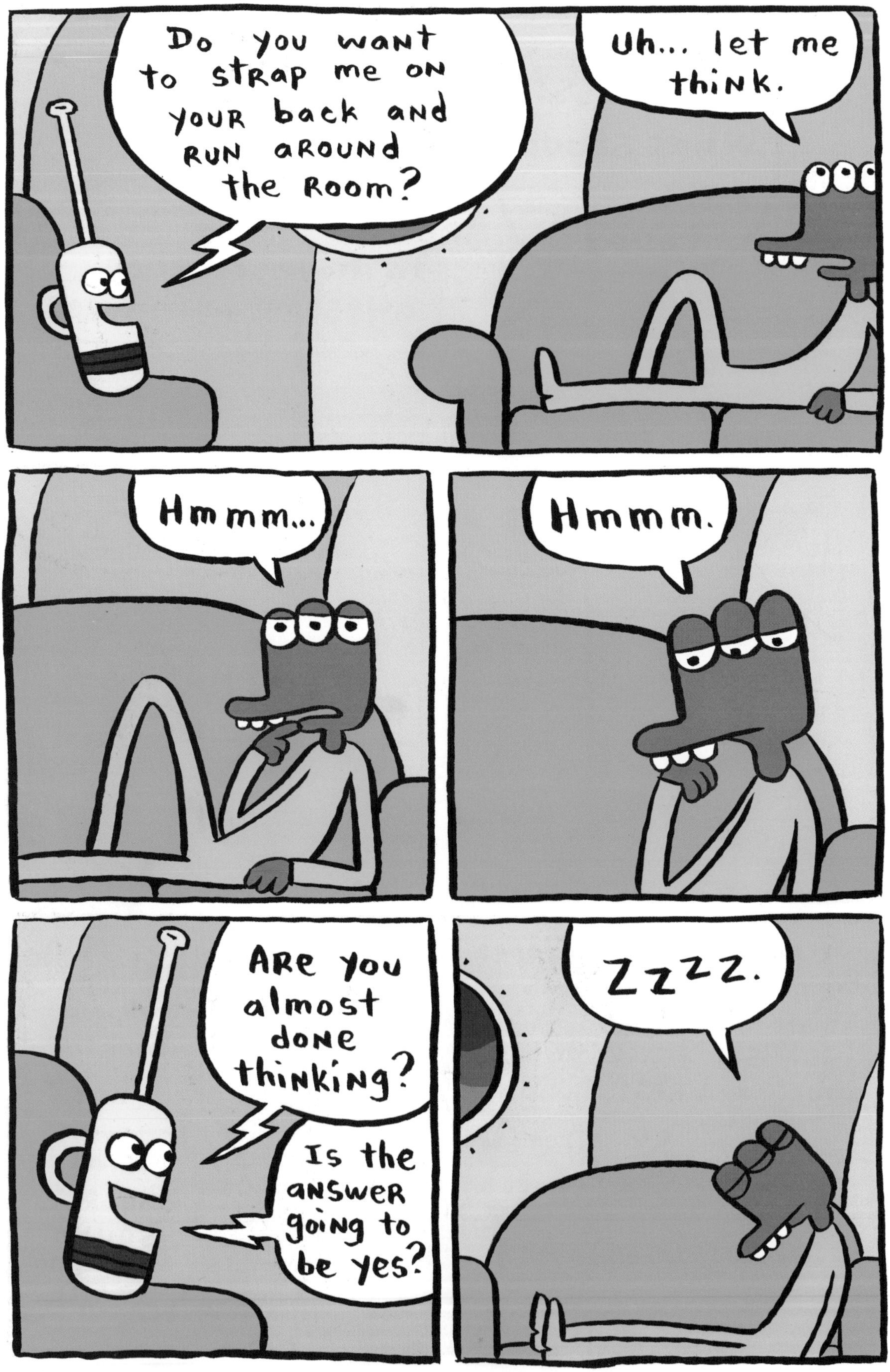
Do you want to strap me on your back and run around the room?
Uh... let me think.
Hmmm...
Hmmm.
Are you almost done thinking?
Is the answer going to be yes?
Zzzz.

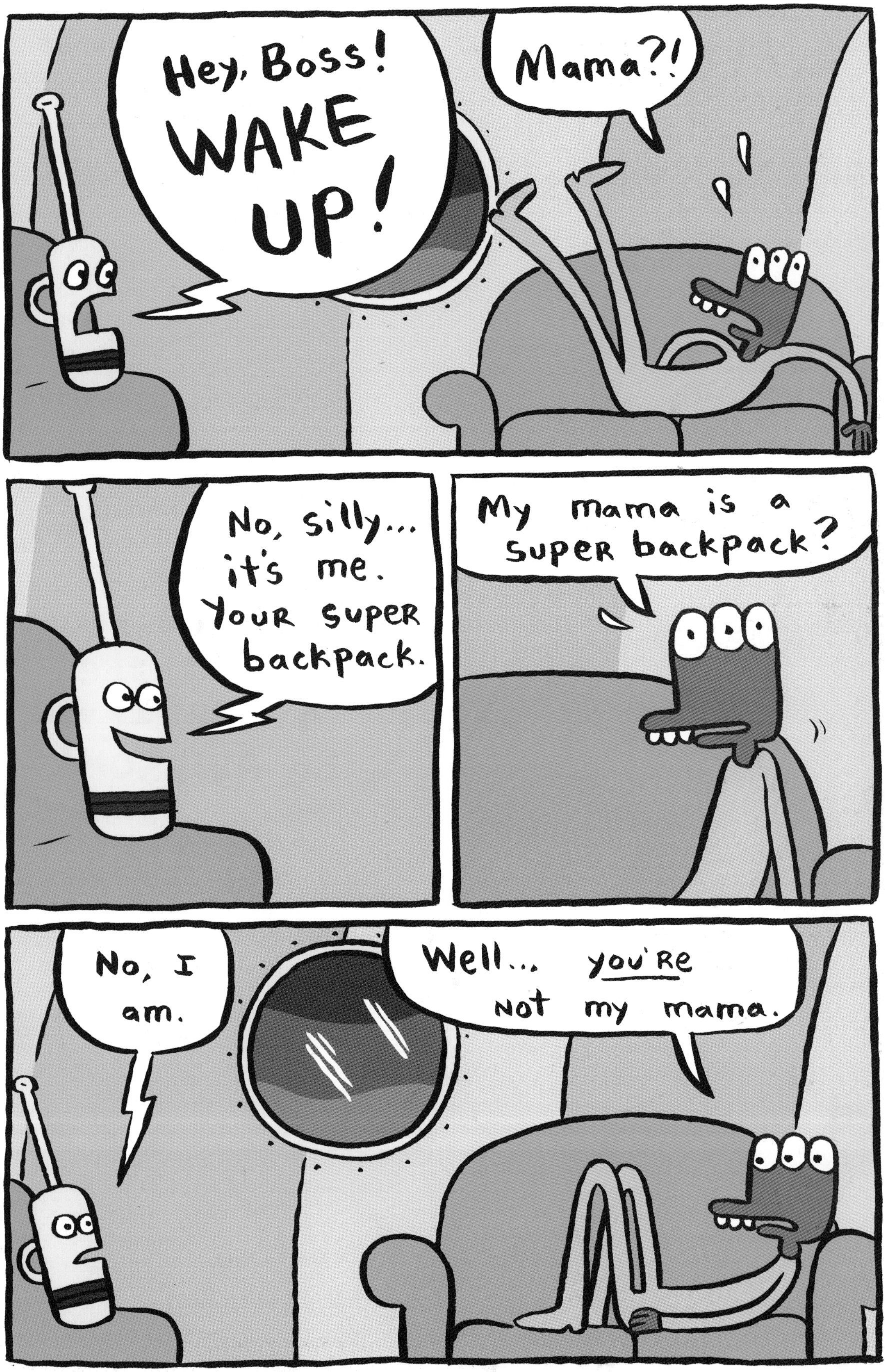
Hey, Boss! WAKE UP!
Mama?!
No, silly... it's me. Your super backpack.
My mama is a super backpack?
No, I am.
Well... you're not my mama.

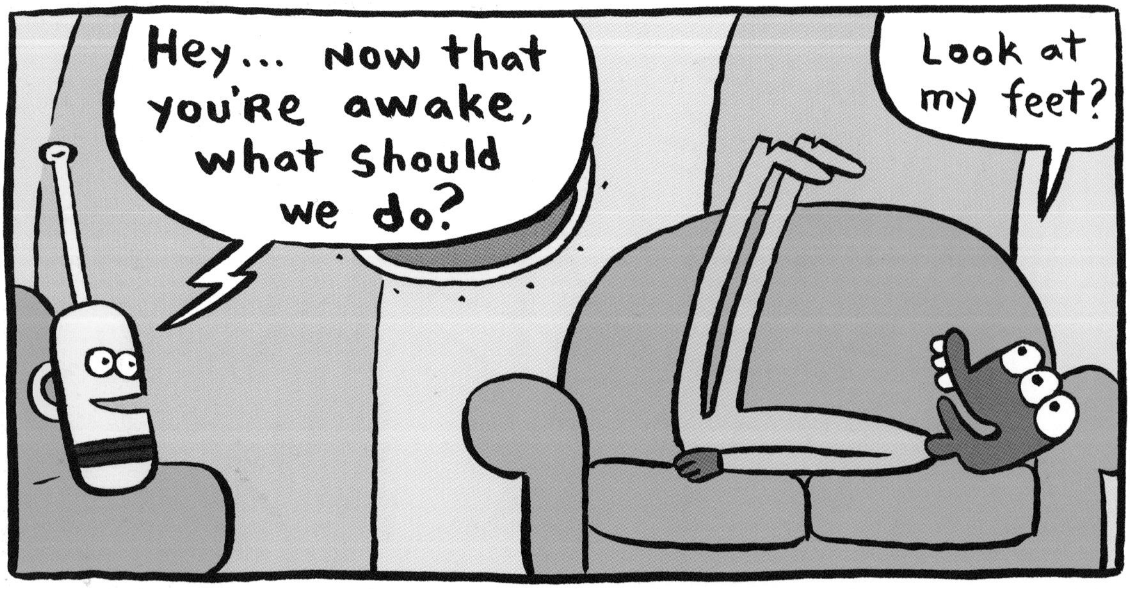
Hey... Now that you're awake, what should we do?
Look at my feet?

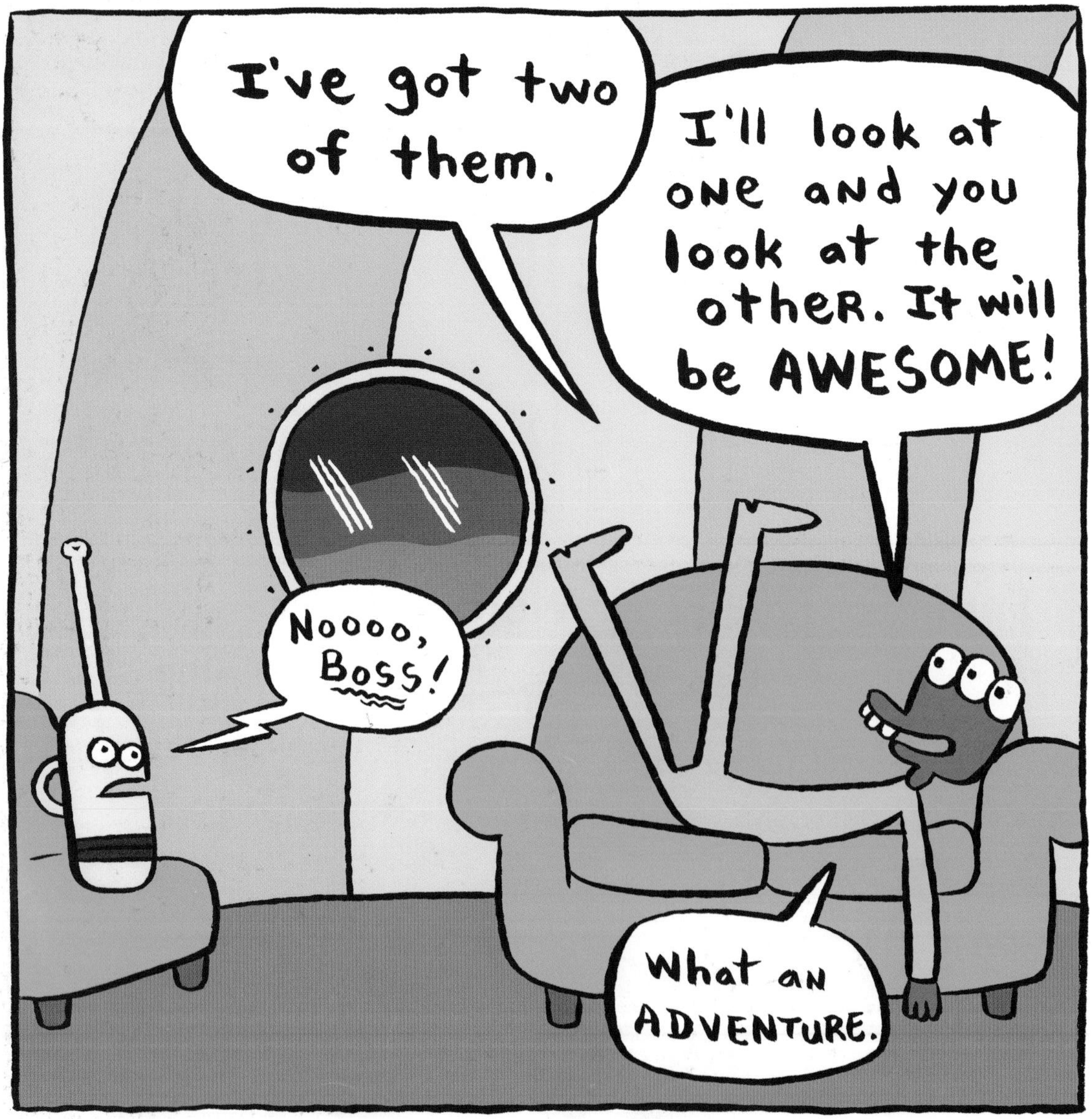
I've got two of them.
I'll look at one and you look at the other. It will be AWESOME!
Noooo, Boss!
What an ADVENTURE.

CHAPTER TWO

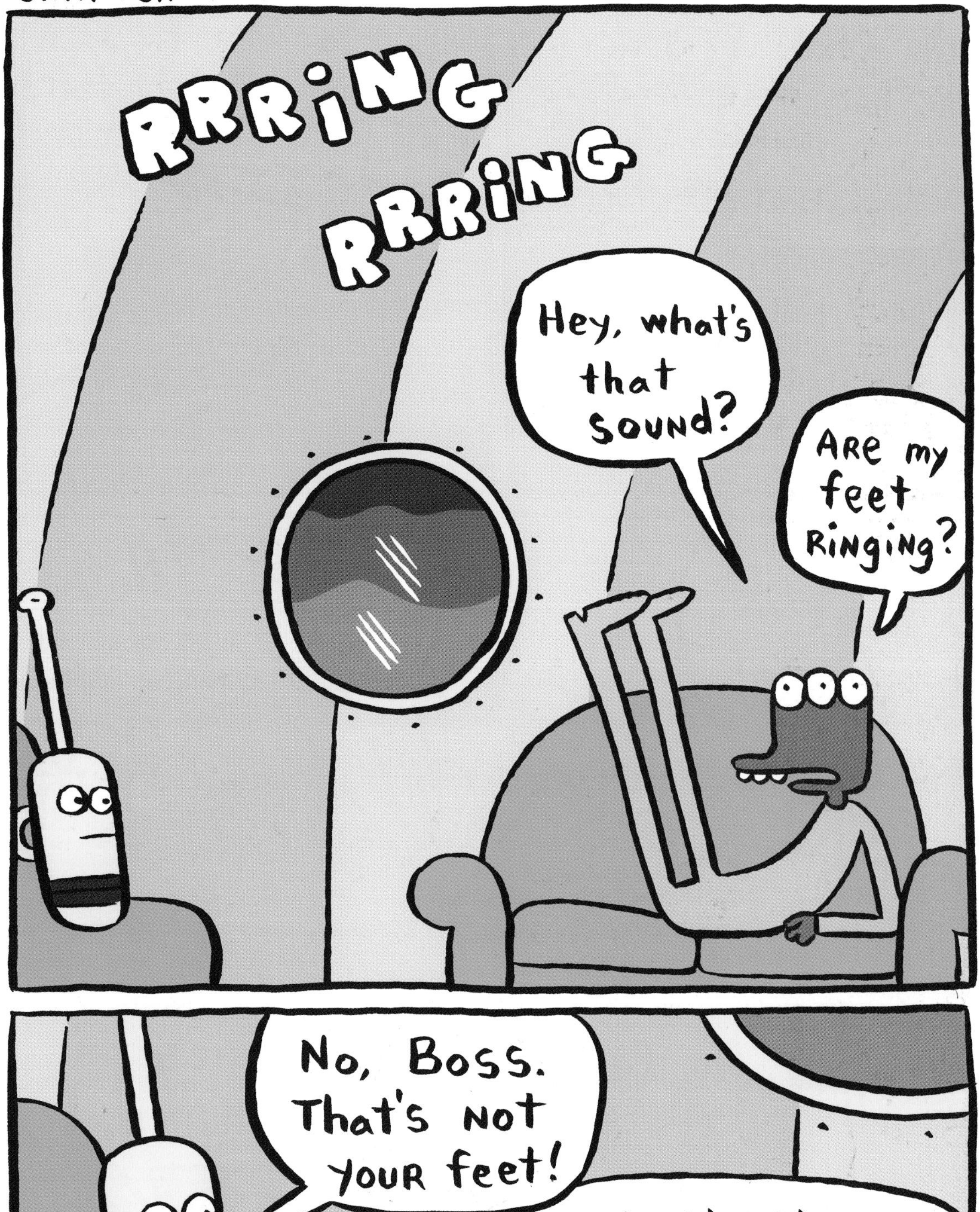
RRRING
RRRING
Hey, what's that sound?
Are my feet ringing?

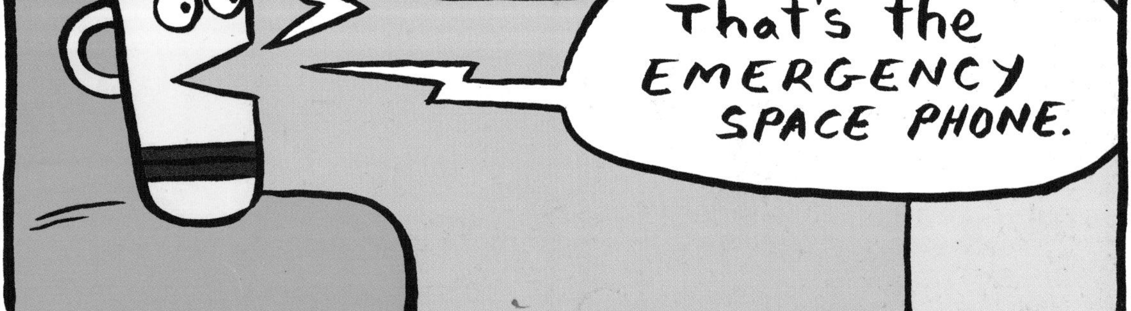
No, Boss. That's not your feet!
That's the EMERGENCY SPACE PHONE.

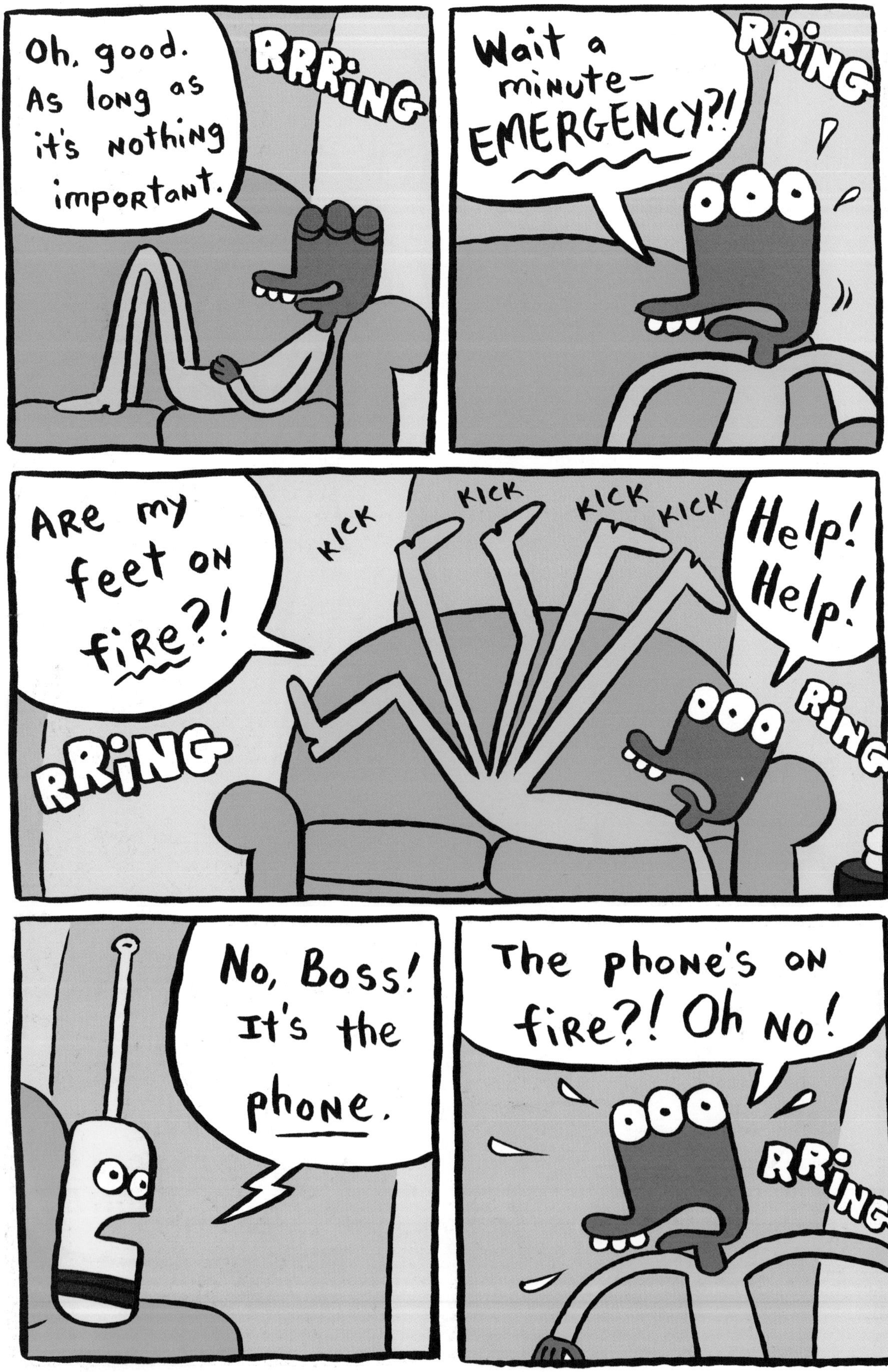
Oh, good. As long as it's nothing important.
RRRiNG
Wait a minute- EMERGENCY?!
RRiNG
Are my feet on fire?!
KICK
KICK
KICK
KICK
Help! Help!
RRiNG
RRiNG
No, Boss! It's the phone.
The phone's on fire?! Oh no!
RRiNG

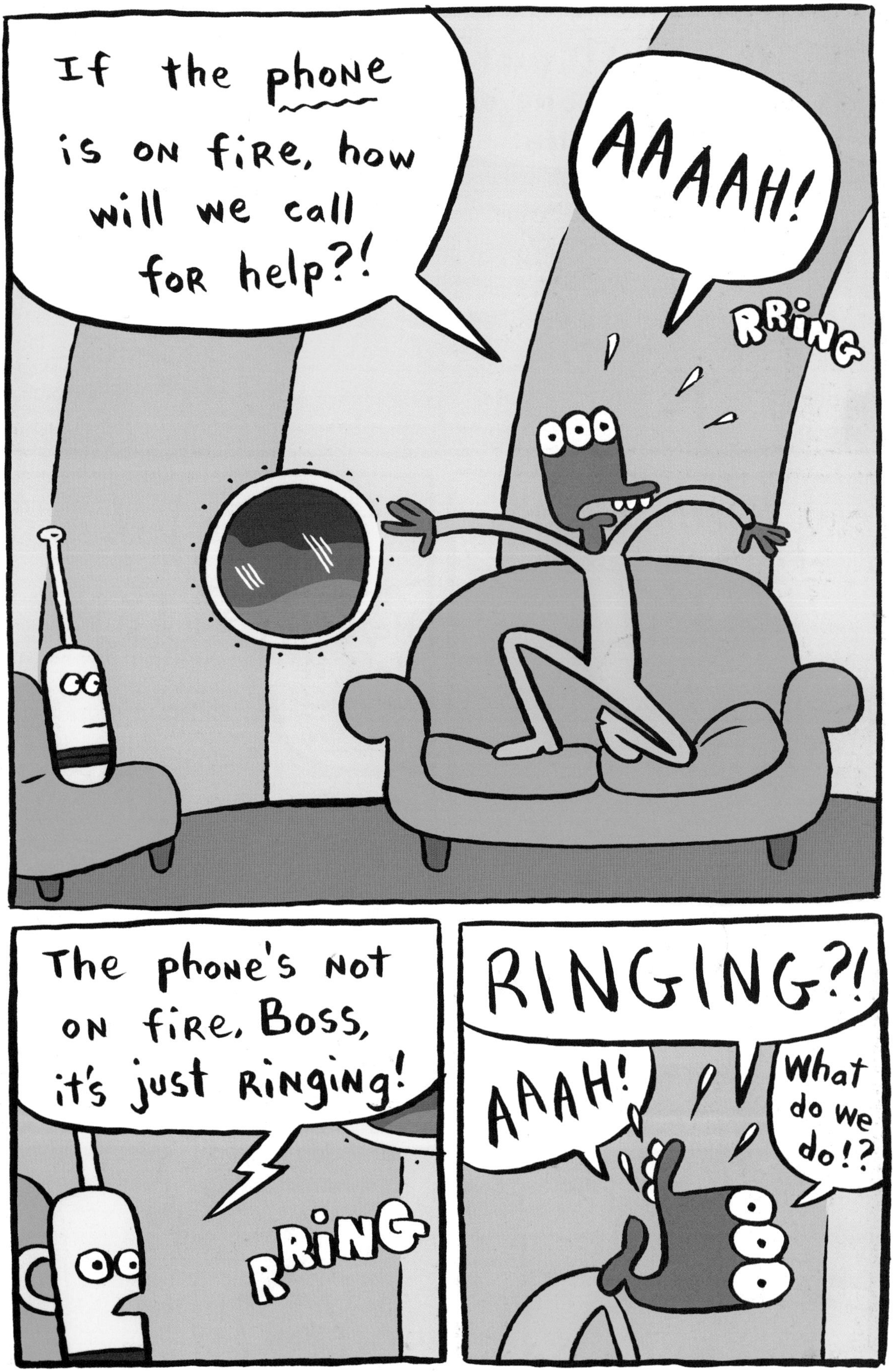

If the phone is on fire, how will we call for help?!
AAAAH!
RRING
The phone's not on fire, Boss, it's just ringing!
RRING
RINGING?!
AAAH!
What do we do!?

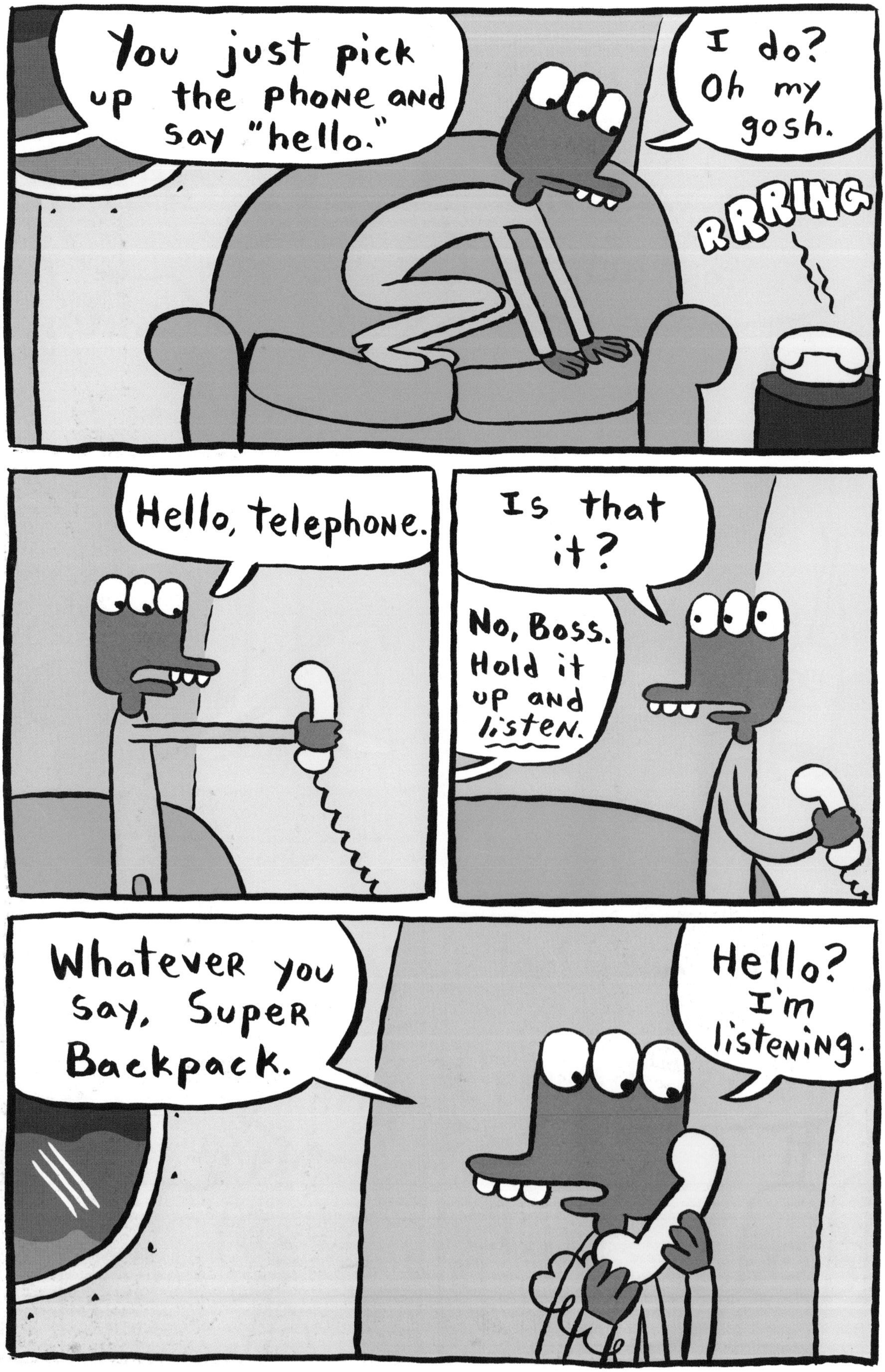

You just pick up the phone and say "hello."
I do? Oh my gosh.
RRRING
Hello, telephone.
Is that it?
No, Boss. Hold it up and listen.
Whatever you say, Super Backpack.
Hello? I'm listening.

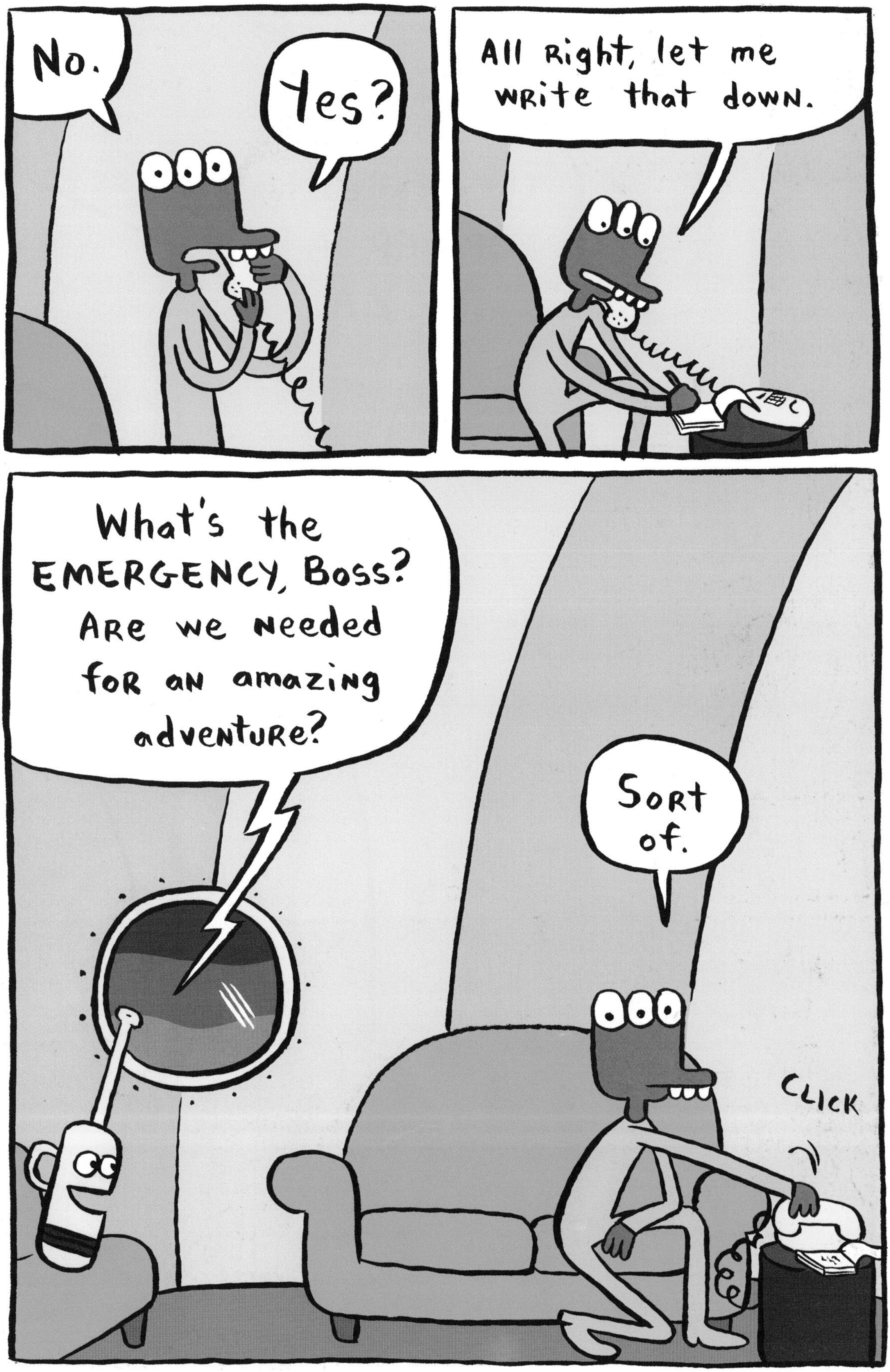

No.
Yes?
All right, let me write that down.
What's the EMERGENCY, Boss? Are we needed for an amazing adventure?
Sort of.
CLICK

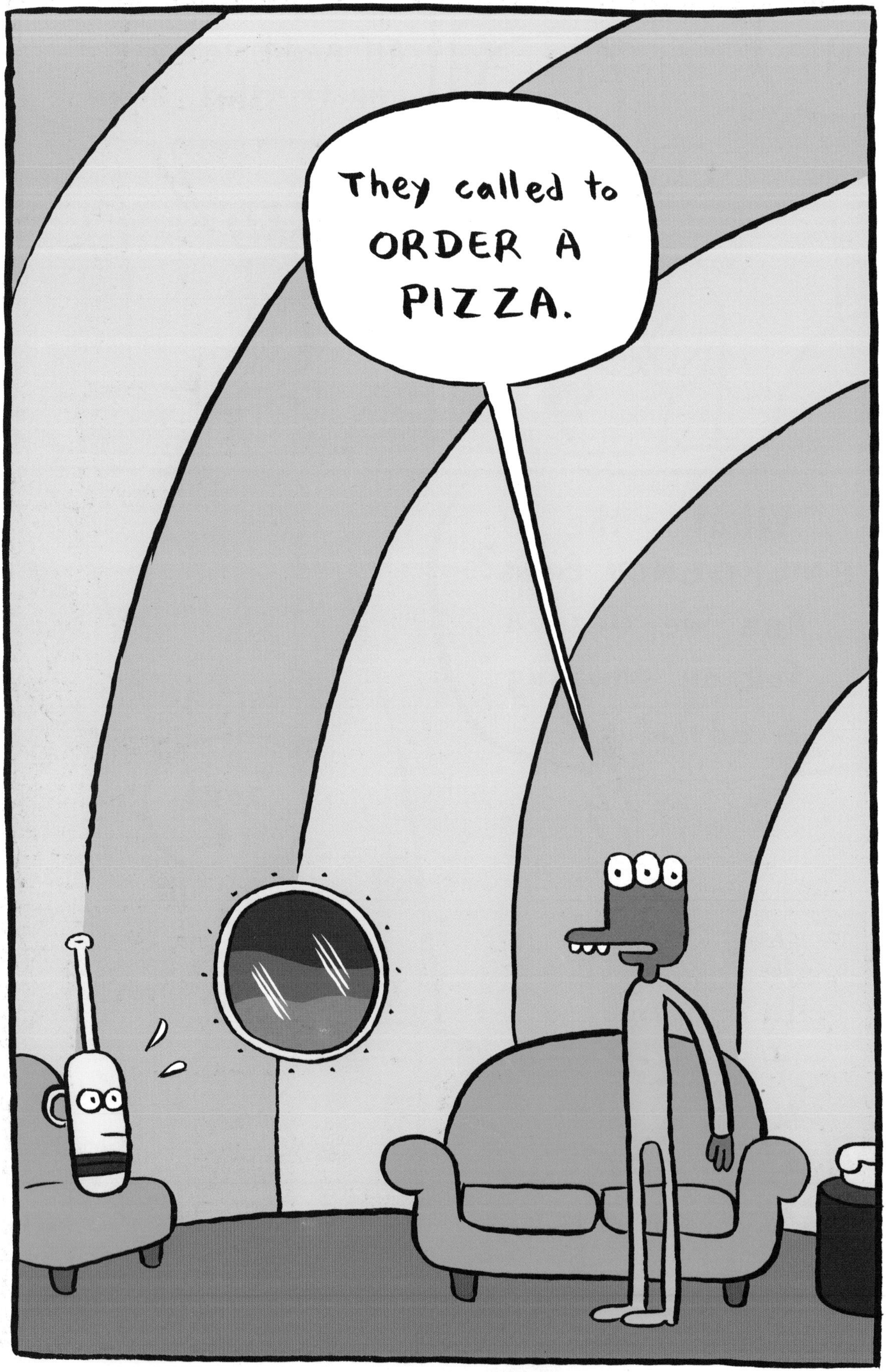
They called to ORDER A PIZZA.

CHAPTER THREE

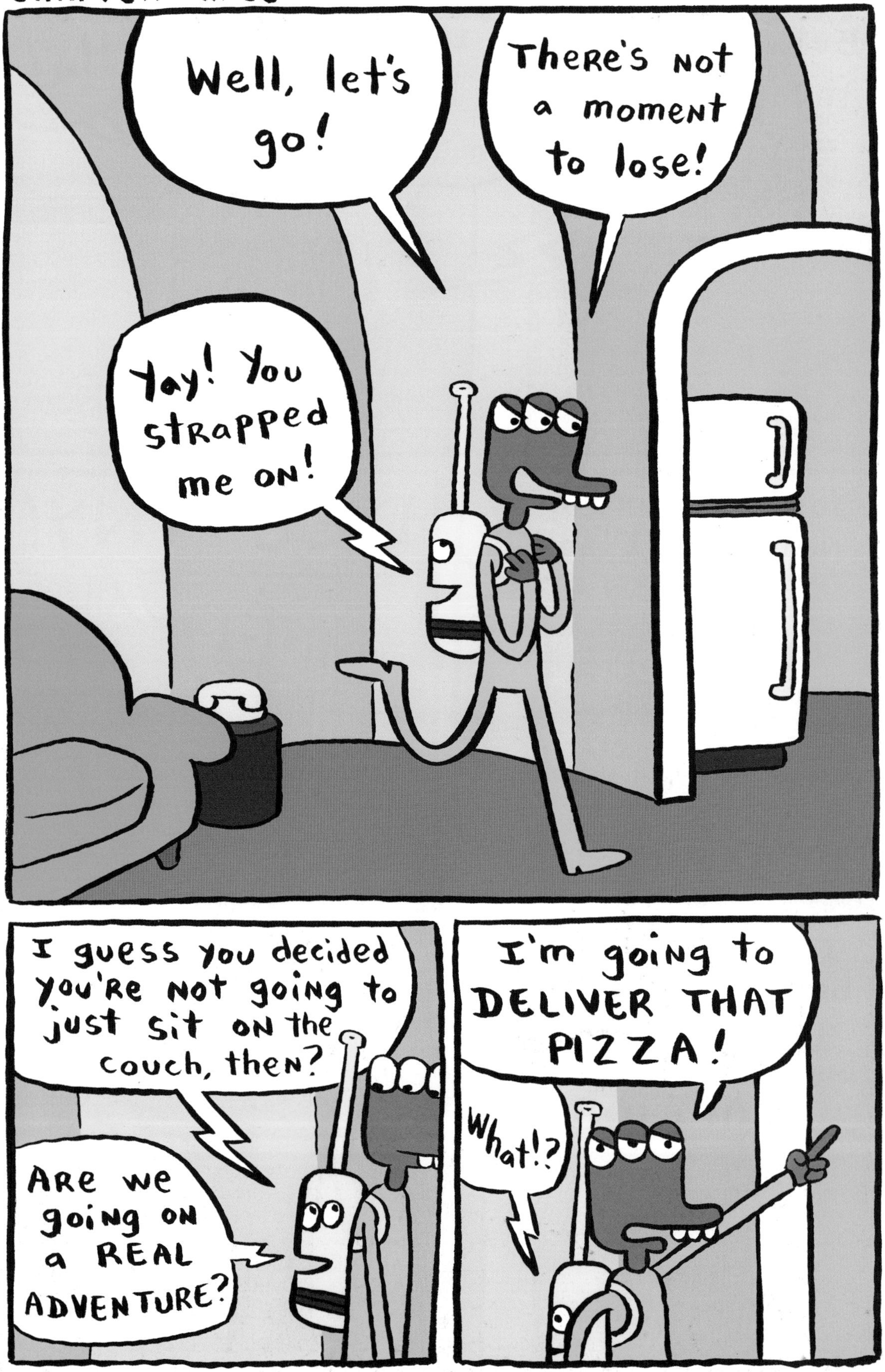

Well, let's go!
There's not a moment to lose!
Yay! You strapped me on!
I guess you decided you're not going to just sit on the couch, then?
Are we going on a REAL ADVENTURE?
I'm going to DELIVER THAT PIZZA!
What!?

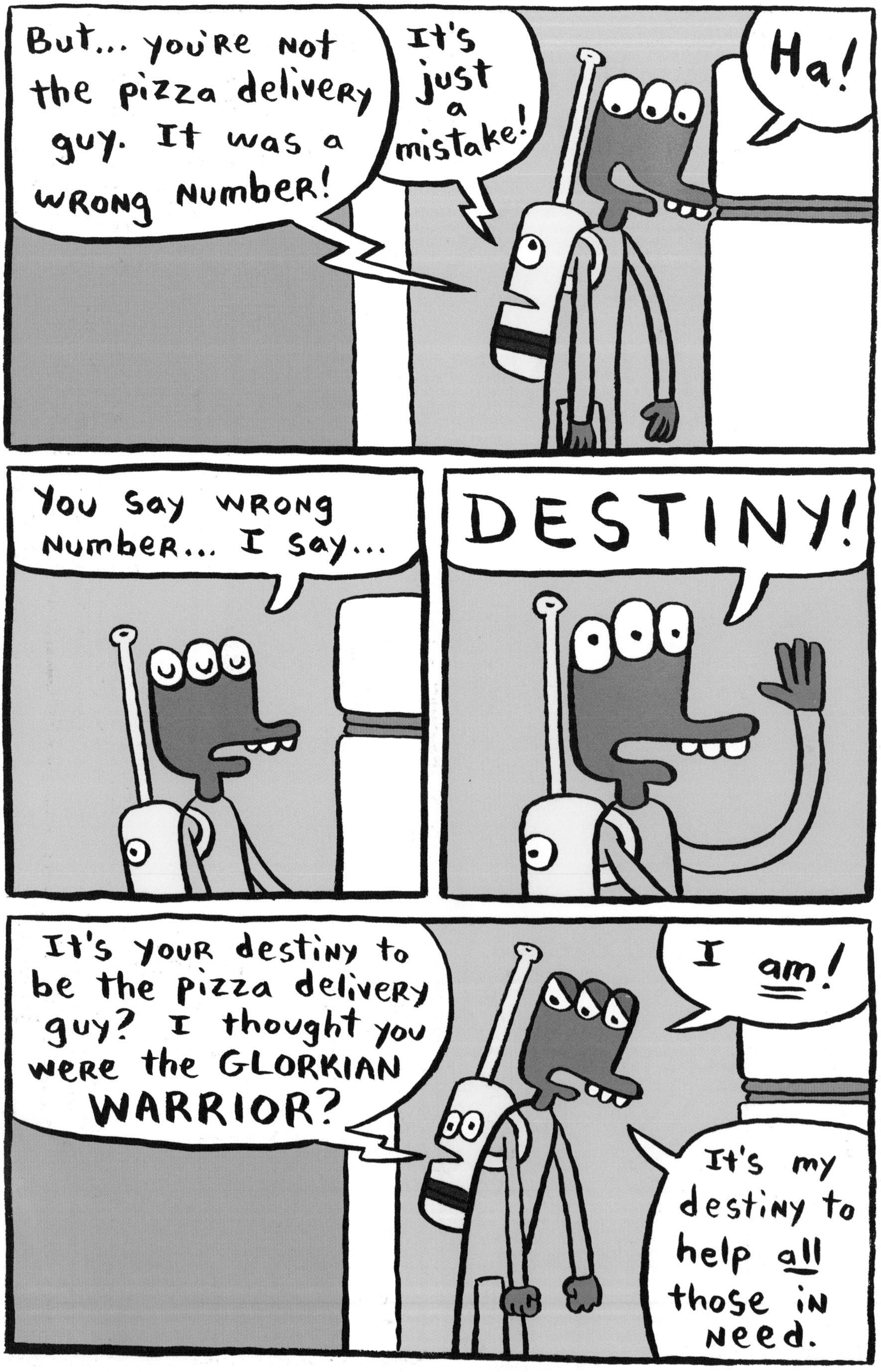
But... you're not the pizza delivery guy. It was a wrong number!
It's just a mistake!
Ha!
You say wrong number... I say...
DESTINY!
It's your destiny to be the pizza delivery guy? I thought you were the GLORKIAN WARRIOR?
I am!
It's my destiny to help all those in need.

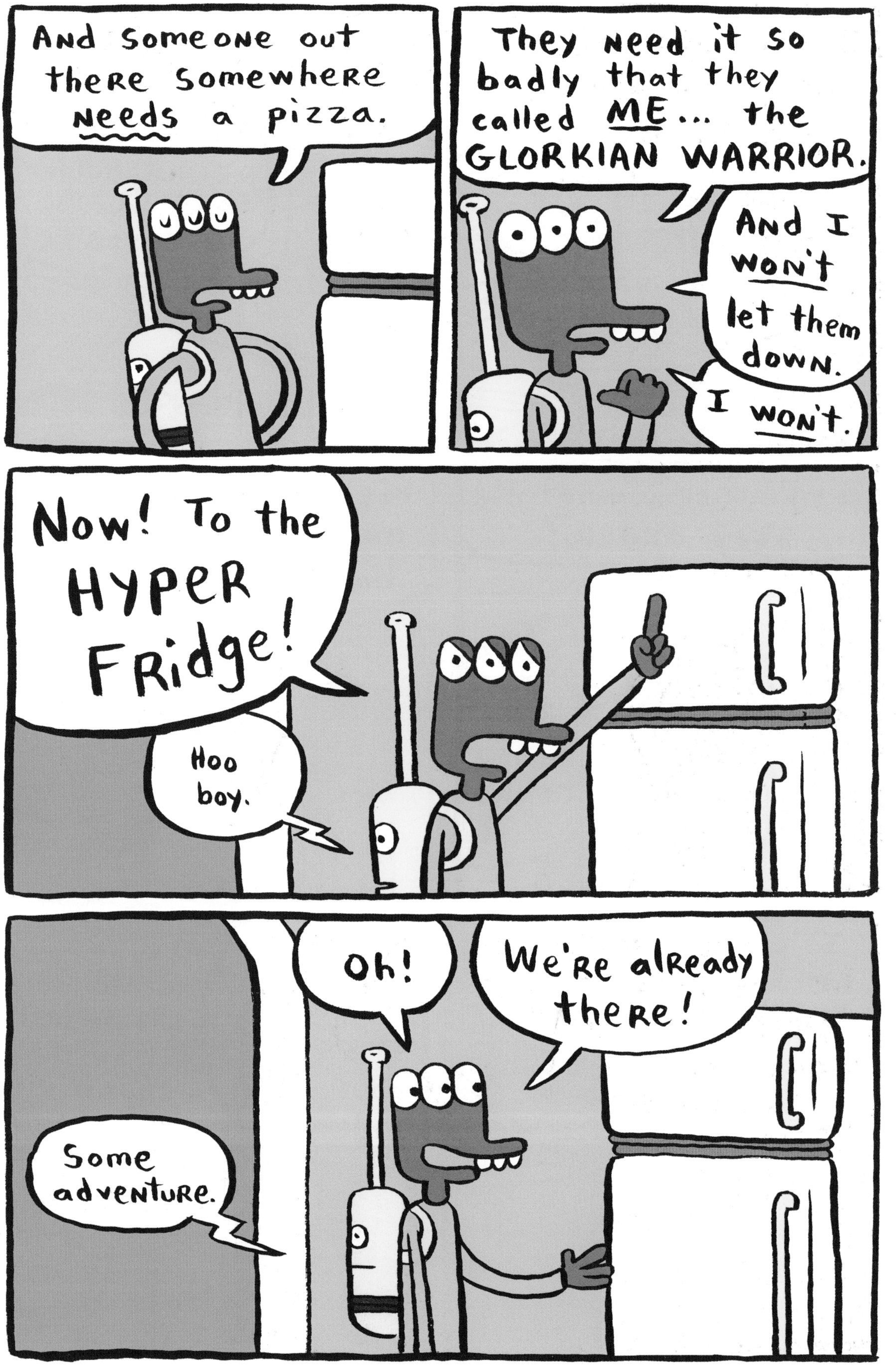
And someone out there somewhere needs a pizza.
They need it so badly that they called ME... the GLORKIAN WARRIOR.
And I won't let them down.
I won't.
Now! To the HYPER Fridge!
Hoo boy.
Oh!
We're already there!
Some adventure.

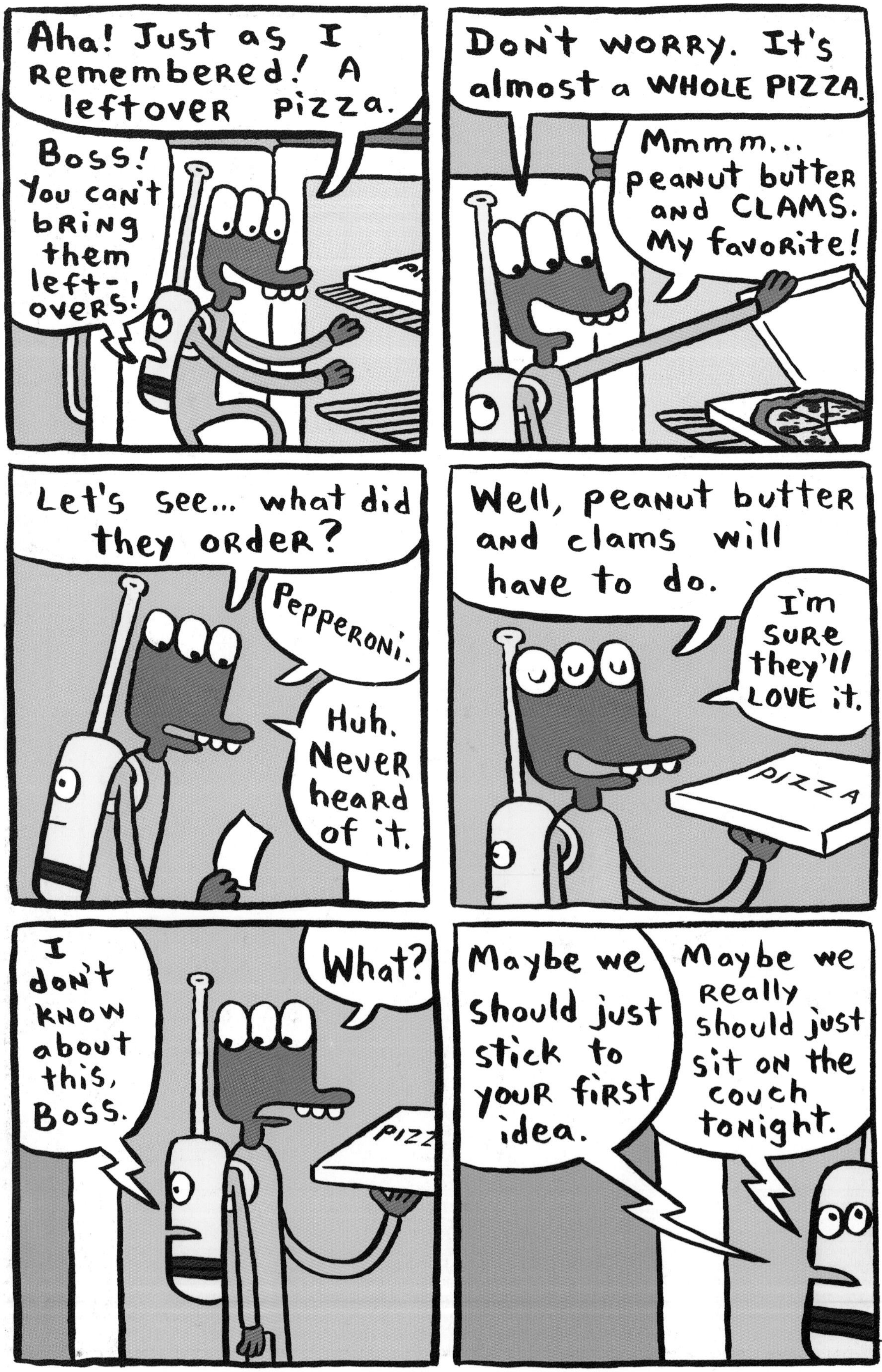
Aha! Just as I remembered! A leftover pizza.
Boss! You can't bring them left-overs!
Don't worry. It's almost a WHOLE PIZZA.
Mmmm... peanut butter and CLAMS. My favorite!
Let's see... what did they order?
Pepperoni.
Huh. Never heard of it.
Well, peanut butter and clams will have to do.
I'm sure they'll LOVE it.
PIZZA
I don't know about this, Boss.
What?
Maybe we should just stick to your first idea.
Maybe we really should just sit on the couch tonight.

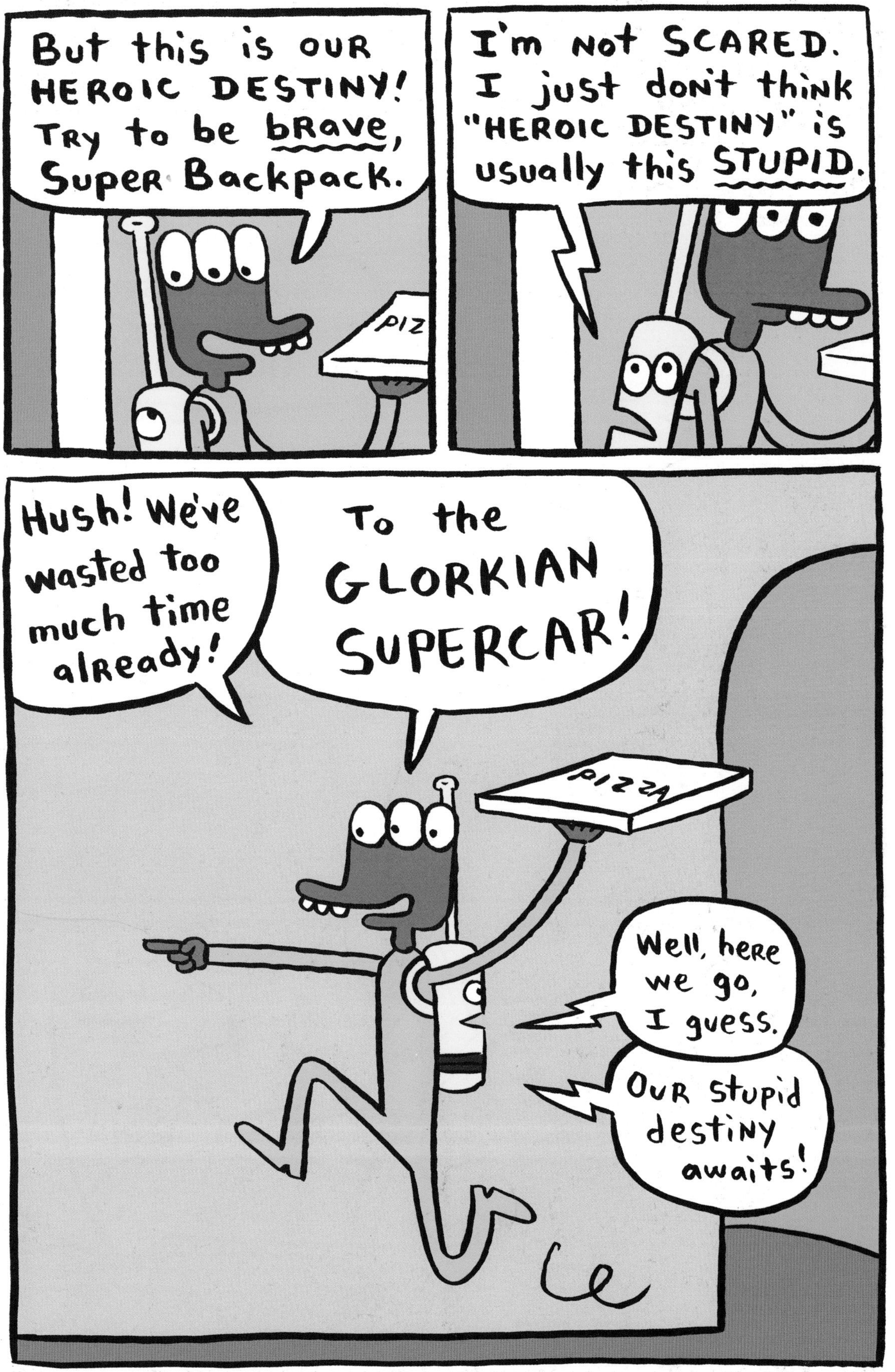
But this is our HEROIC DESTINY! Try to be brave, Super Backpack.
PIZ
I'm not SCARED. I just don't think "HEROIC DESTINY" is usually this STUPID.
Hush! We've wasted too much time already!
To the GLORKIAN SUPERCAR!
PIZZA
Well, here we go, I guess.
Our stupid destiny awaits!

CHAPTER FOUR

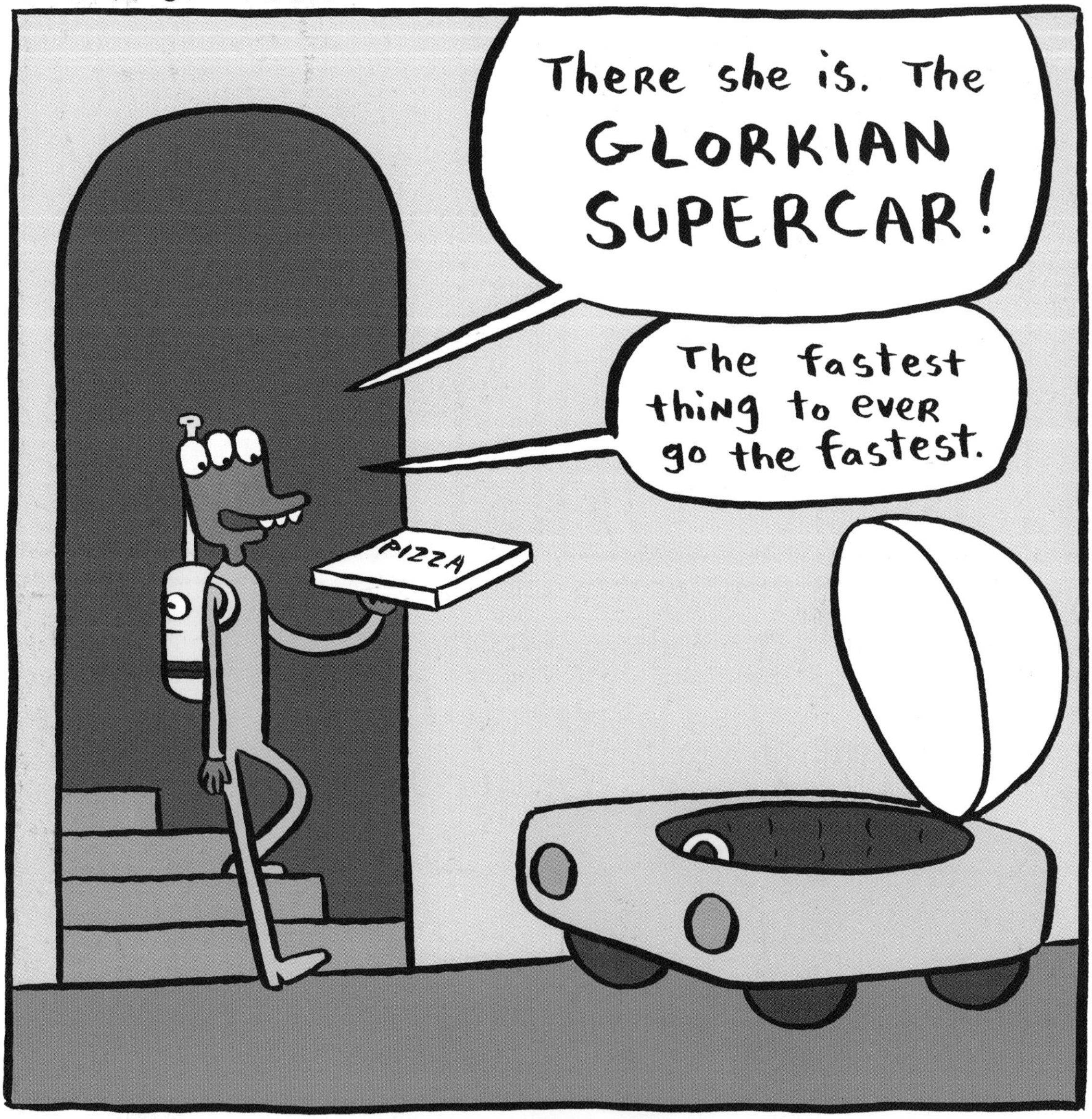
There she is. The GLORKIAN SUPERCAR!
The fastest thing to ever go the fastest.
PIZZA

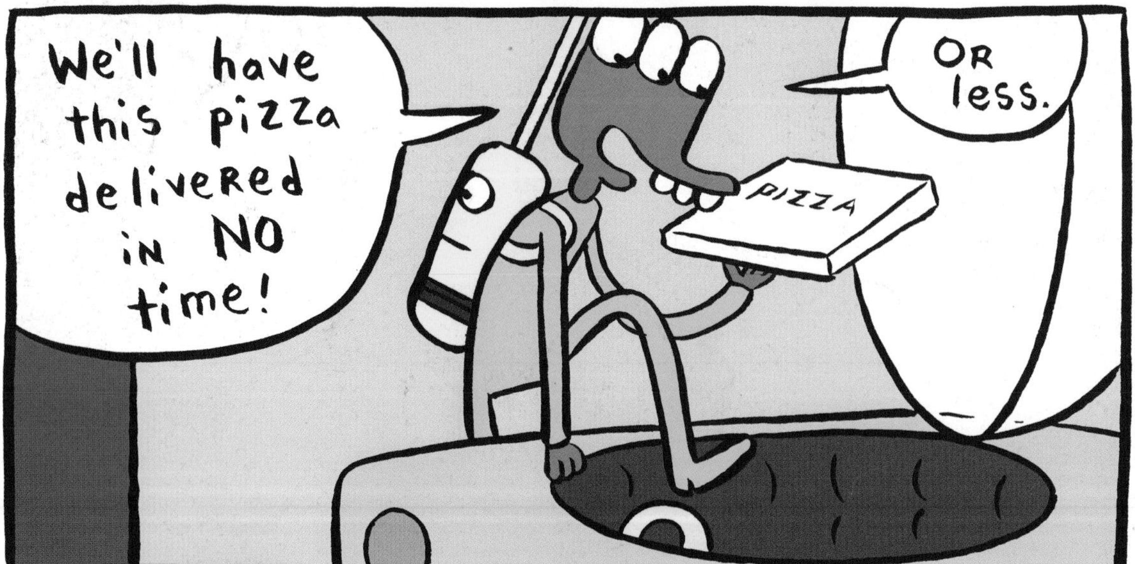
We'll have this pizza delivered in NO time!
OR less.
PIZZA

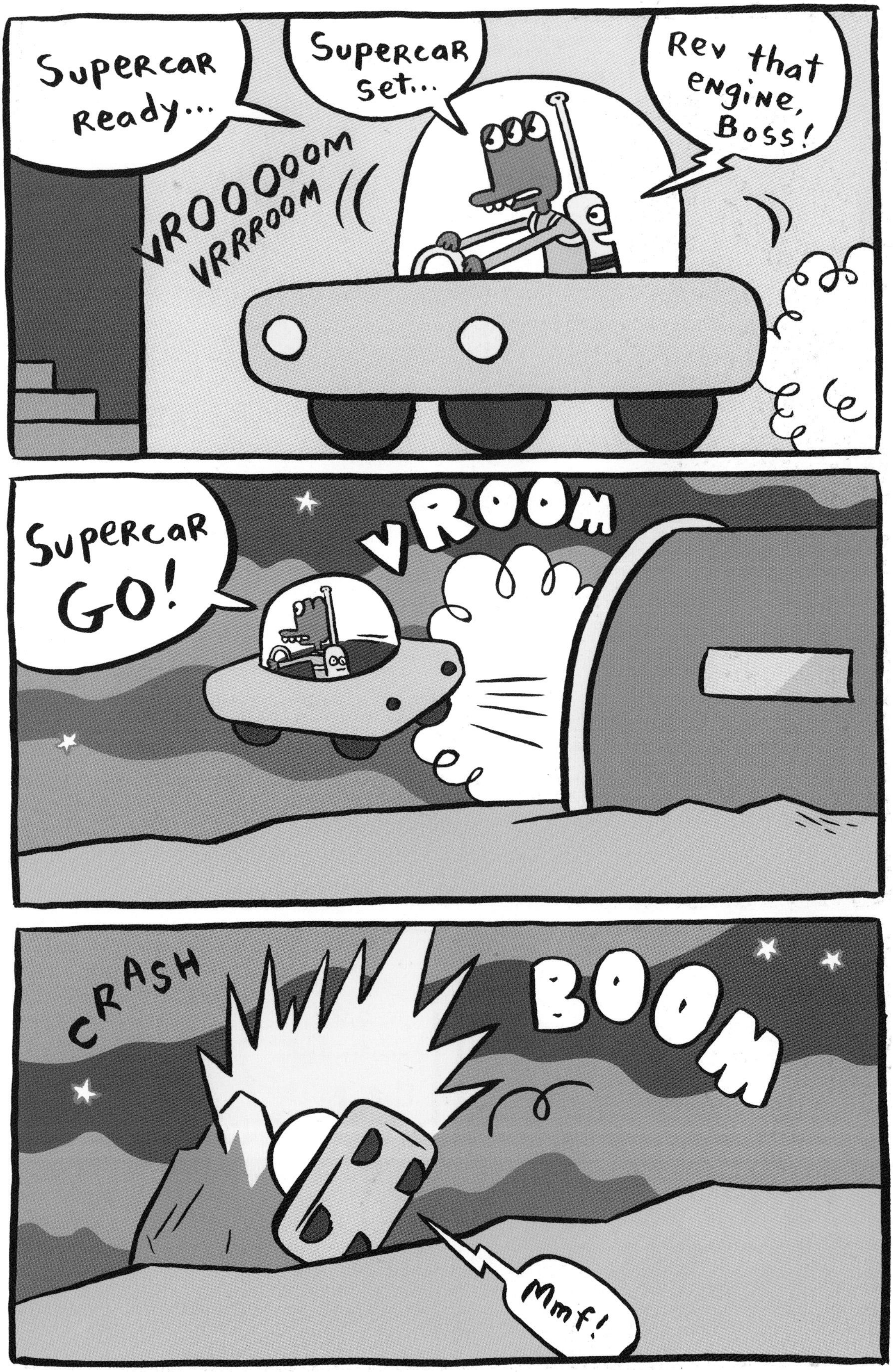
Supercar ready...
Supercar set...
Rev that engine, Boss!
VROOOOOOM
VRRROOM
Supercar GO!
VROOM
CRASH
BOOM
Mmf!

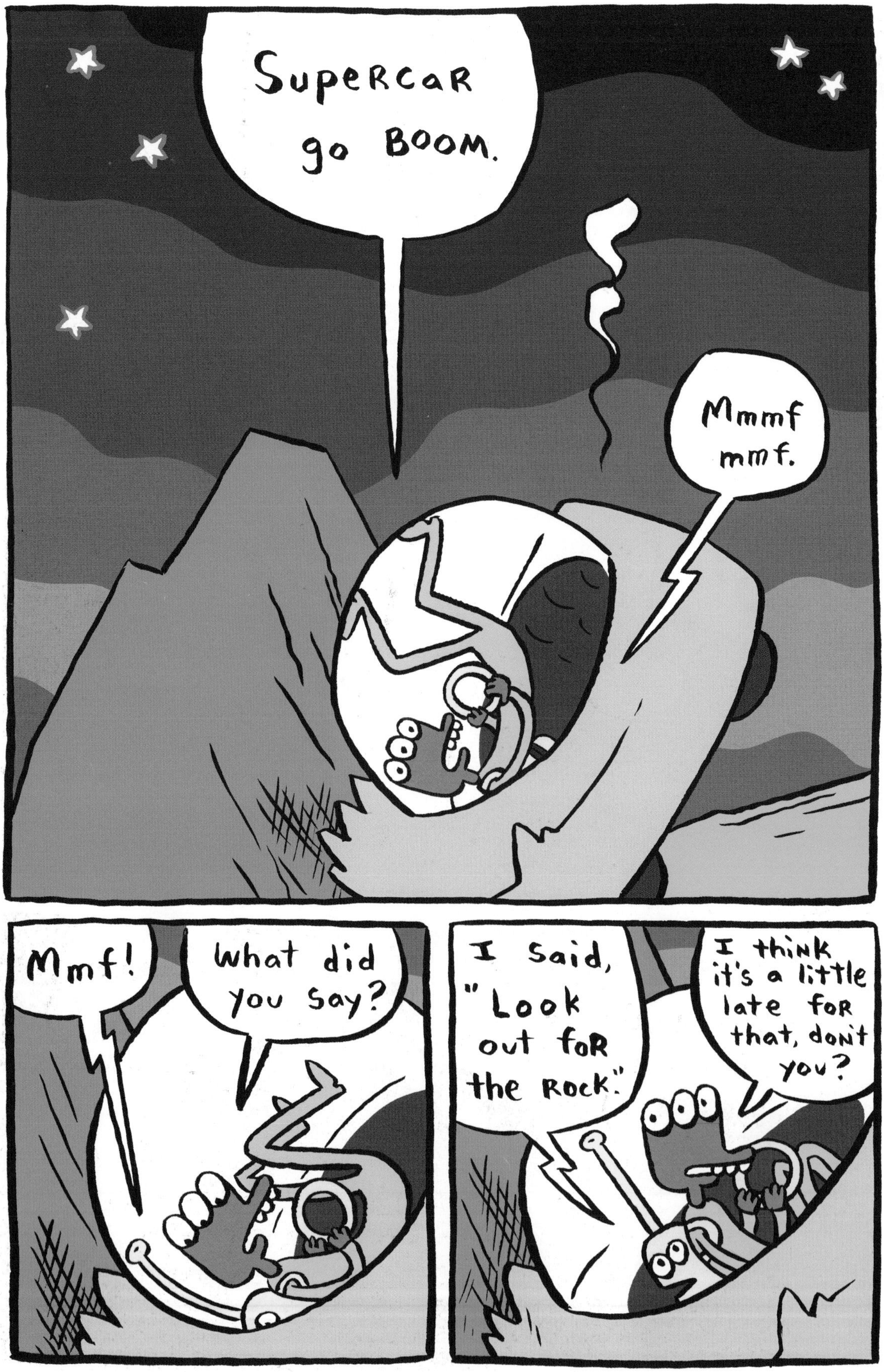

Supercar go BOOM.
Mmmf mmf.
Mmf!
What did you say?
I said, "Look out for the rock."
I think it's a little late for that, don't you?

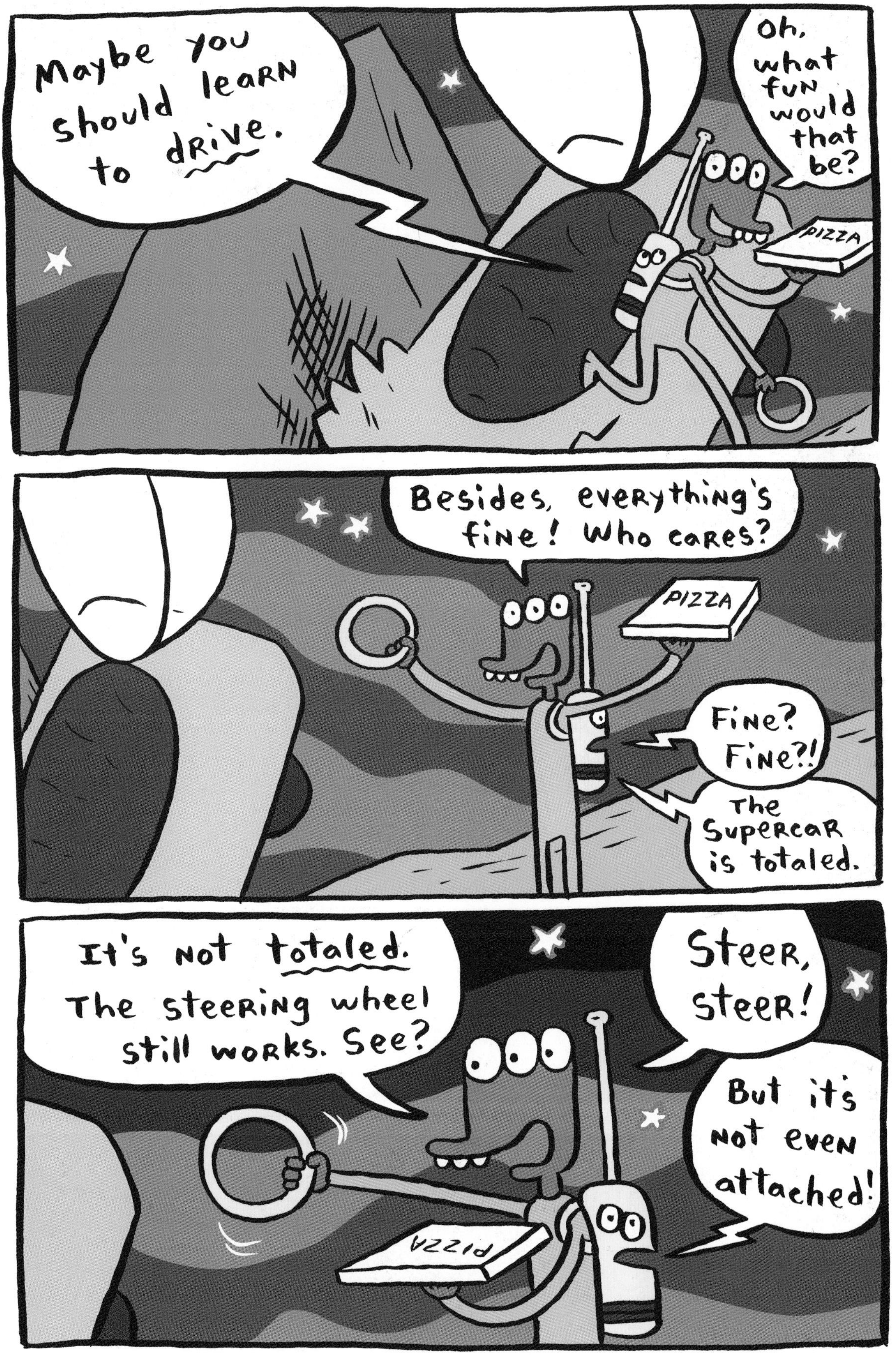
Maybe you should learn to drive.
Oh, what fun would that be?
Besides, everything's fine! Who cares?
PIZZA
Fine? Fine?!
The Supercar is totaled.
It's not totaled. The steering wheel still works. See?
Steer, steer!
But it's not even attached!
PIZZA

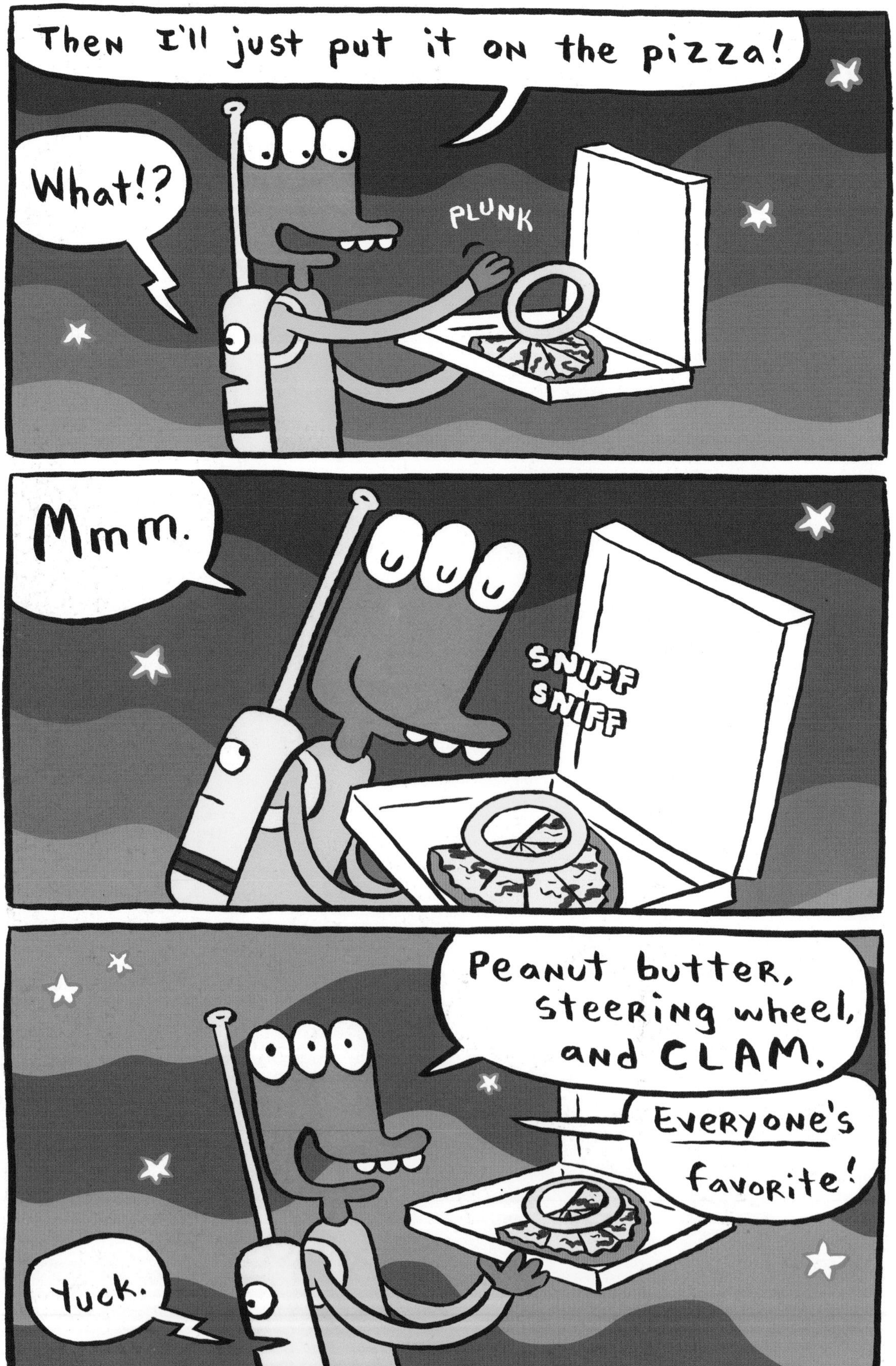
Then I'll just put it on the pizza!
What!?
PLUNK
Mmm.
SNIFF
SNIFF
Peanut butter, steering wheel, and CLAM.
Everyone's favorite!
Yuck.

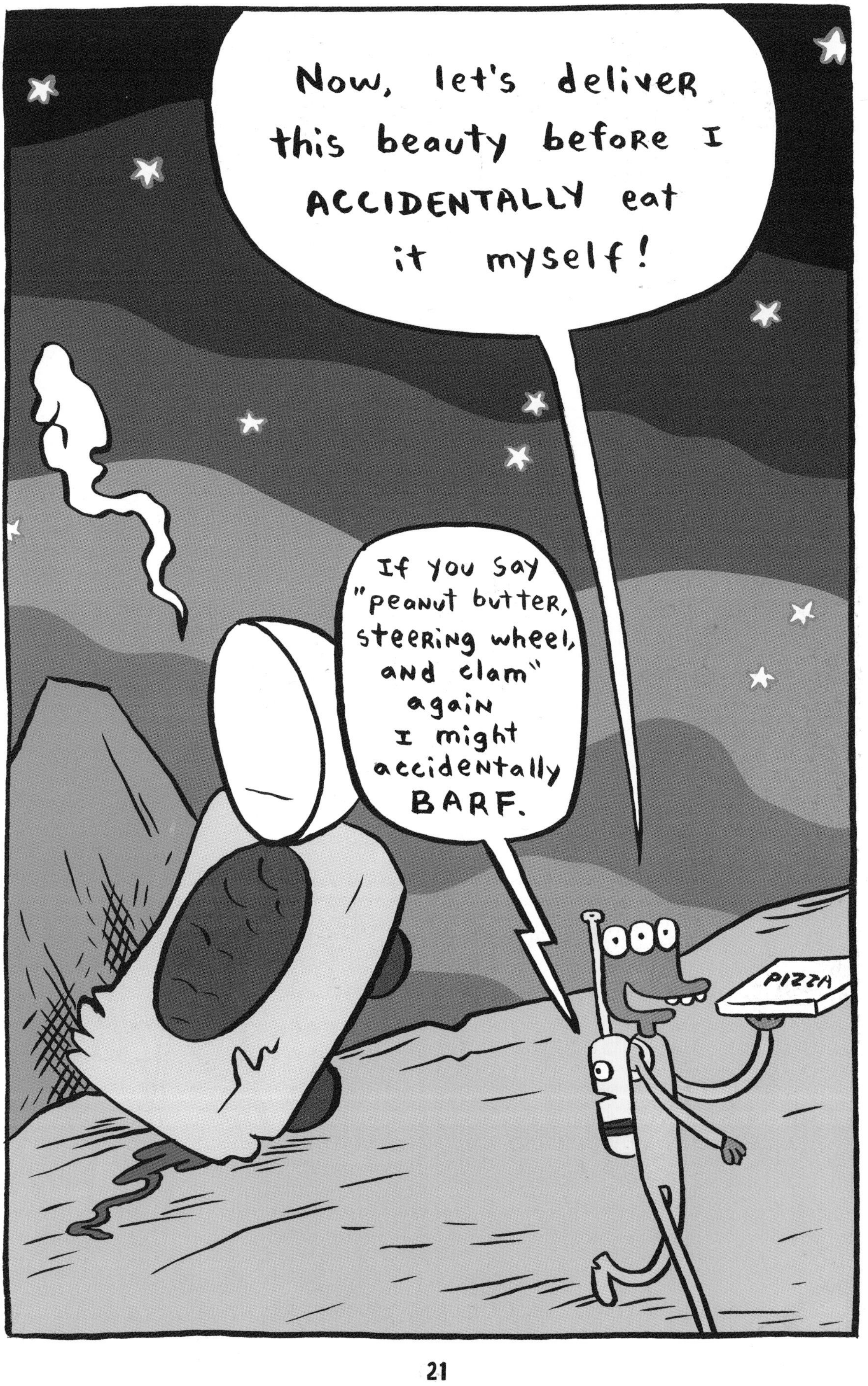
Now, let's deliver this beauty before I ACCIDENTALLY eat it myself!
If you say "peanut butter, steering wheel, and clam" again I might accidentally BARF.
PIZZA

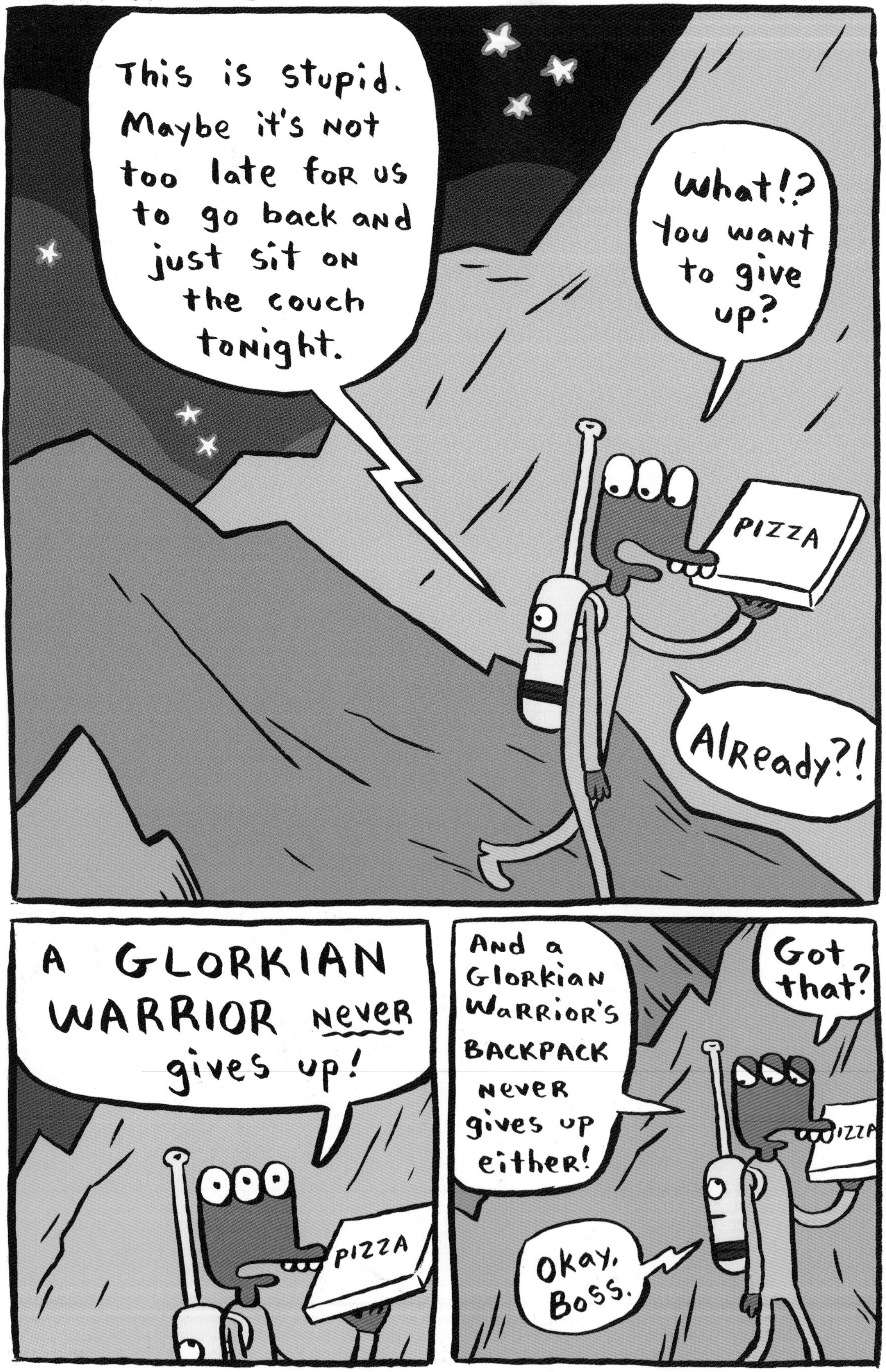
This is stupid. Maybe it's not too late for us to go back and just sit on the couch tonight.
What!? You want to give up?
PIZZA
Already?!
A GLORKIAN WARRIOR never gives up!
PIZZA
And a Glorkian Warrior's BACKPACK never gives up either!
Got that?
IZZA
Okay, Boss.

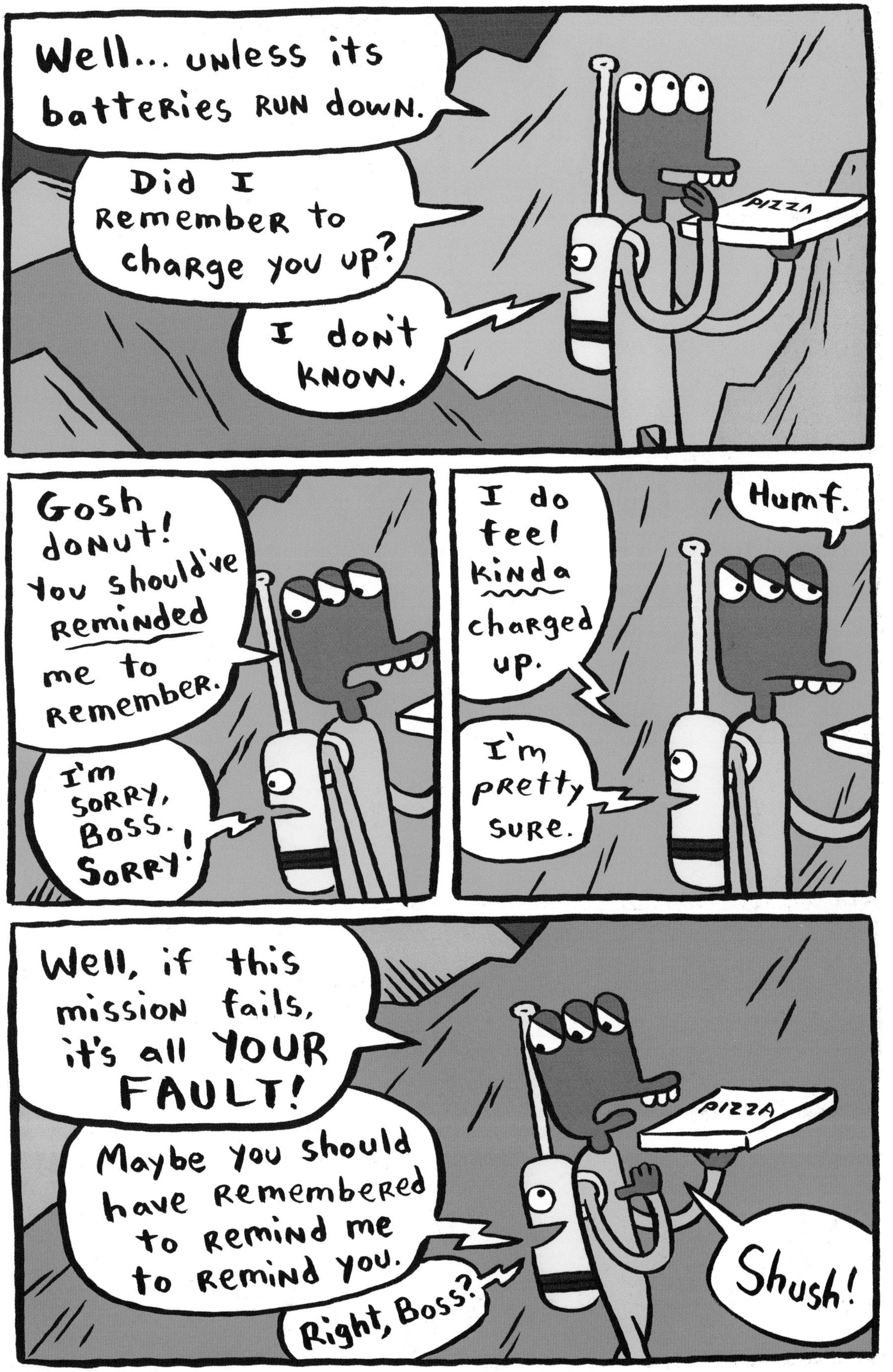

Well... unless its batteries RUN down.
Did I Remember to charge you up?
I don't know.
Gosh donut! You should've reminded me to remember.
I'm sorry, Boss. Sorry!
I do feel kinda charged up.
Humf.
I'm pretty sure.
Well, if this mission fails, it's all YOUR FAULT!
Maybe you should have remembered to remind me to remind you.
Right, Boss?
Shush!
PIZZA

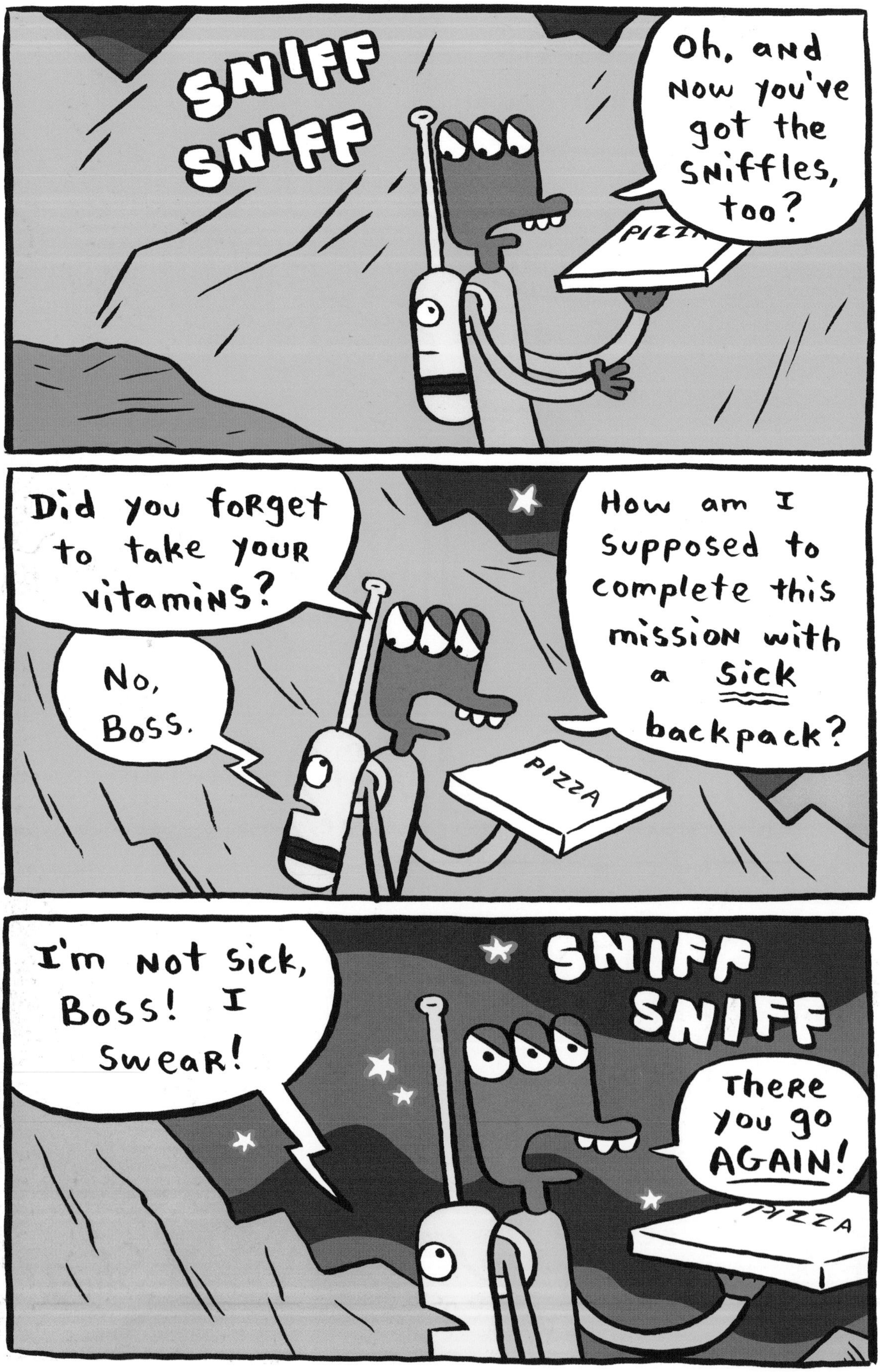
SNIFF SNIFF
Oh, and now you've got the sniffles, too?
PIZZA
Did you forget to take your vitamins?
How am I supposed to complete this mission with a sick backpack?
No, Boss.
PIZZA
I'm not sick, Boss! I swear!
SNIFF SNIFF
There you go AGAIN!
PIZZA

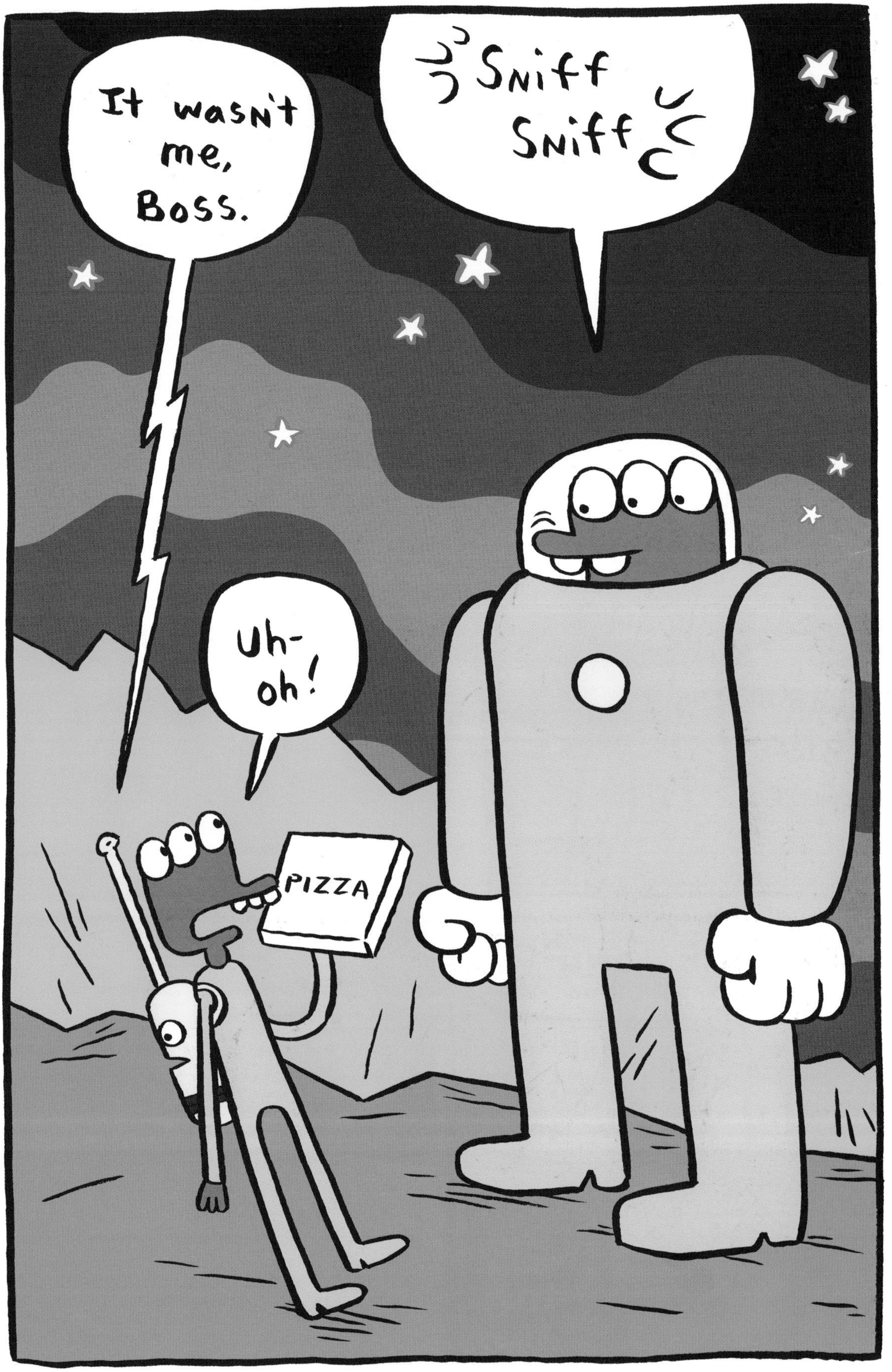
Sniff
Sniff
It wasn't me, Boss.
Uh-oh!
PIZZA

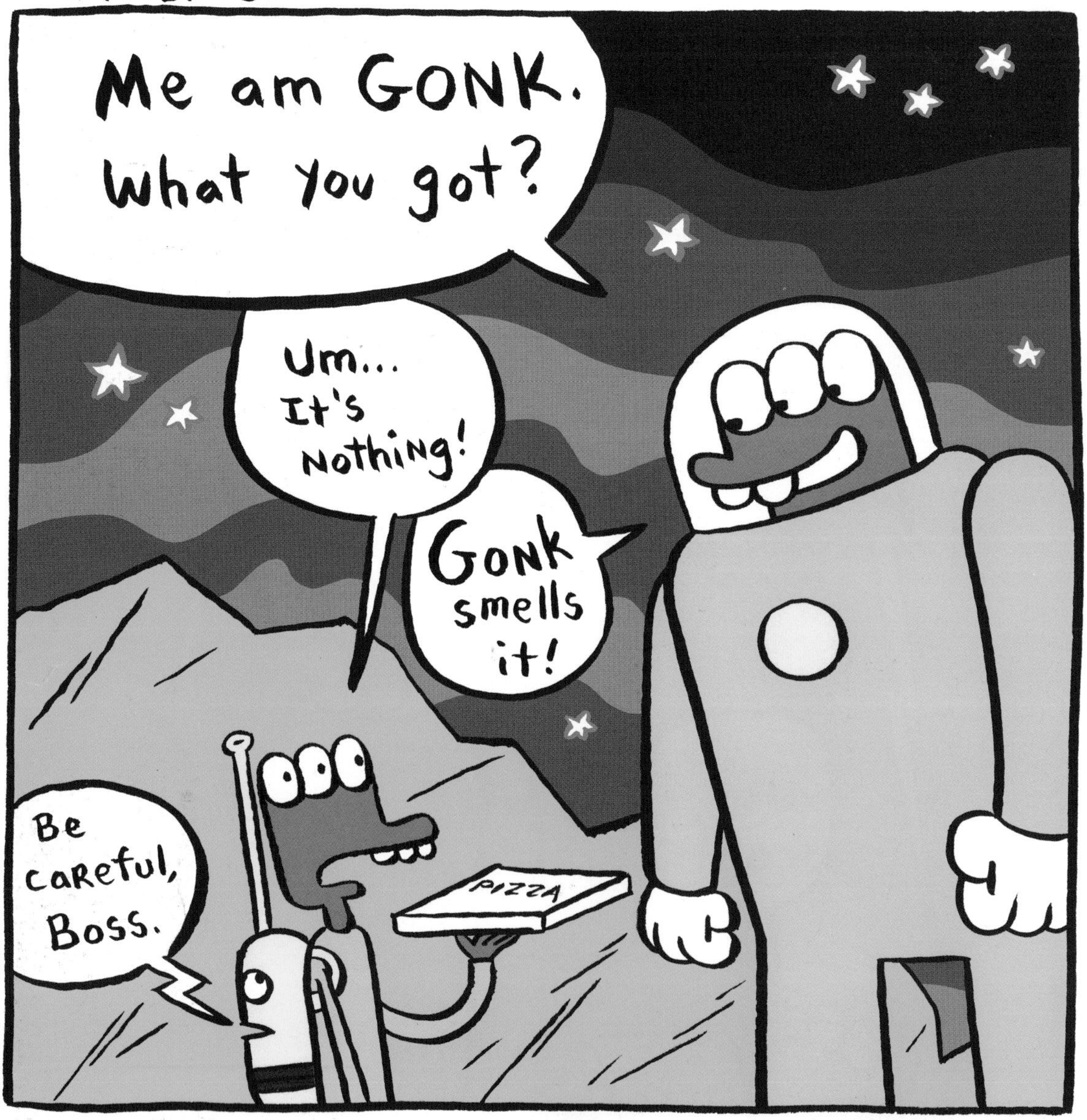
Me am GONK. What you got?
Um... It's Nothing!
Gonk smells it!
Be careful, Boss.
PIZZA

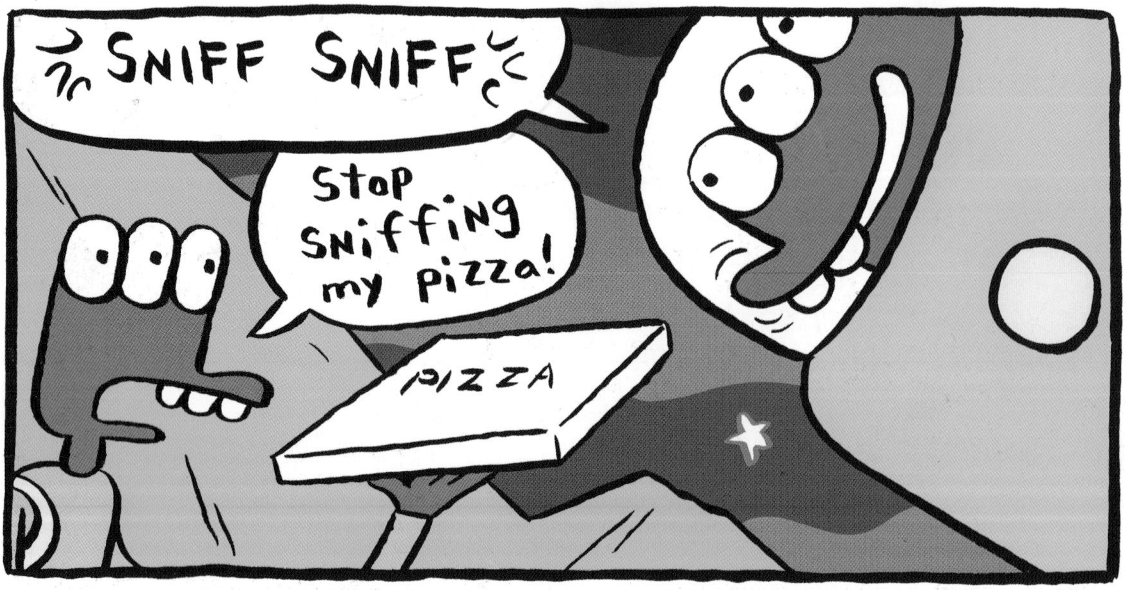
SNIFF SNIFF
Stop sniffing my pizza!
PIZZA

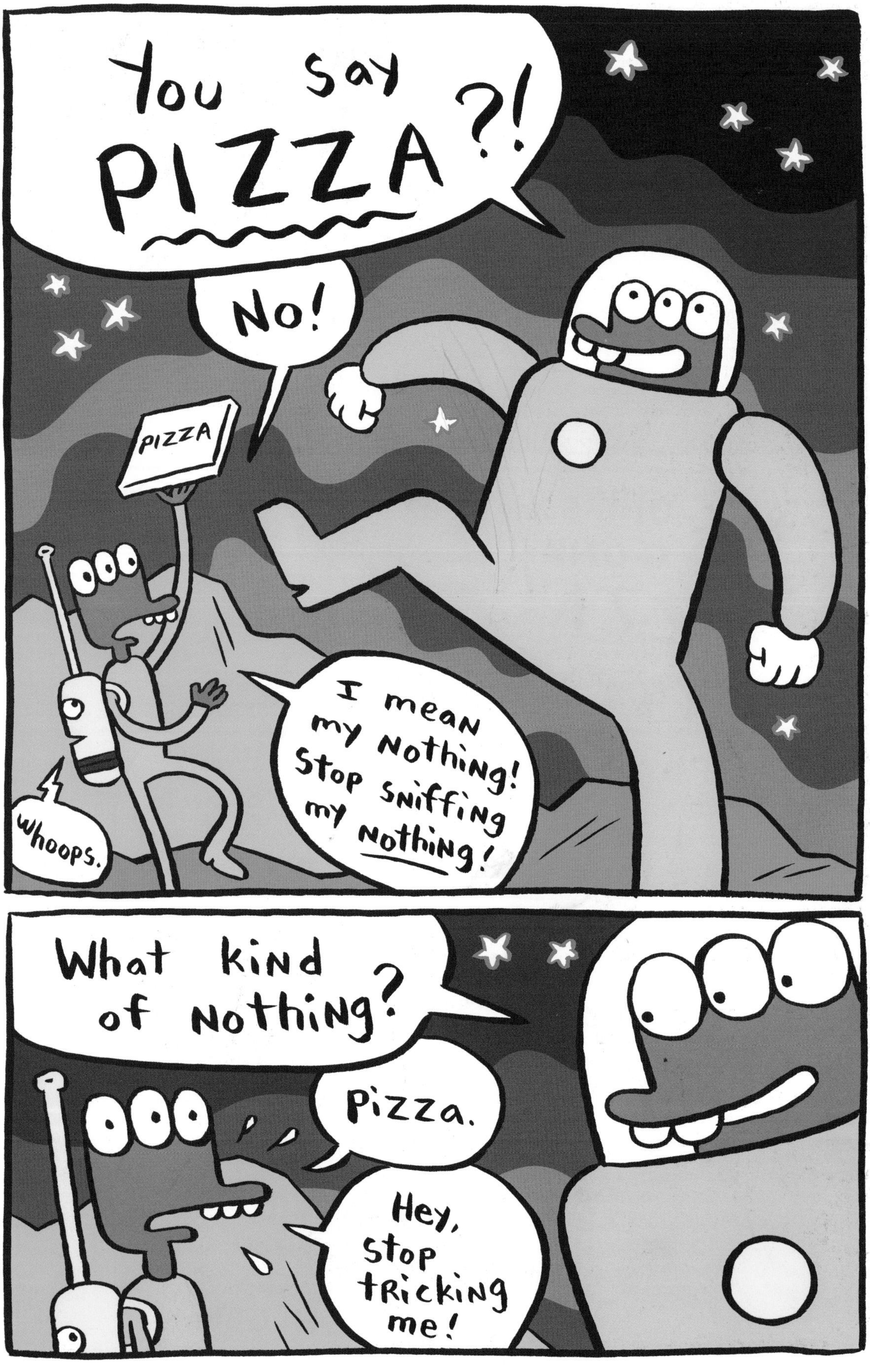
You say PIZZA?!
No!
PIZZA
I mean my Nothing! Stop sniffing my nothing!
Whoops.
What kind of Nothing?
Pizza.
Hey, stop tricking me!

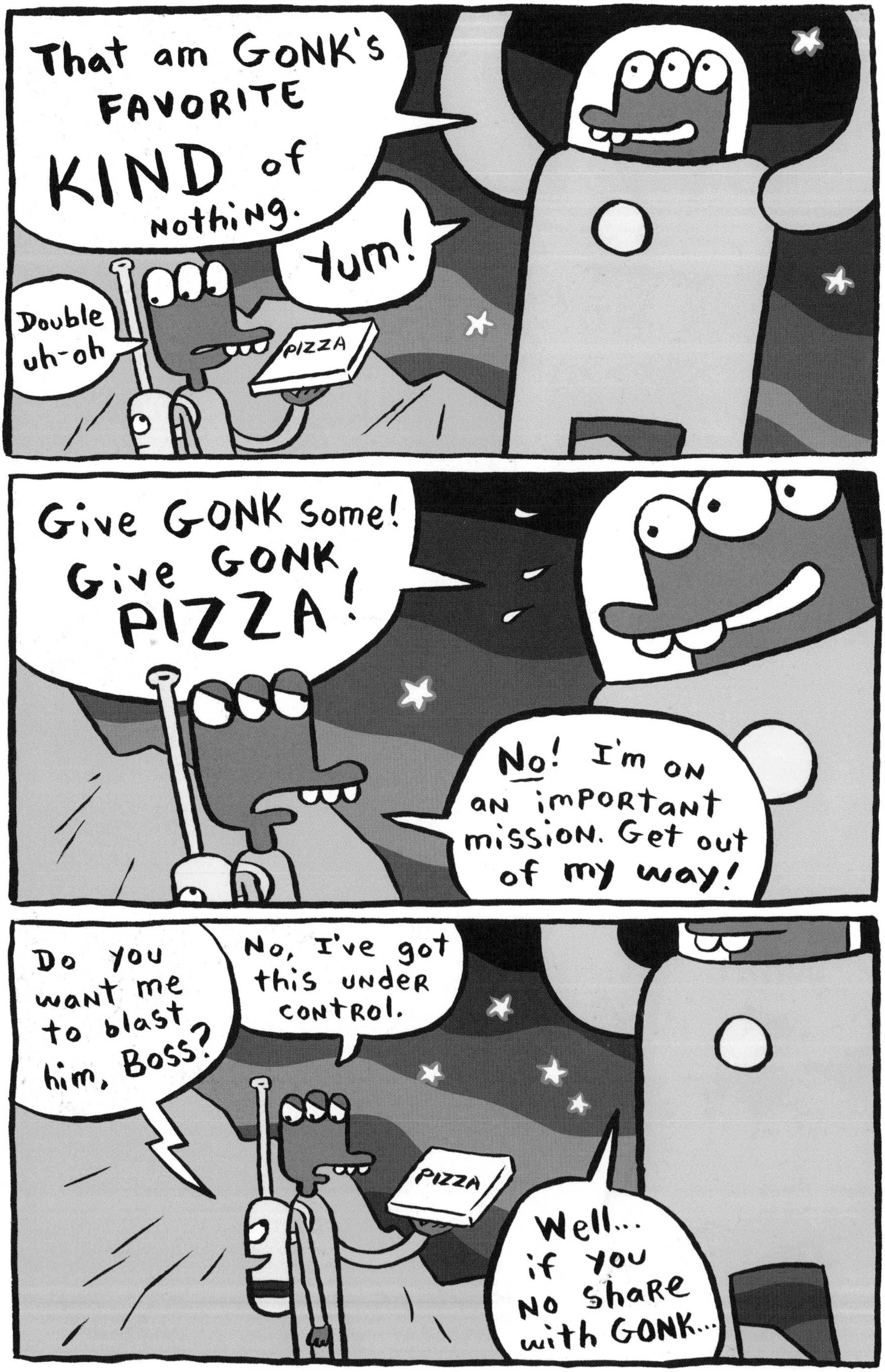

That am GONK's FAVORITE KIND of nothing.
Yum!
Double uh-oh
PIZZA
Give GONK some! Give GONK PIZZA!
No! I'm on an important mission. Get out of my way!
Do you want me to blast him, Boss?
No, I've got this under control.
PIZZA
Well... if you no share with GONK...

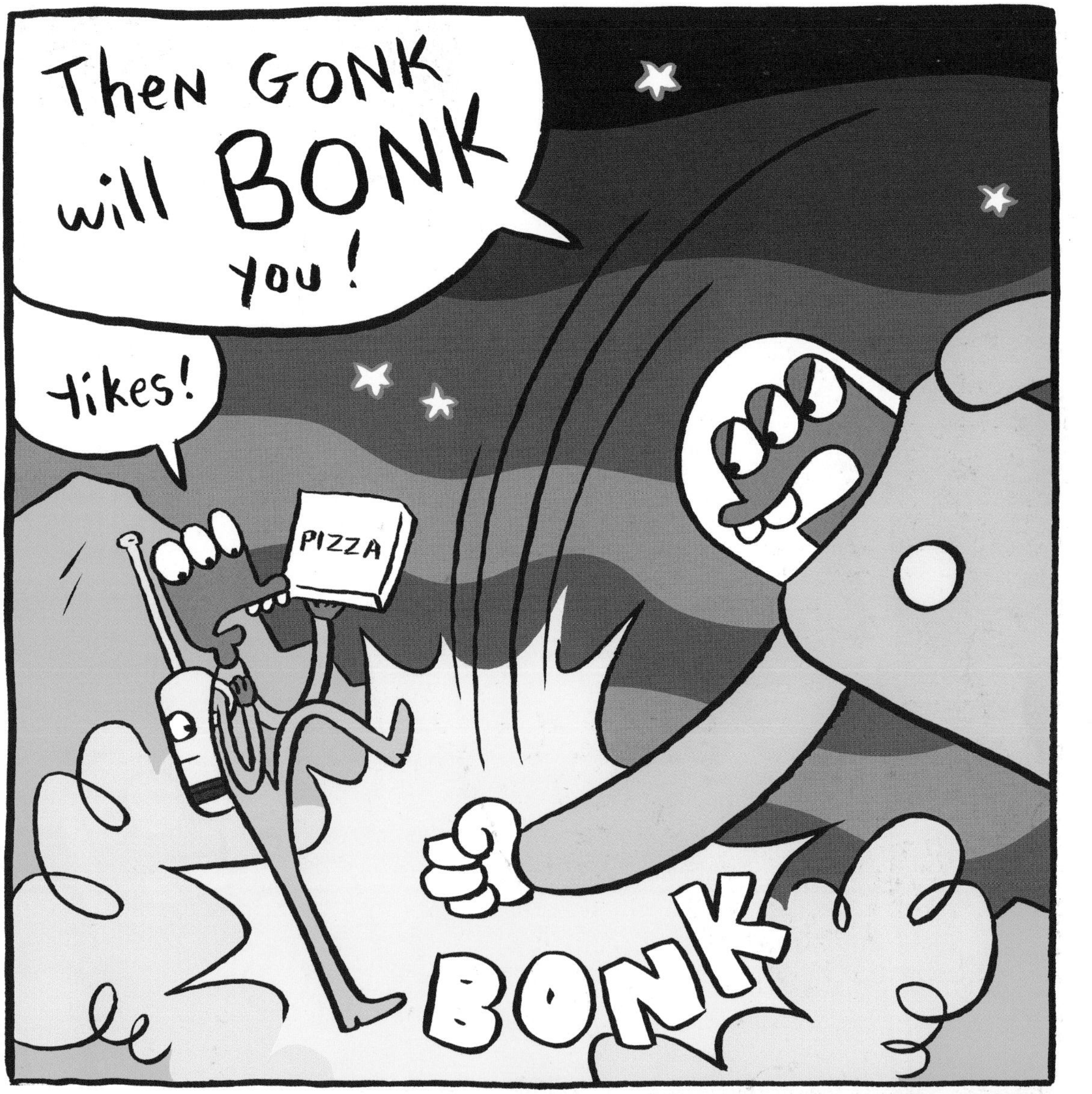
Then GONK will BONK you!
Yikes!
PIZZA
BONK

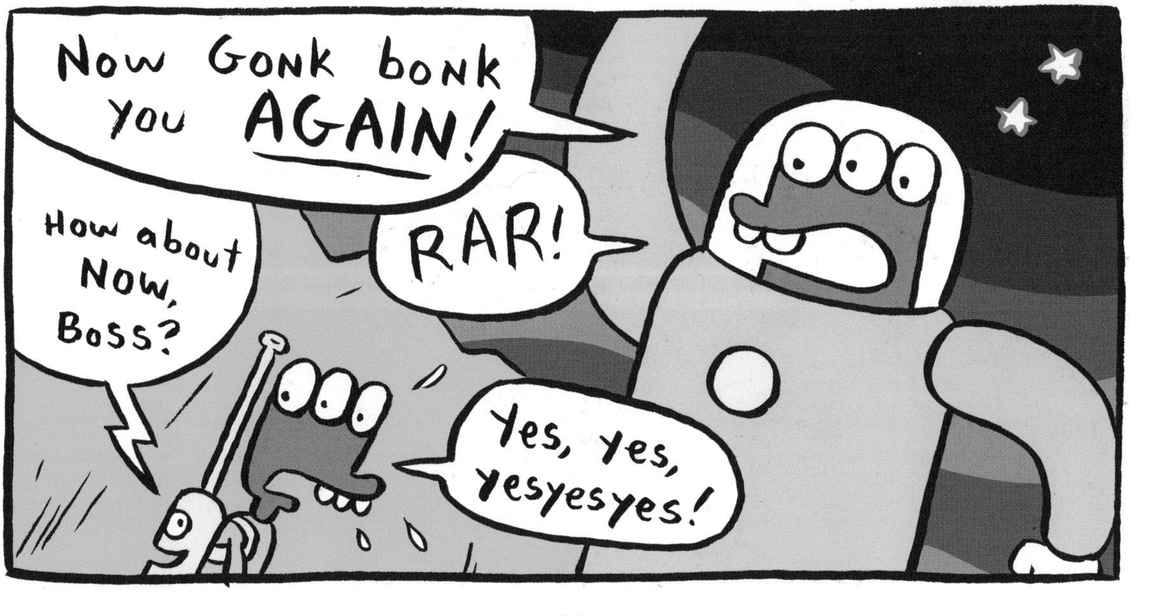
Now Gonk bonk you AGAIN!
RAR!
How about NOW, Boss?
Yes, yes, yesyesyes!

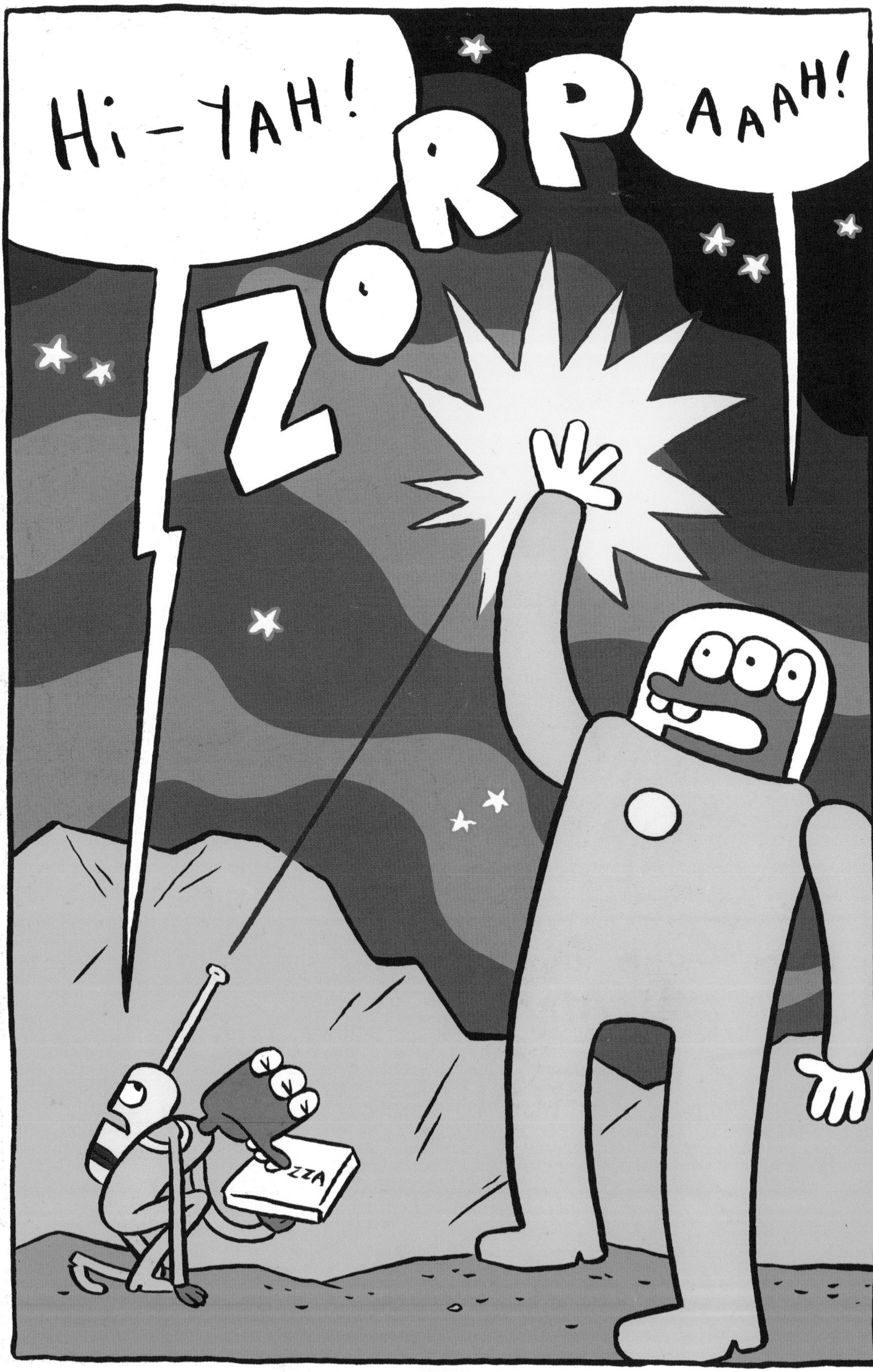
HI-YAH!
ZORP
AAAAH!
ZZA

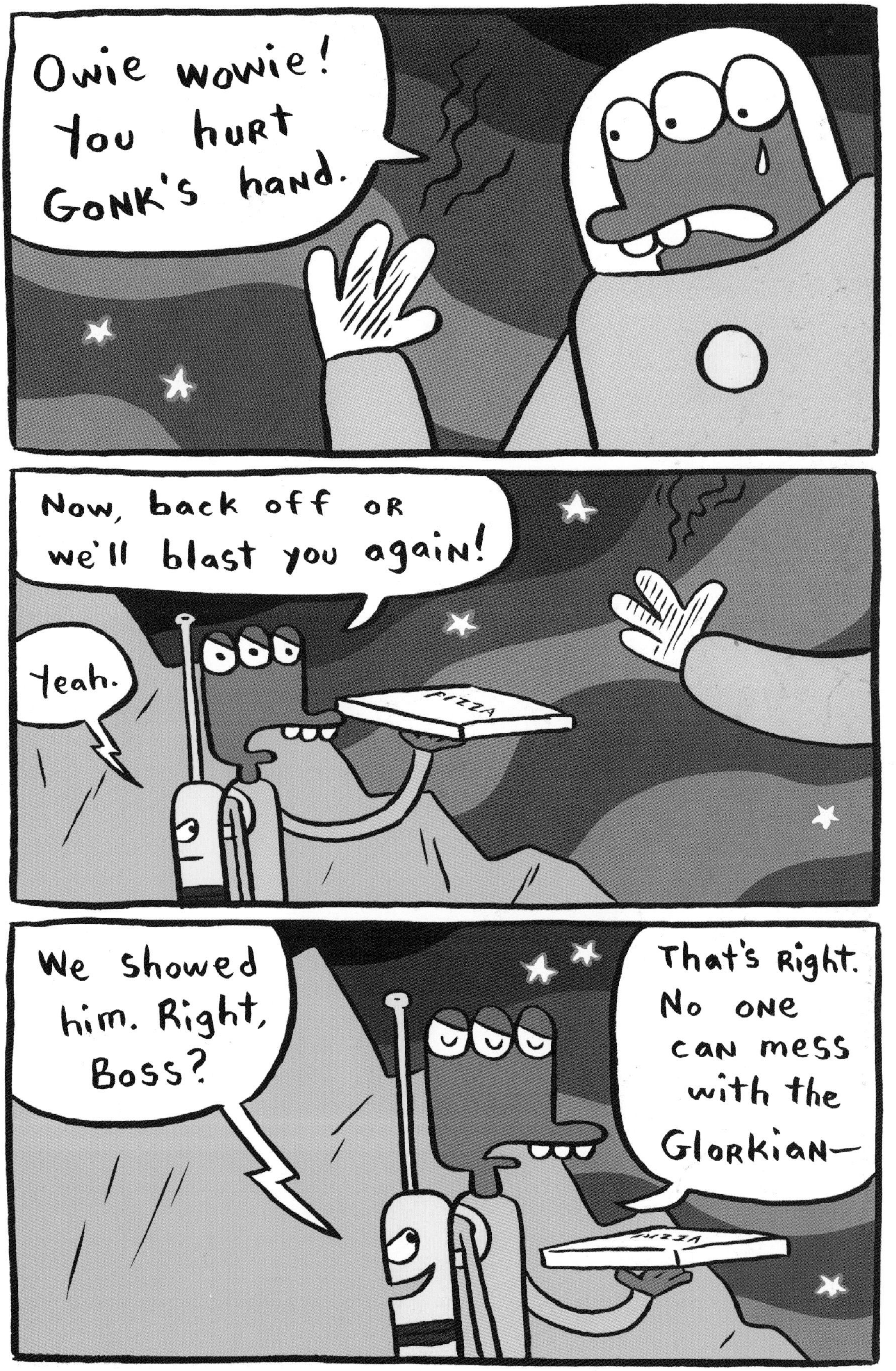
Owie wowie! You hurt GONK's hand.
Now, back off or we'll blast you again!
Yeah.
PIZZA
We showed him. Right, Boss?
That's Right. No one can mess with the Glorkian—
PIZZA

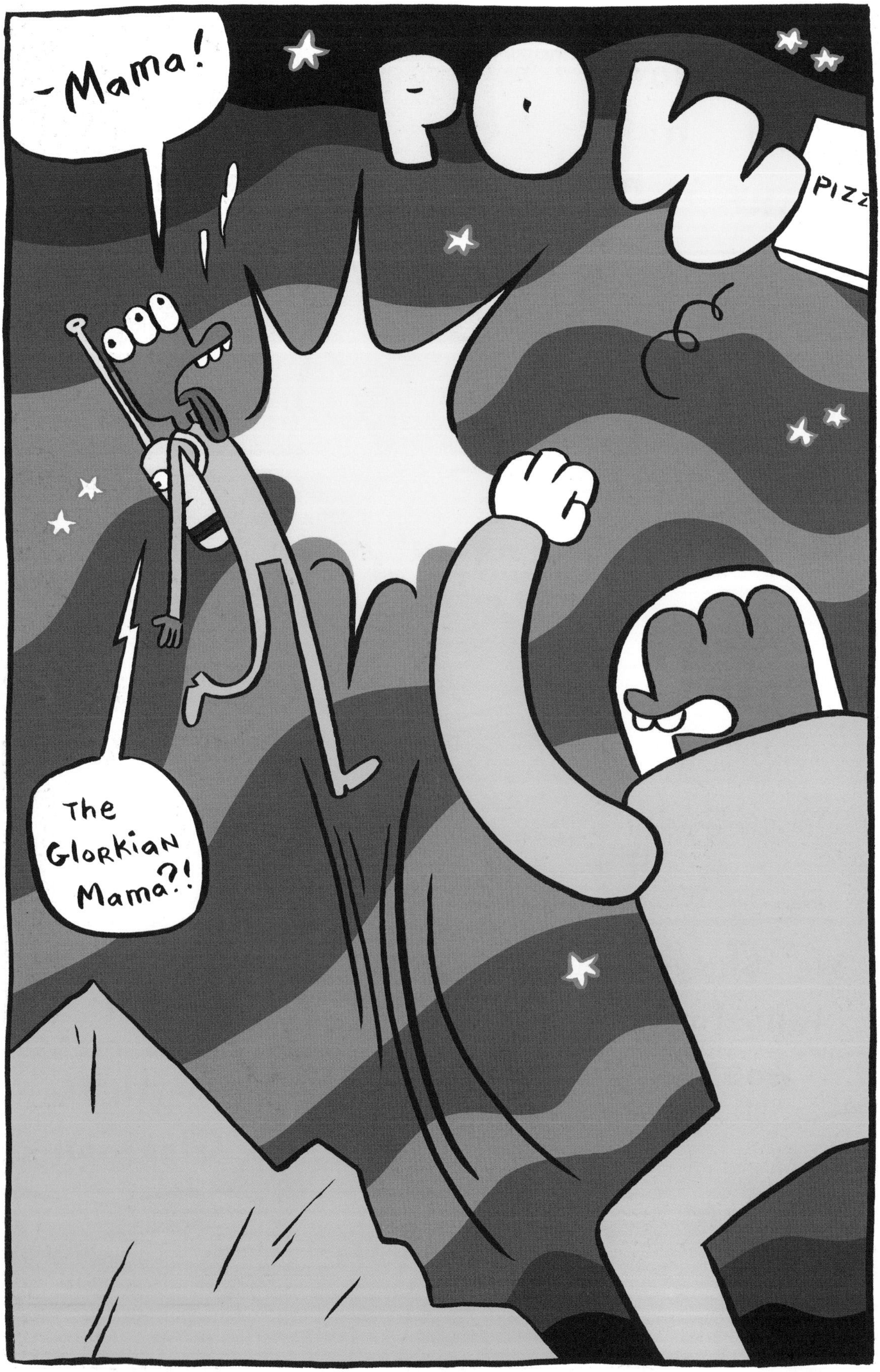
-Mama!
POW
PIZZ
The Glorkian Mama?!

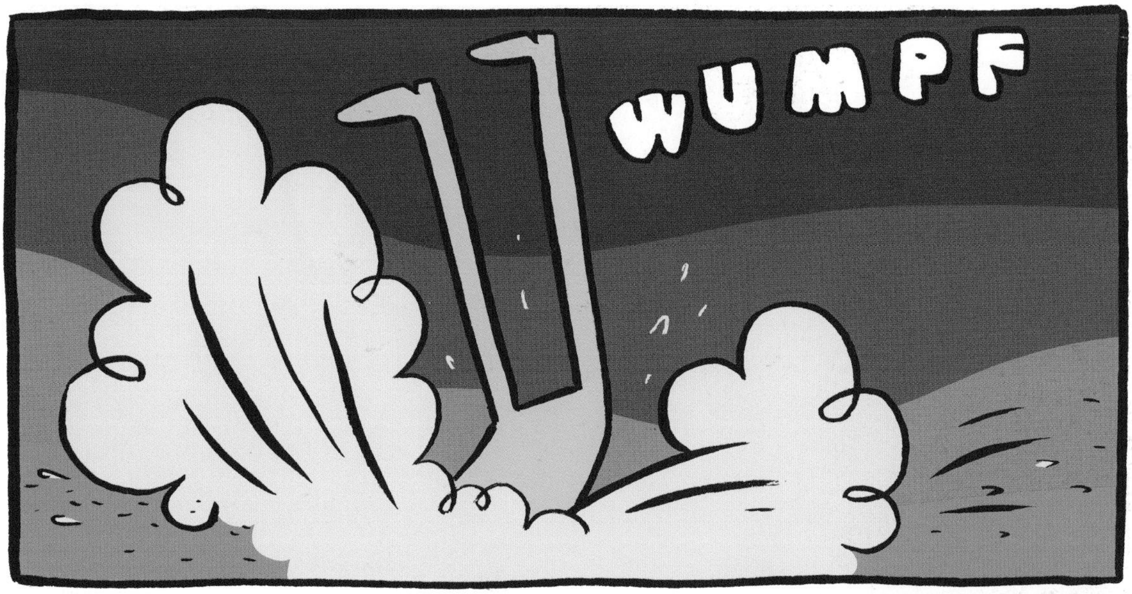
WUMPF

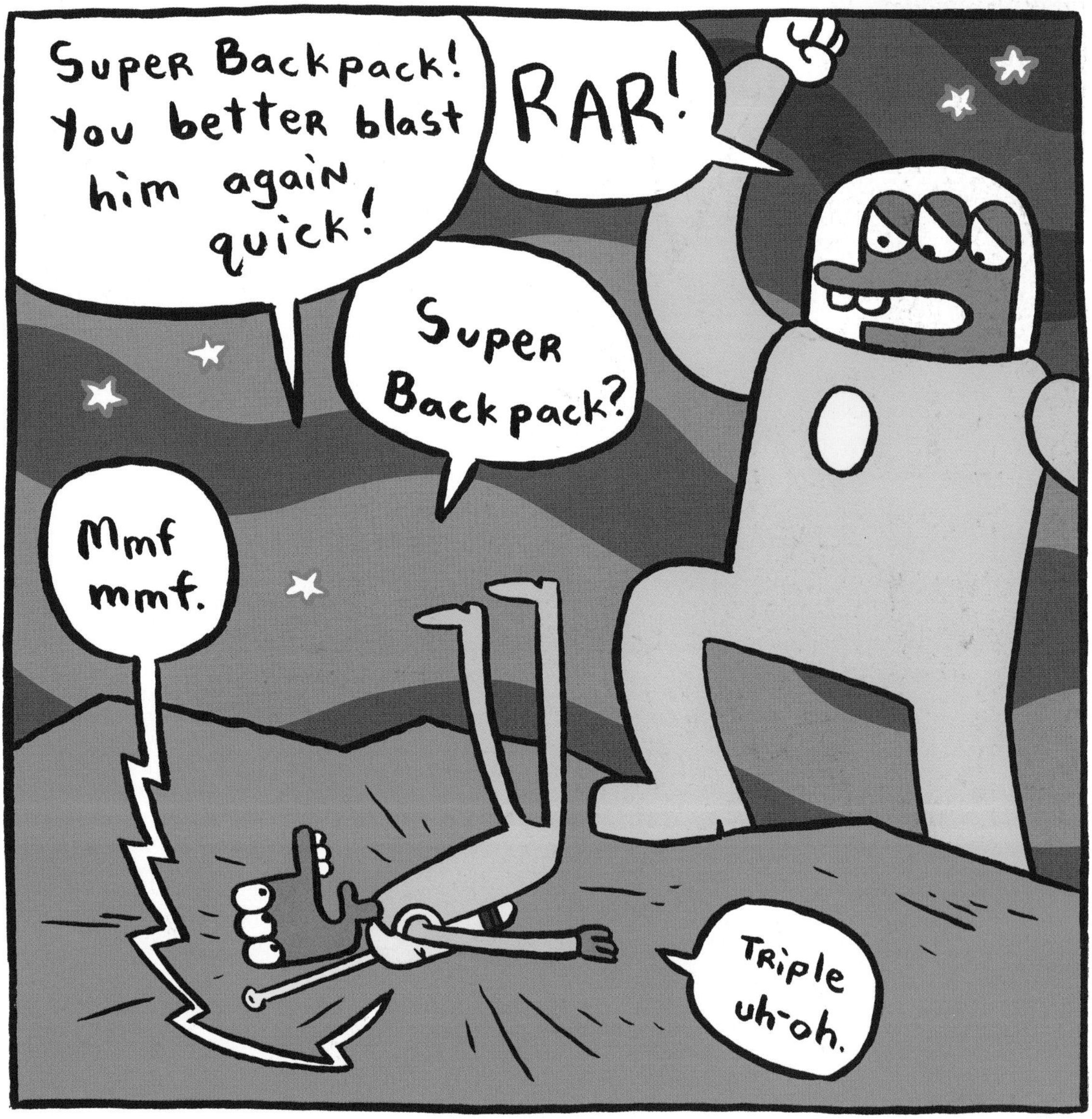
Super Backpack! You better blast him again quick!
RAR!
Super Backpack?
Mmf mmf.
Triple uh-oh.

CHAPTER SEVEN

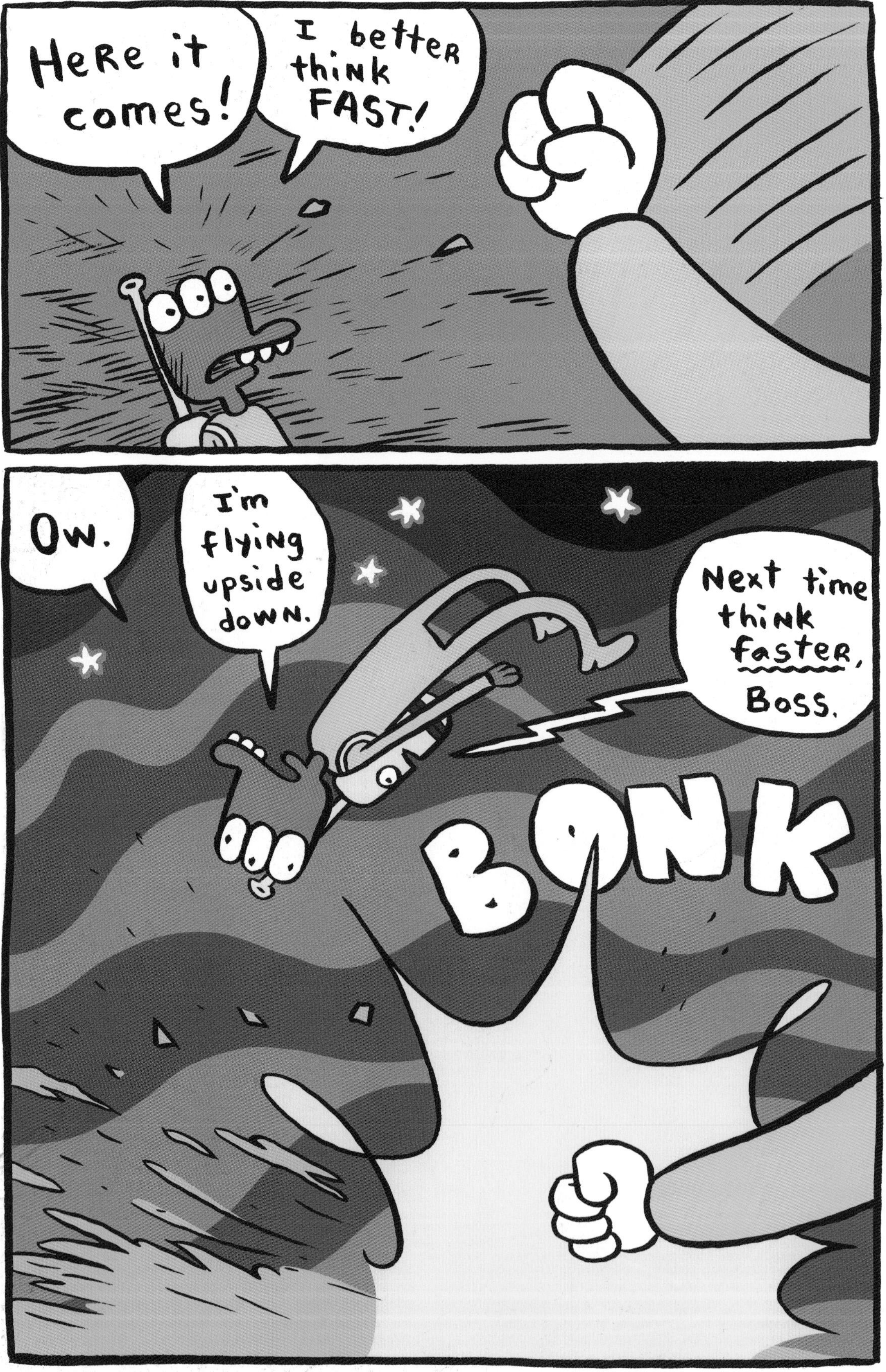
Here it comes!
I better think FAST!
Ow.
I'm flying upside down.
Next time think faster, Boss.
BONK

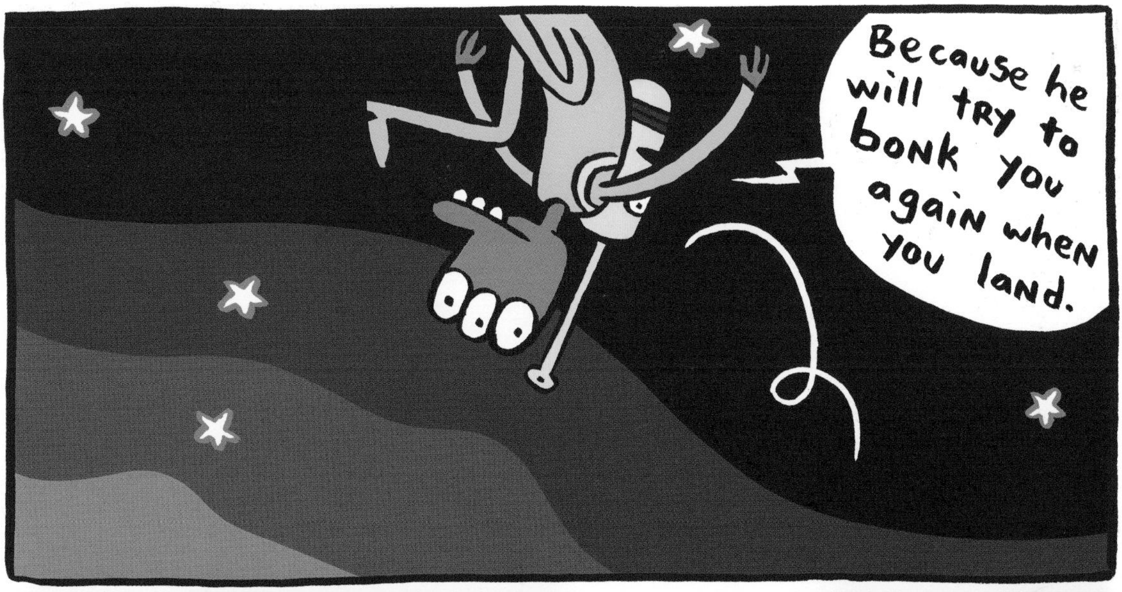
Because he will TRY to bonk you again when you land.

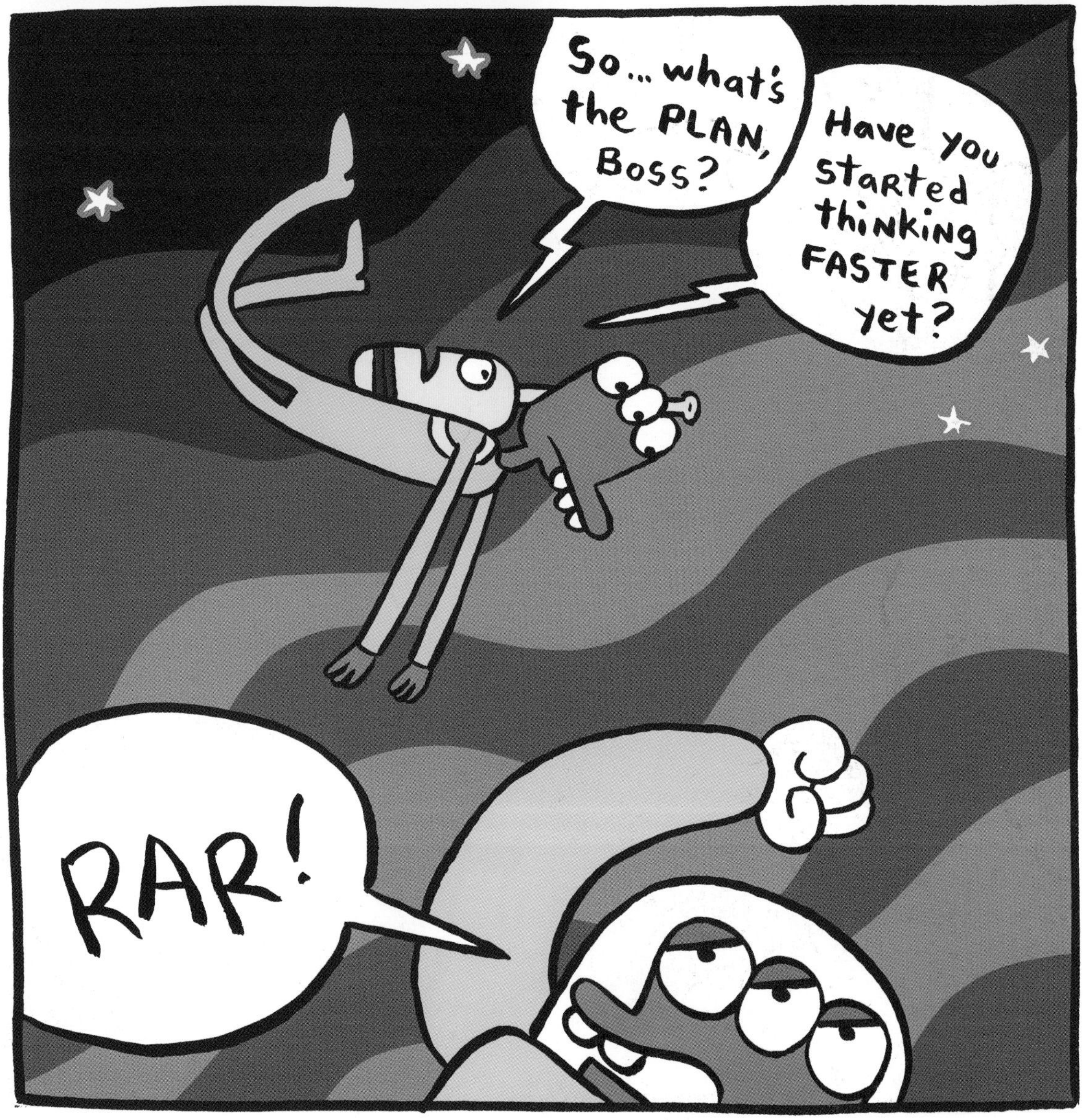
So... what's the PLAN, Boss?
Have you started thinking FASTER yet?
RAR!

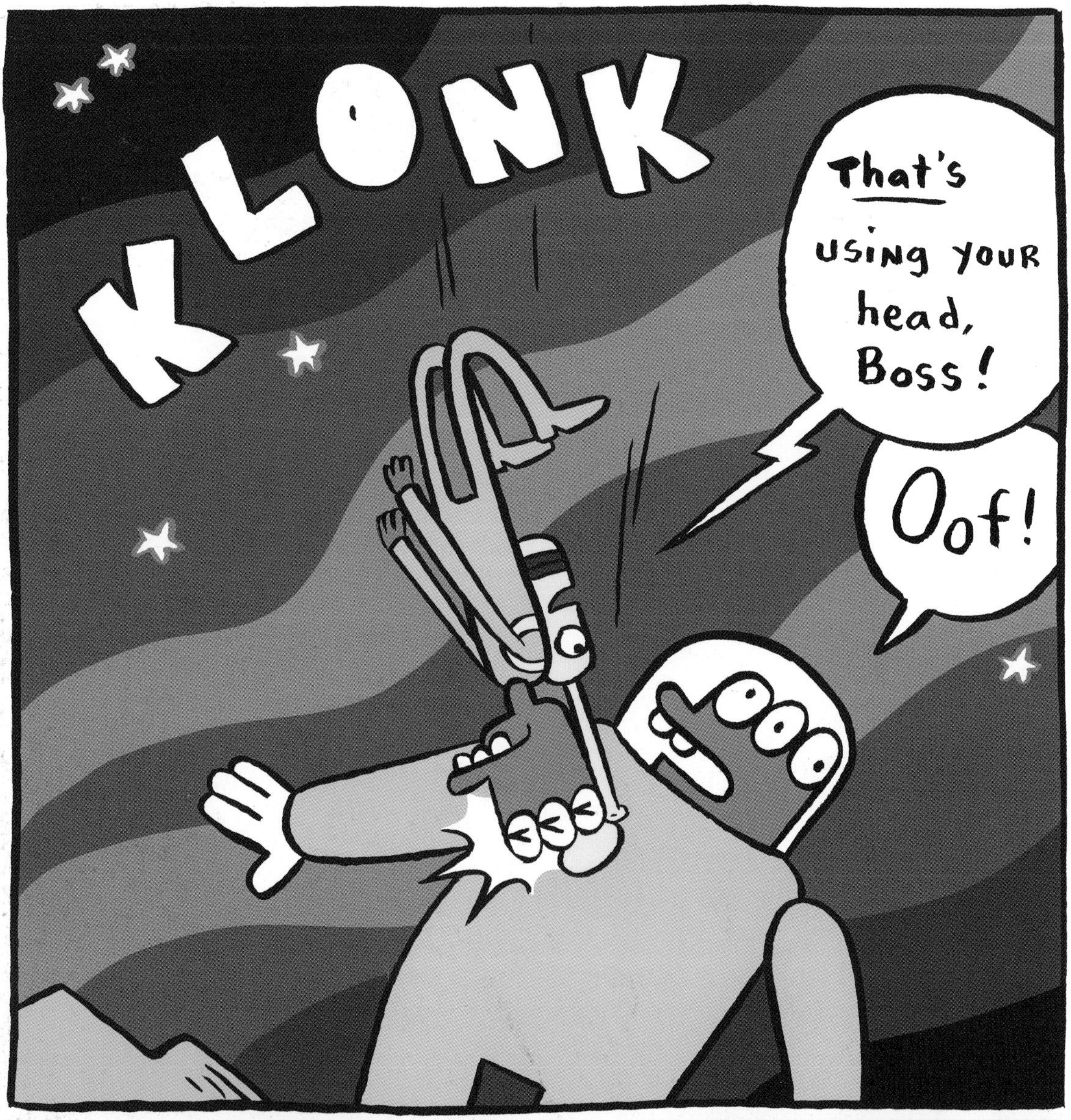
KLONK
That's using your head, Boss!
Oof!

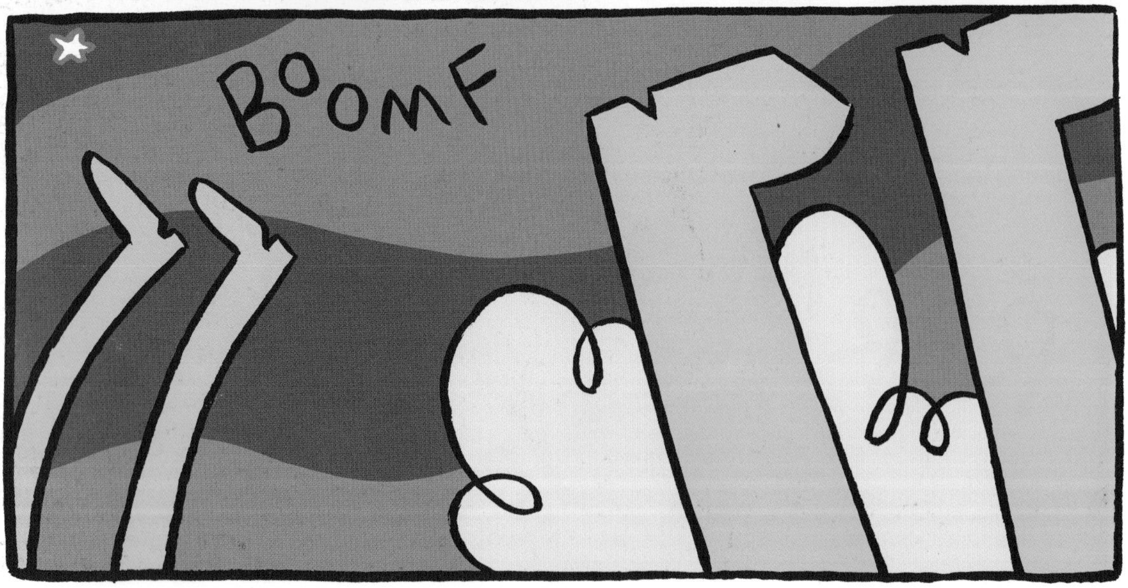
BOOMF

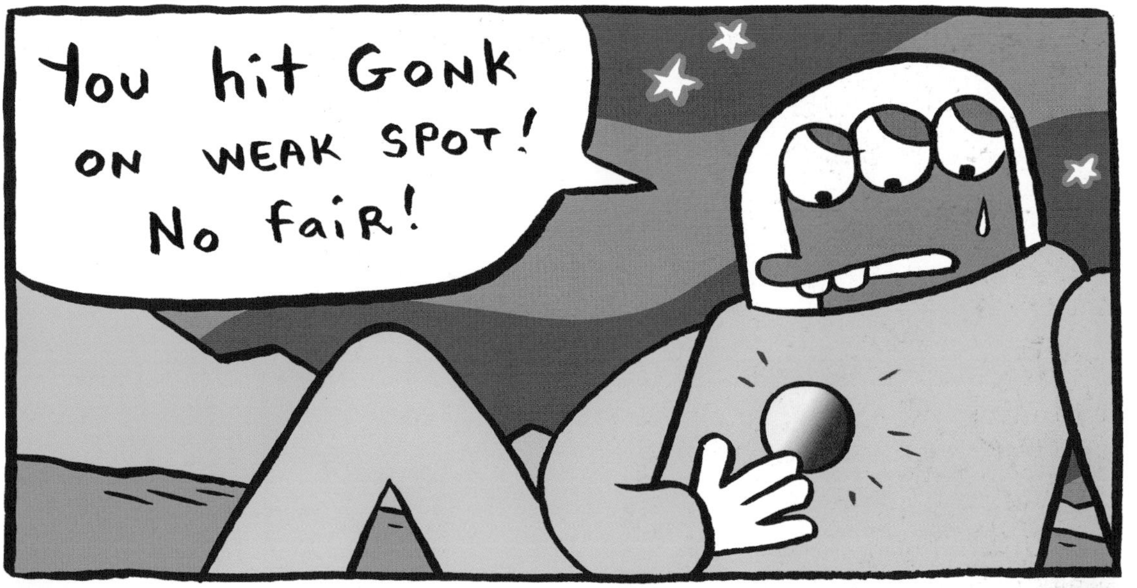
You hit Gonk on weak spot! No fair!

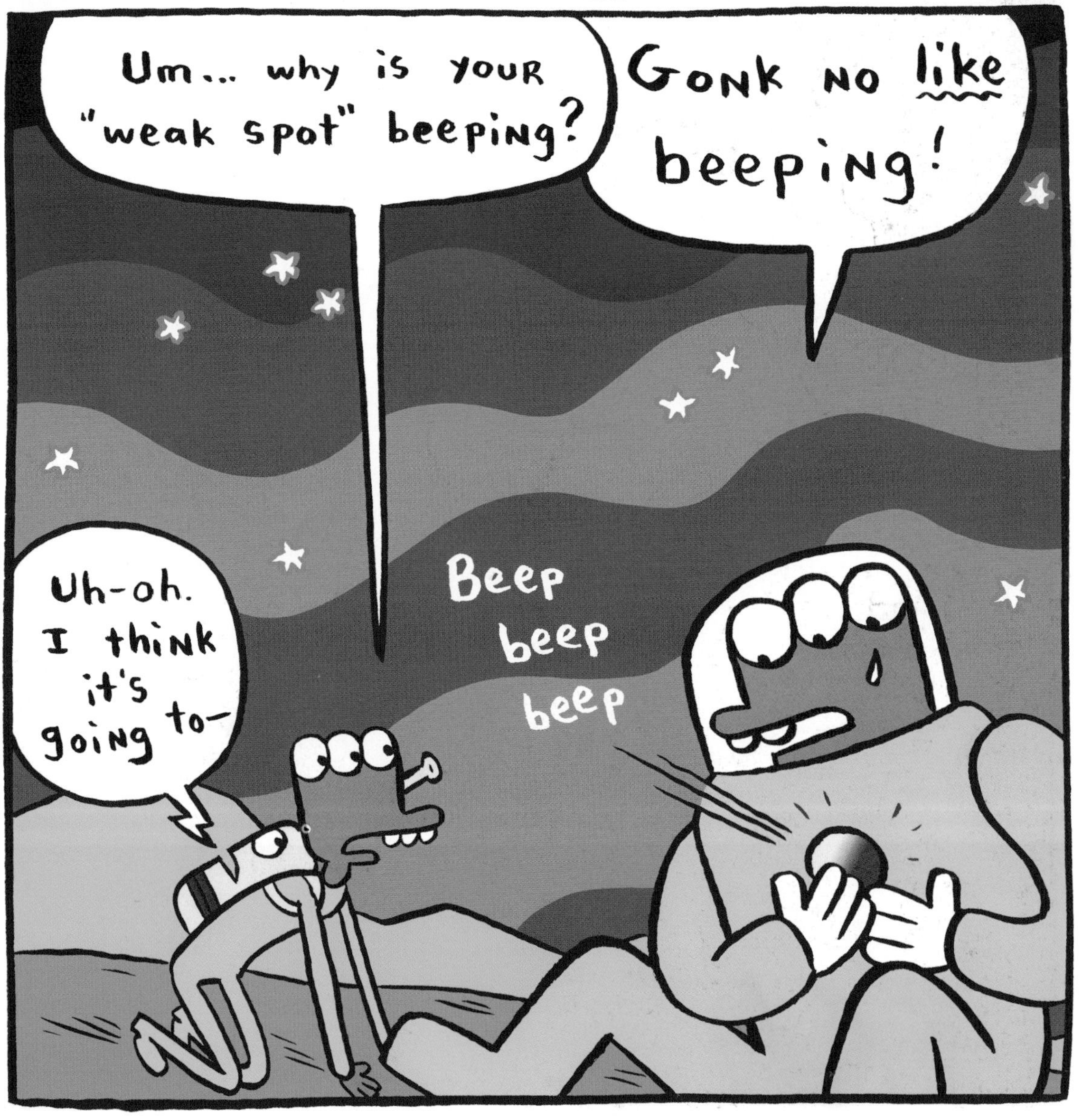
Um... why is your "weak spot" beeping?
Gonk no like beeping!
Uh-oh. I think it's going to-
Beep beep beep

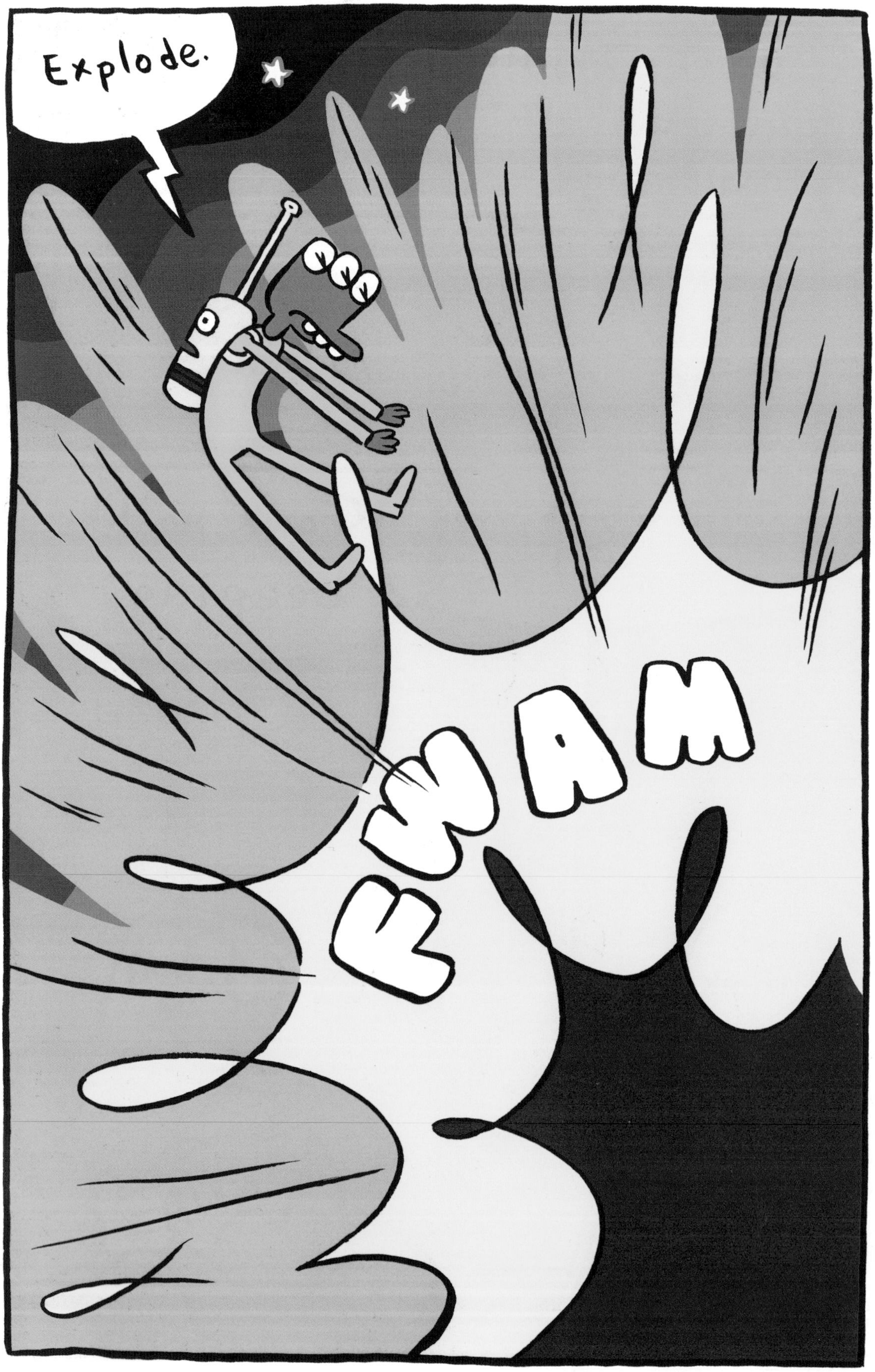
Explode.
FWAM

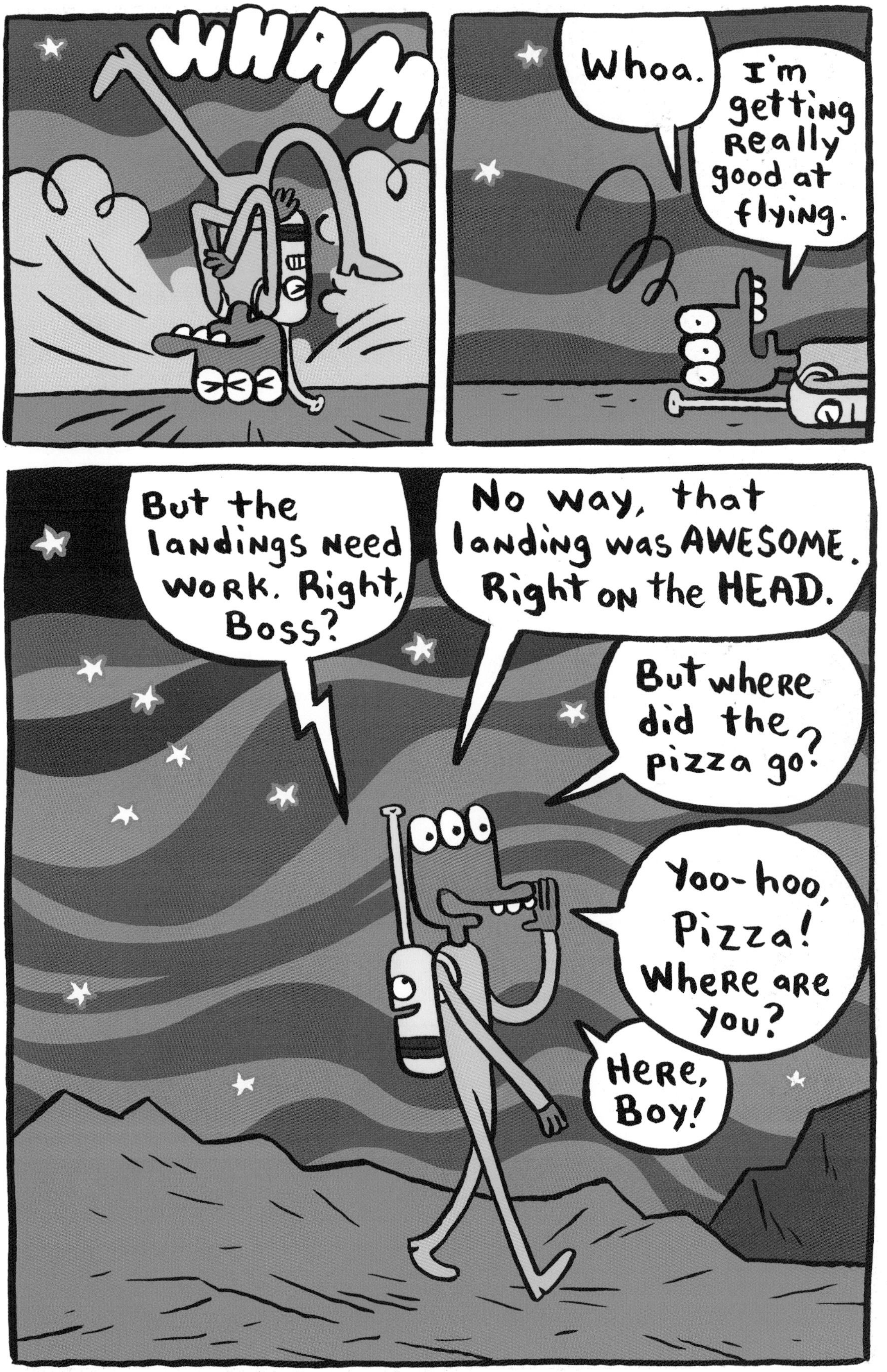
WHAM
Whoa.
I'm getting really good at flying.
But the landings need work. Right, Boss?
No way, that landing was AWESOME. Right on the HEAD.
But where did the pizza go?
Yoo-hoo, Pizza! Where are you?
Here, Boy!

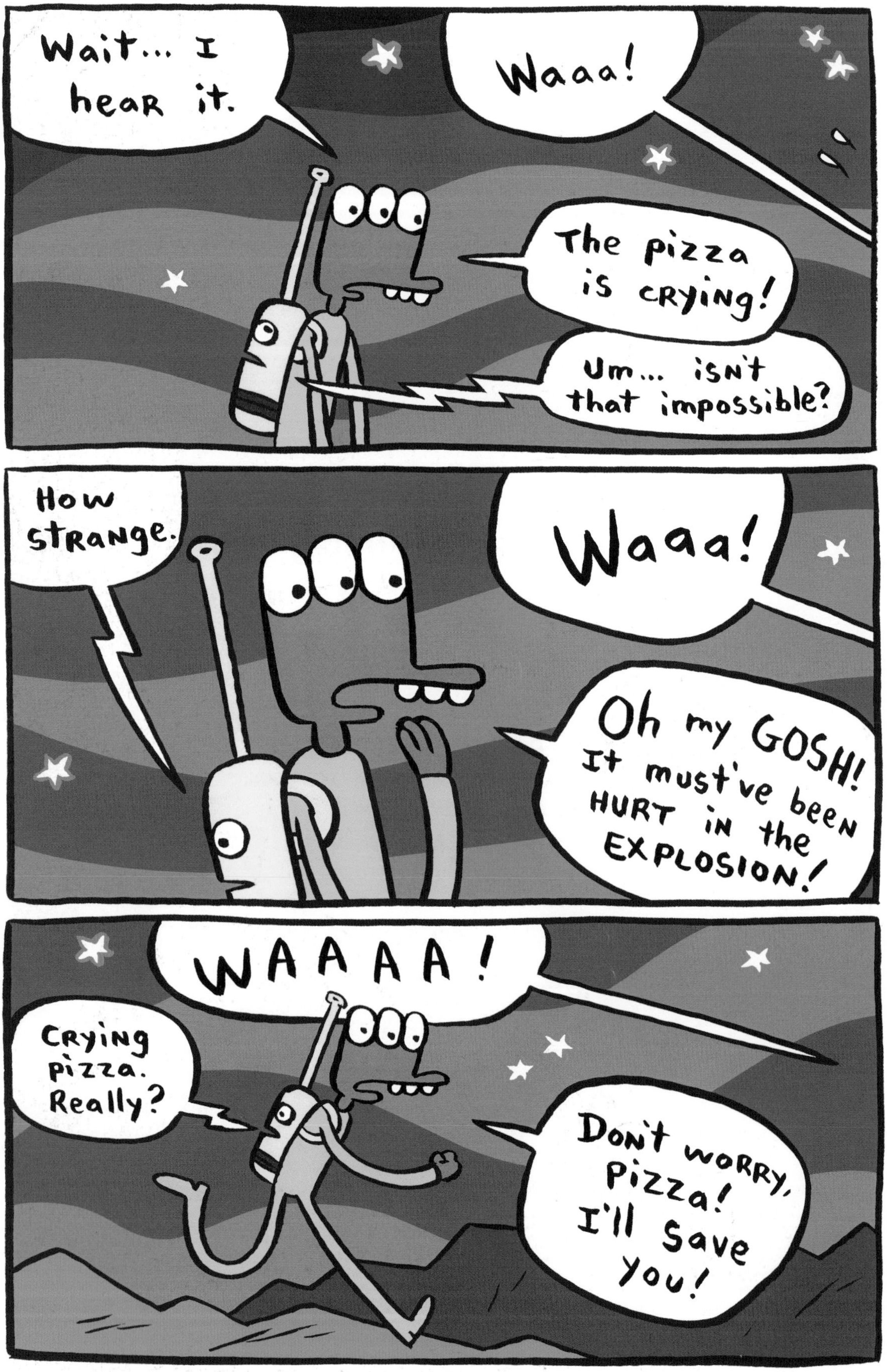
Wait... I hear it.
Waaa!
The pizza is crying!
Um... isn't that impossible?
How strange.
Waaa!
Oh my GOSH! It must've been HURT in the EXPLOSION!
WAAAA!
Crying pizza. Really?
Don't worry, Pizza! I'll save you!

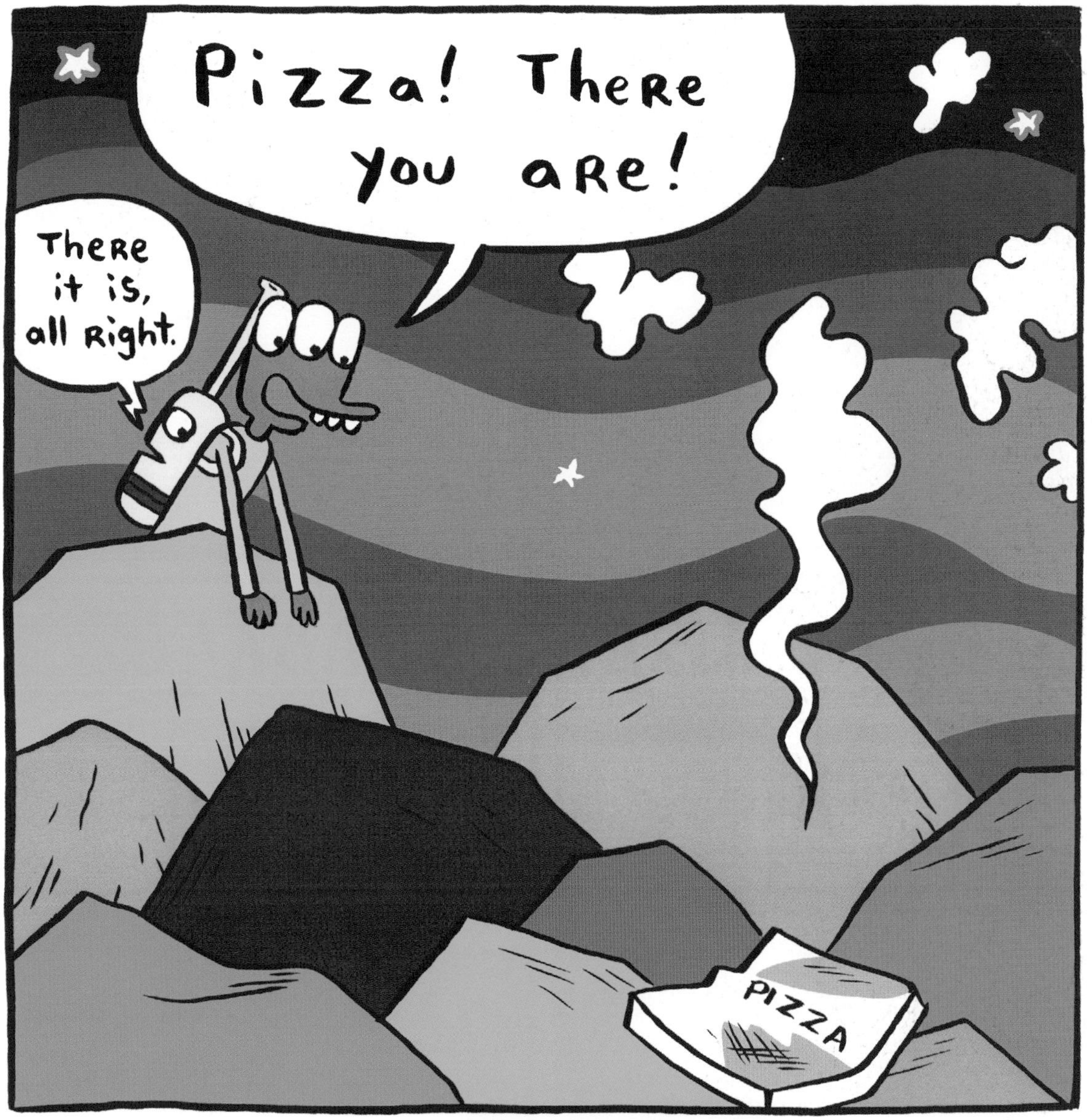
Pizza! There you are!
There it is, all right.
PIZZA

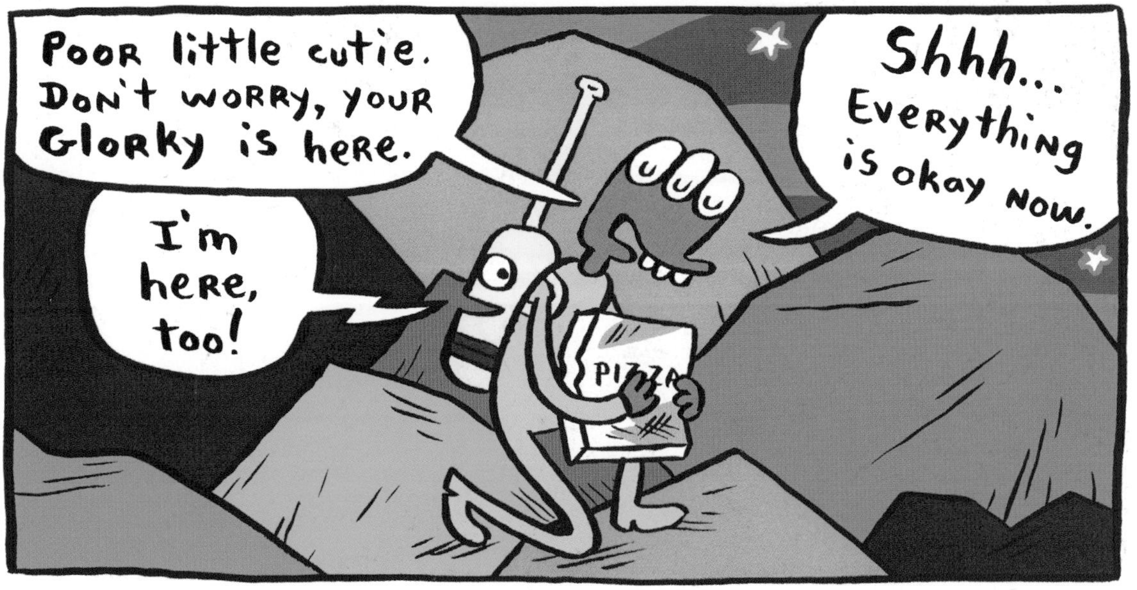
Poor little cutie. Don't worry, your Glorky is here.
I'm here, too!
Shhh... Everything is okay now.

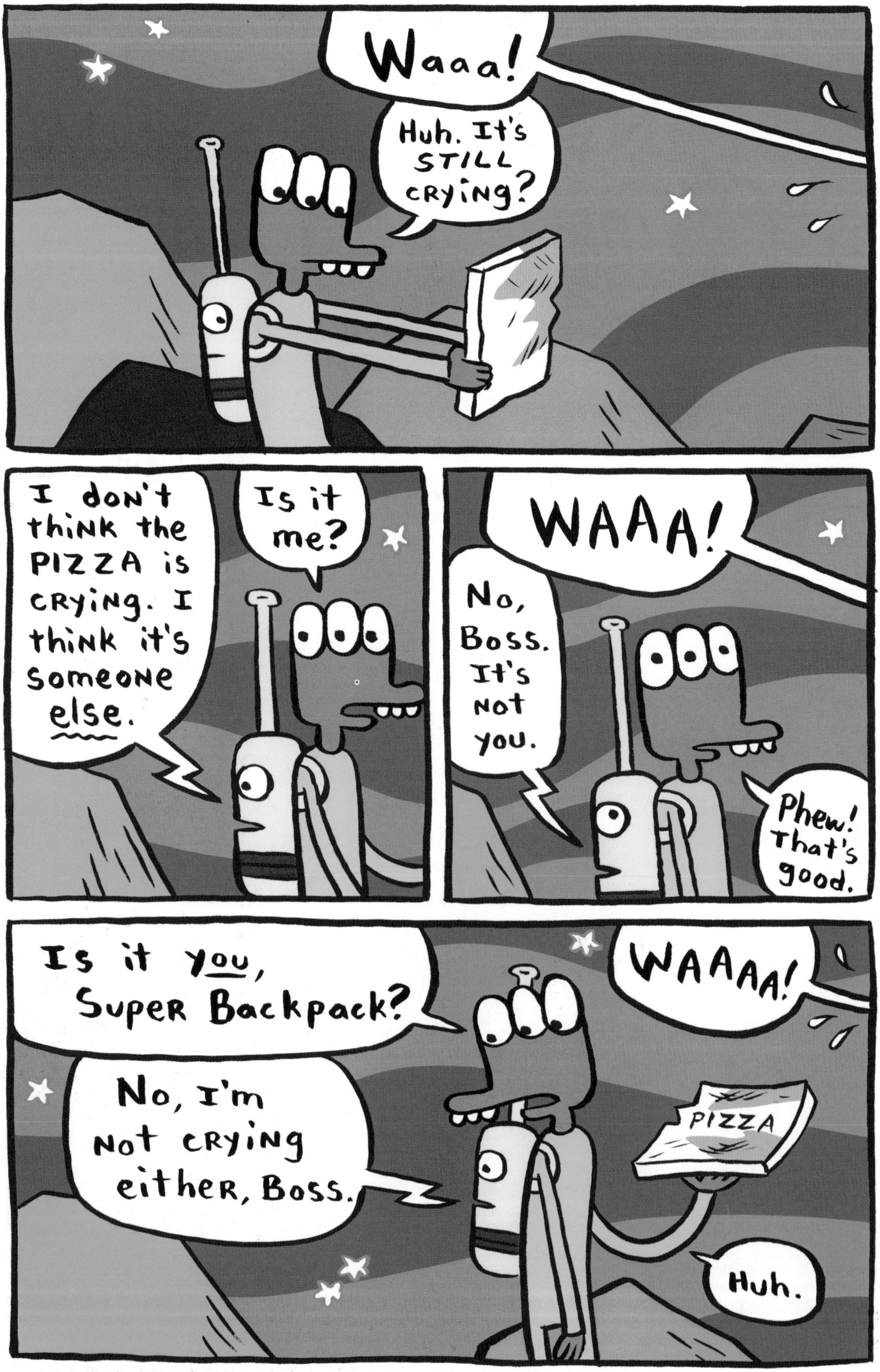
Waaa!
Huh. It's STILL crying?
I don't think the PIZZA is crying. I think it's someone else.
Is it me?
WAAA!
No, Boss. It's not you.
Phew! That's good.
Is it you, Super Backpack?
WAAAA!
No, I'm not crying either, Boss.
PIZZA
Huh.

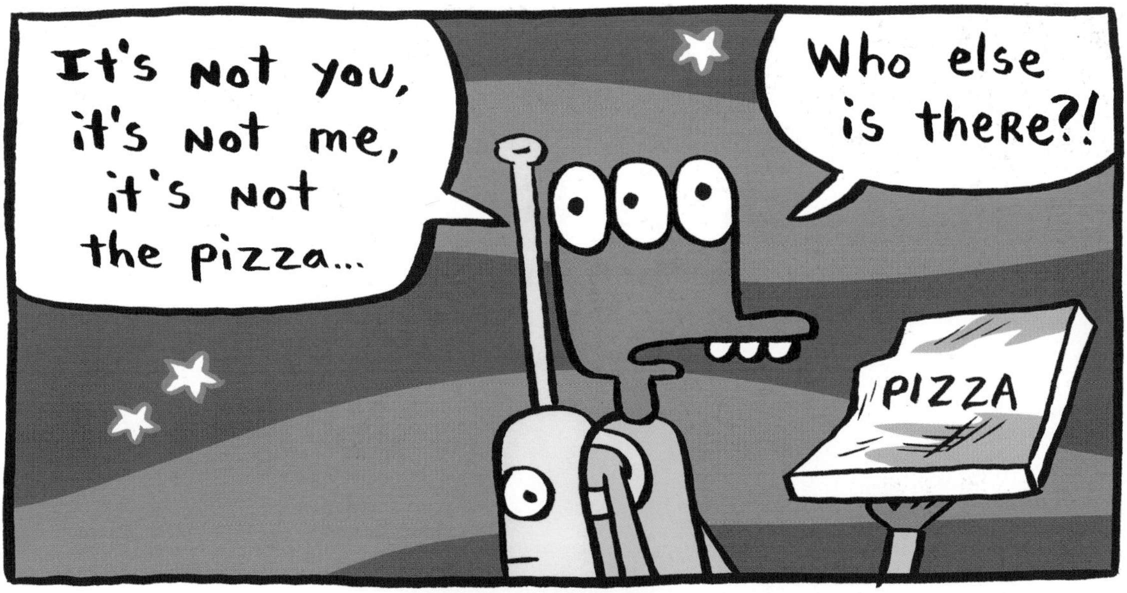
It's not you, it's not me, it's not the pizza...
Who else is there?!
PIZZA

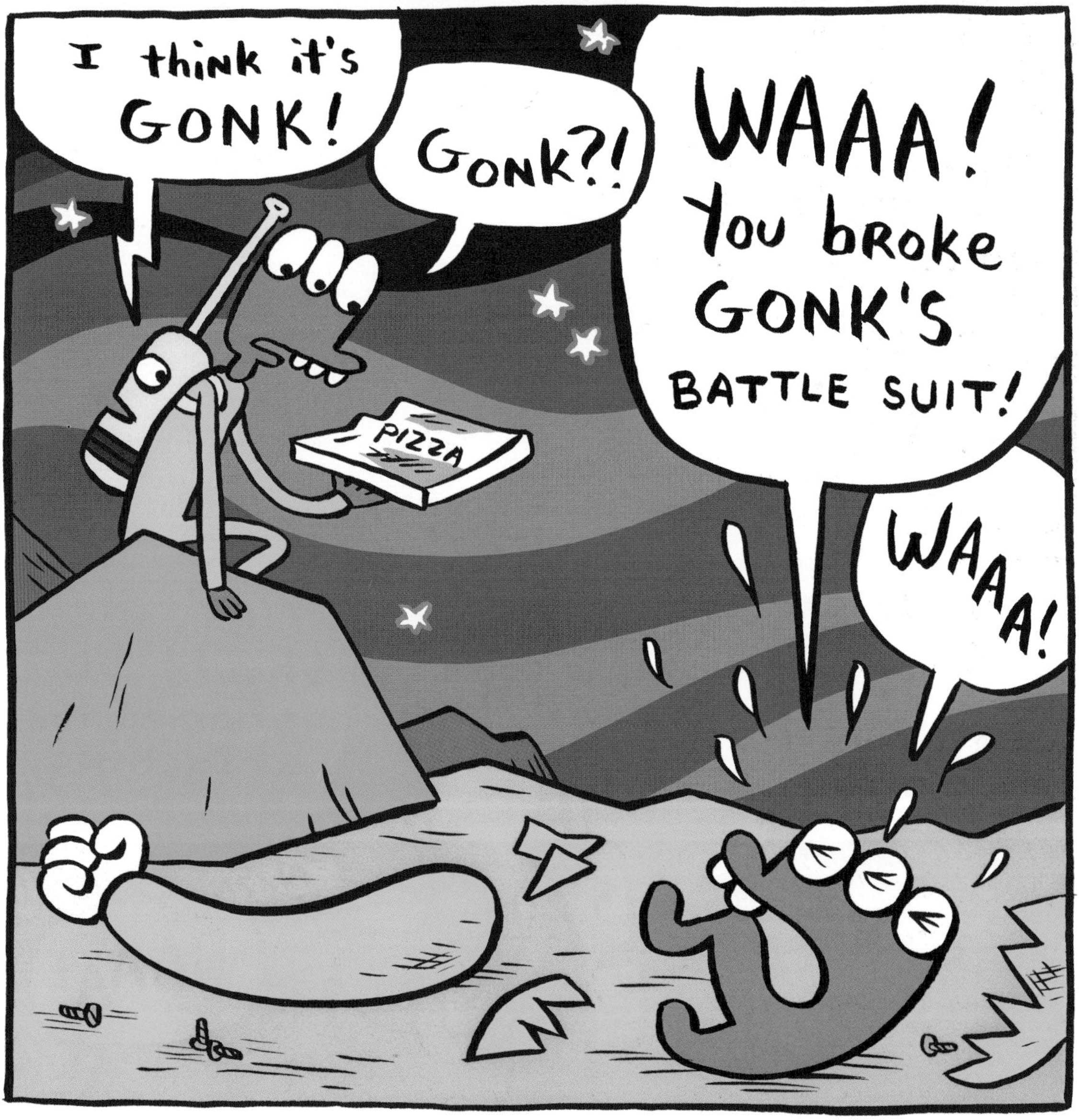
I think it's GONK!
GONK?!
WAAAA! You broke GONK'S BATTLE SUIT!
WAAAA!
PIZZA

CHAPTER NINE

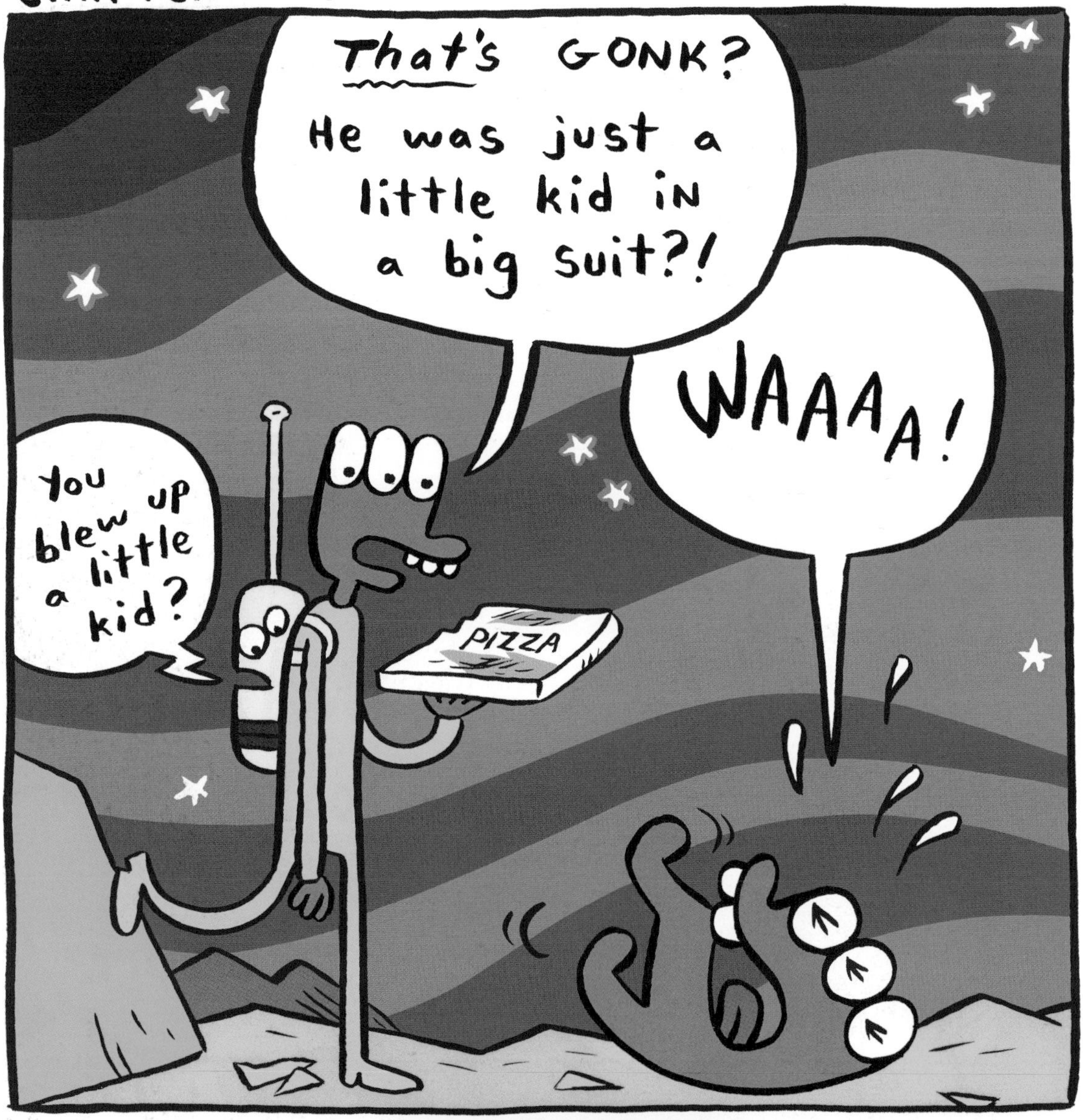
That's GONK? He was just a little kid in a big suit?!
You blew up a little kid?
PIZZA
WAAAAA!

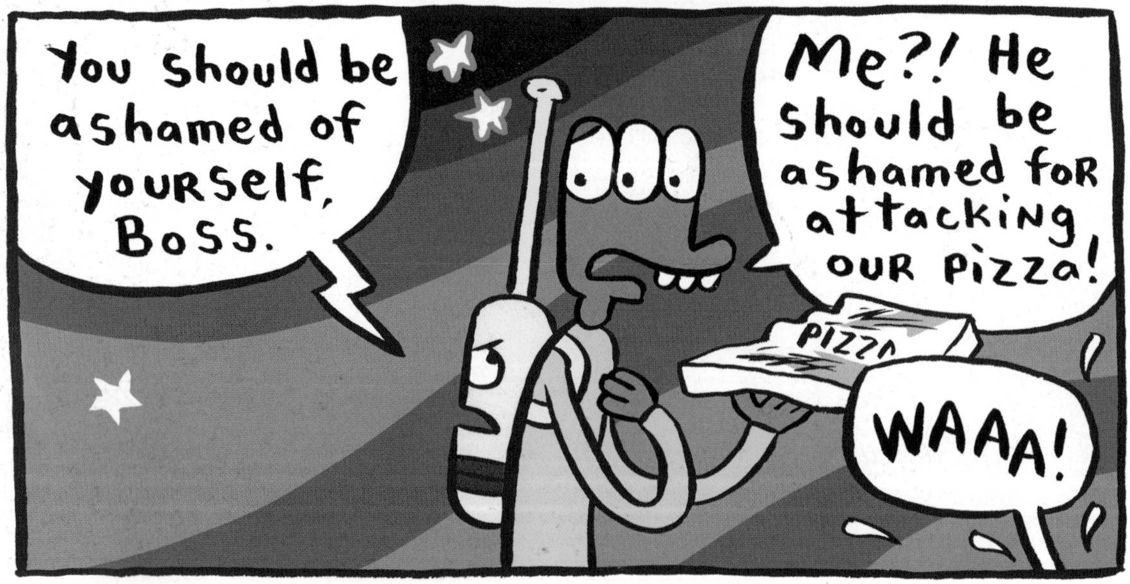
You should be ashamed of yourself, BOSS.
Me?! He should be ashamed for attacking our pizza!
WAAA!

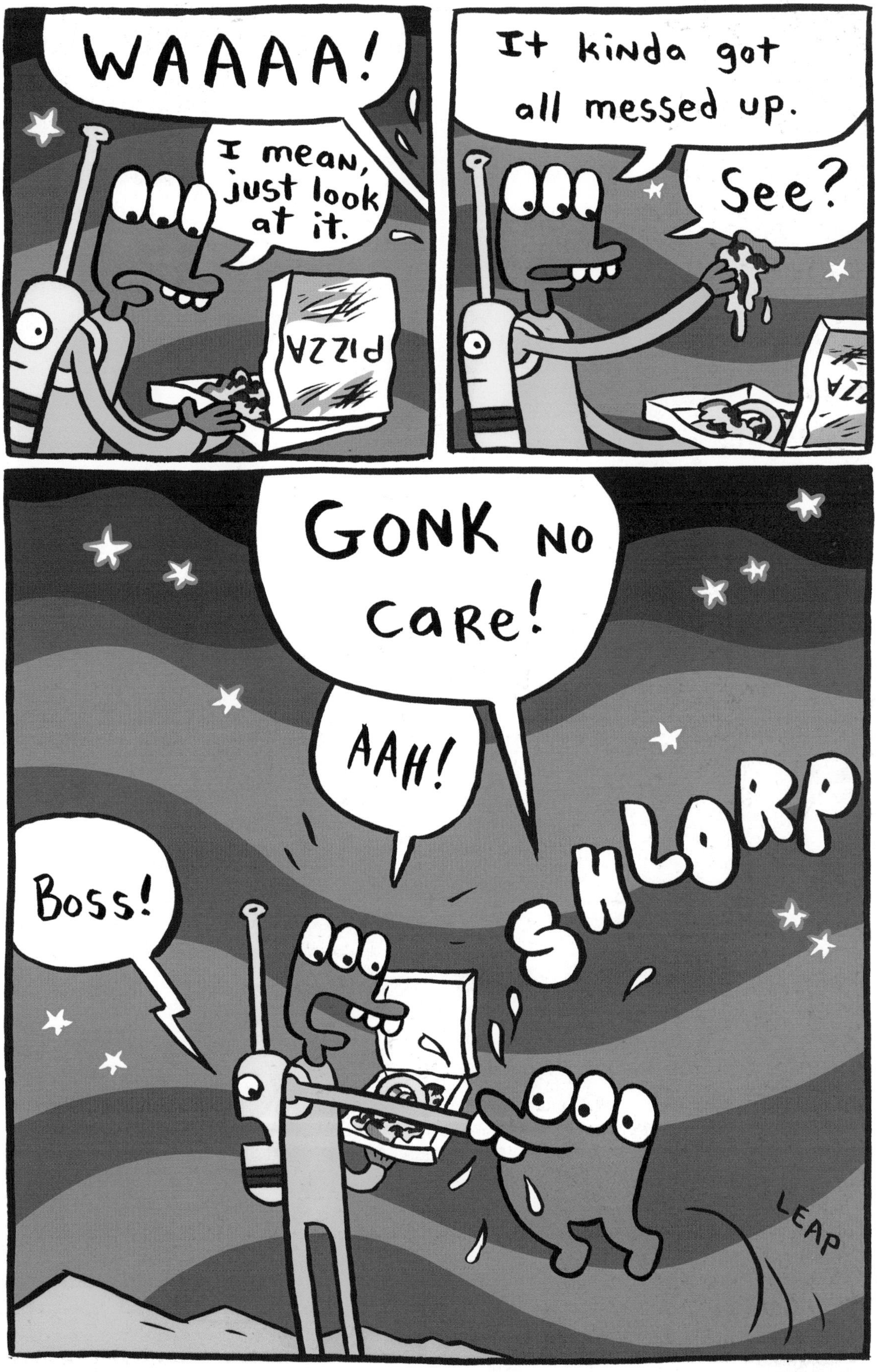
WAAAA!
I mean, just look at it.
PIZZA
It kinda got all messed up.
See?
GONK NO CARE!
AAH!
Boss!
SHLORP
LEAP

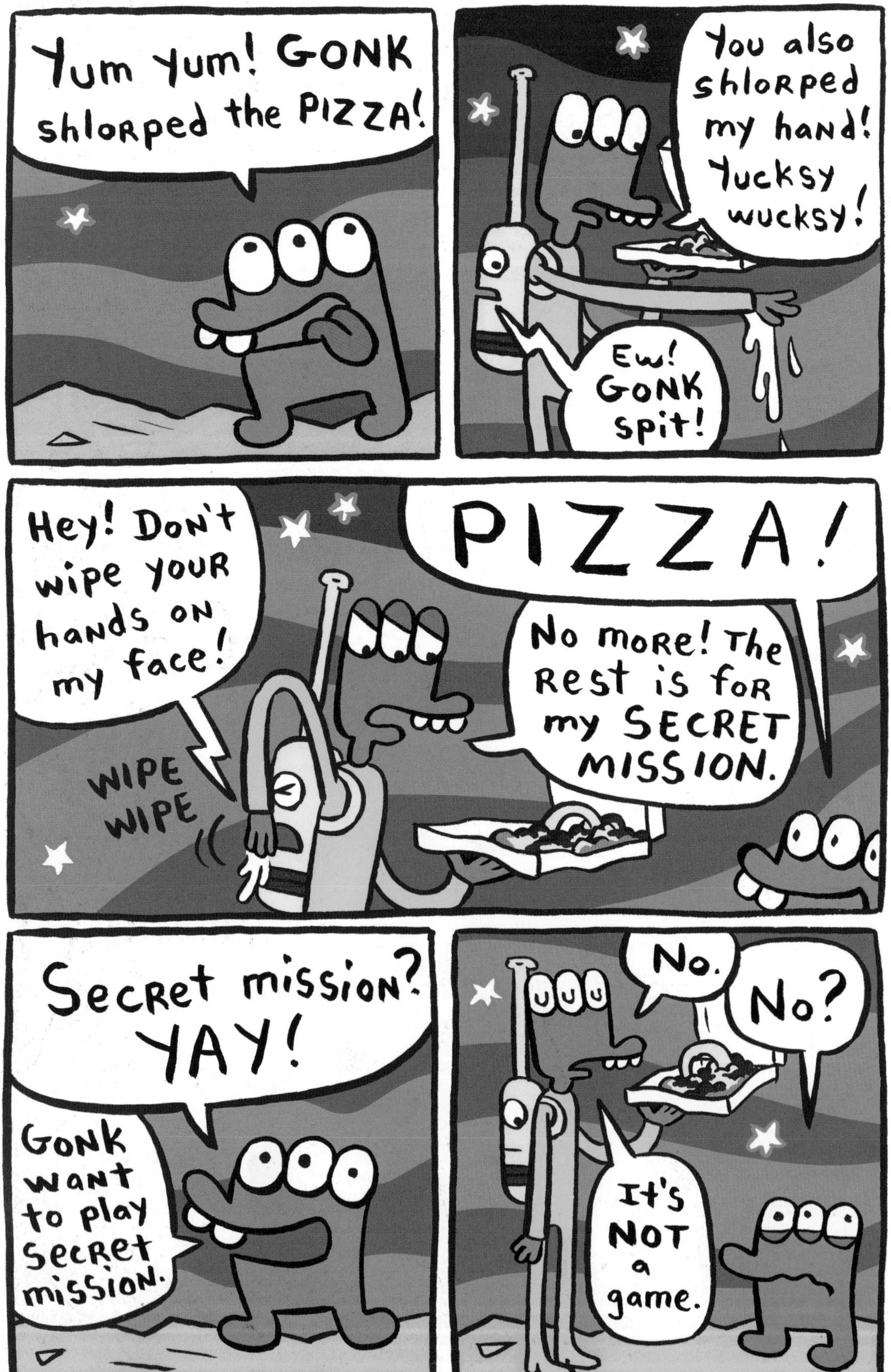

Yum Yum! GONK shlorped the PIZZA!
You also shlorped my hand! Yucksy wucksy!
Ew! GONK spit!
Hey! Don't wipe your hands on my face!
PIZZA!
No more! The rest is for my SECRET MISSION.
WIPE WIPE
Secret mission? YAY!
GONK want to play secret mission.
No.
No?
It's NOT a game.

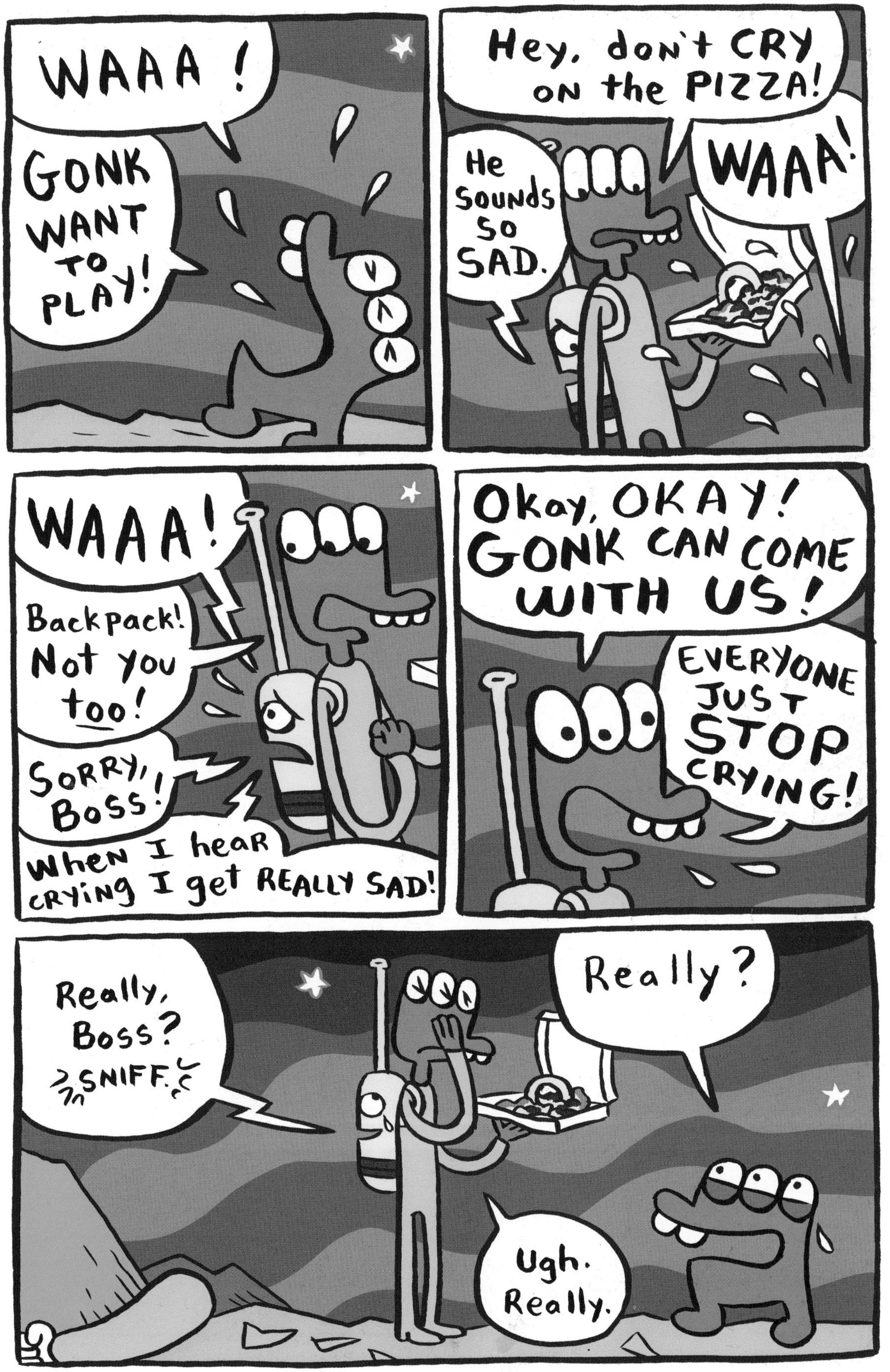
WAAA!
GONK WANT TO PLAY!
Hey, don't CRY on the PIZZA!
He sounds so SAD.
WAAA!
WAAA!
Backpack! Not you too!
SORRY, BOSS!
When I hear crying I get REALLY SAD!
Okay, OKAY! GONK CAN COME WITH US!
EVERYONE JUST STOP CRYING!
Really, Boss?
SNIFF.
Really?
Ugh. Really.

All Right, GONK! You made our team!
Good for you!
One time, GONK made poopy in the toilet.
Hmm... Peanutbutter, steering wheel, clams, and tears.
We might really be onto something here!
Looks GOOD.

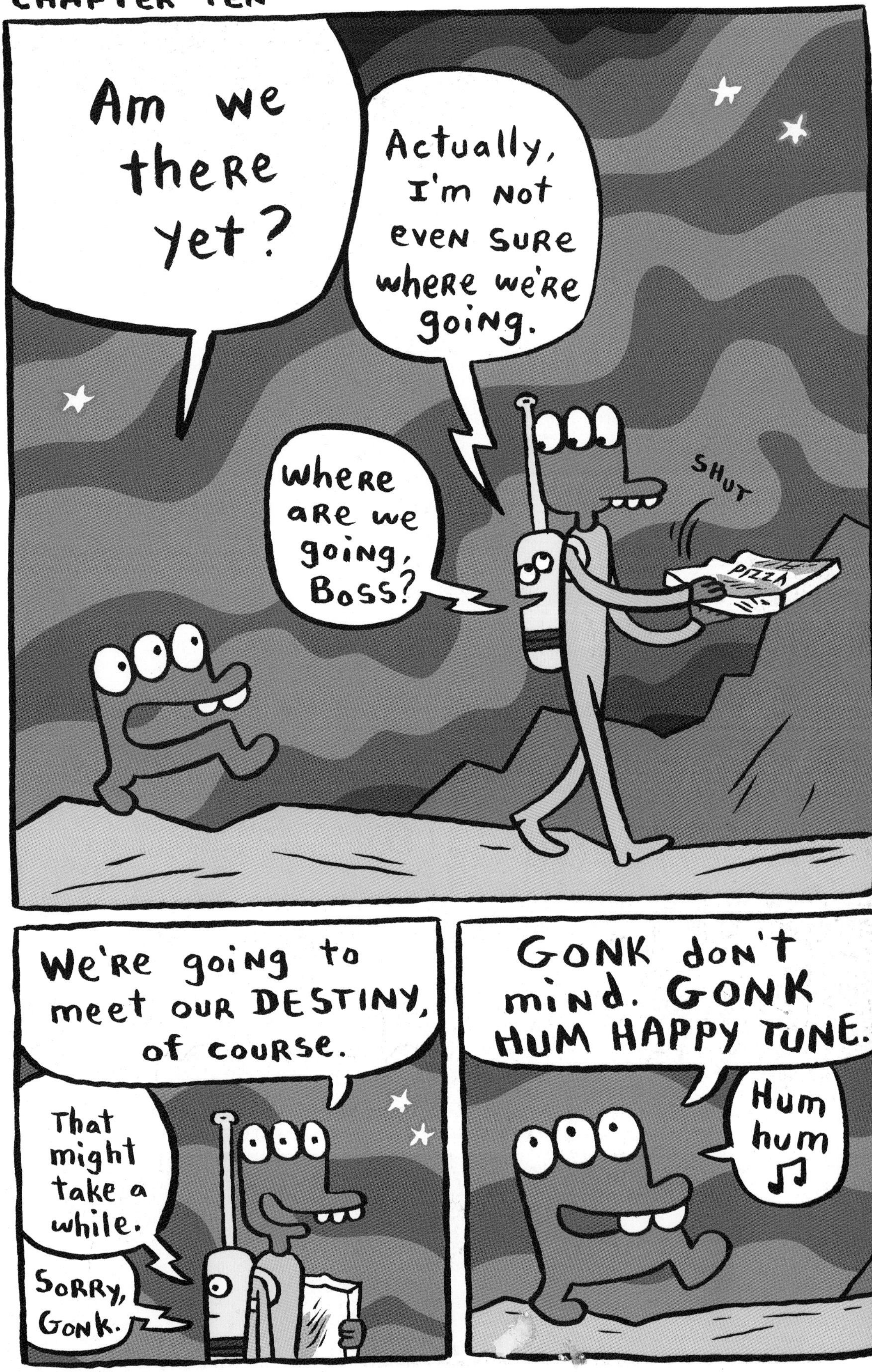
Am we there yet?
Actually, I'm not even sure where we're going.
where are we going, Boss?
SHUT
PIZZA
We're going to meet our DESTINY, of course.
That might take a while.
Sorry, Gonk.
GONK don't mind. GONK HUM HAPPY TUNE.
Hum hum ♫

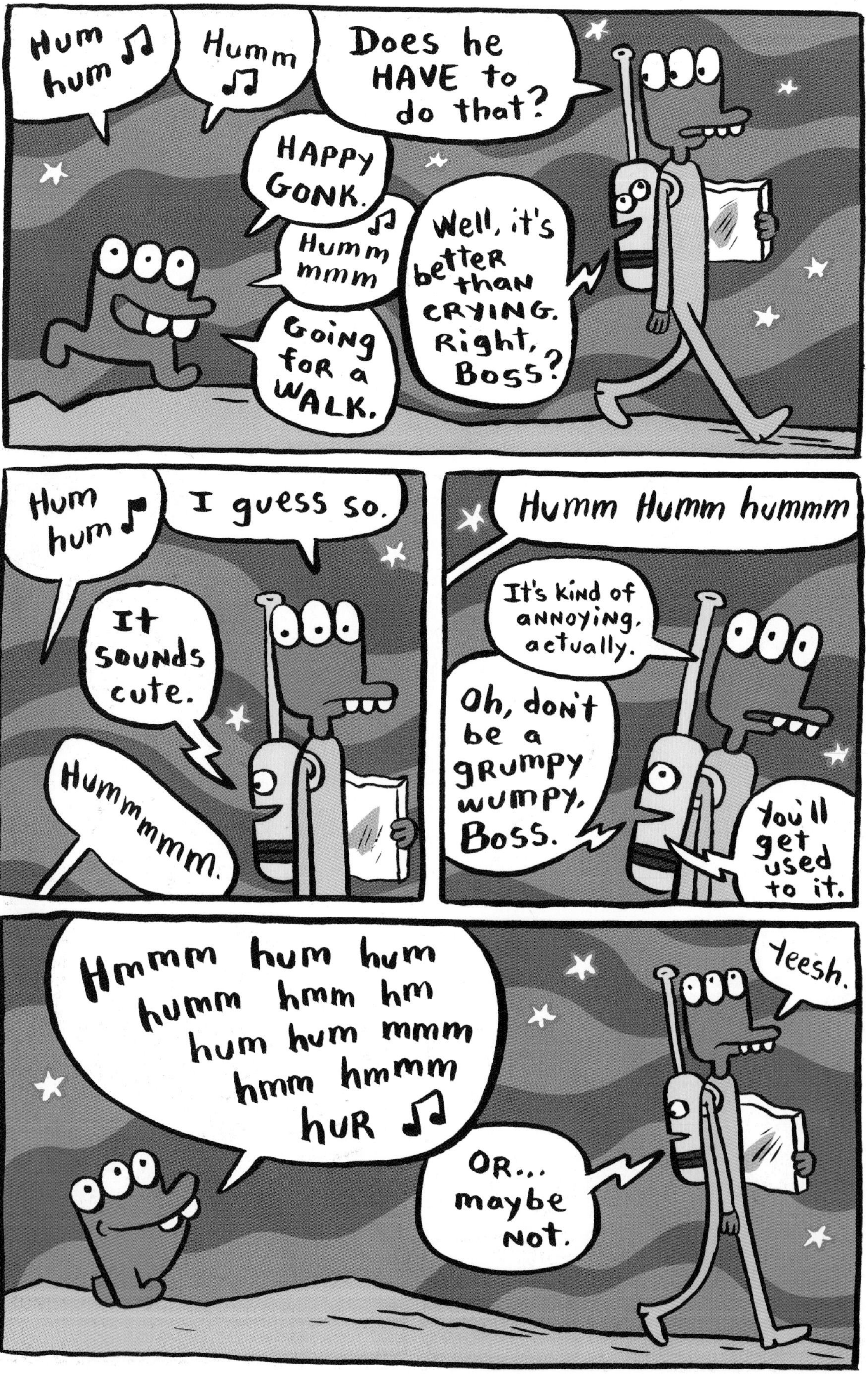
Hum hum ♫
Humm ♫
Does he HAVE to do that?
HAPPY GONK.
♫ Humm mmm
Well, it's better than CRYING. Right, BOSS?
Going for a WALK.
Hum hum ♪
I guess so.
It sounds cute.
Hummmmm.
Humm Humm hummm
It's kind of annoying, actually.
Oh, don't be a grumpy wumpy, BOSS.
You'll get used to it.
Hmmm hum hum humm hmm hm hum hum mmm hmm hmmm huR ♫
Yeesh.
OR... maybe NOT.

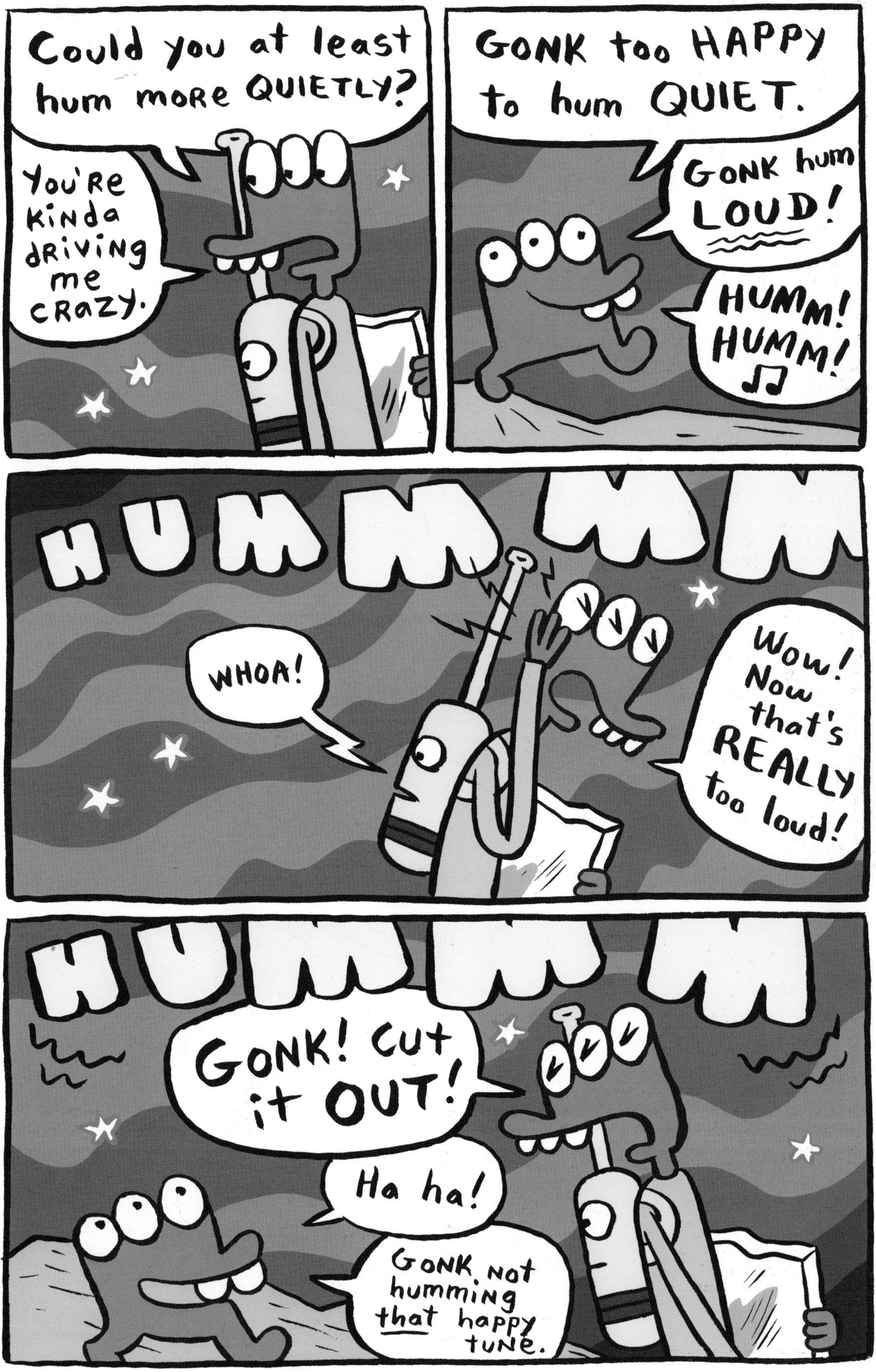

Could you at least hum more QUIETLY?
You're kinda driving me crazy.
GONK too HAPPY to hum QUIET.
GONK hum LOUD!
HUMM! HUMM!
HUMMMM
WHOA!
Wow! Now that's REALLY too loud!
HUMMM
GONK! Cut it OUT!
Ha ha!
GONK not humming that happy tune.

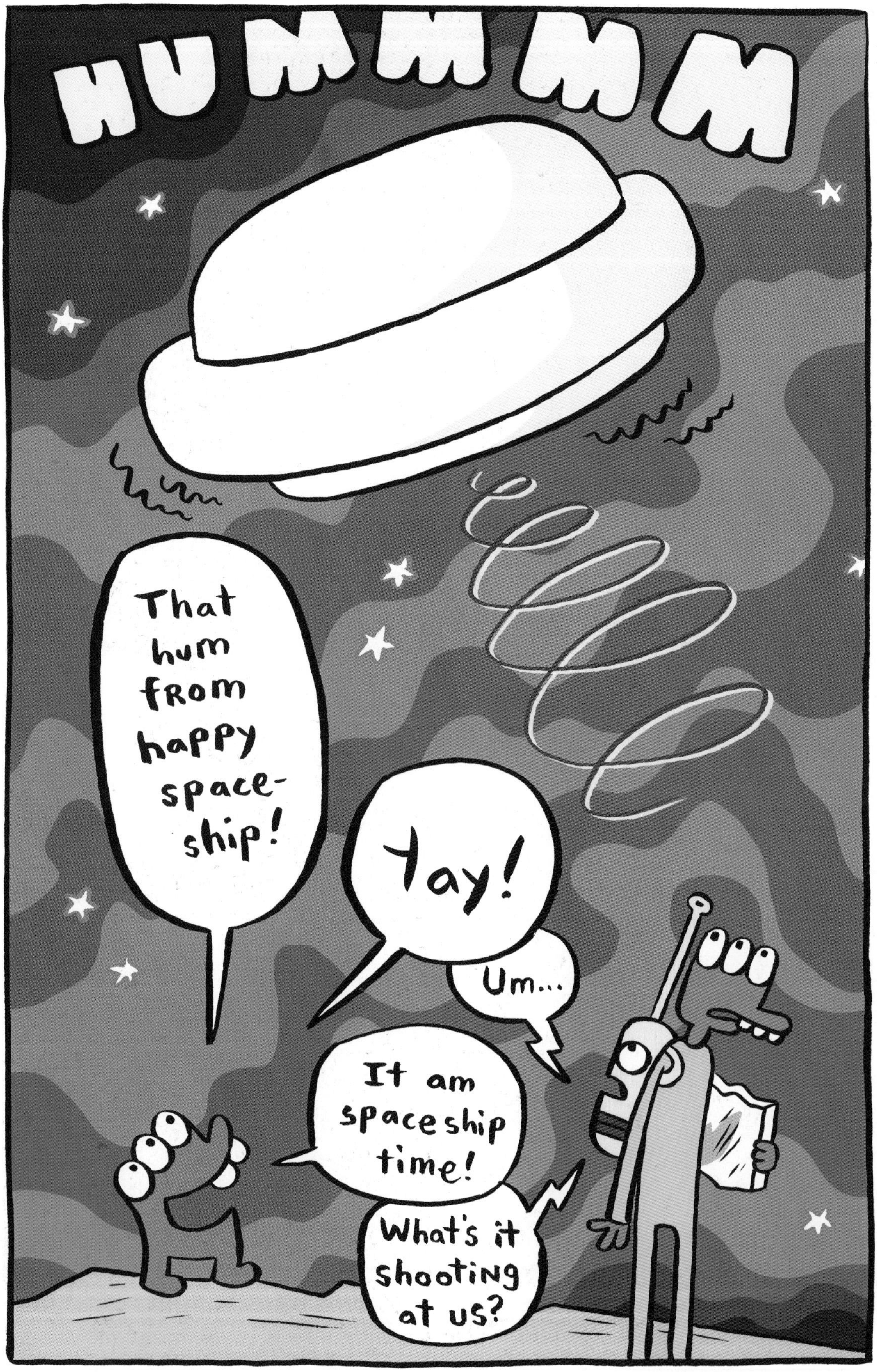
HUMMMM
That hum from happy space-ship!
Yay!
Um...
It am spaceship time!
What's it shooting at us?

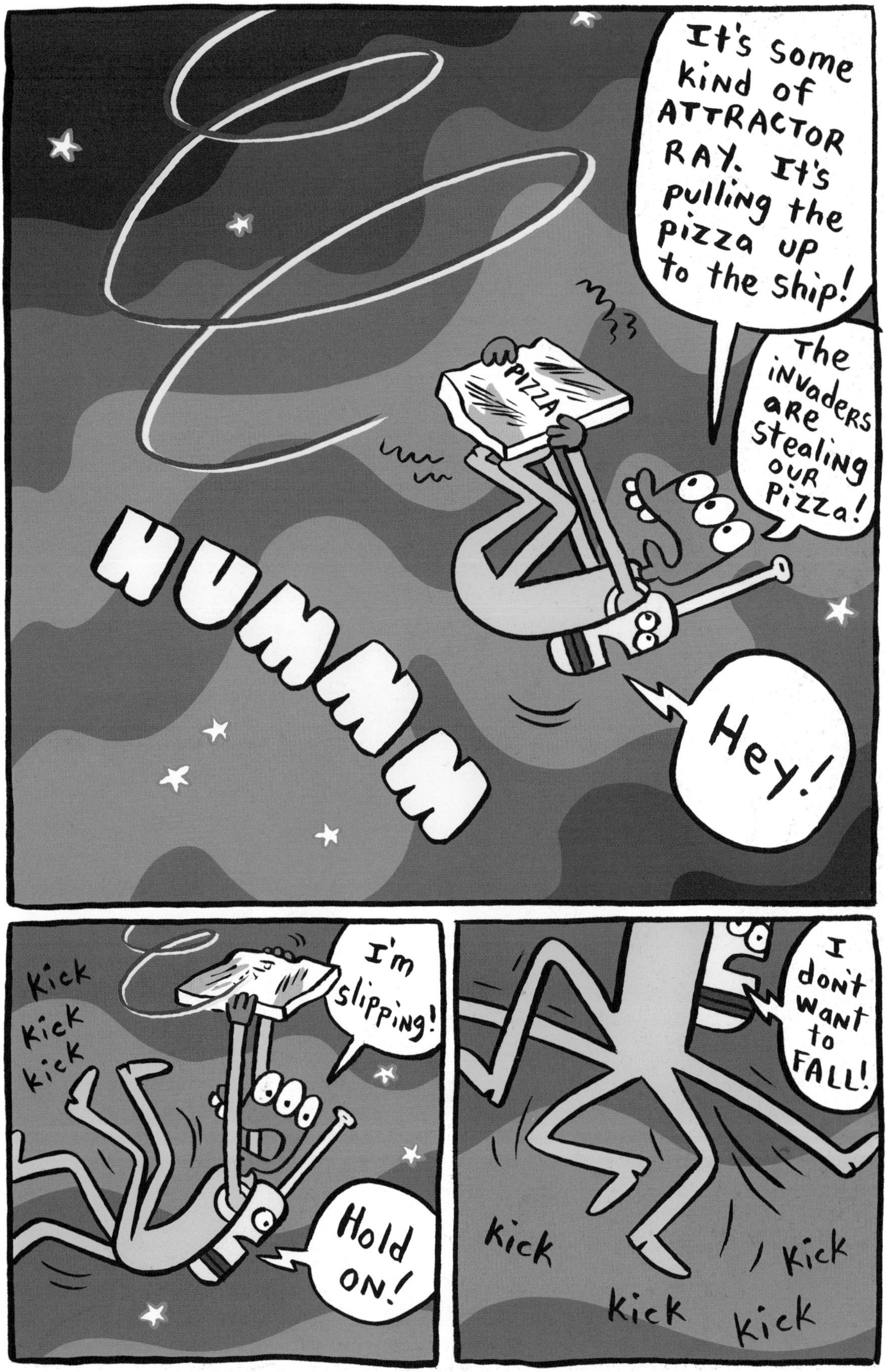
It's some kind of ATTRACTOR RAY. It's pulling the pizza up to the ship!
The invaders are stealing our pizza!
PIZZA
HUMMMM
Hey!
Kick kick kick
I'm slipping!
Hold ON!
I don't want to FALL!
Kick Kick Kick Kick

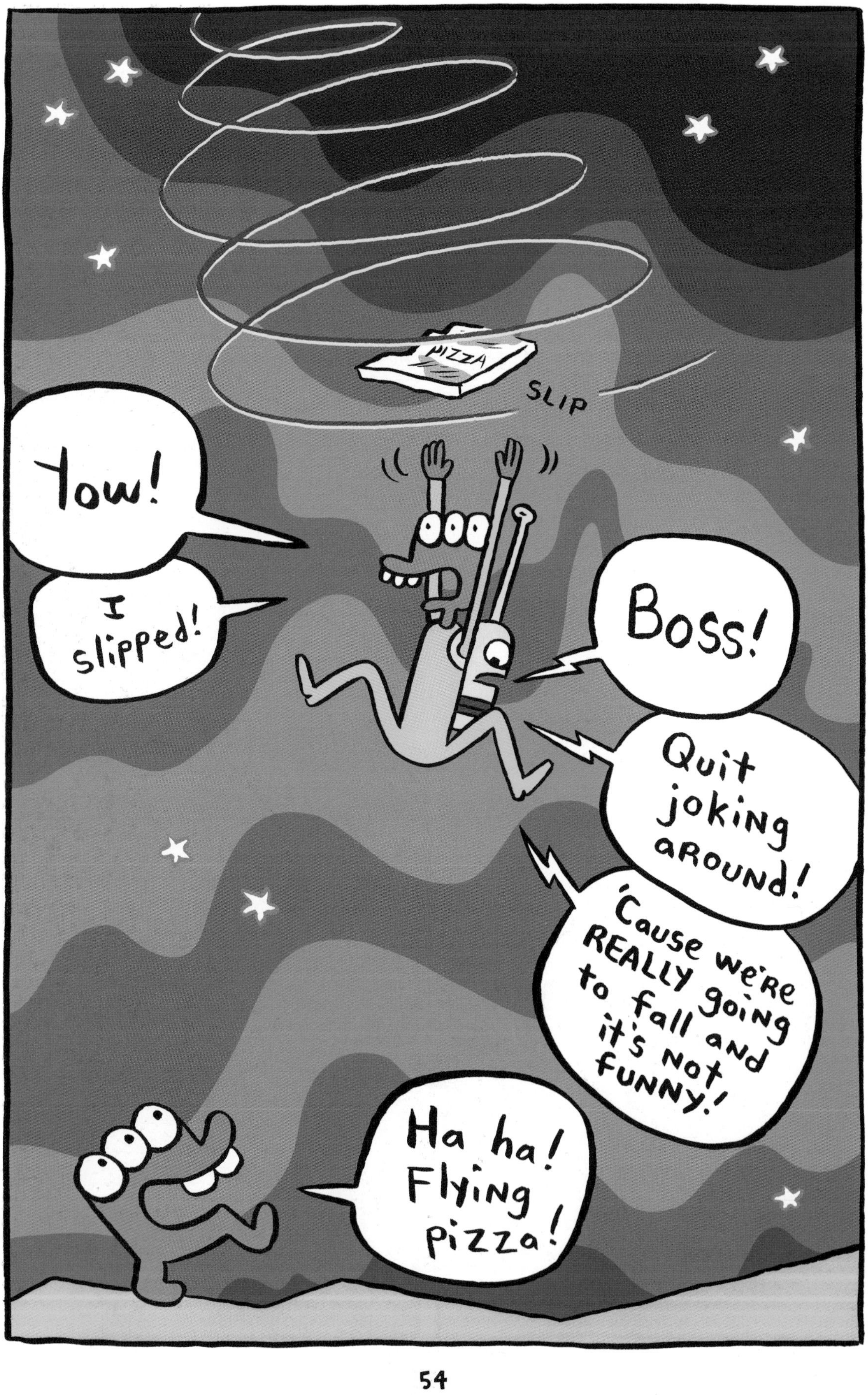
PIZZA
SLIP
Yow!
I slipped!
Boss!
Quit joking around!
'Cause we're REALLY going to fall and it's not FUNNY!
Ha ha! Flying pizza!

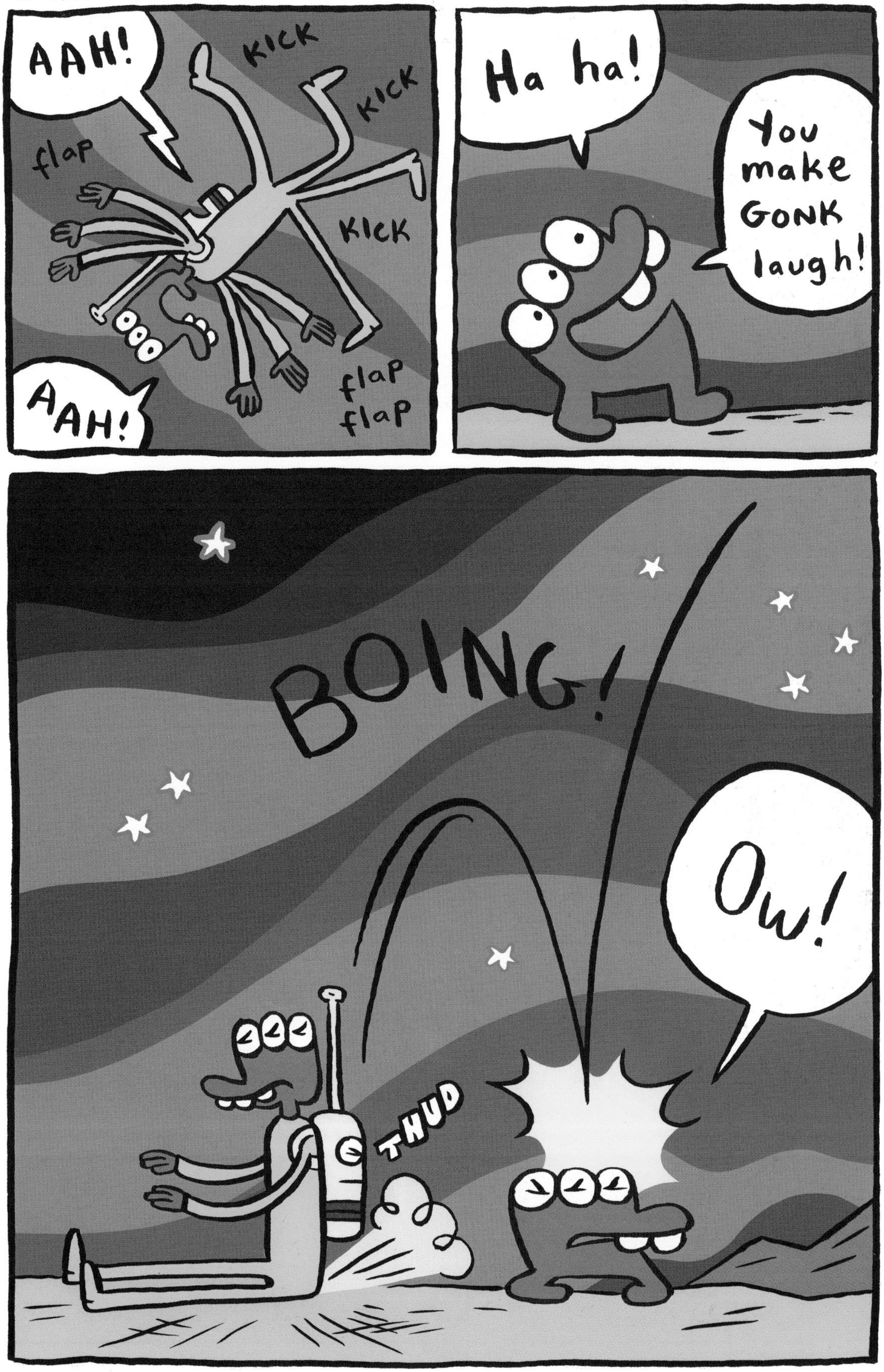
AAH!
KICK
KICK
flap
KICK
flap
flap
AAH!
Ha ha!
You make GONK laugh!
BOING!
Ow!
THUD

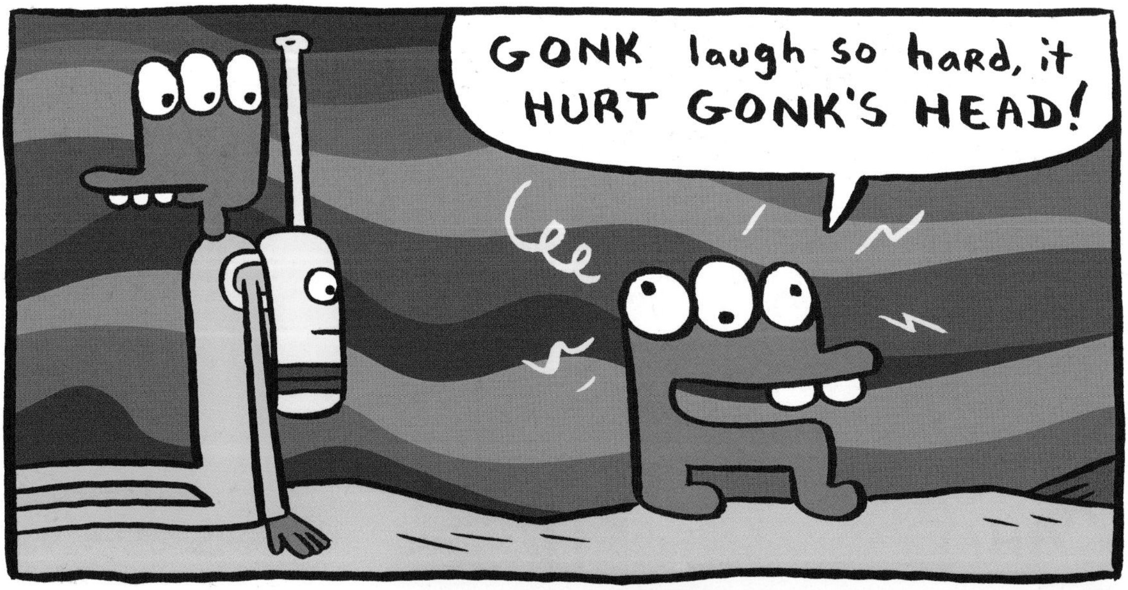
GONK laugh so hard, it HURT GONK'S HEAD!

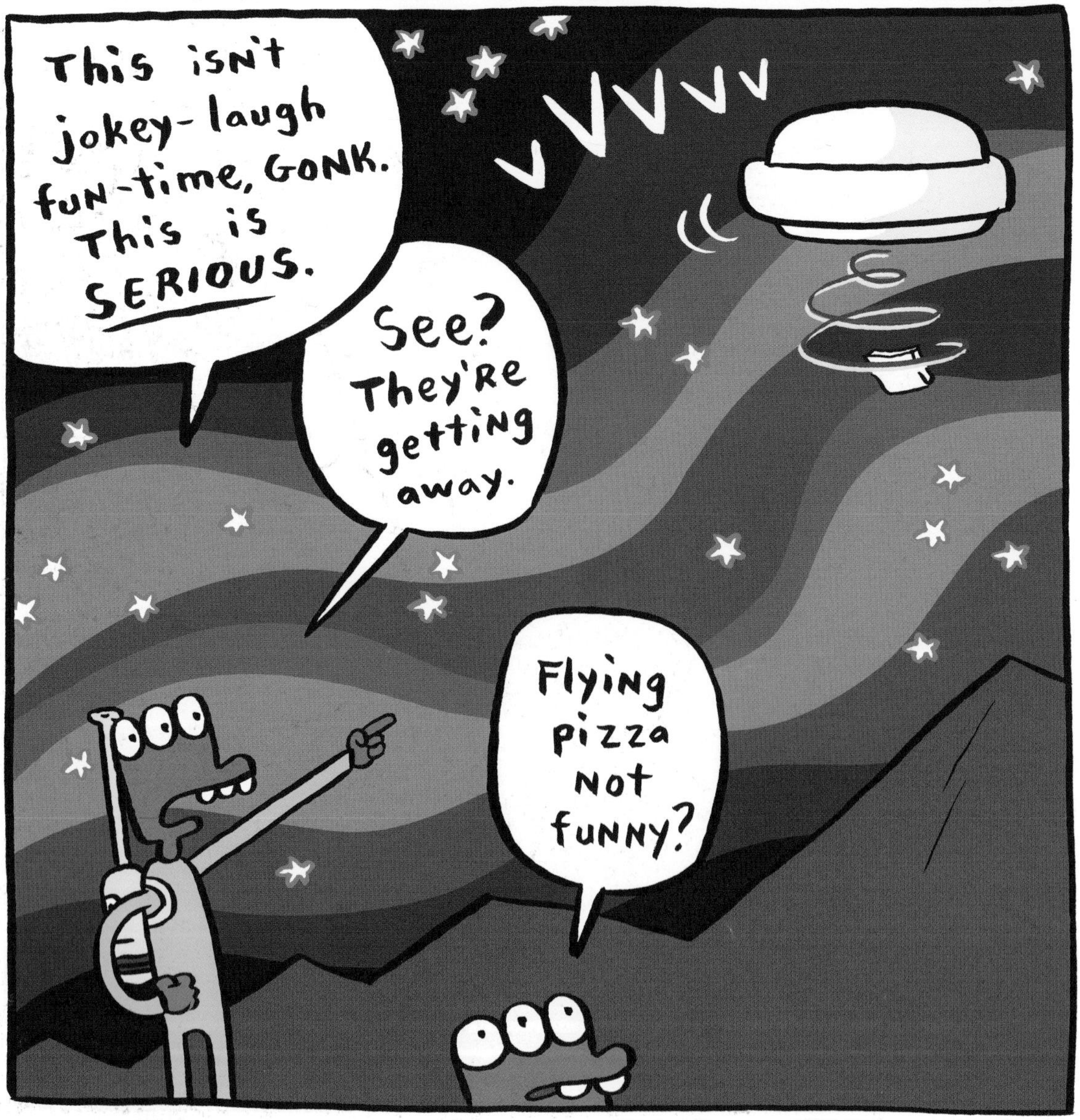
This isn't jokey-laugh fun-time, GONK. This is SERIOUS.
VVVVVV
See? They're getting away.
Flying pizza not funny?

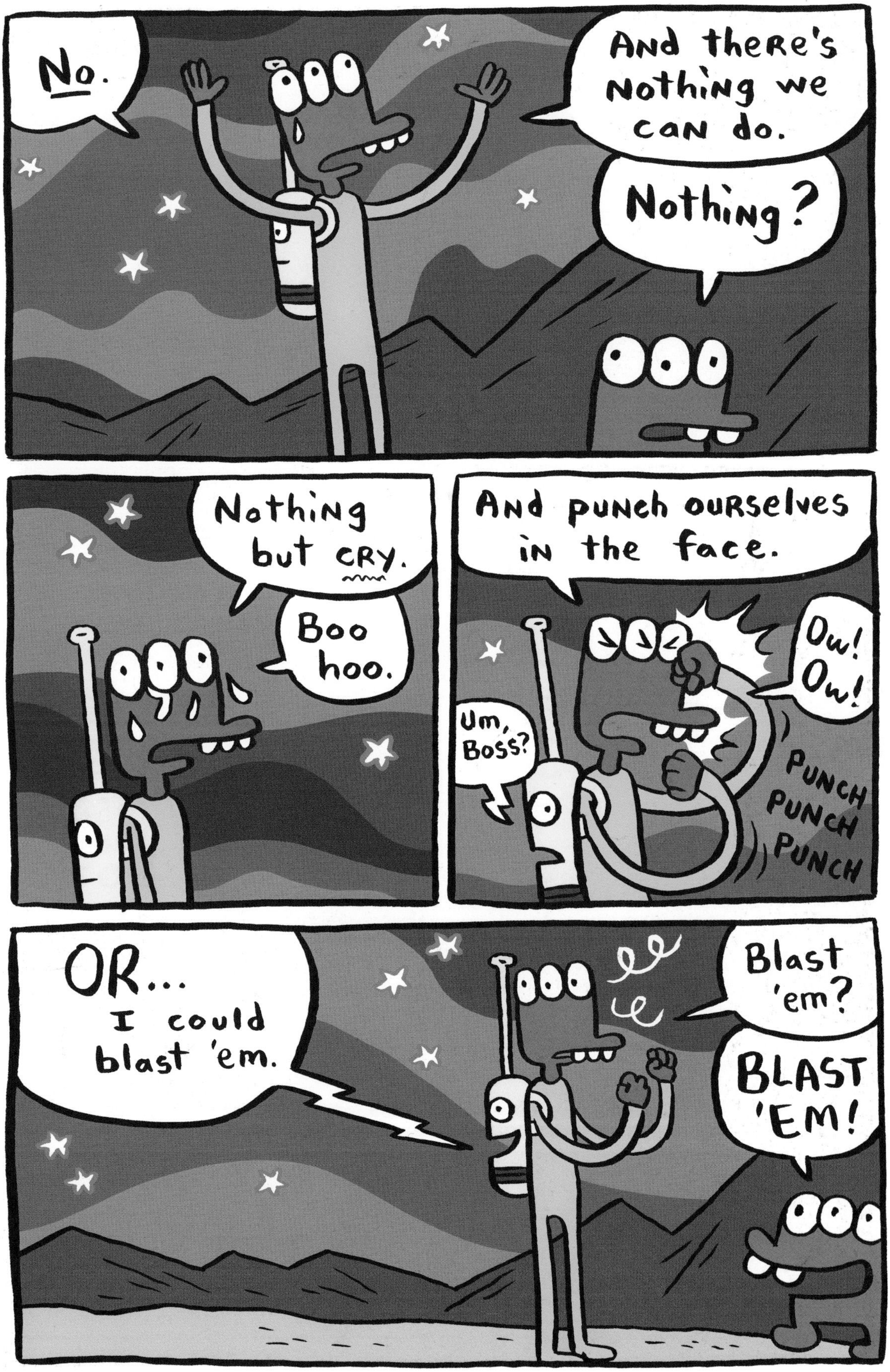
No.
And there's Nothing we can do.
Nothing?
Nothing but CRY.
Boo hoo.
And punch ourselves in the face.
Um, Boss?
Ow! Ow!
PUNCH PUNCH PUNCH
OR... I could blast 'em.
Blast 'em?
BLAST 'EM!

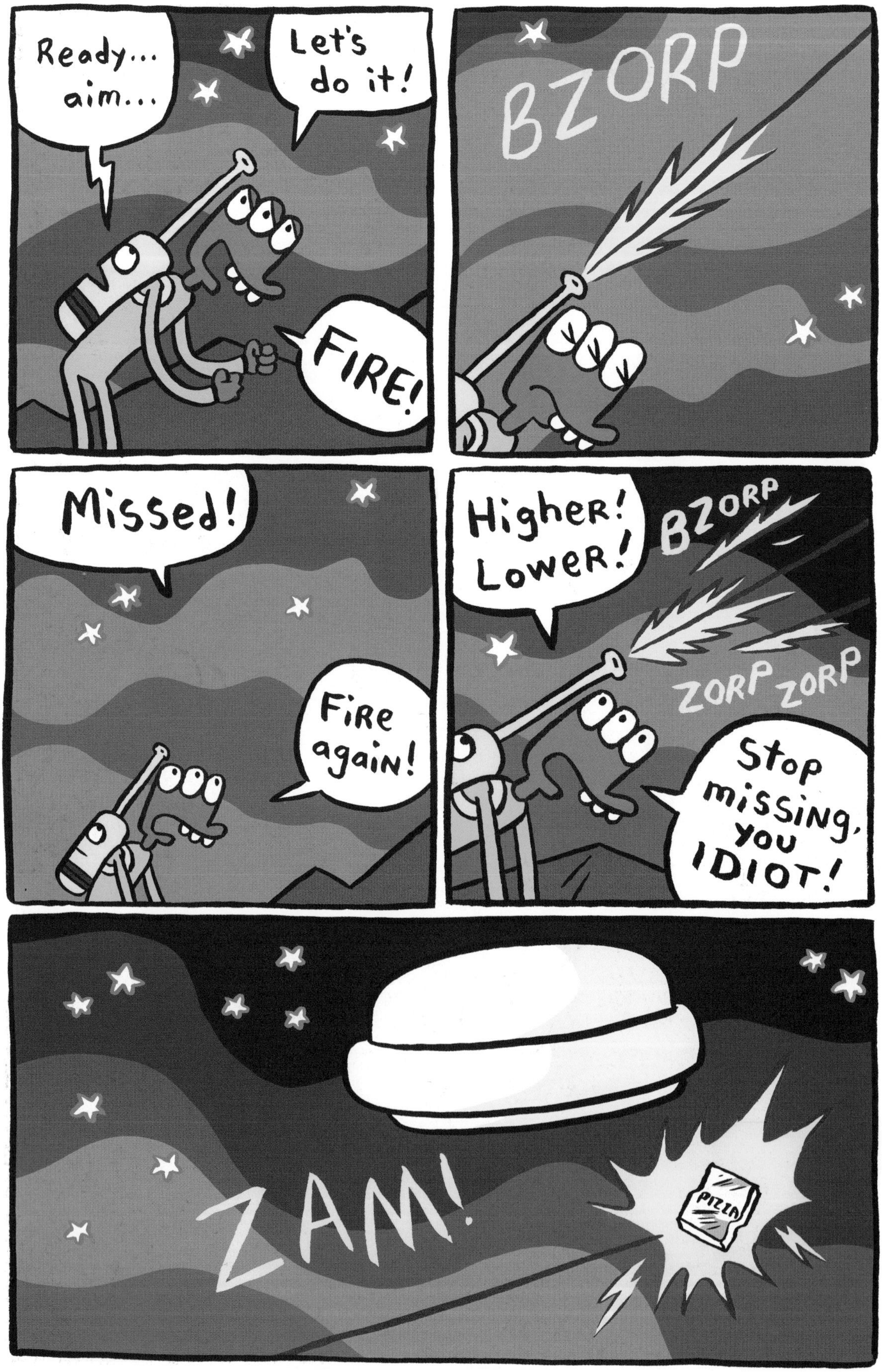

Ready... aim...
Let's do it!
FIRE!
BZORP
Missed!
Fire again!
Higher! Lower!
BZORP
ZORP ZORP
Stop missing, you IDIOT!
ZAM!
PIZZA

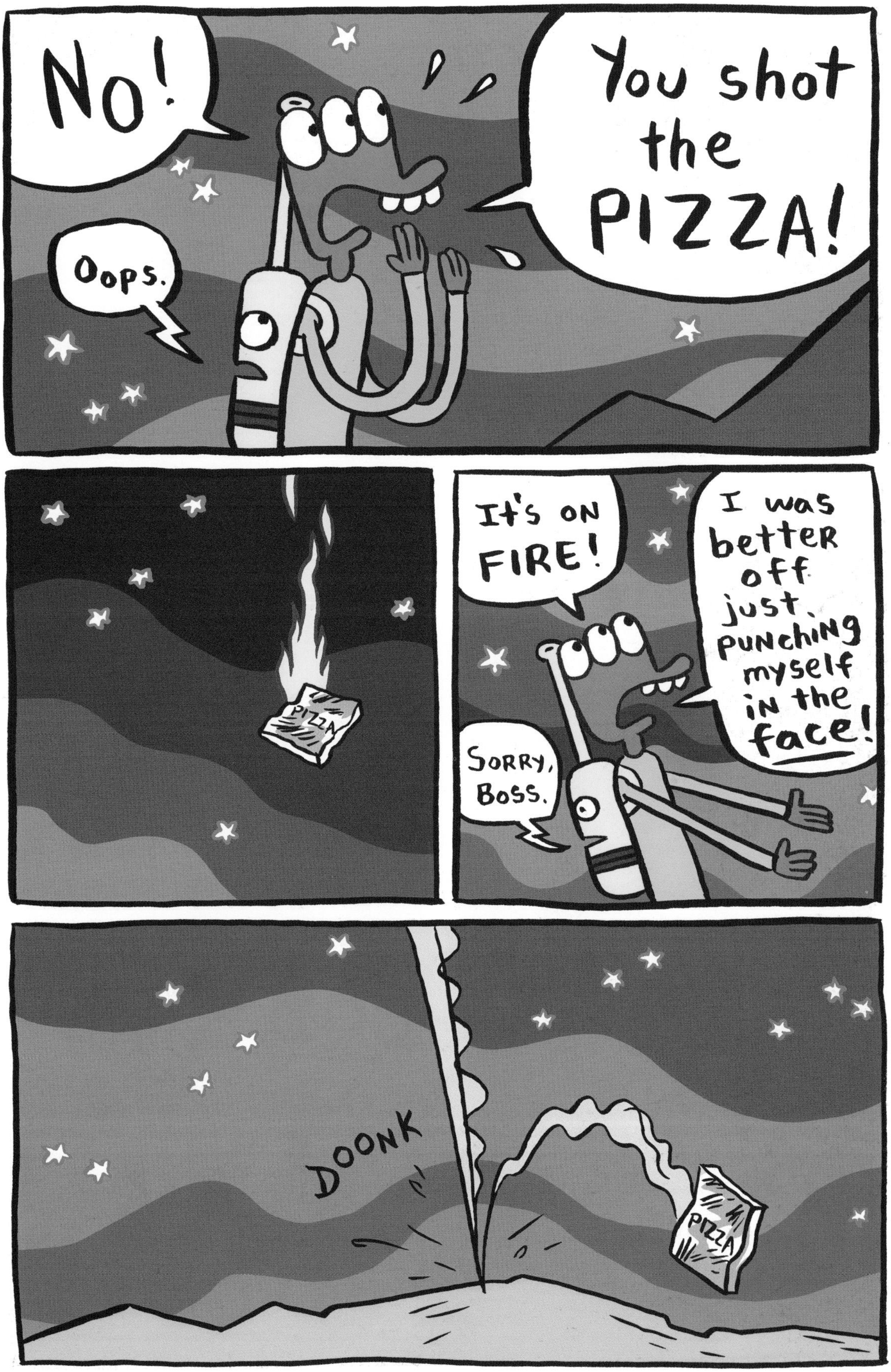
No!
Oops.
You shot the PIZZA!
PIZZA
It's ON FIRE!
I was better off just punching myself in the face!
SORRY, BOSS.
DOONK
PIZZA

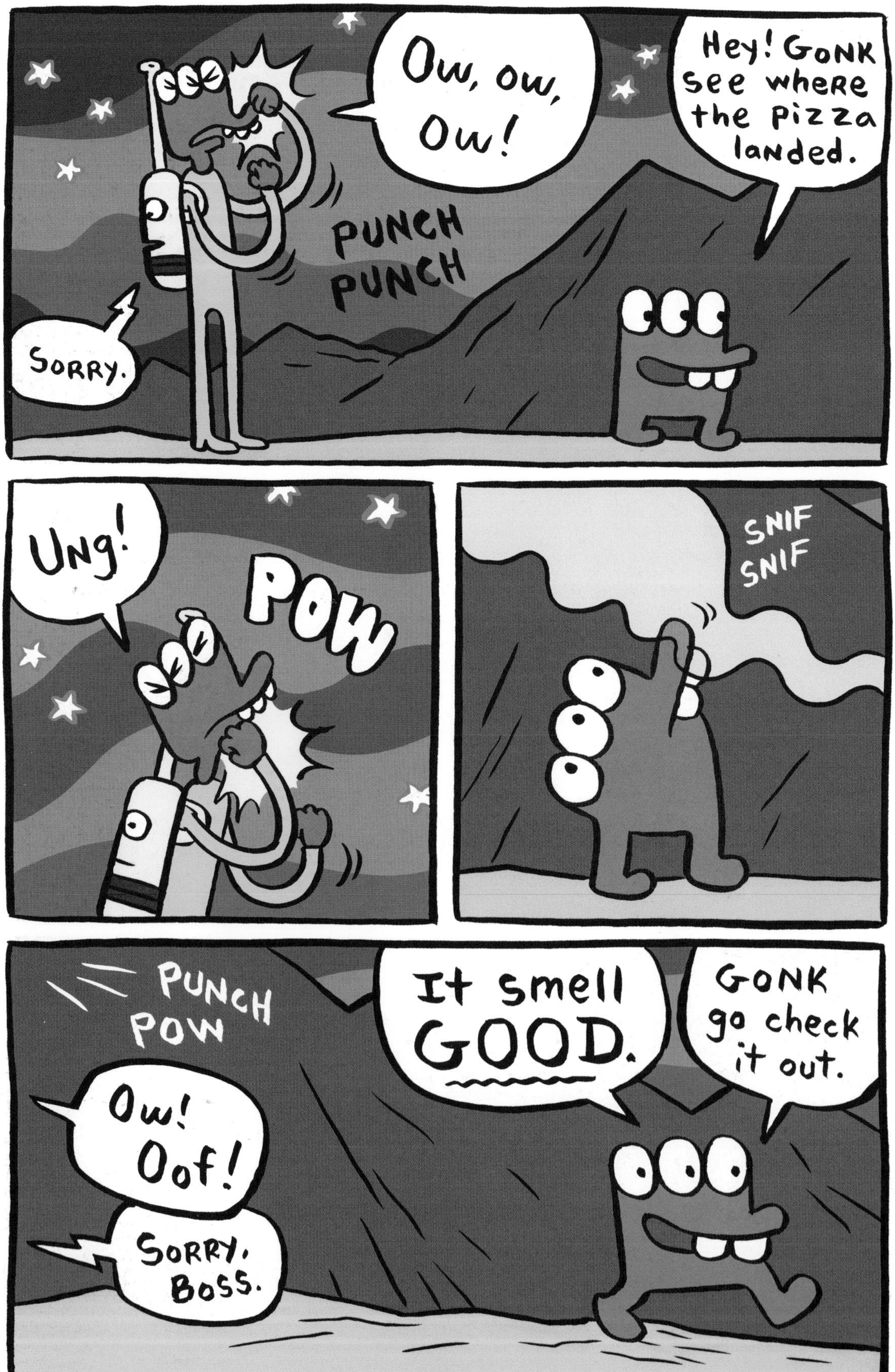
Ow, ow, Ow!
Hey! GONK see where the pizza landed.
PUNCH PUNCH
SORRY.
Ung!
POW
SNIF SNIF
PUNCH POW
Ow! Oof!
SORRY, BOSS.
It smell GOOD.
GONK go check it out.

CHAPTER TWELVE

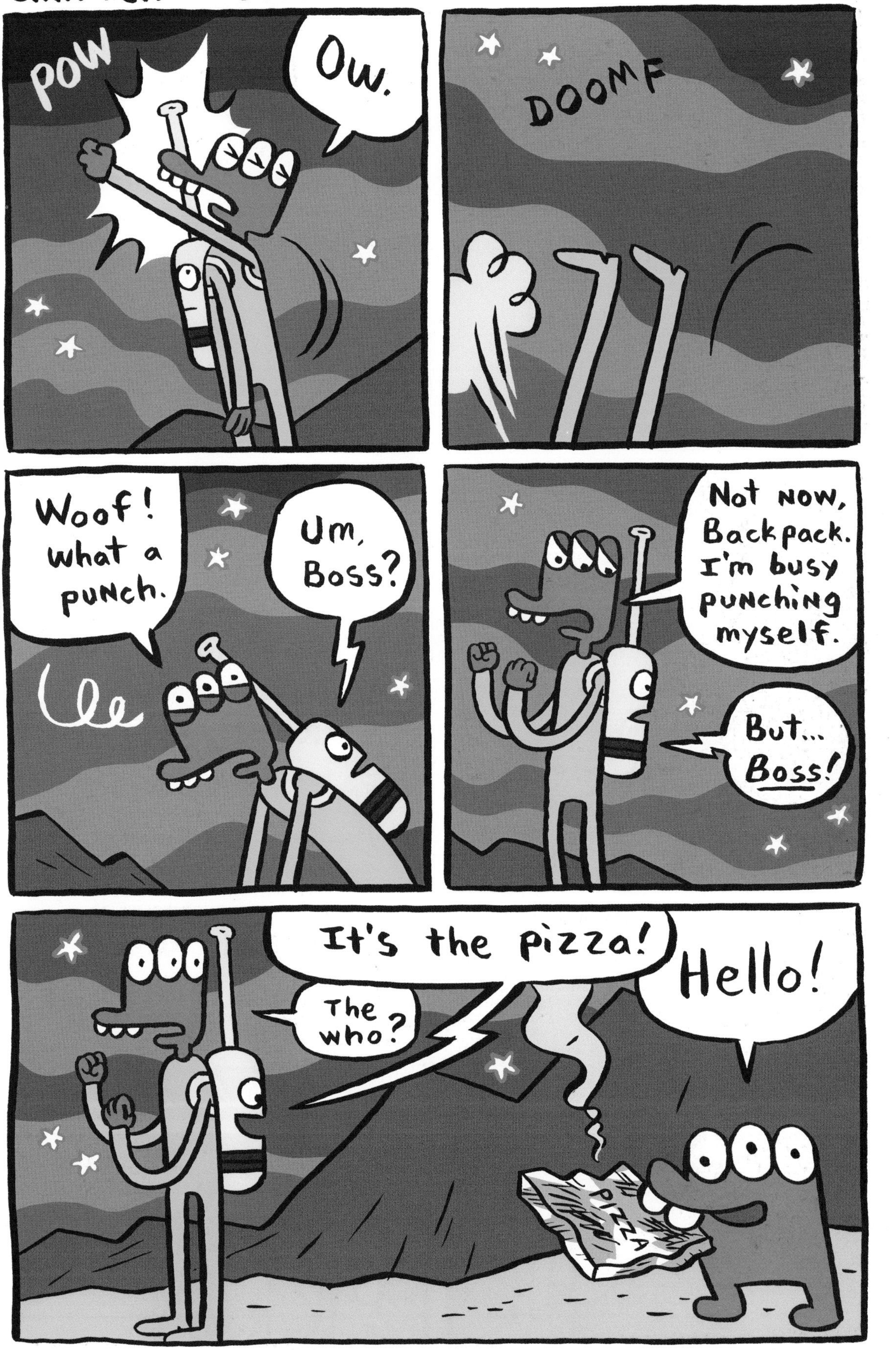
POW
Ow.
DOOMF
Woof! what a punch.
Um, Boss?
Not now, Backpack. I'm busy punching myself.
But... Boss!
It's the pizza!
The who?
Hello!
PIZZA

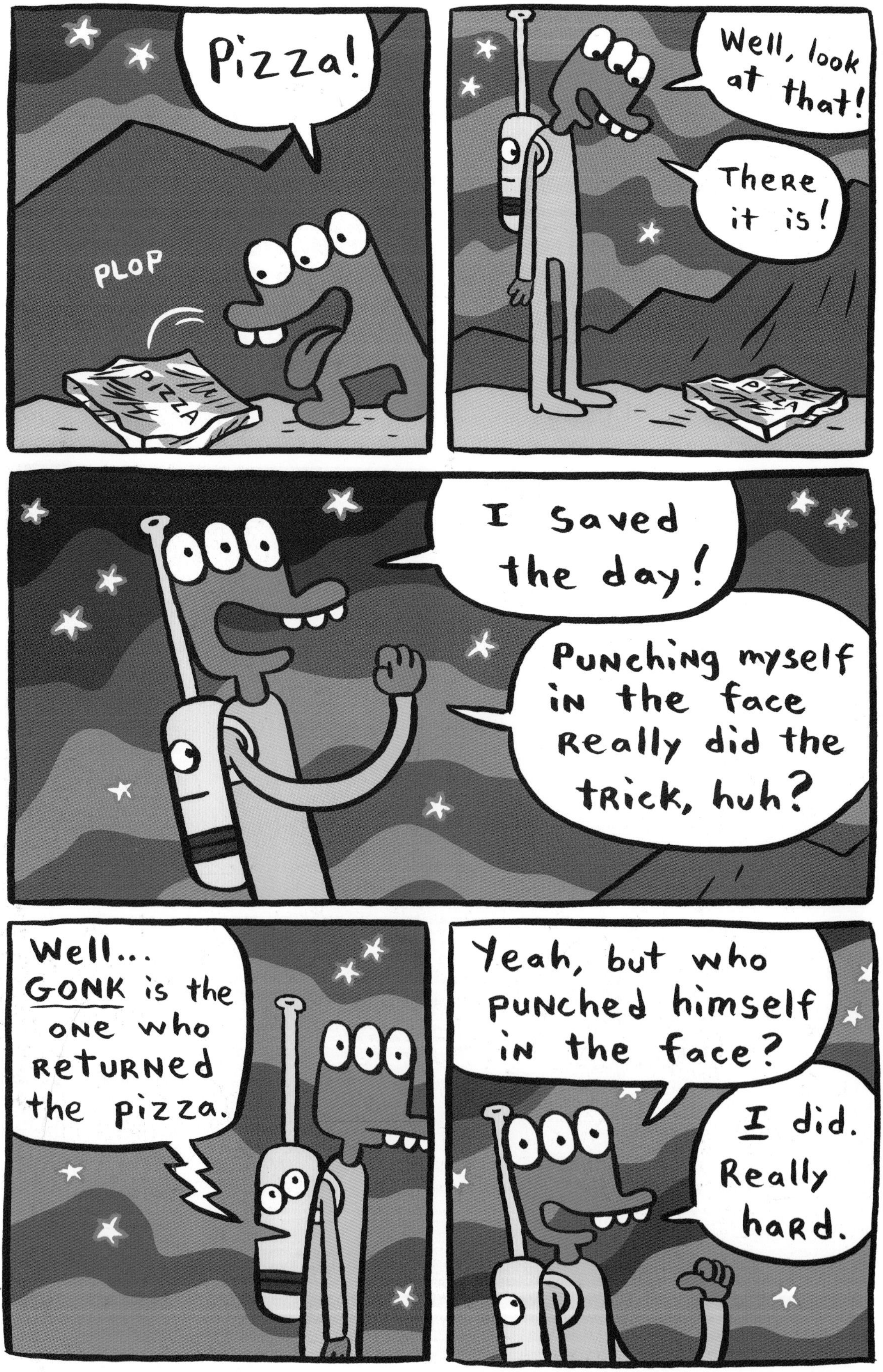
Pizza!
PLOP
PIZZA
Well, look at that!
There it is!
I saved the day!
Punching myself in the face really did the trick, huh?
Well... GONK is the one who returned the pizza.
Yeah, but who punched himself in the face?
I did. Really hard.

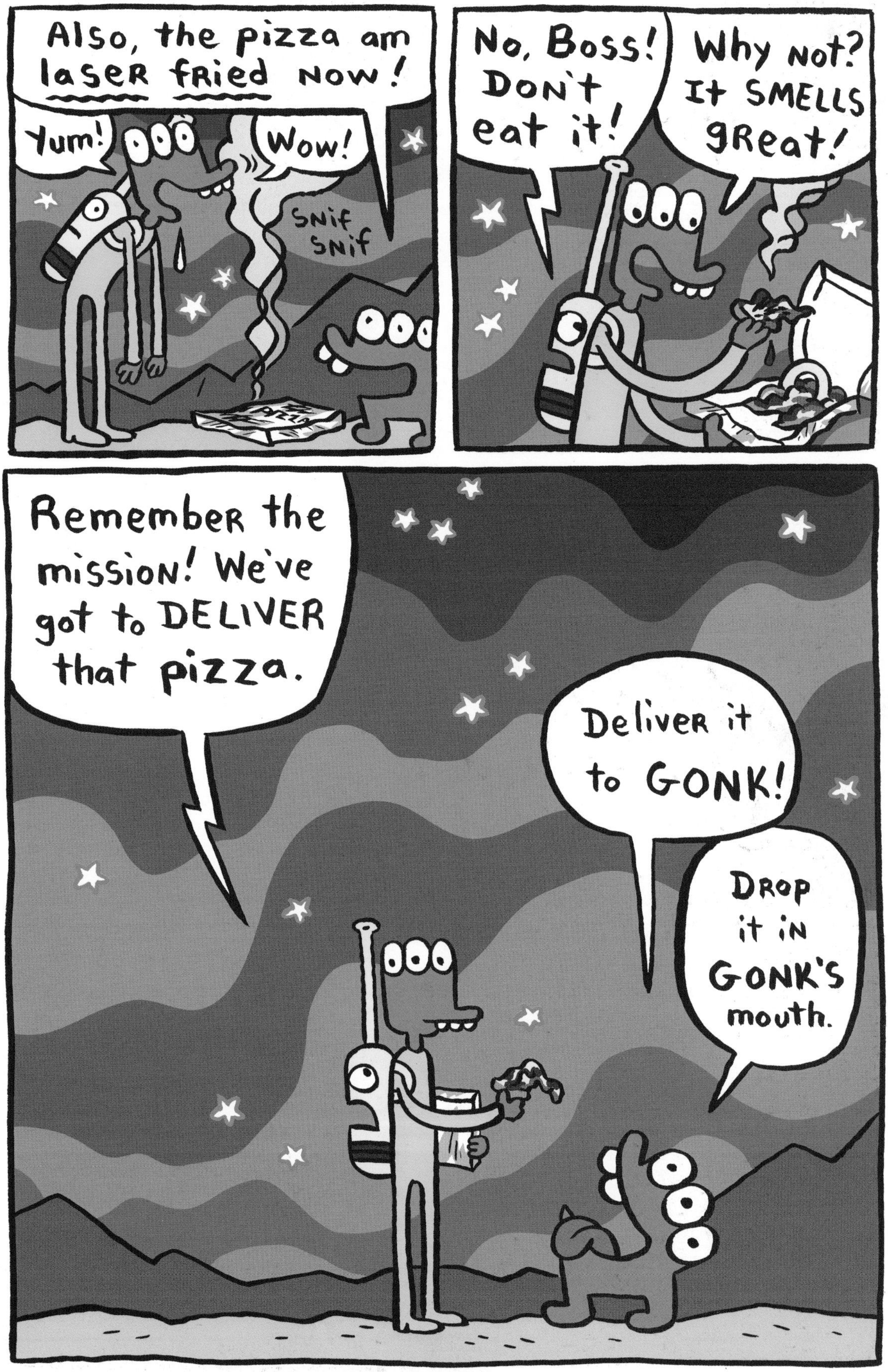

Also, the pizza am laser fried now!
Yum!
Wow!
SNIF SNIF
No, Boss! Don't eat it!
Why not? It SMELLS great!
Remember the mission! We've got to DELIVER that pizza.
Deliver it to GONK!
Drop it in GONK'S mouth.

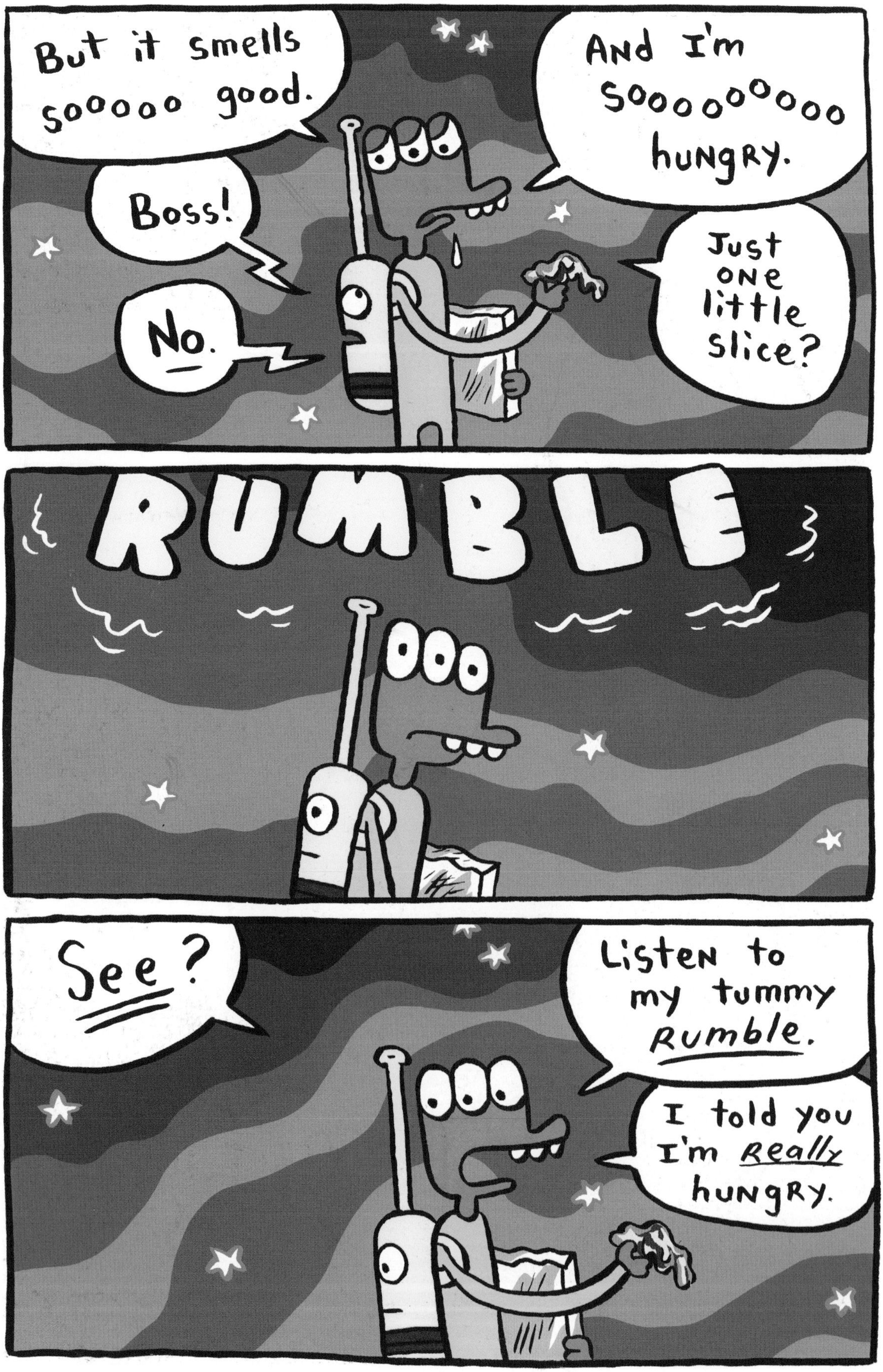
But it smells sooooo good.
And I'm sooooooooo hungry.
Boss!
No.
Just one little slice?
RUMBLE
See?
Listen to my tummy Rumble.
I told you I'm Really hungry.

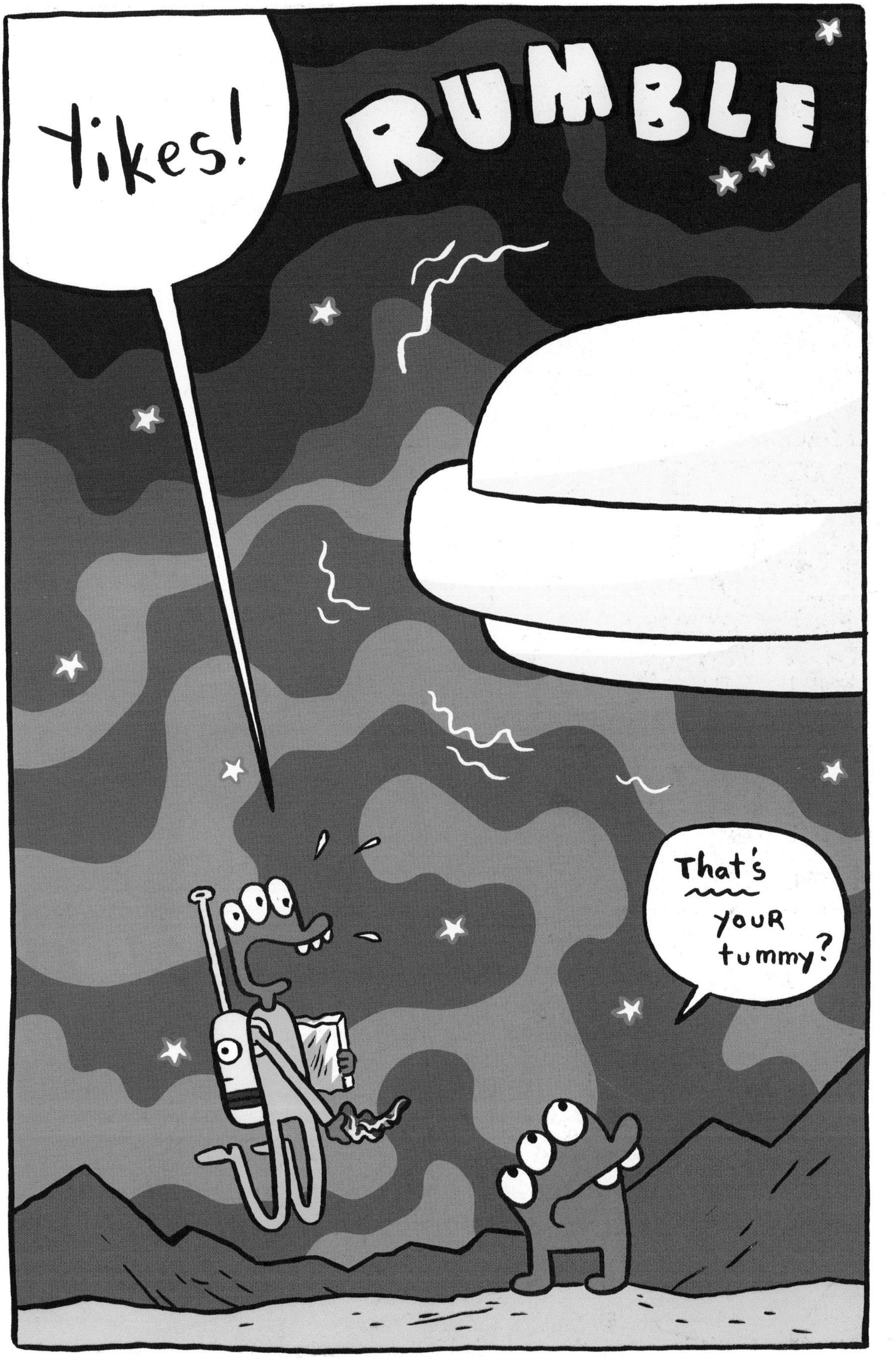
Yikes!
RUMBLE
That's your tummy?

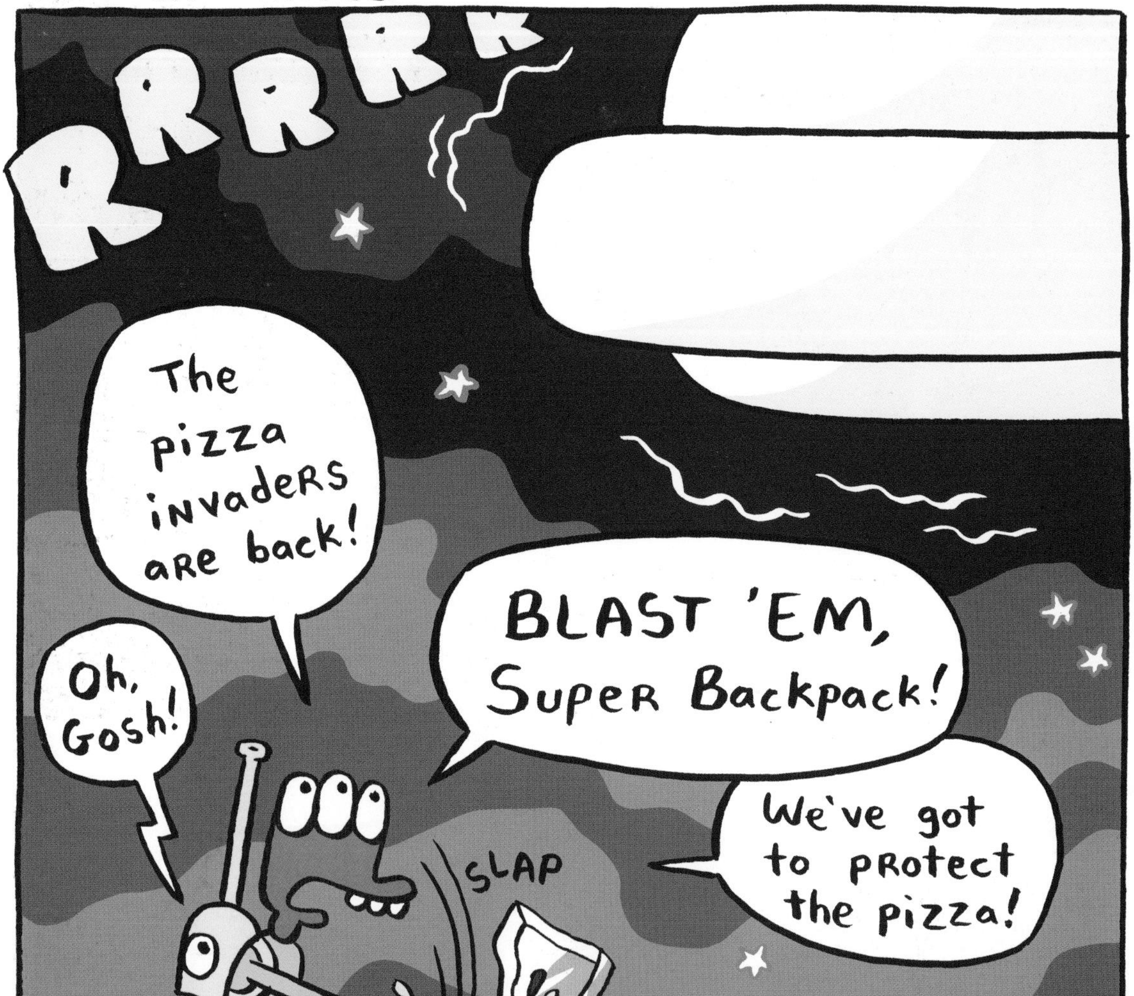
RRRRK
The pizza invaders are back!
Oh, Gosh!
BLAST 'EM, Super Backpack!
SLAP
We've got to protect the pizza!

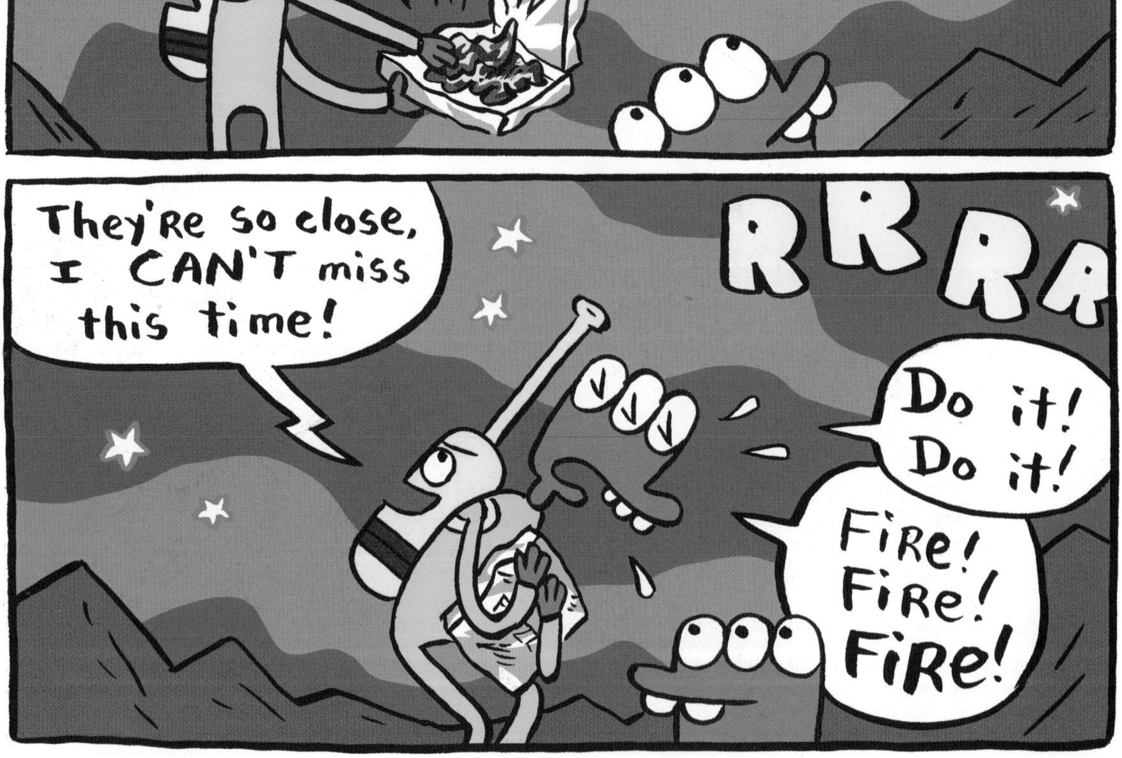
RRRR
They're so close, I CAN'T miss this time!
Do it! Do it!
Fire! Fire! FiRe!

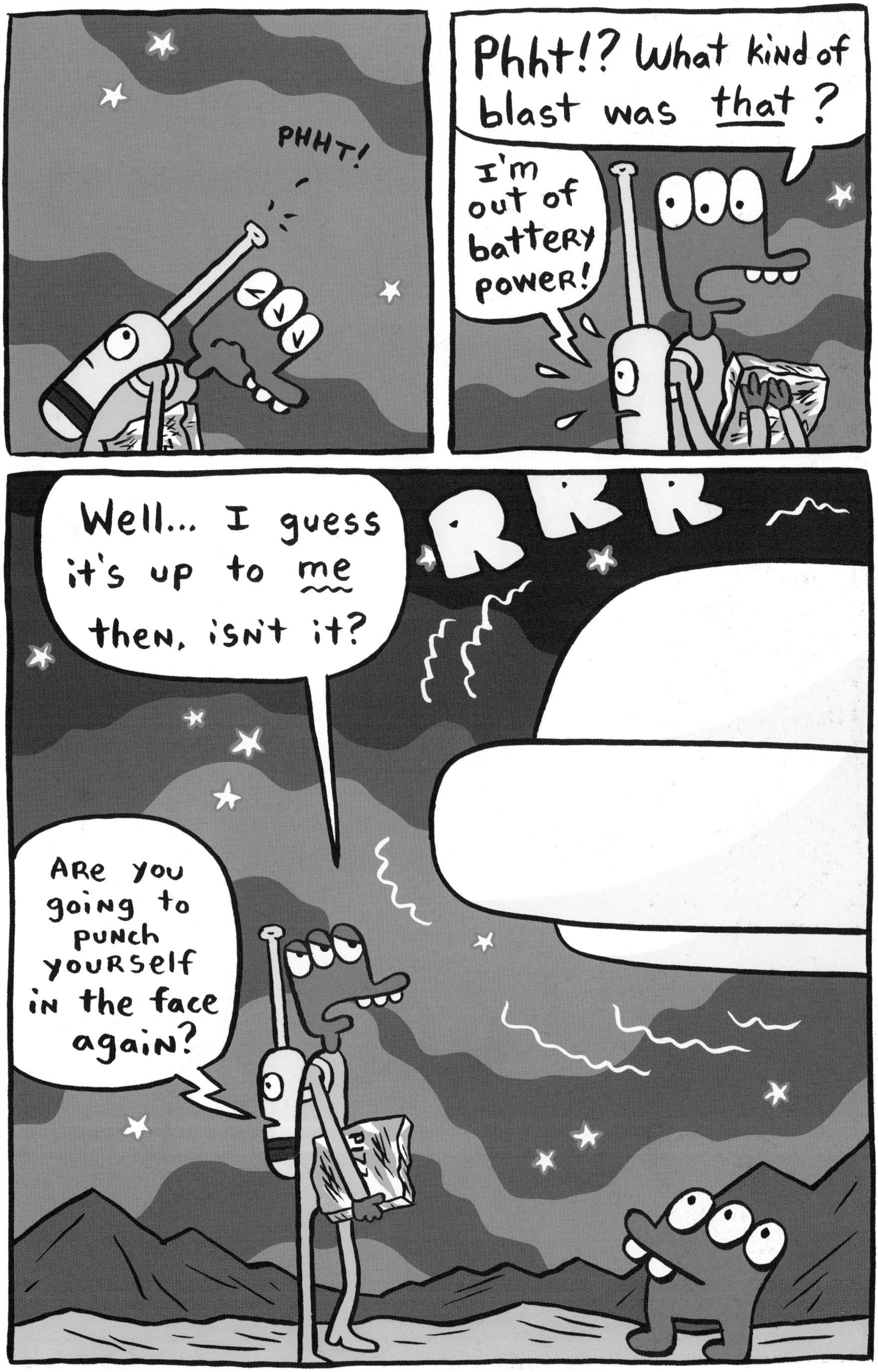
PHHT!
Phht!? What kind of blast was that?
I'm out of battery power!
RRR
Well... I guess it's up to me then, isn't it?
Are you going to punch yourself in the face again?

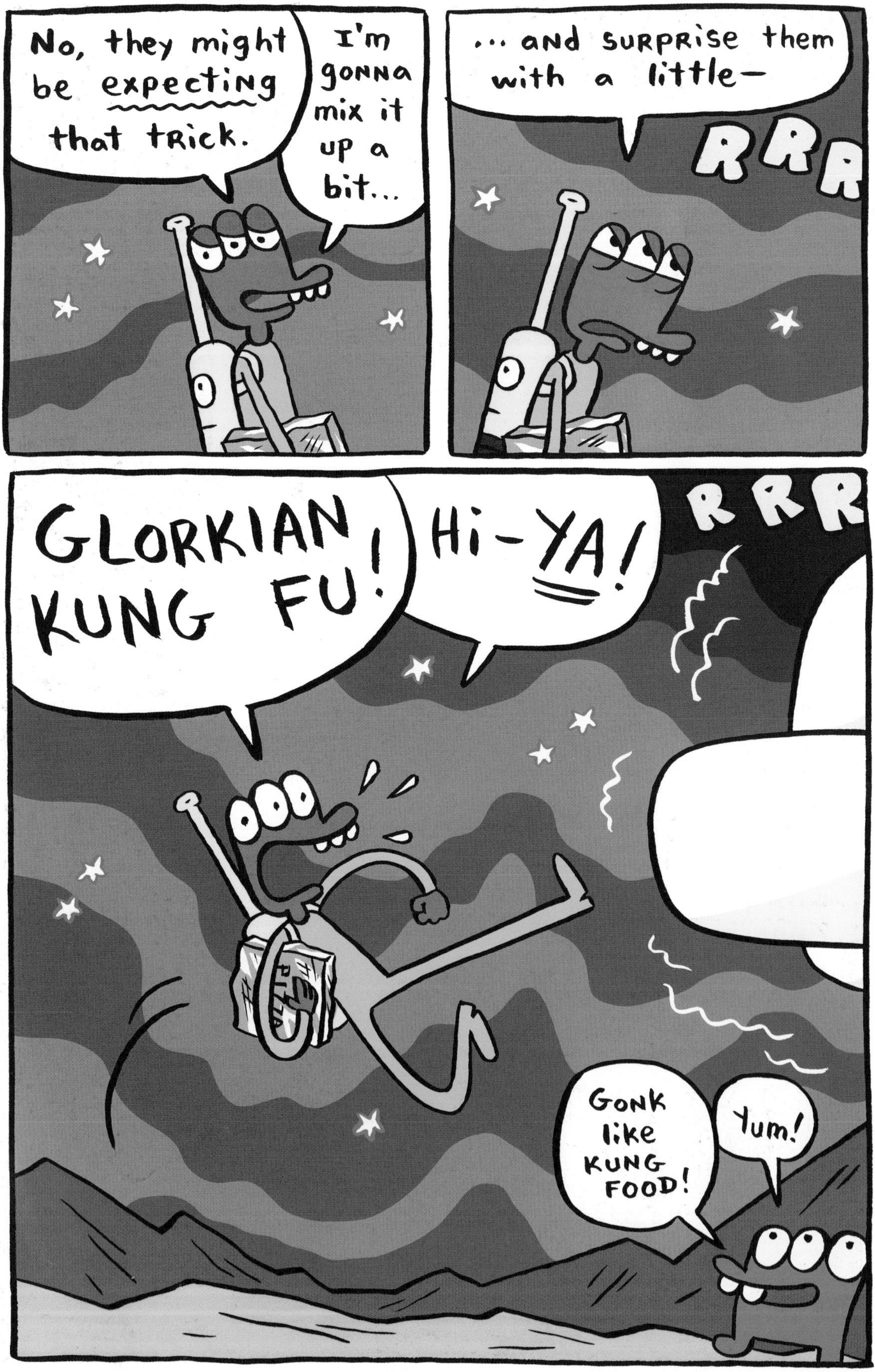
No, they might be expecting that trick.
I'm gonna mix it up a bit...
... and surprise them with a little—
RRR
RRR
GLORKIAN KUNG FU!
Hi-YA!
Gonk like KUNG FOOD!
Yum!

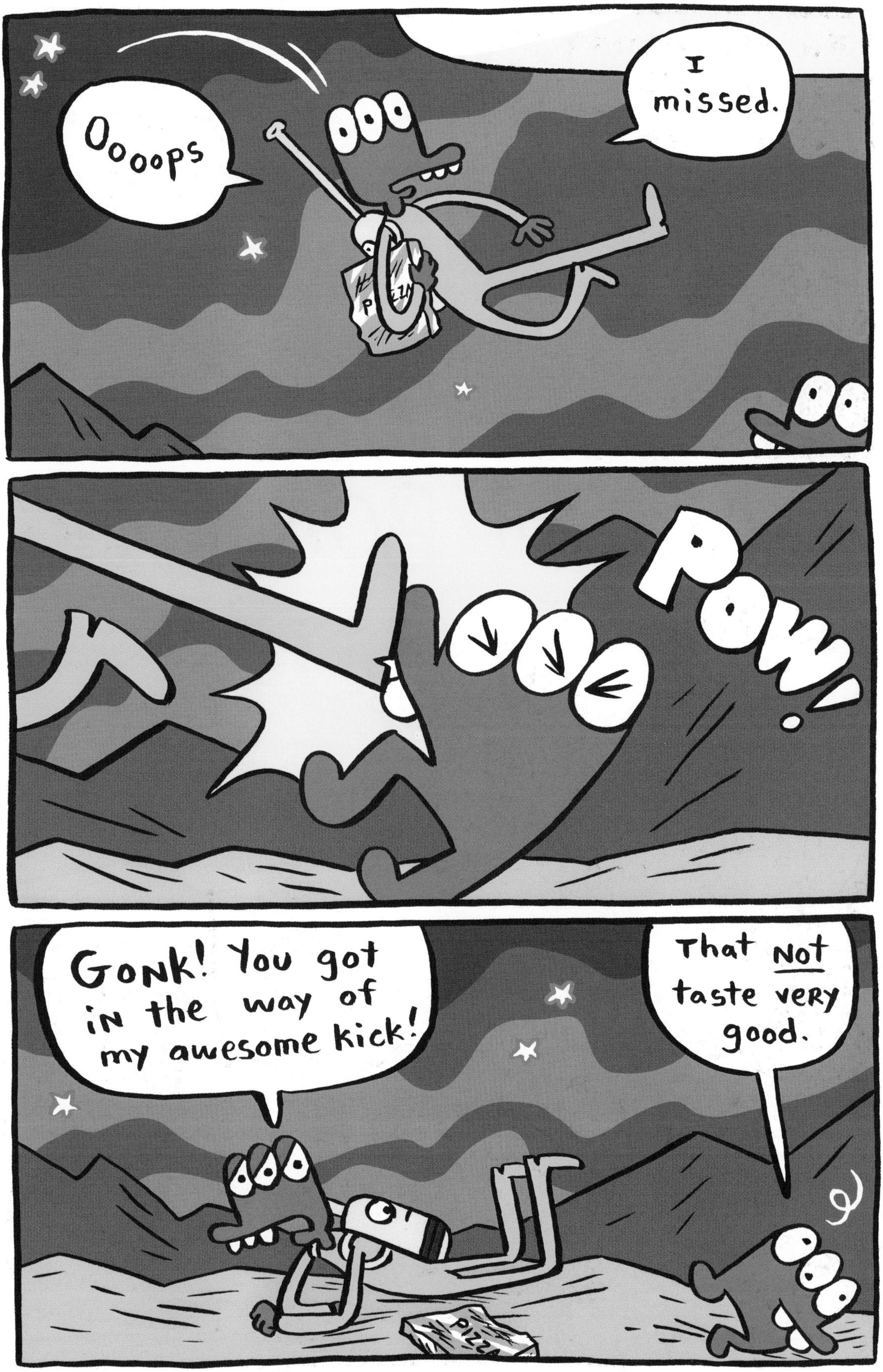
Oooops
I missed.
POW!
GONK! You got in the way of my awesome kick!
That NOT taste very good.

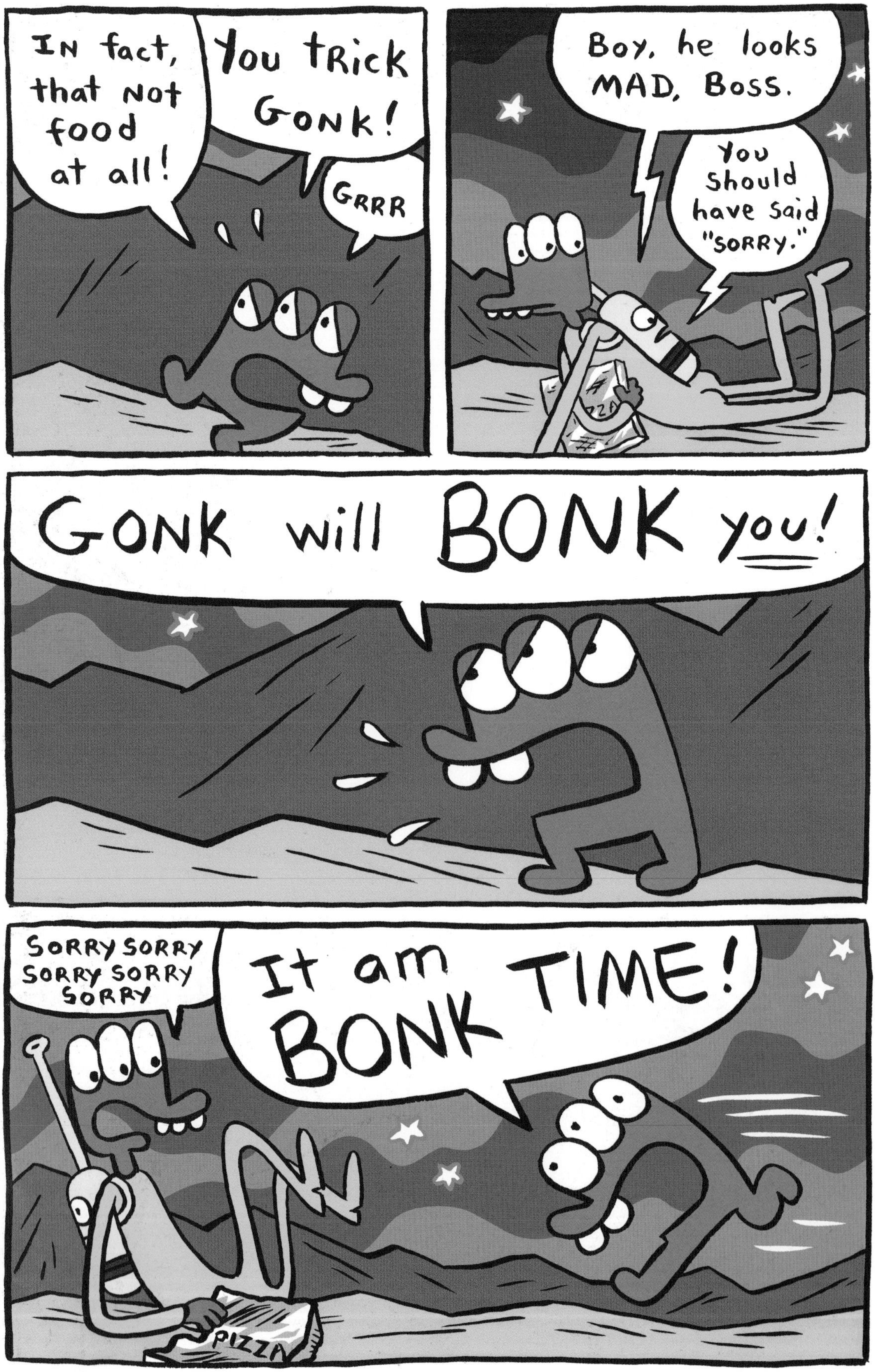

IN fact, that not food at all!
You trick Gonk!
GRRR
Boy, he looks MAD, Boss.
You should have said "SORRY."
PIZZA
GONK will BONK you!
SORRY SORRY SORRY SORRY SORRY
It am BONK TIME!
PIZZA

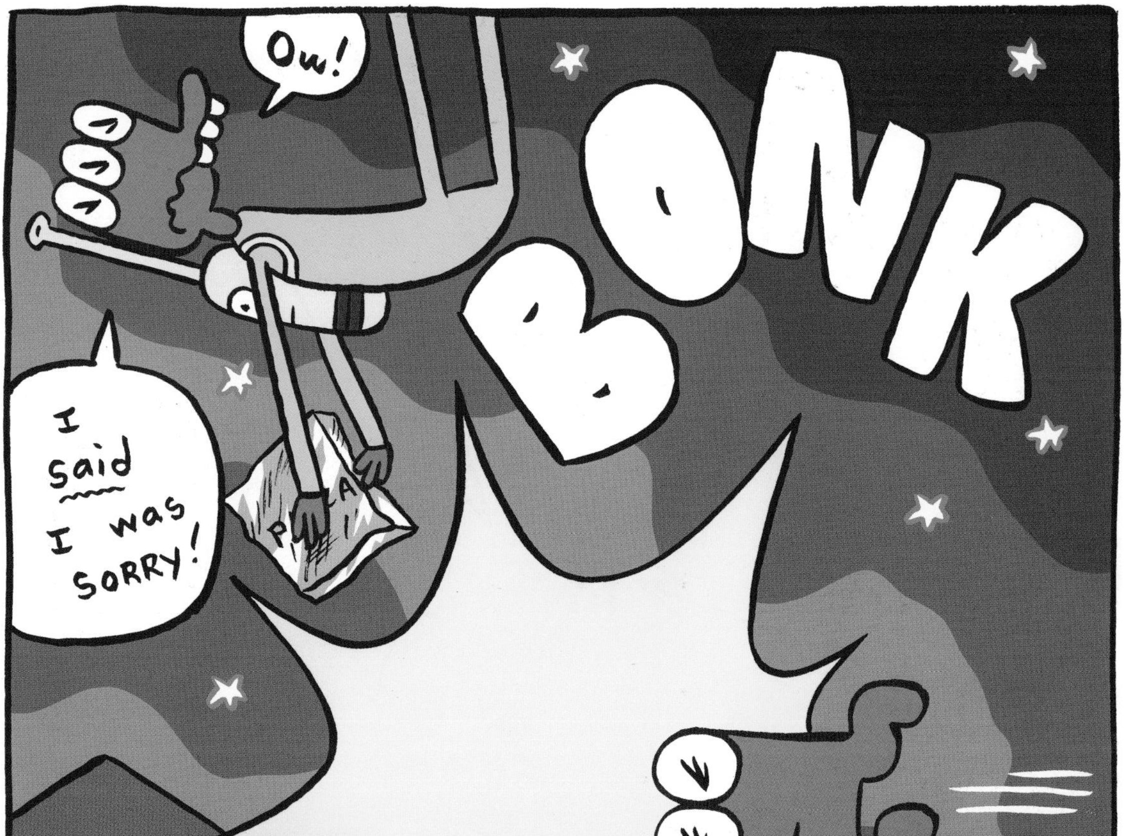
Ow!
BONK
I said I was SORRY!

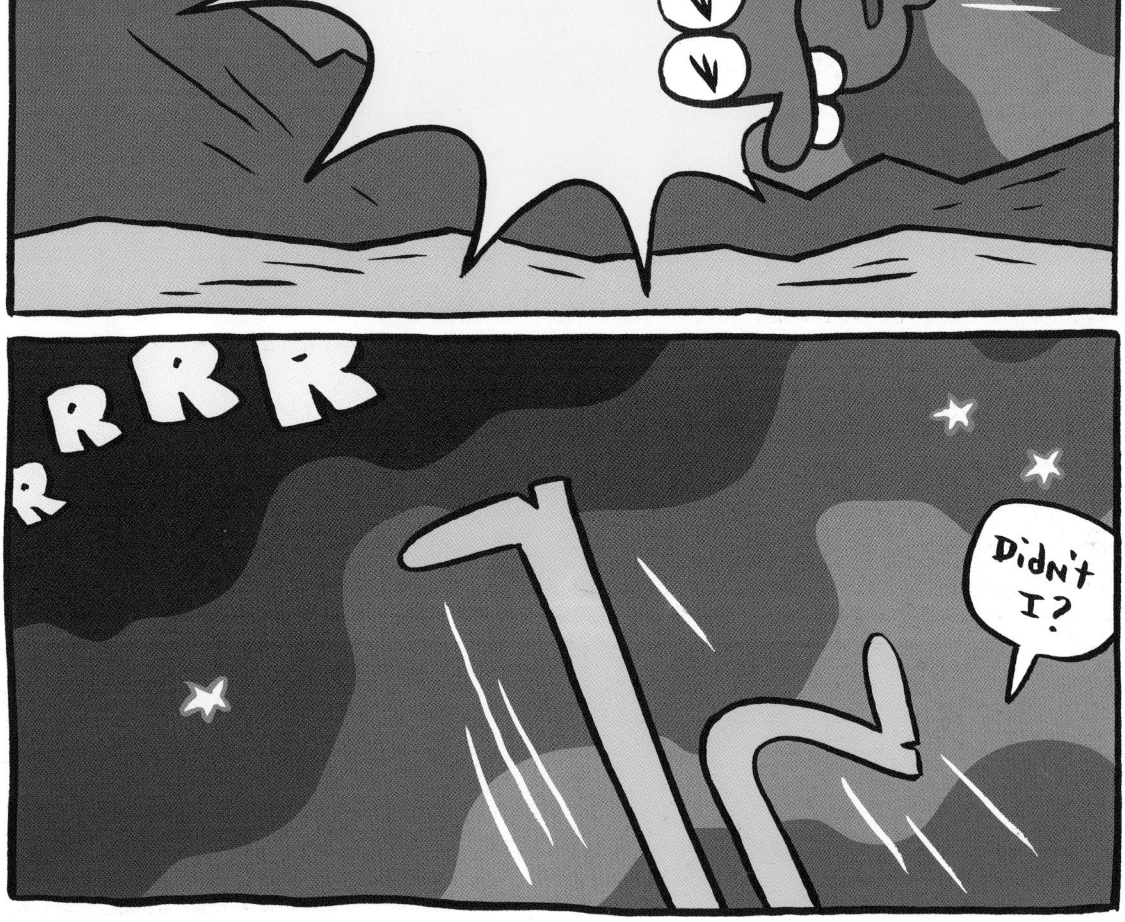
RRRR
Didn't I?

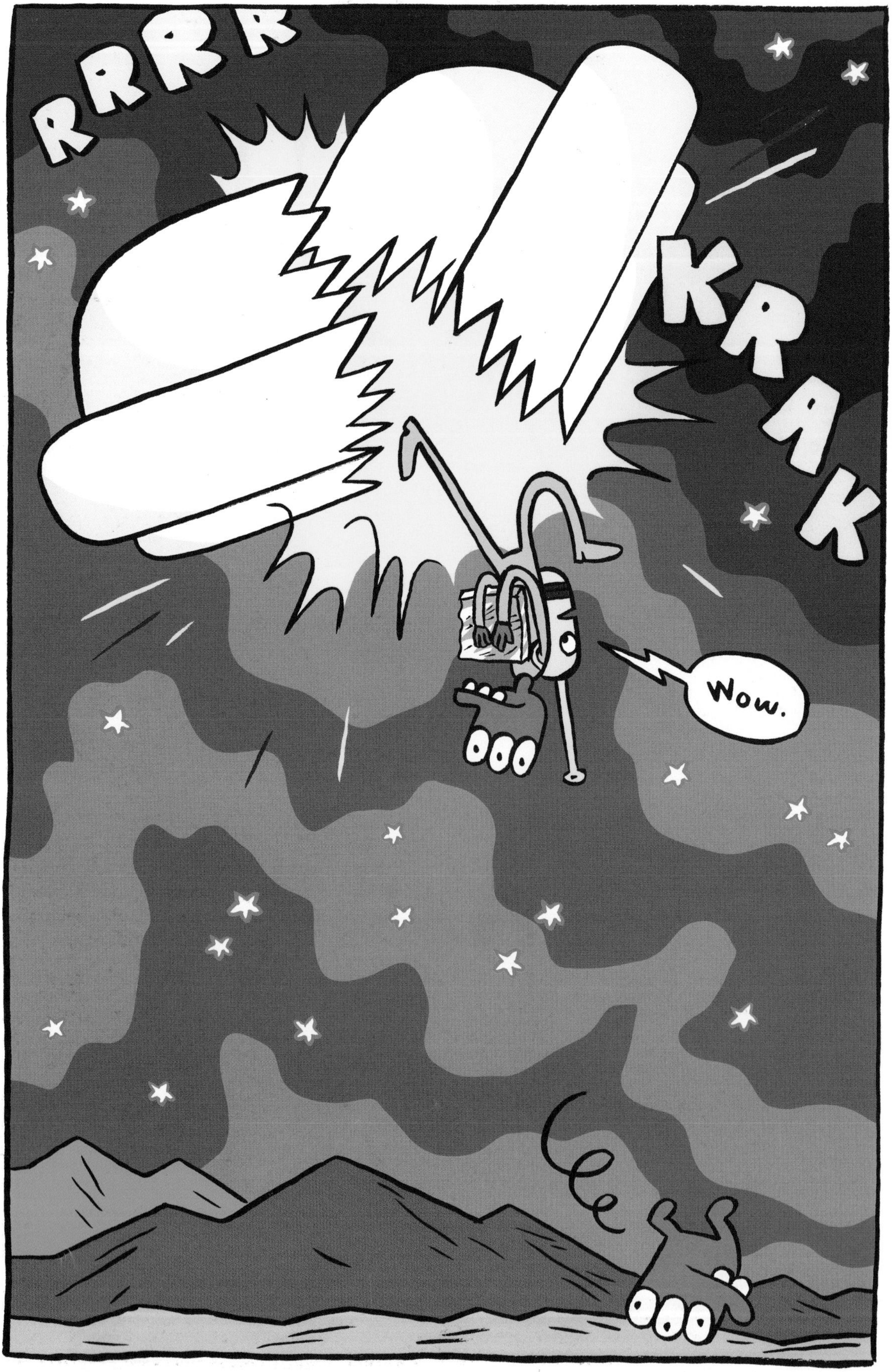
RRRR
KRAK
Wow.

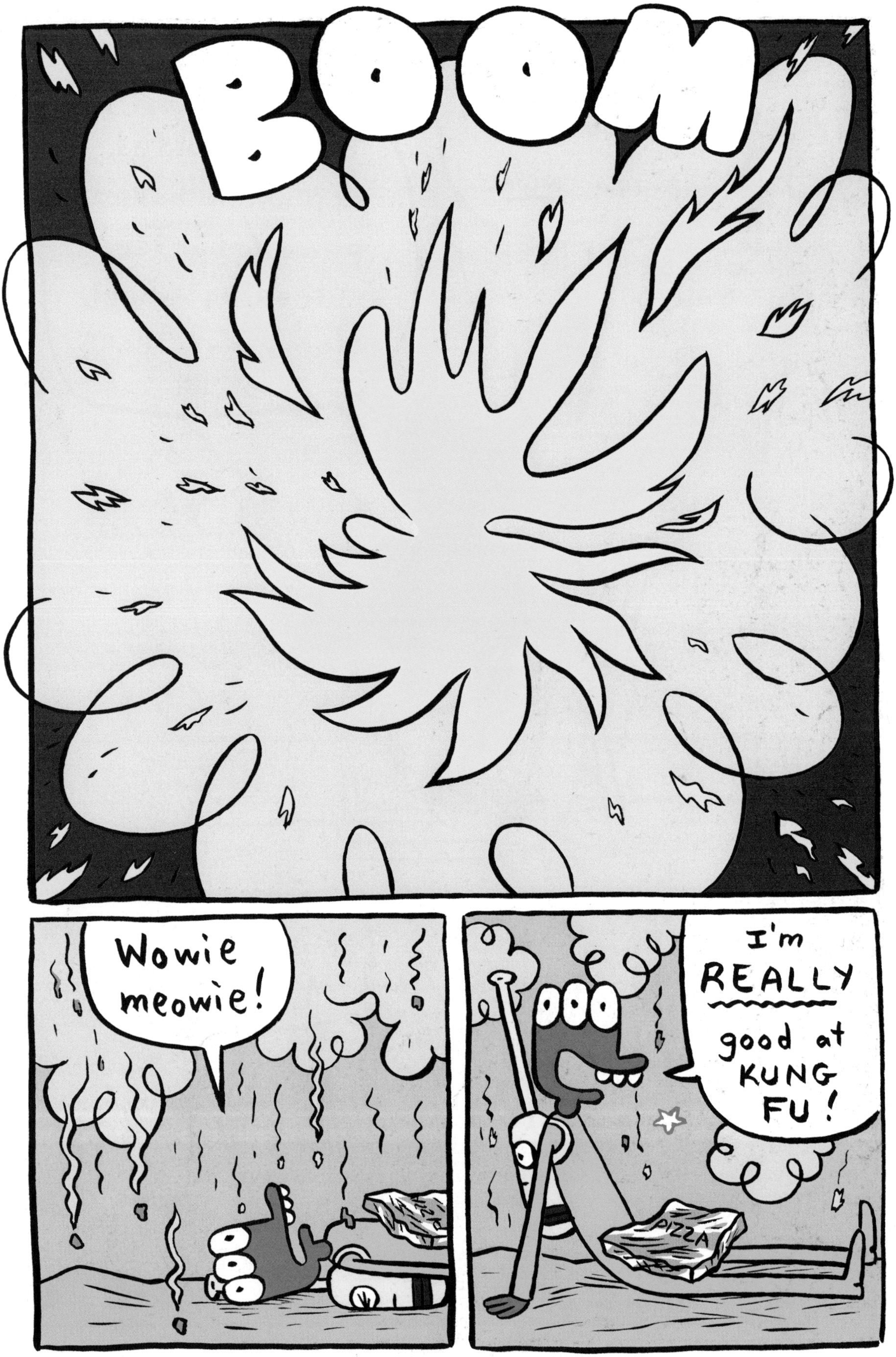
BOOM
Wowie meowie!
I'm REALLY good at KUNG FU!
PIZZA

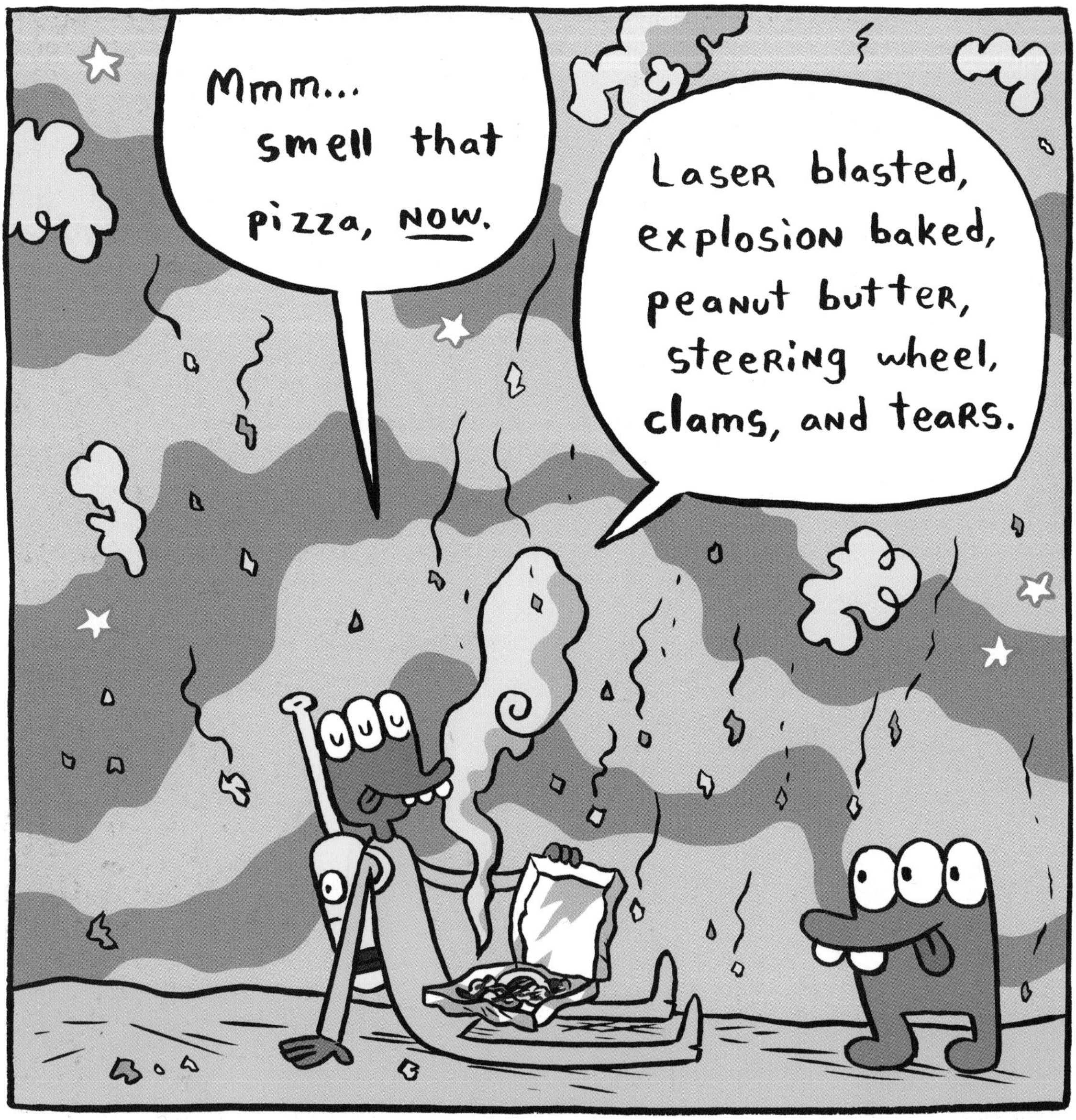
Mmm... smell that pizza, NOW.
Laser blasted, explosion baked, peanut butter, steering wheel, clams, and tears.

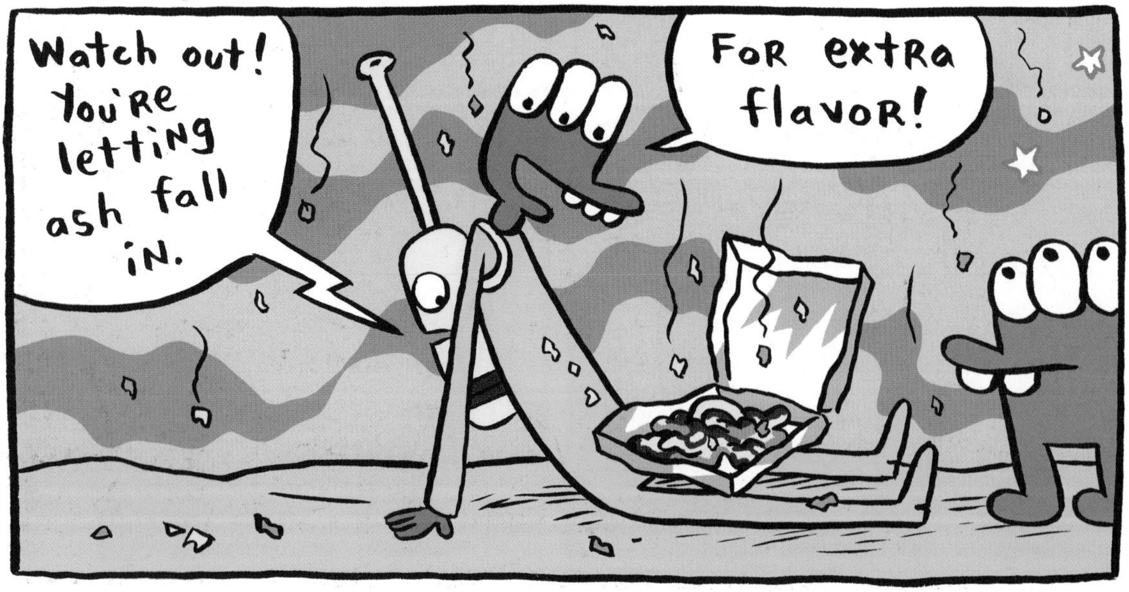
Watch out! You're letting ash fall in.
For extra flavor!

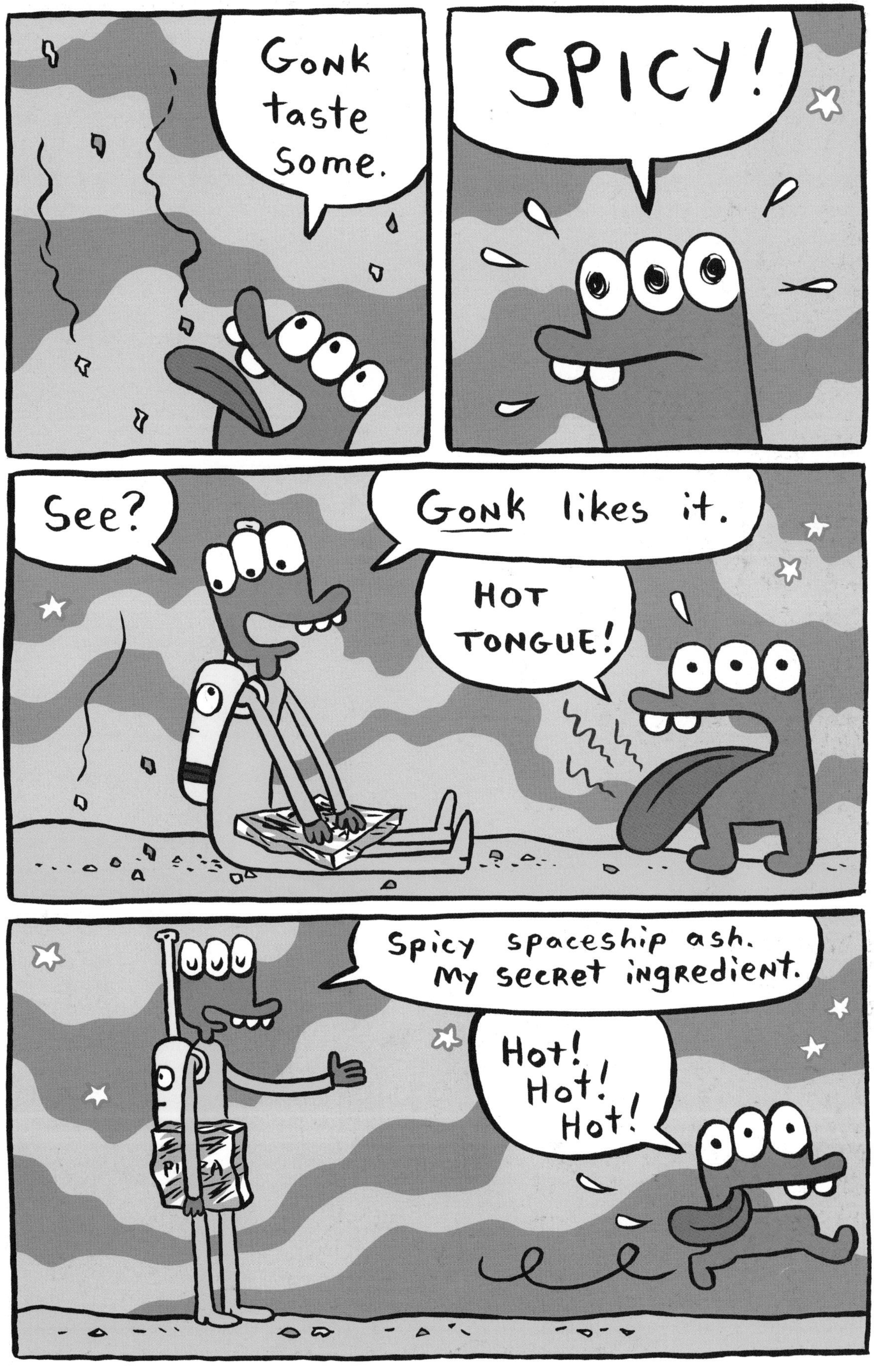
Gonk taste some.
SPICY!
See?
Gonk likes it.
HOT TONGUE!
Spicy spaceship ash. My secret ingredient.
Hot! Hot! Hot!
PIZZA

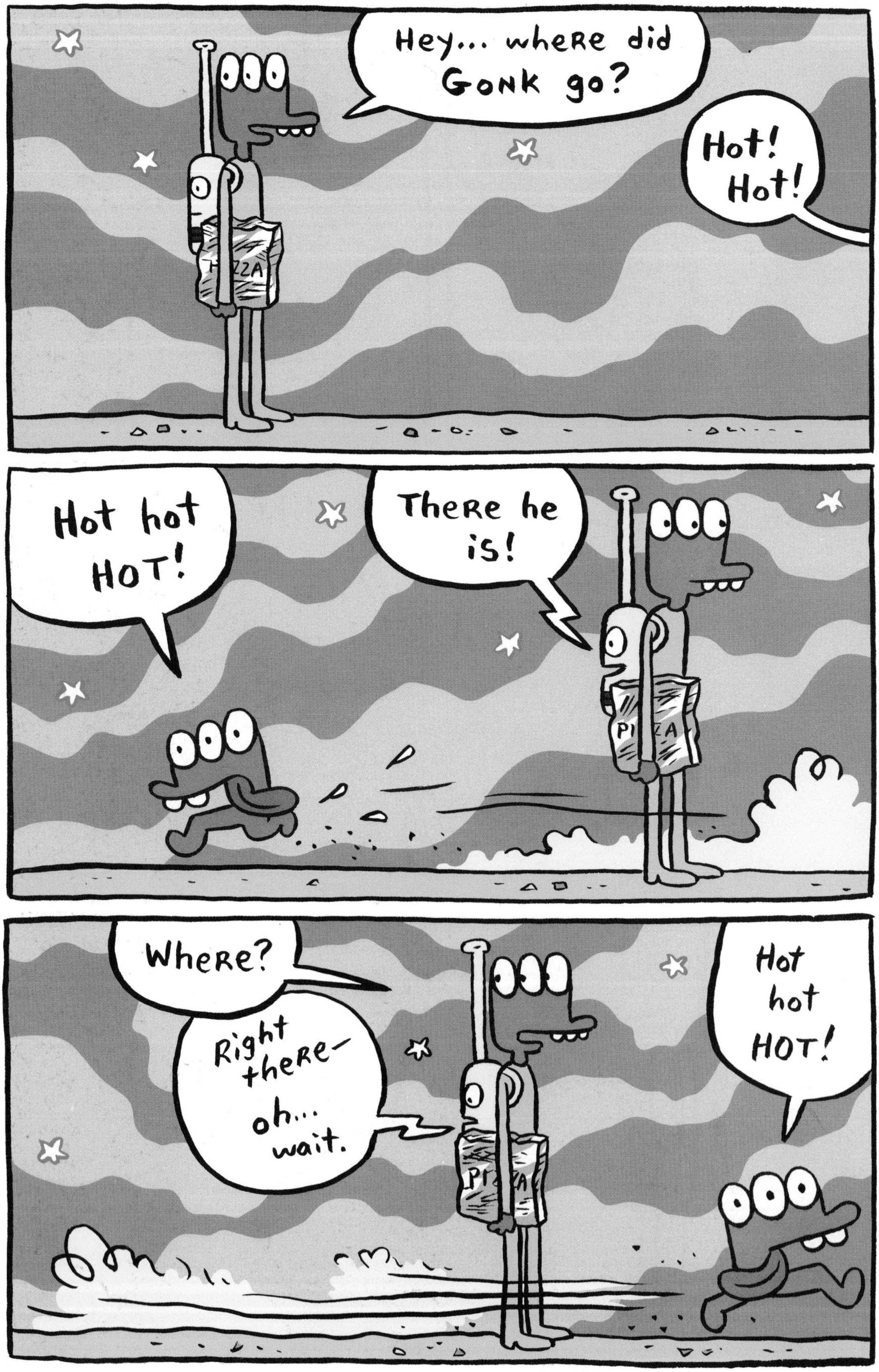
Hey... where did Gonk go?
Hot! Hot!
PIZZA
Hot hot HOT!
There he is!
PIZZA
Where?
Right there- oh... wait.
Hot hot HOT!
PIZZA

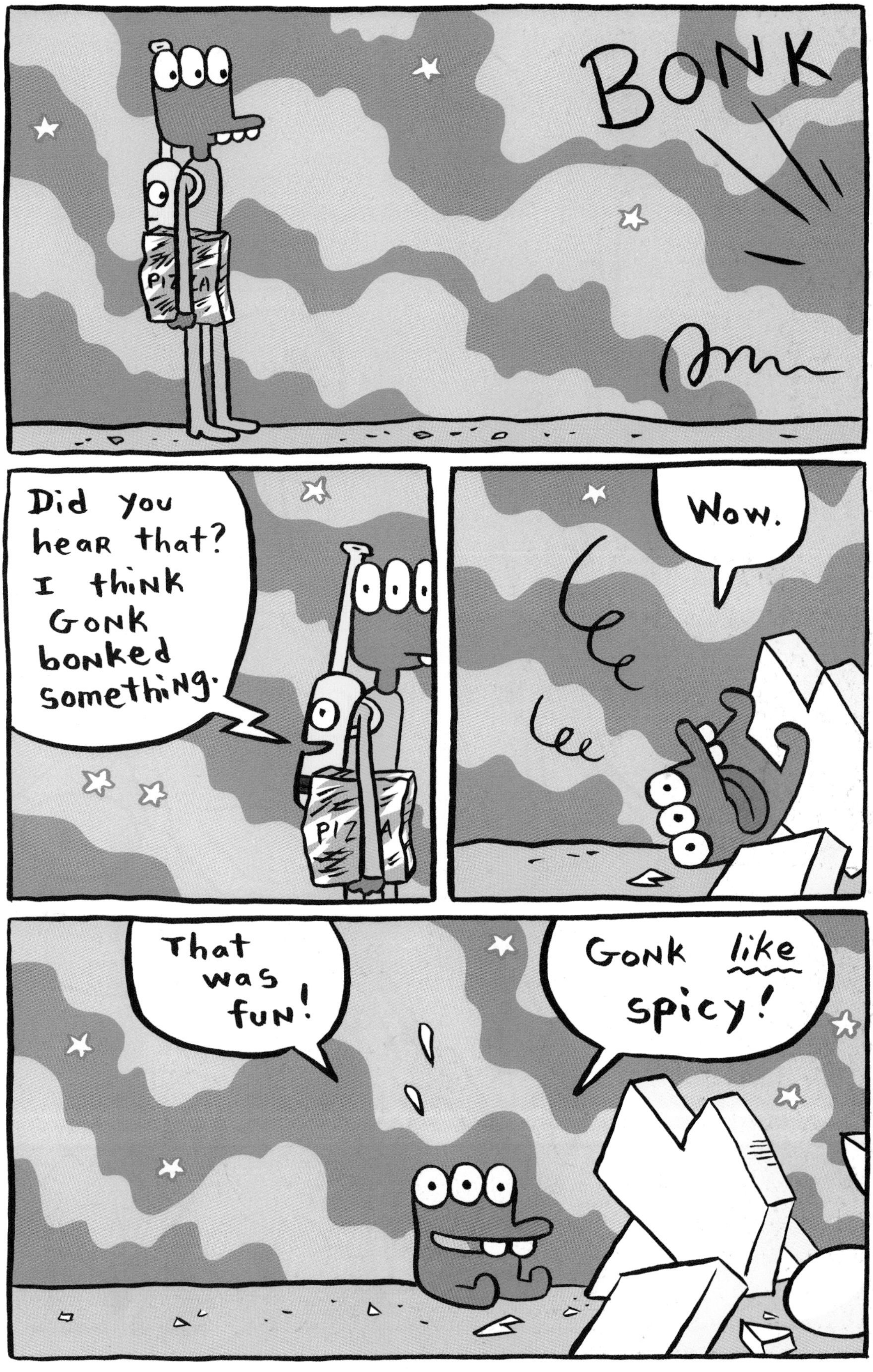
BONK
Did you hear that? I think GONK bonked something.
Wow.
That was fun!
GONK like spicy!

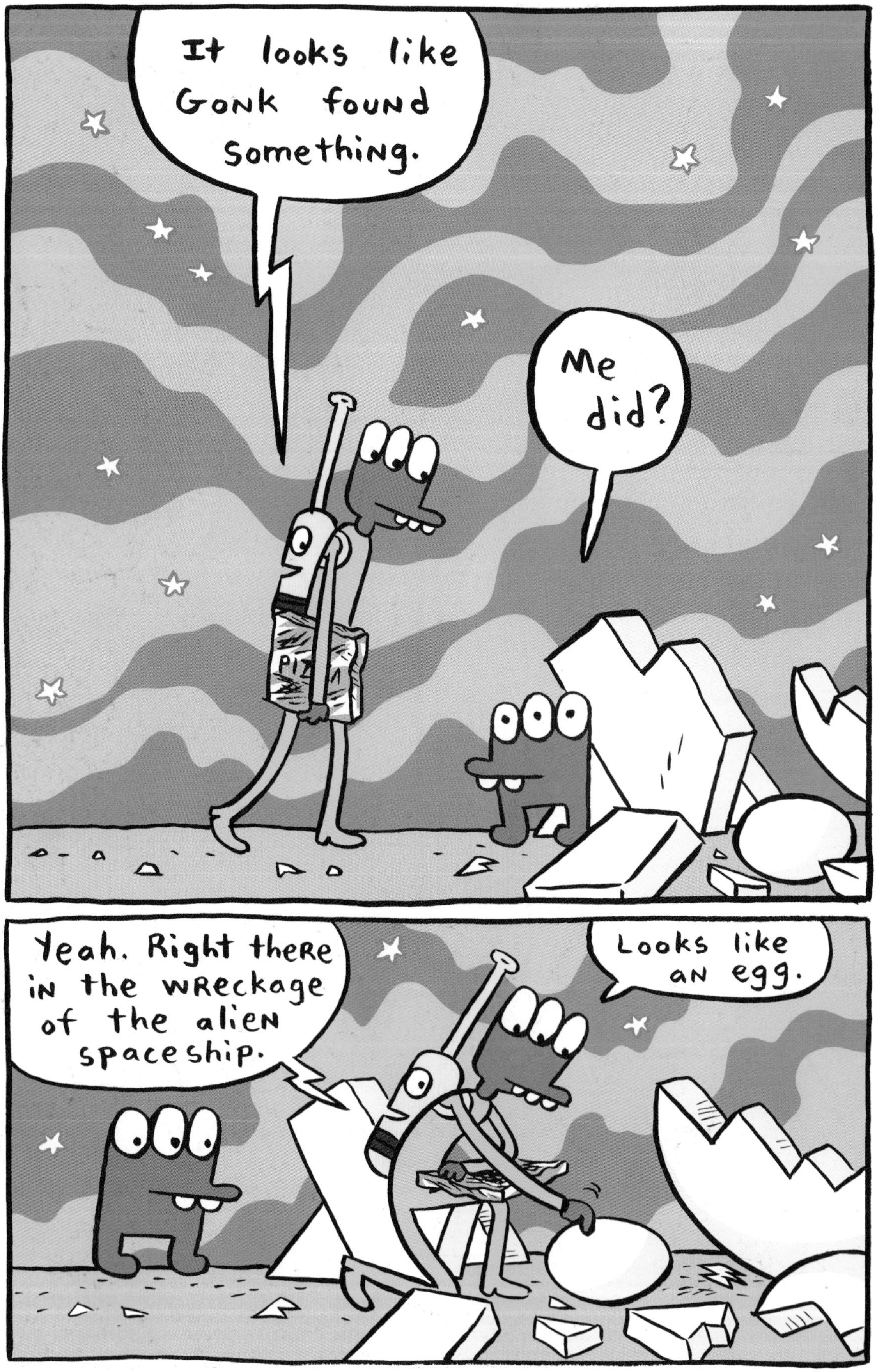
It looks like Gonk found something.
Me did?
PIZ
Yeah. Right there in the wreckage of the alien spaceship.
Looks like an egg.

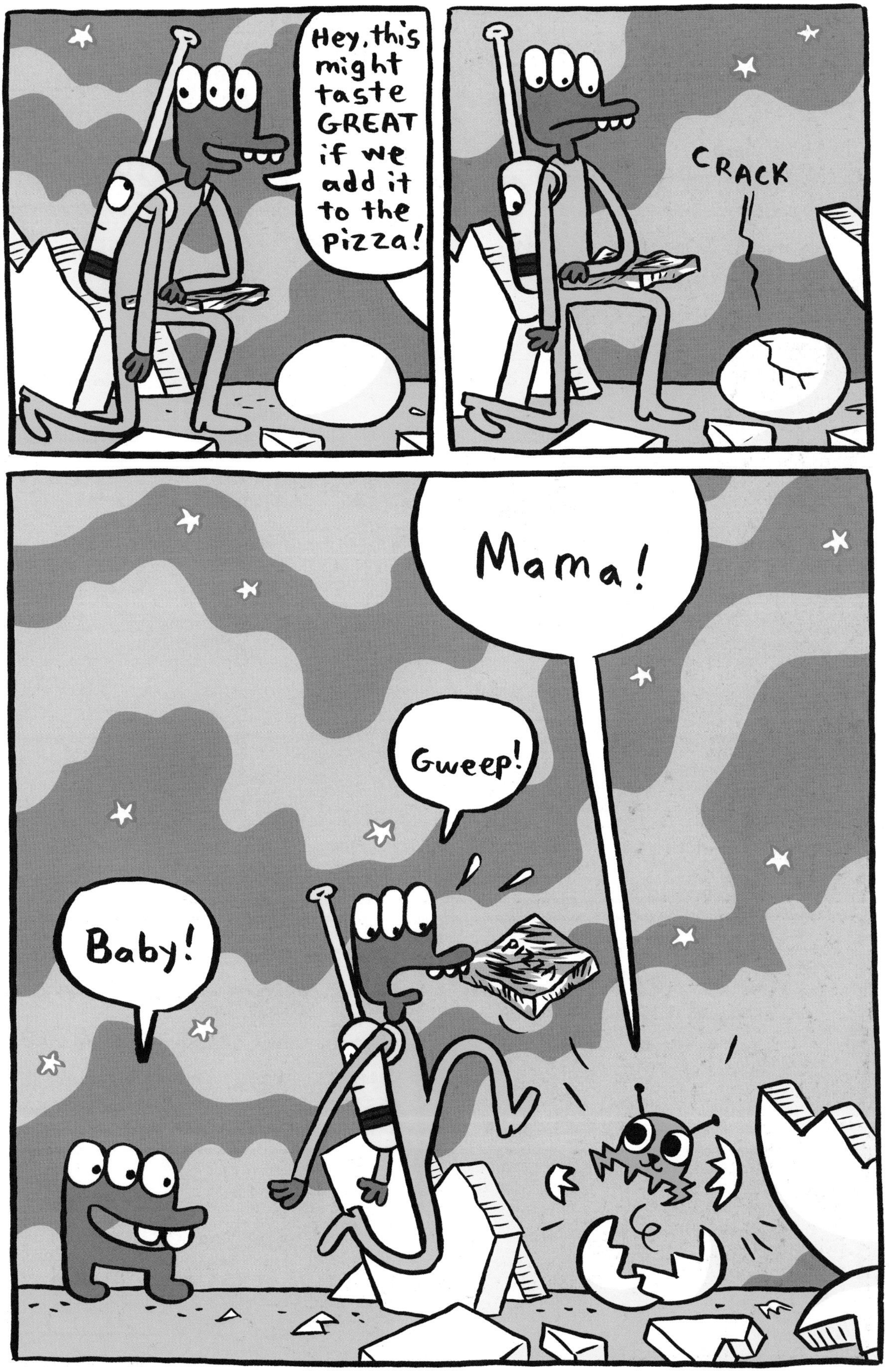
Hey, this might taste GREAT if we add it to the pizza!
CRACK
Mama!
Gweep!
Baby!

CHAPTER FIFTEEN

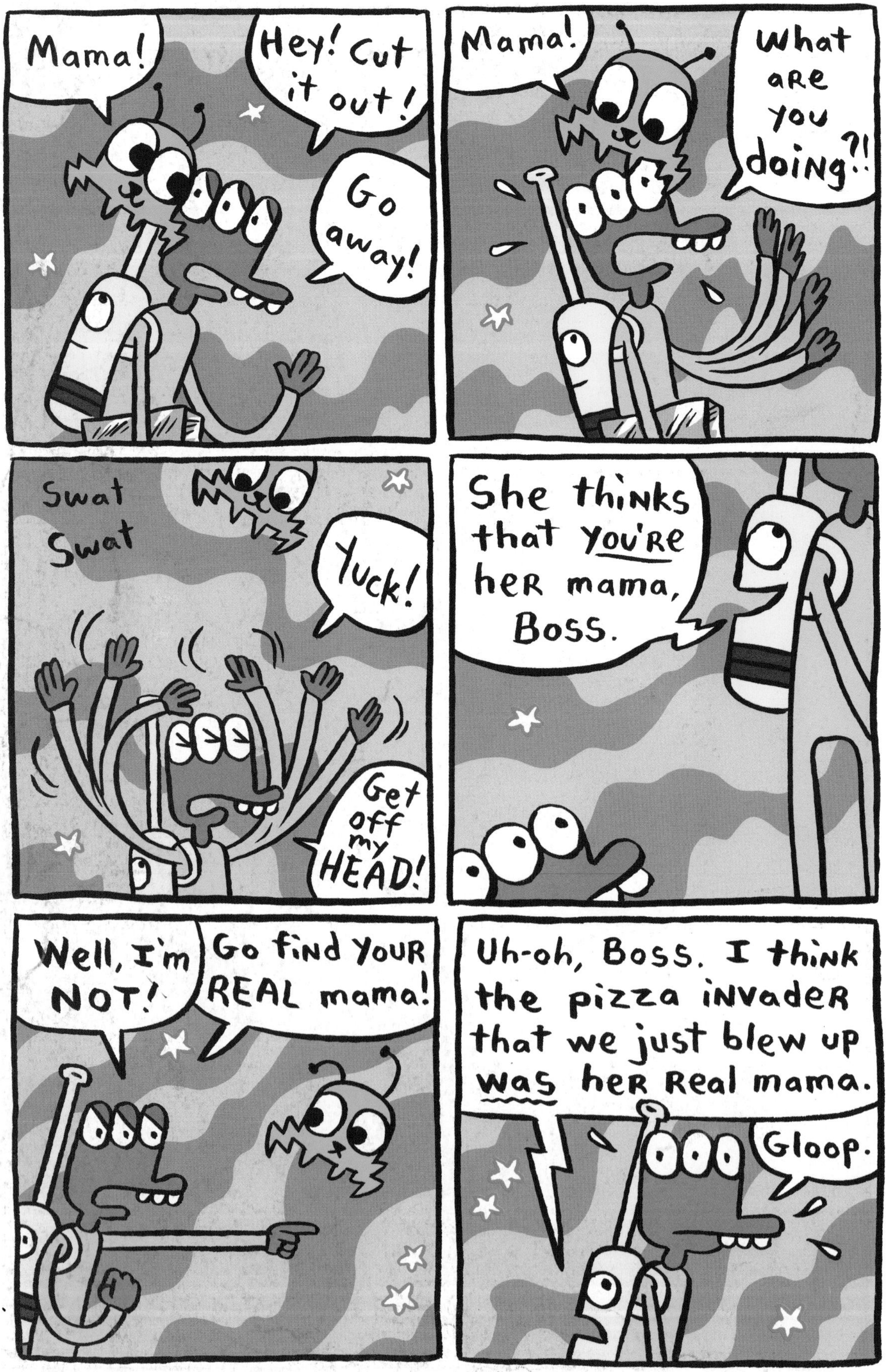
Mama!
Hey! Cut it out!
Go away!
Mama!
What are you doing?!
Swat Swat
Yuck!
Get off my HEAD!
She thinks that YOU'RE her mama, Boss.
Well, I'm NOT!
Go find YOUR REAL mama!
Uh-oh, Boss. I think the pizza invader that we just blew up was her real mama.
Gloop.

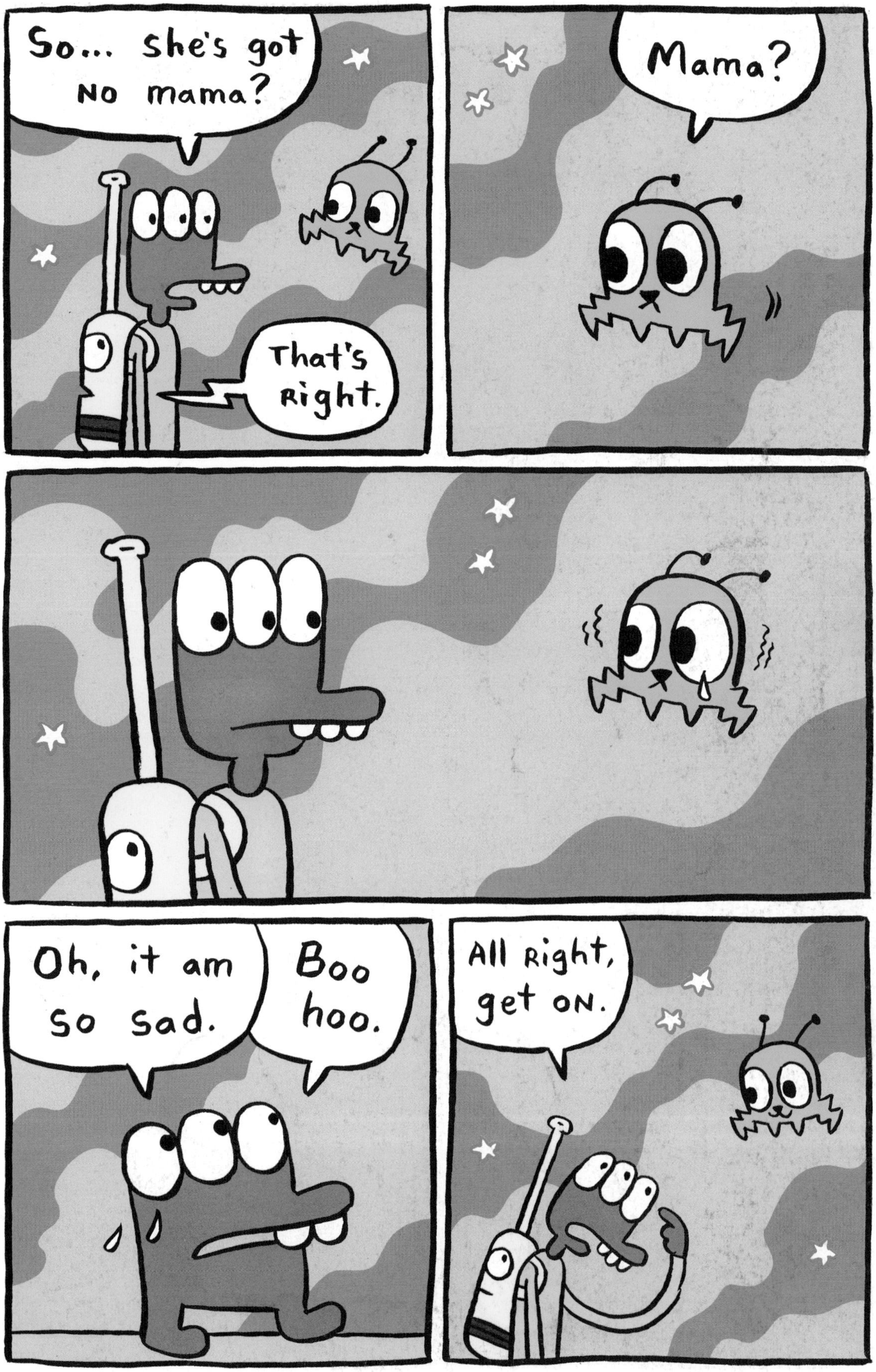
So... she's got no mama?
That's right.
Mama?
Oh, it am so sad.
Boo hoo.
All right, get on.

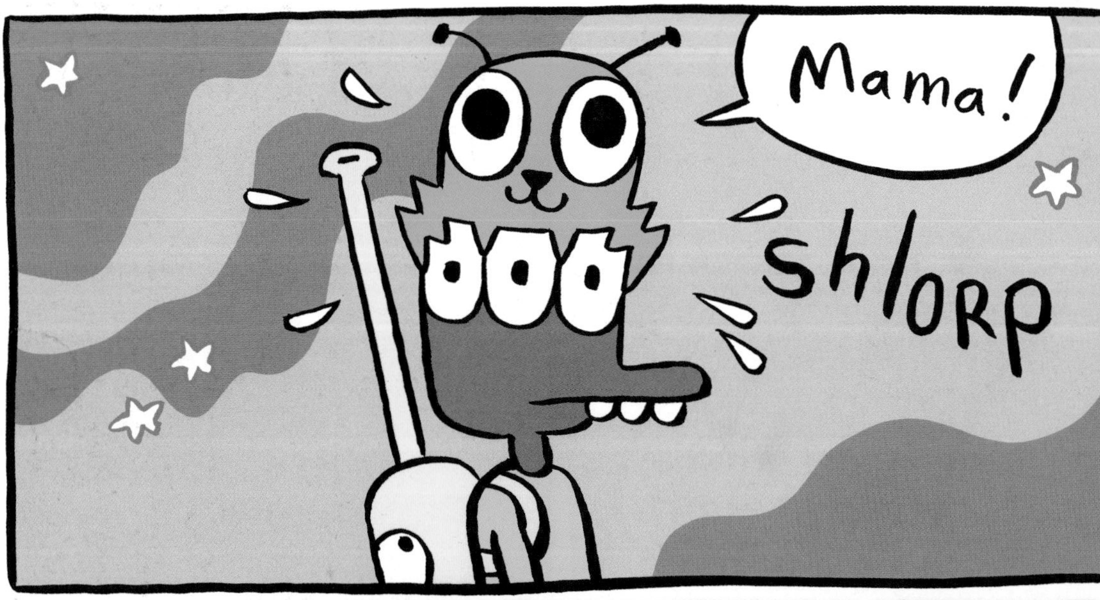
Mama!
shlorp

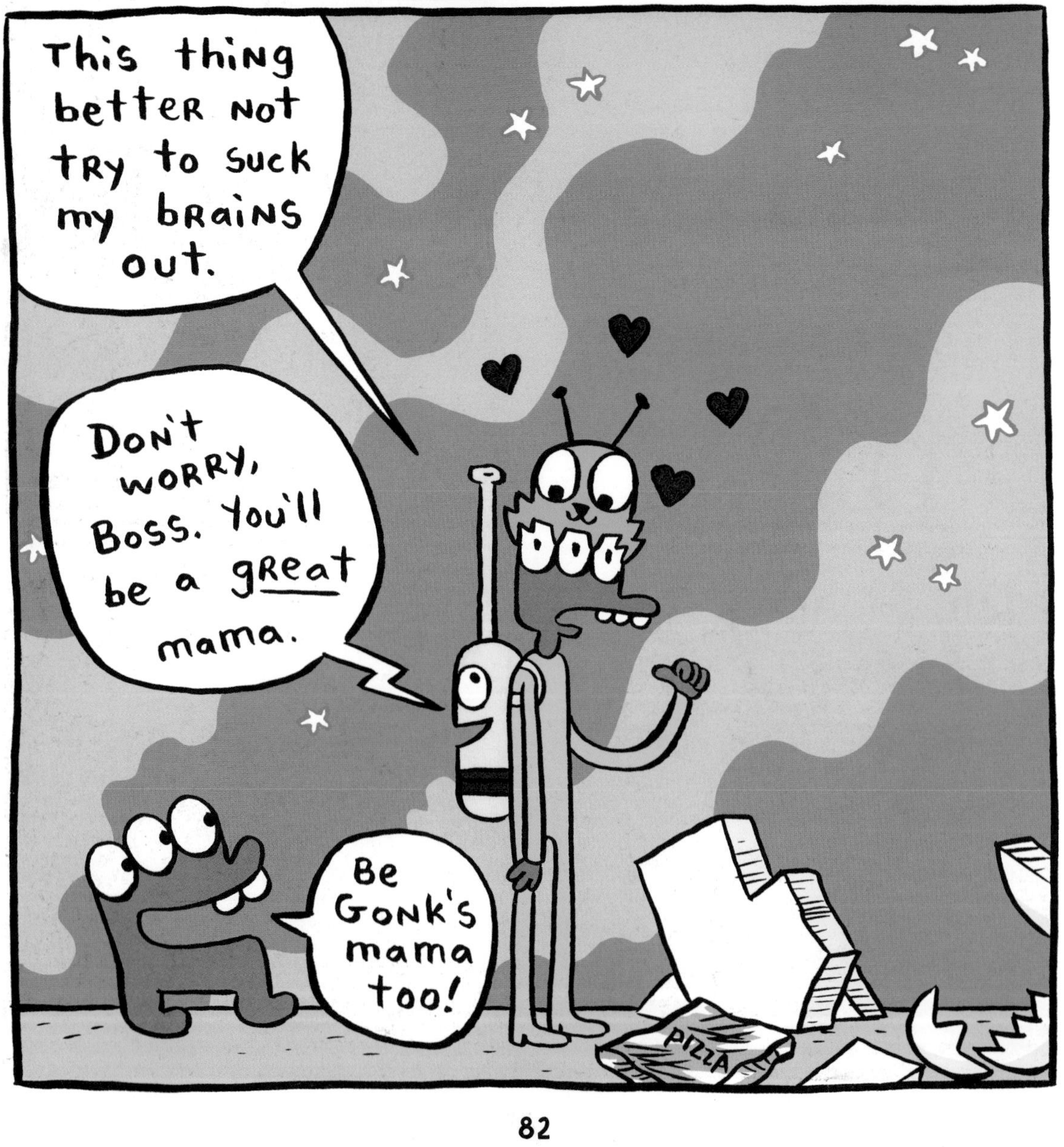
This thing better not try to suck my brains out.
Don't worry, Boss. You'll be a great mama.
Be Gonk's mama too!
PIZZA

CHAPTER SIXTEEN

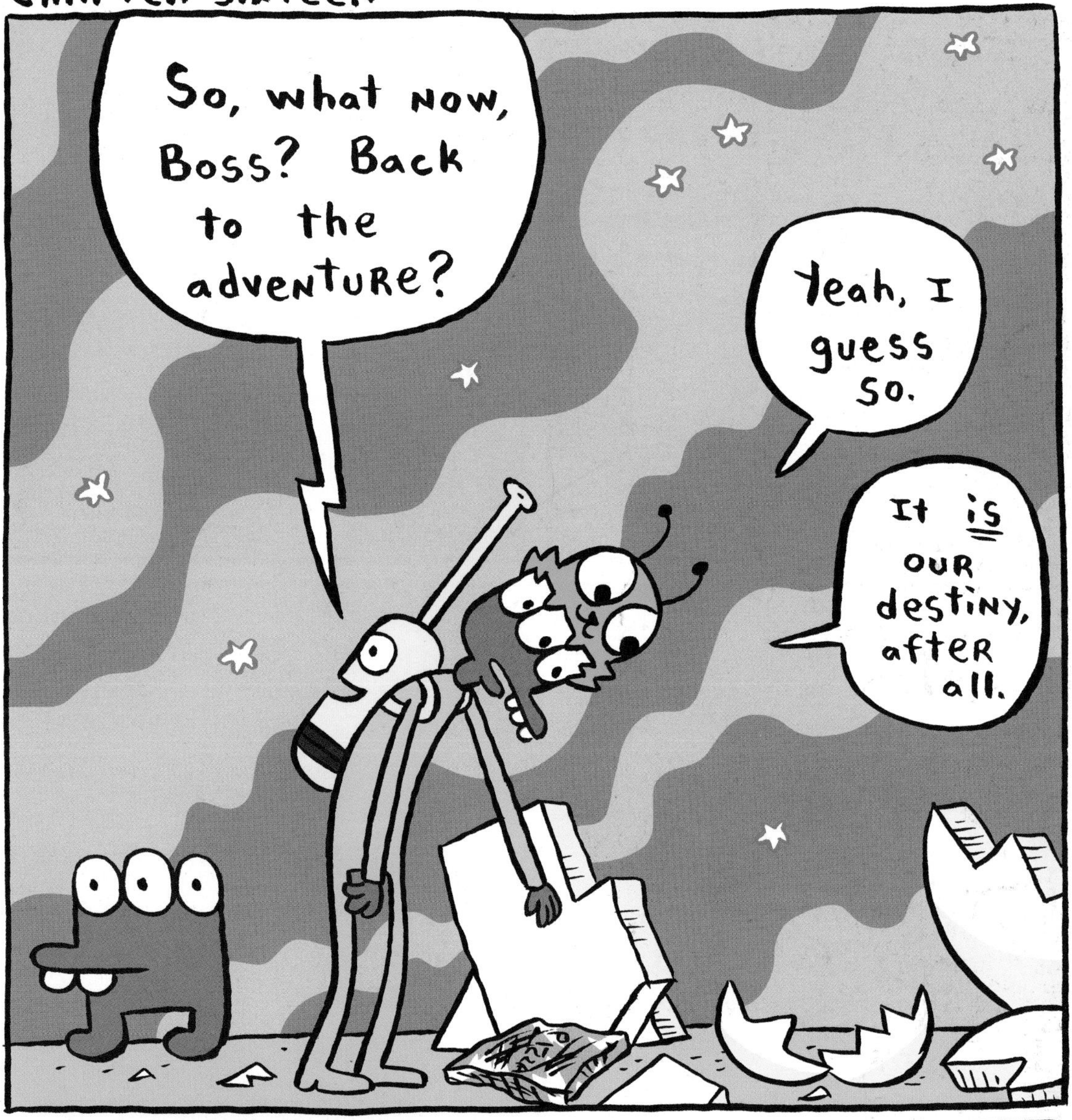

So, what now, Boss? Back to the adventure?
Yeah, I guess so.
It *is* our destiny, after all.

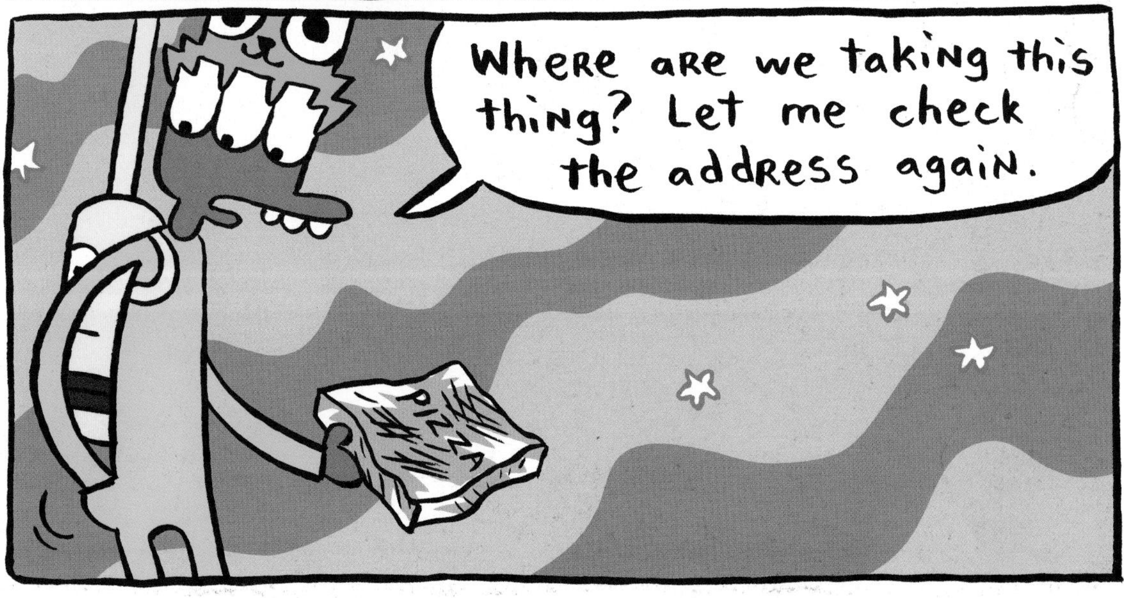

Where are we taking this thing? Let me check the address again.
PIZZA

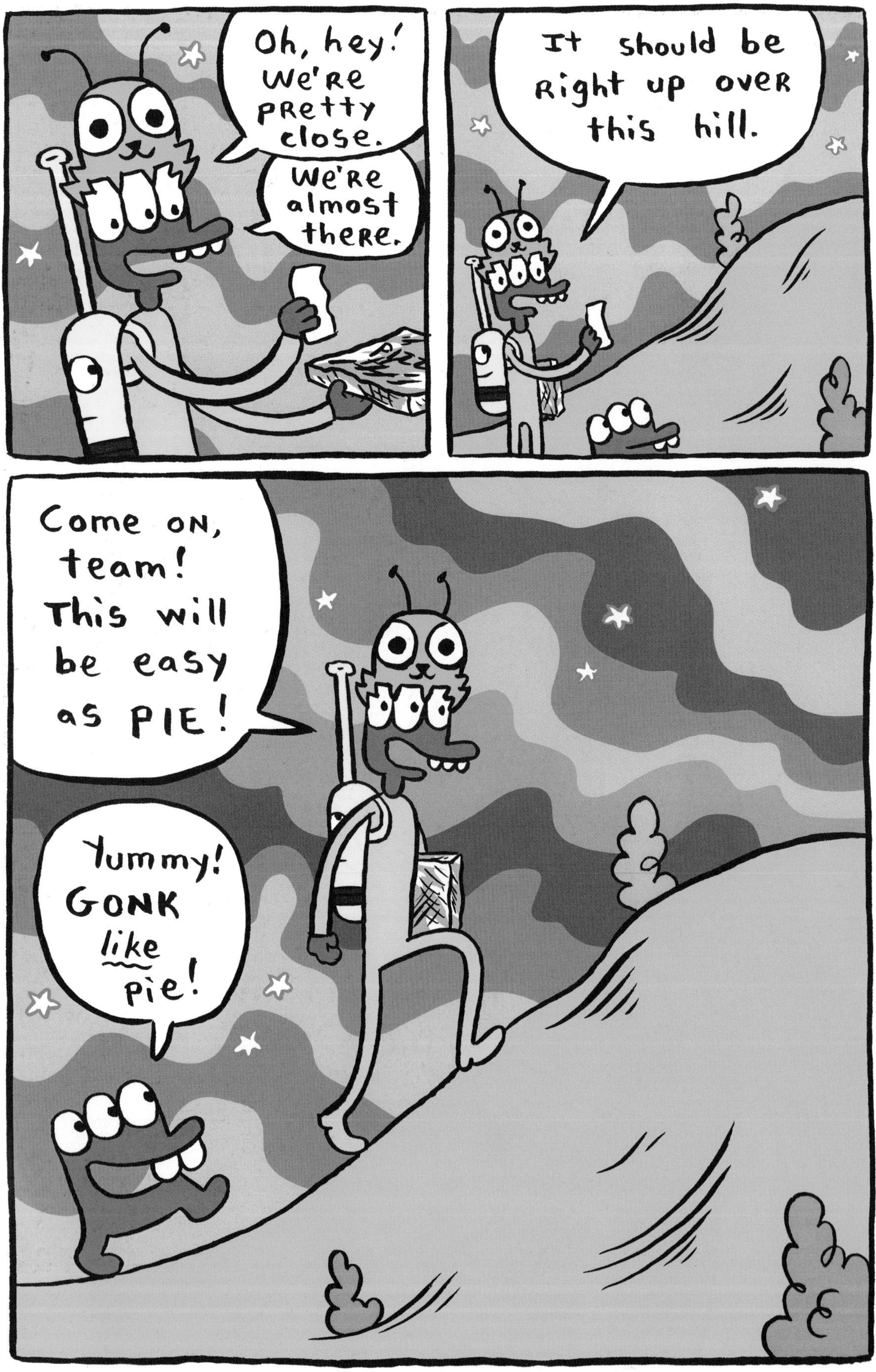
Oh, hey! We're pretty close.
We're almost there.
It should be right up over this hill.
Come on, team! This will be easy as PIE!
Yummy! GONK like pie!

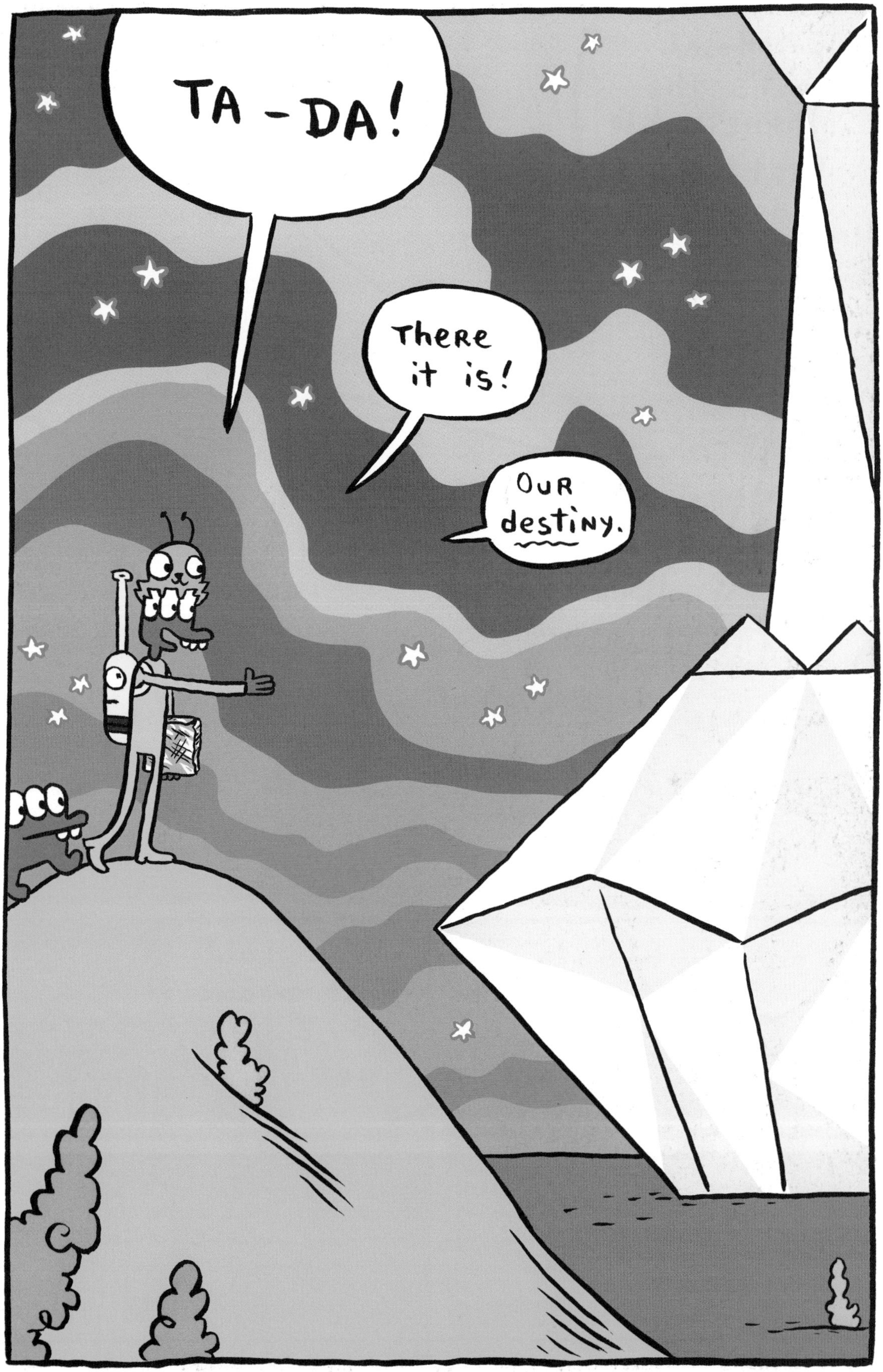
TA-DA!
There it is!
Our destiny.

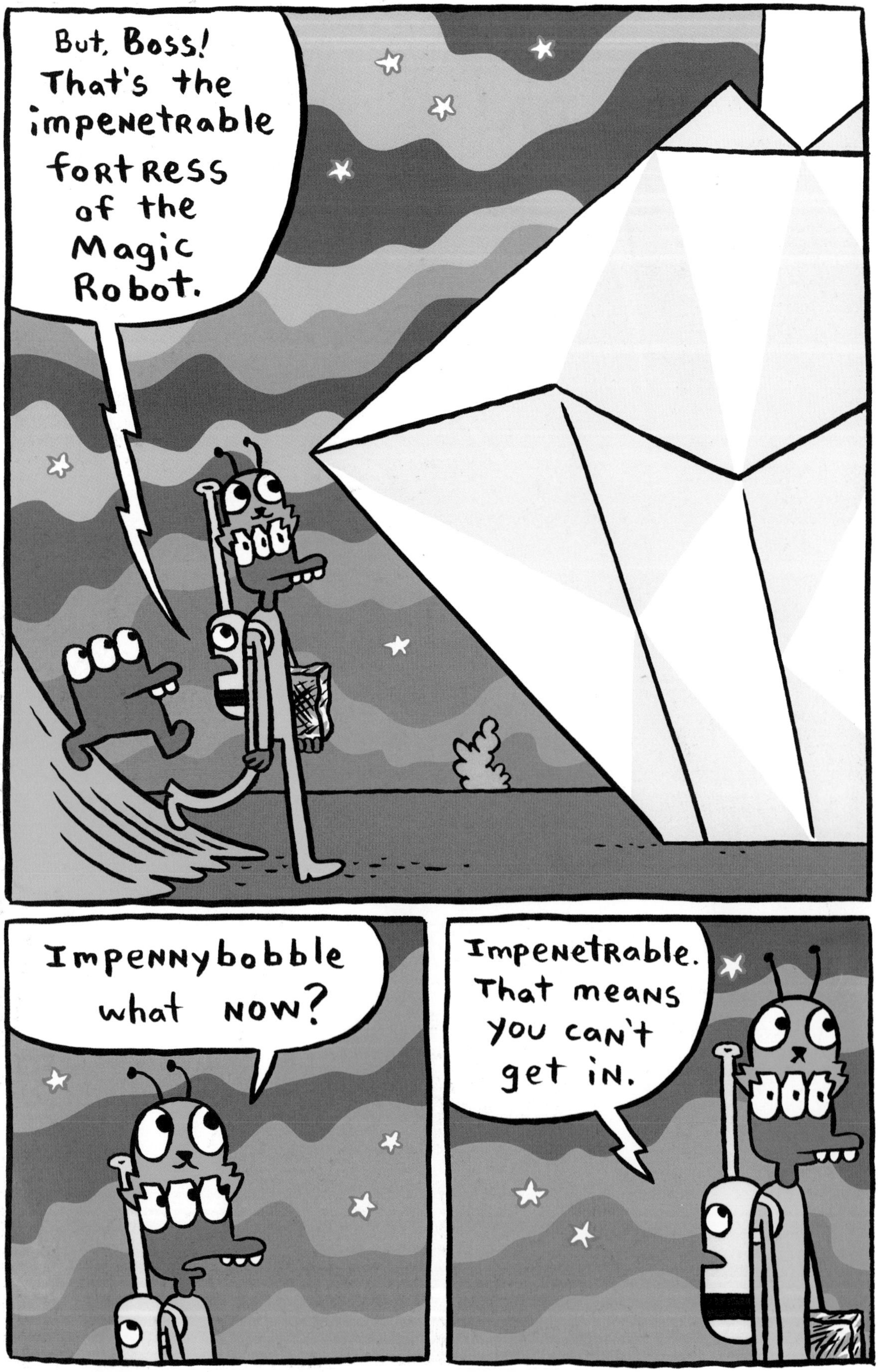
But, Boss! That's the impenetrable fortress of the Magic Robot.
Impennybobble what now?
Impenetrable. That means you can't get in.

Try the doorbell.
Good idea, GONK.

But this stupid place doesn't seem to have a doorbell.
Phew! Thank goodness!
"Never ring the doorbell of the Magic Robot." That's my motto.

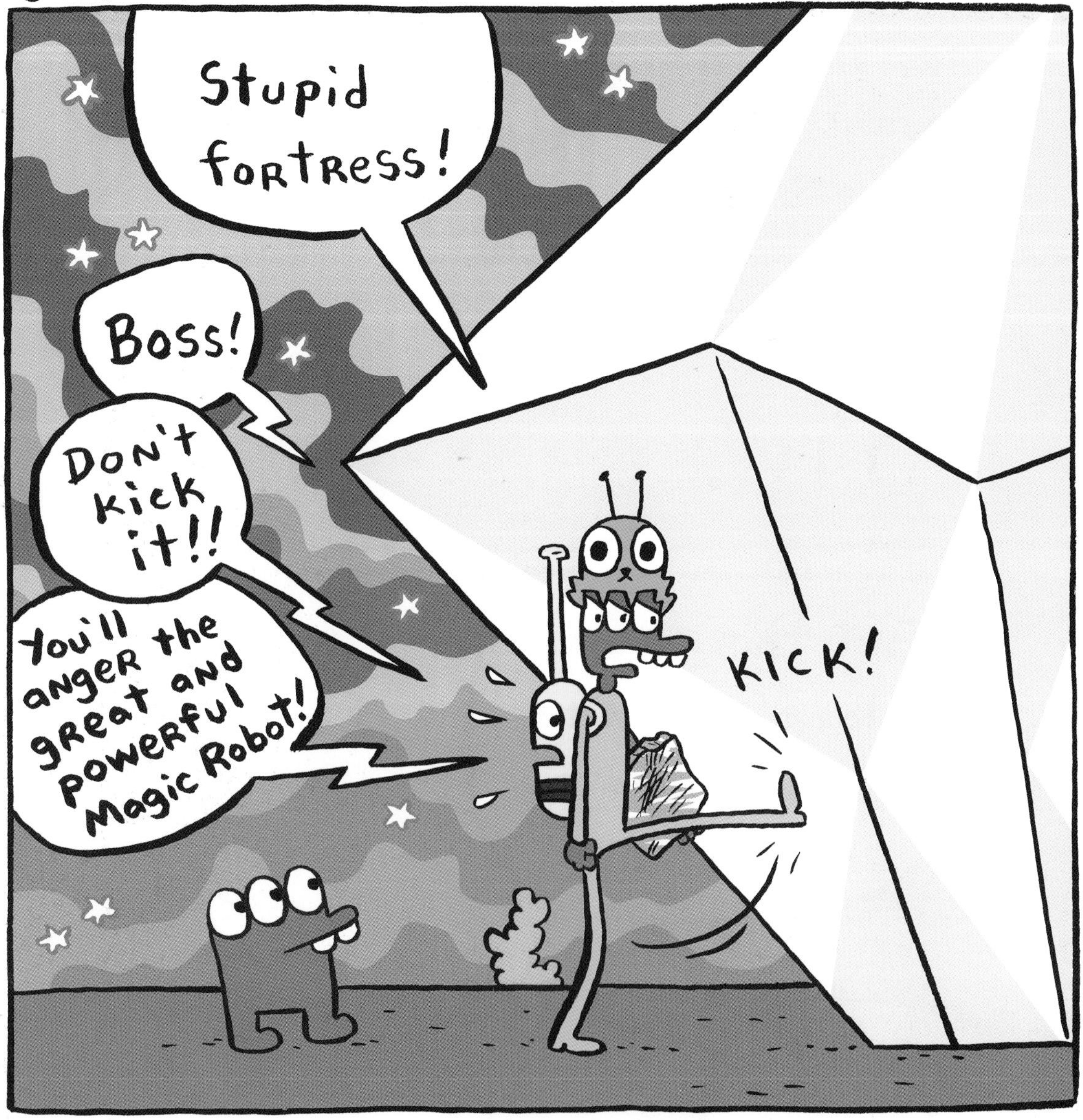
Stupid fortress!
Boss!
Don't kick it!!
You'll anger the great and powerful Magic Robot!
KICK!

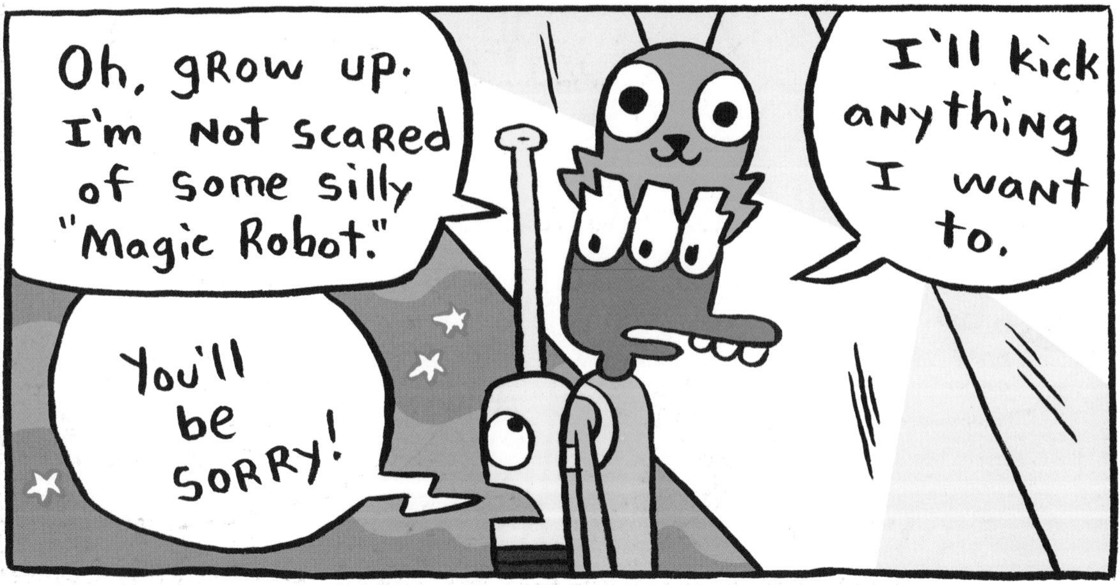
Oh, grow up. I'm not scared of some silly "Magic Robot."
I'll kick anything I want to.
You'll be SORRY!

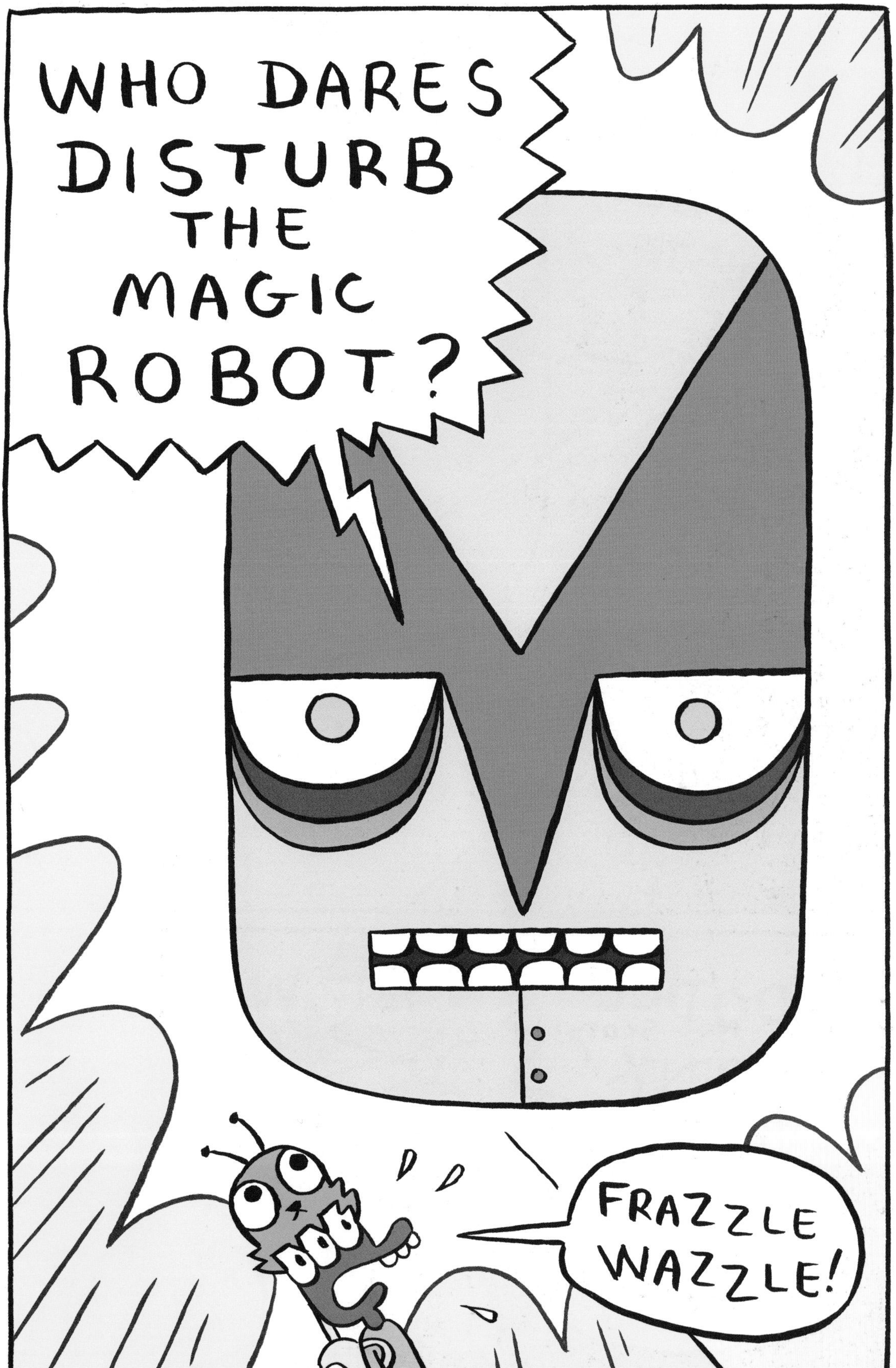
WHO DARES DISTURB THE MAGIC ROBOT?
FRAZZLE WAZZLE!

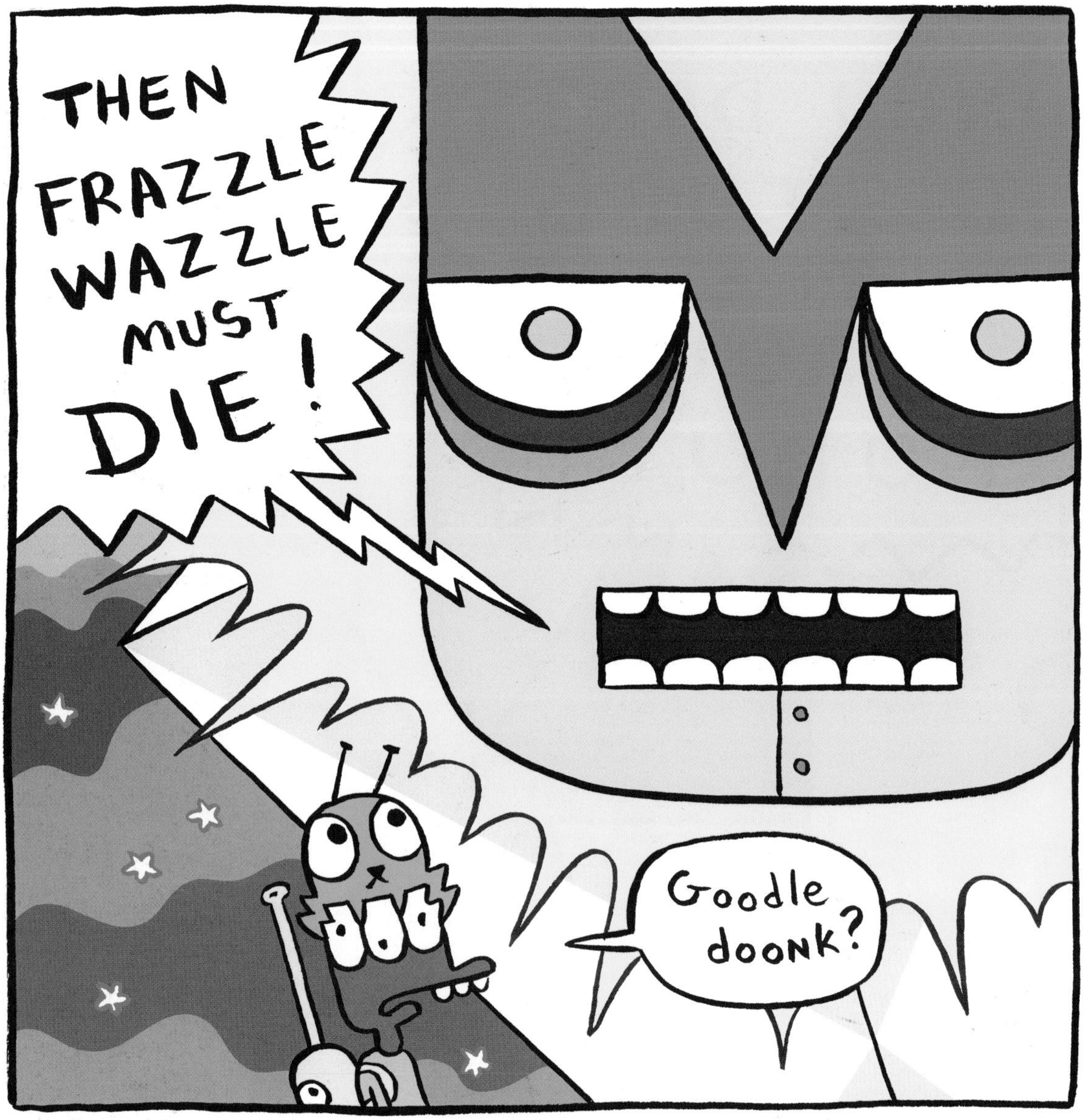
THEN FRAZZLE WAZZLE MUST DIE!
Goodle doonk?

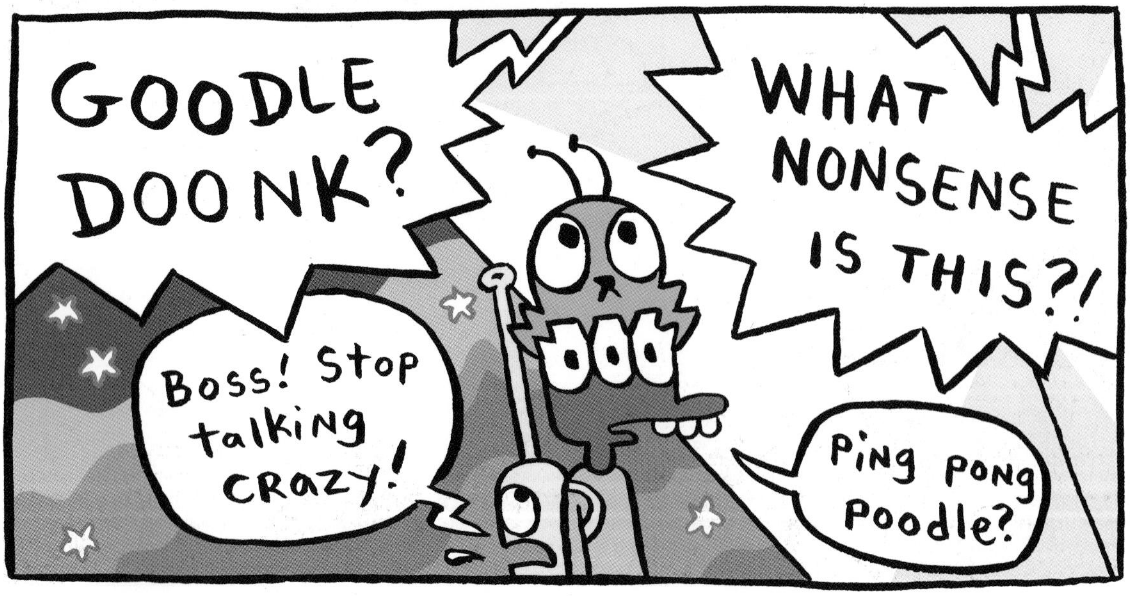
GOODLE DOONK?
WHAT NONSENSE IS THIS?!
Boss! Stop talking crazy!
Ping pong poodle?

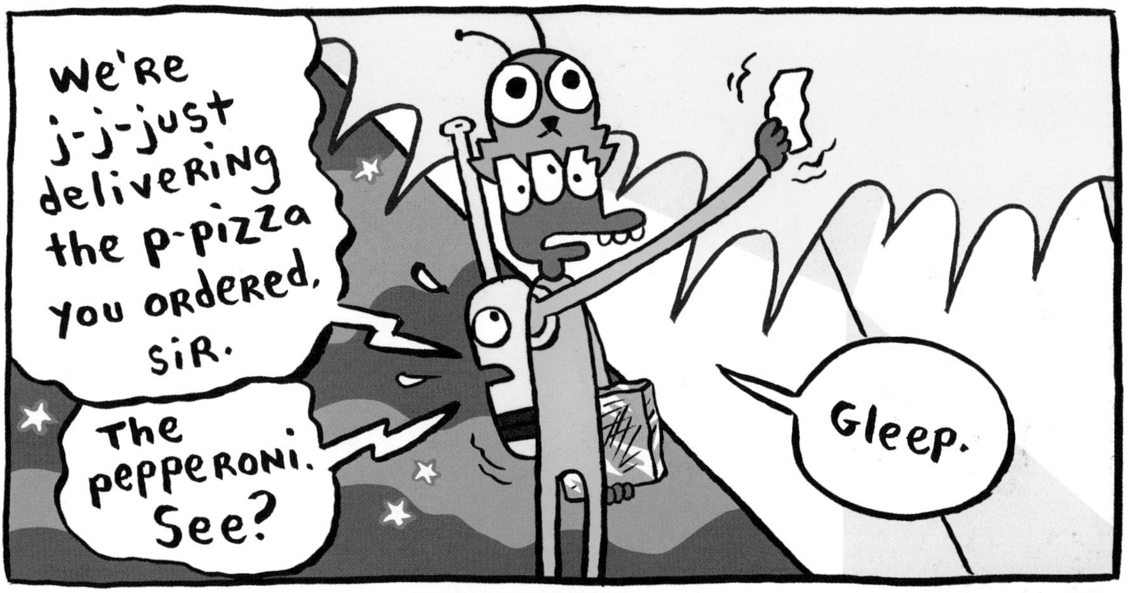
We're j-j-just delivering the p-pizza you ordered, sir.
The pepperoni. See?
Gleep.

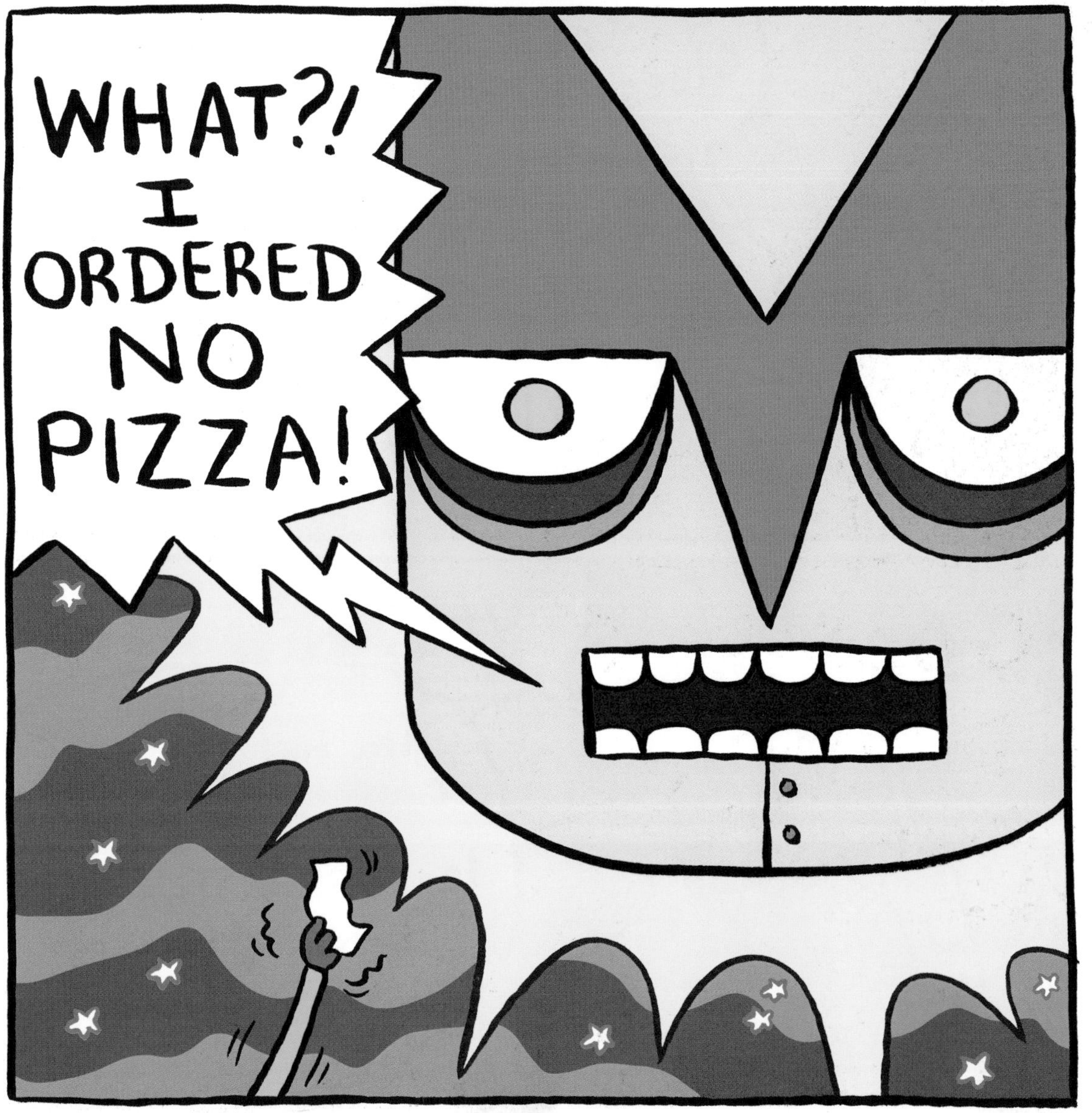
WHAT?! I ORDERED NO PIZZA!

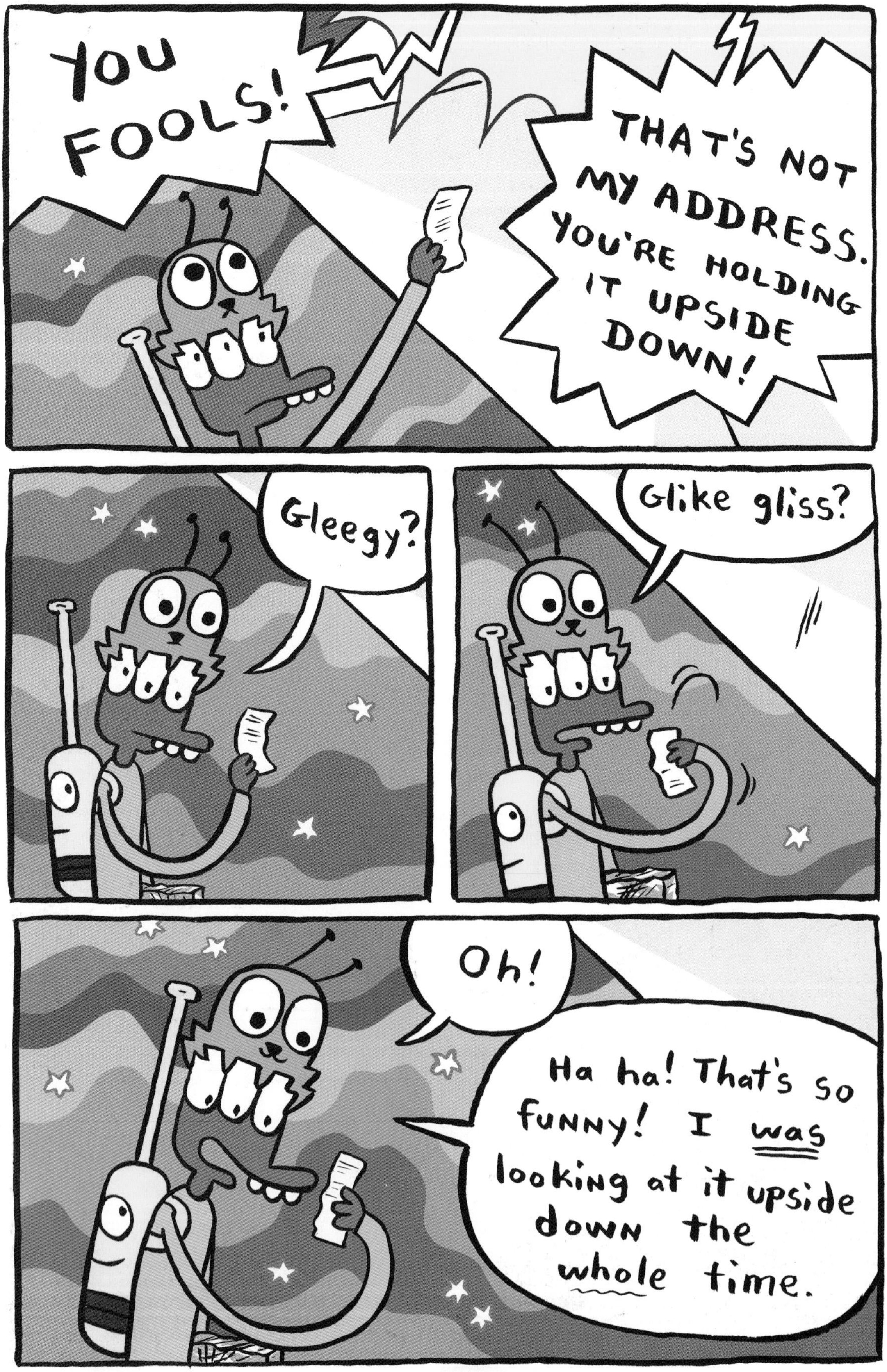
YOU FOOLS!
THAT'S NOT MY ADDRESS. YOU'RE HOLDING IT UPSIDE DOWN!
Gleegy?
Glike gliss?
Oh!
Ha ha! That's so funny! I was looking at it upside down the whole time.

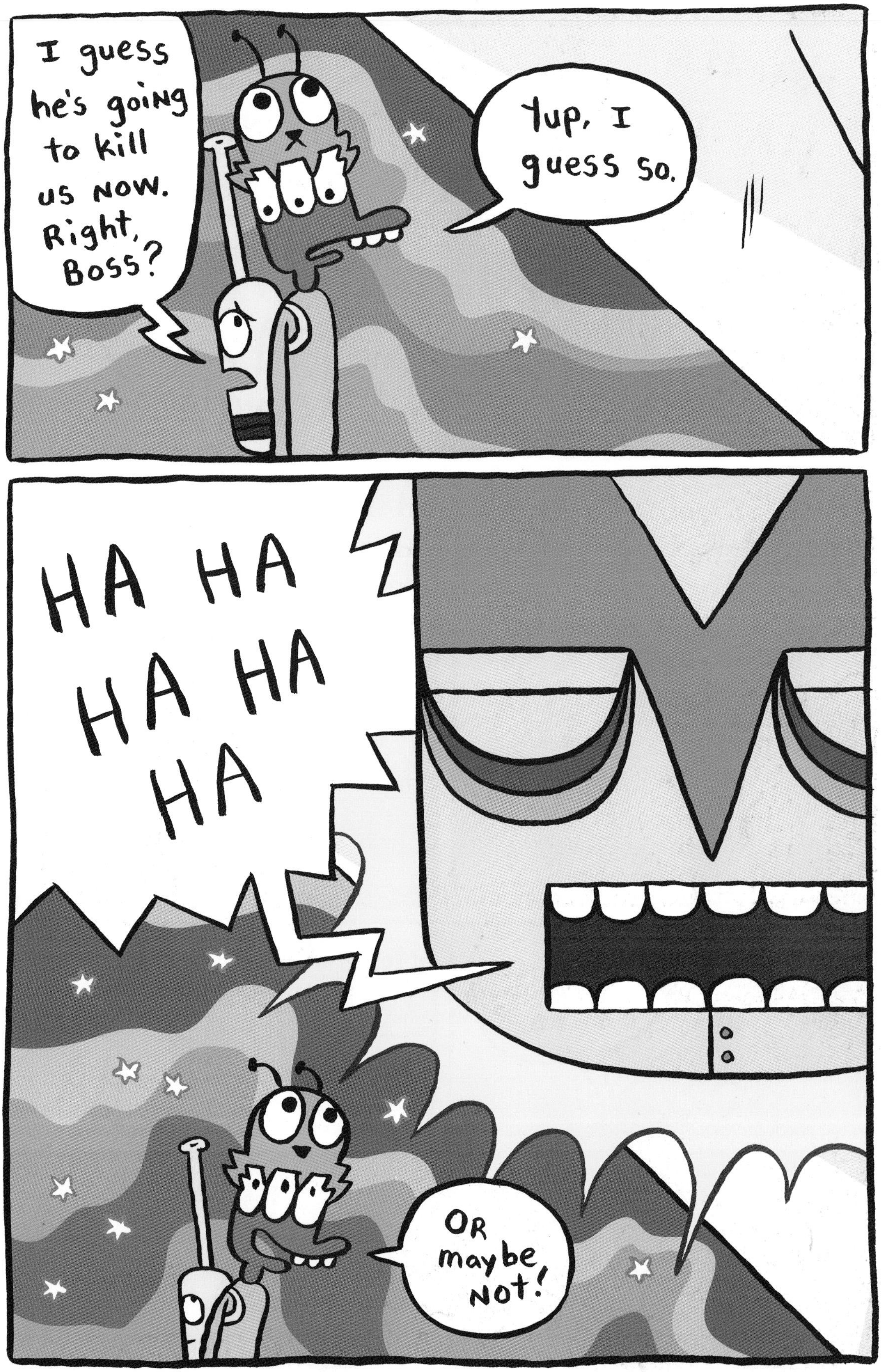
I guess he's going to kill us now. Right, Boss?
Yup, I guess so.
HA HA HA HA HA
Or maybe not!

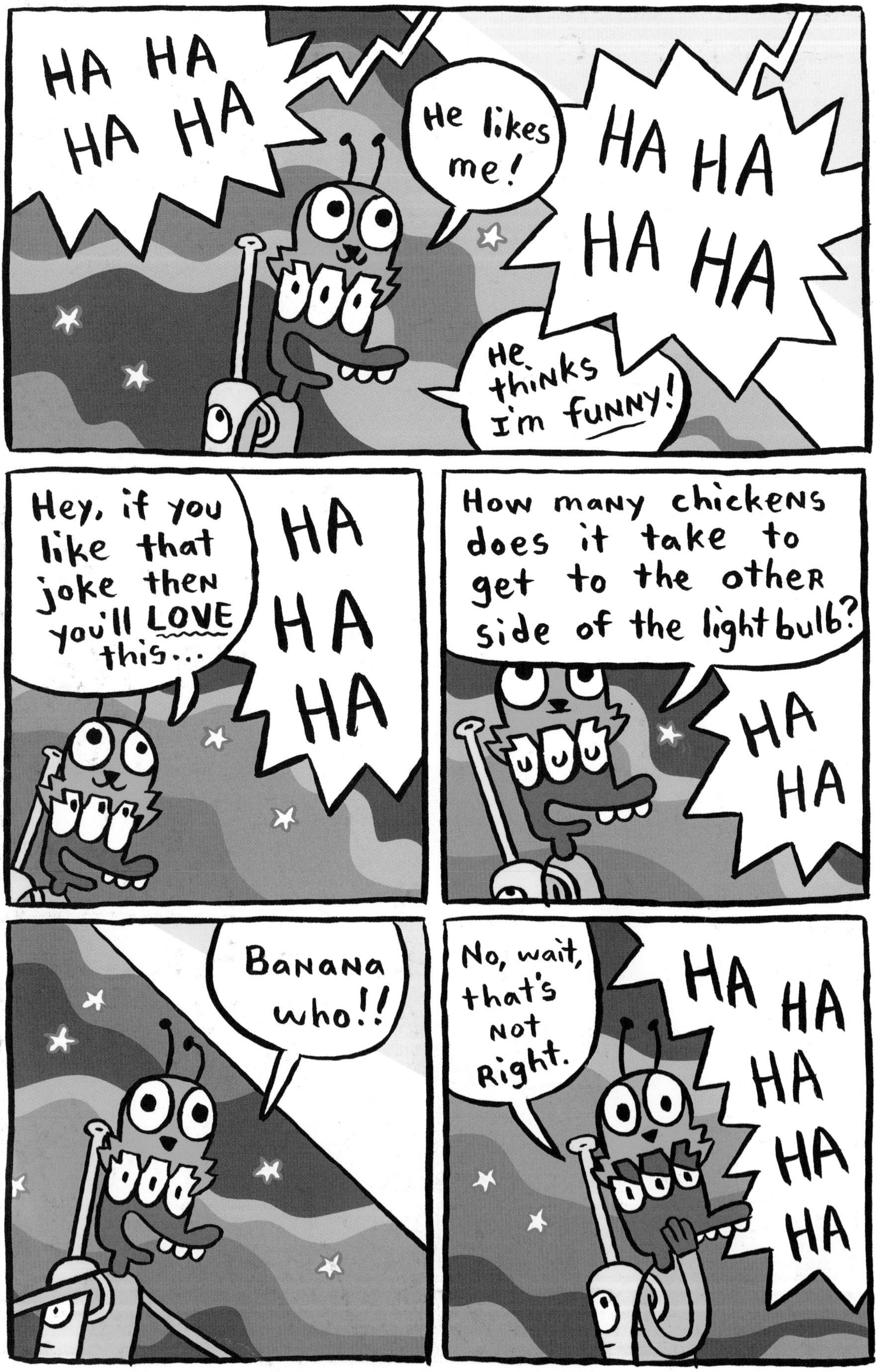
HA HA
HA HA
He likes me!
HA HA
HA HA
He thinks I'm FUNNY!
Hey, if you like that joke then you'll LOVE this...
HA
HA
HA
How many chickens does it take to get to the other side of the lightbulb?
HA
HA
Banana who!!
No, wait, that's not right.
HA HA
HA
HA
HA

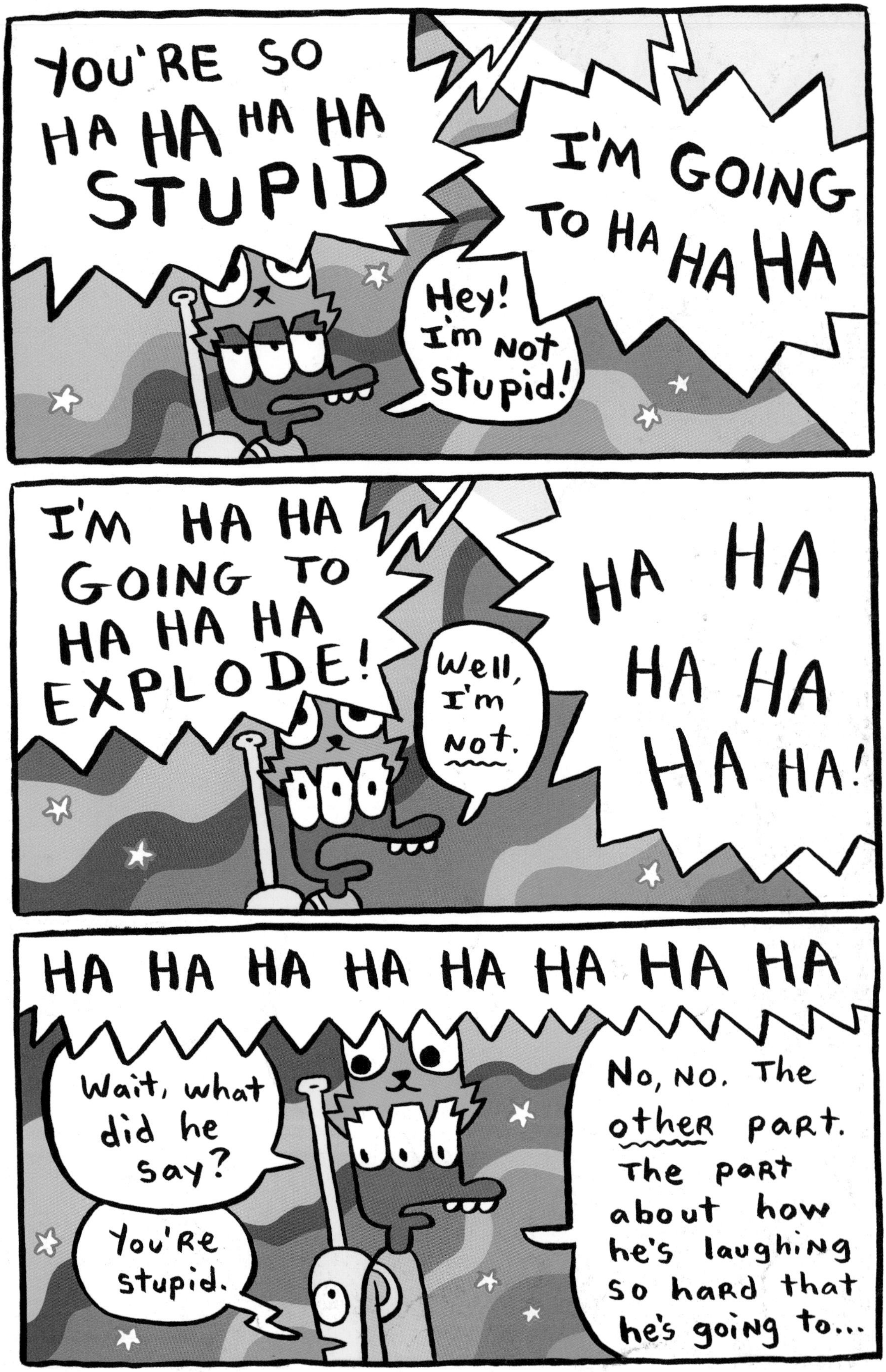

YOU'RE SO HA HA HA HA HA STUPID
I'M GOING TO HA HA HA HA
Hey! I'm not stupid!
I'M HA HA GOING TO HA HA HA EXPLODE!
Well, I'm not.
HA HA HA HA HA HA HA!
HA HA HA HA HA HA HA HA
Wait, what did he say?
You're stupid.
No, no. The other part. The part about how he's laughing so hard that he's going to...

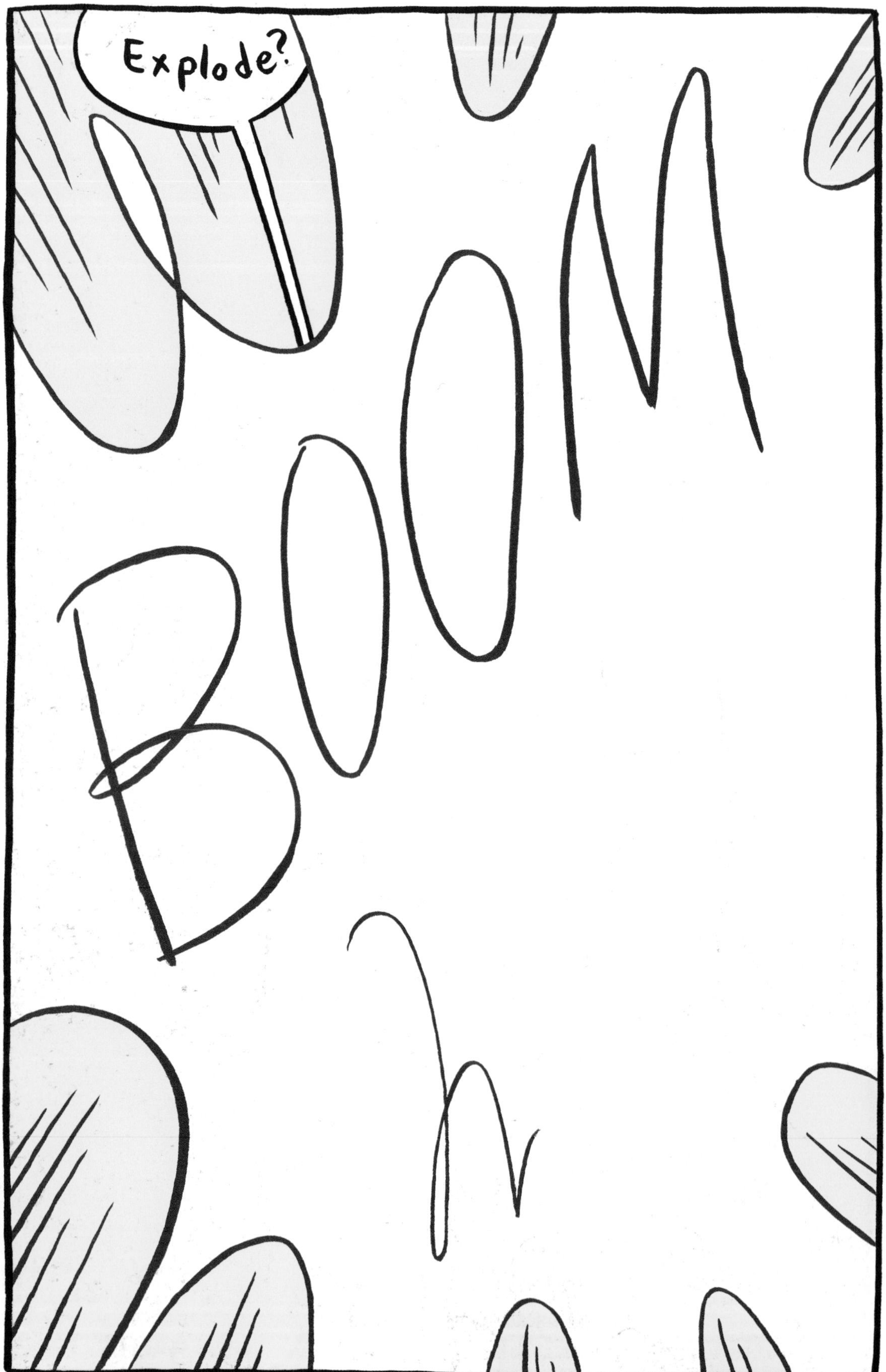
Explode?
BOOM

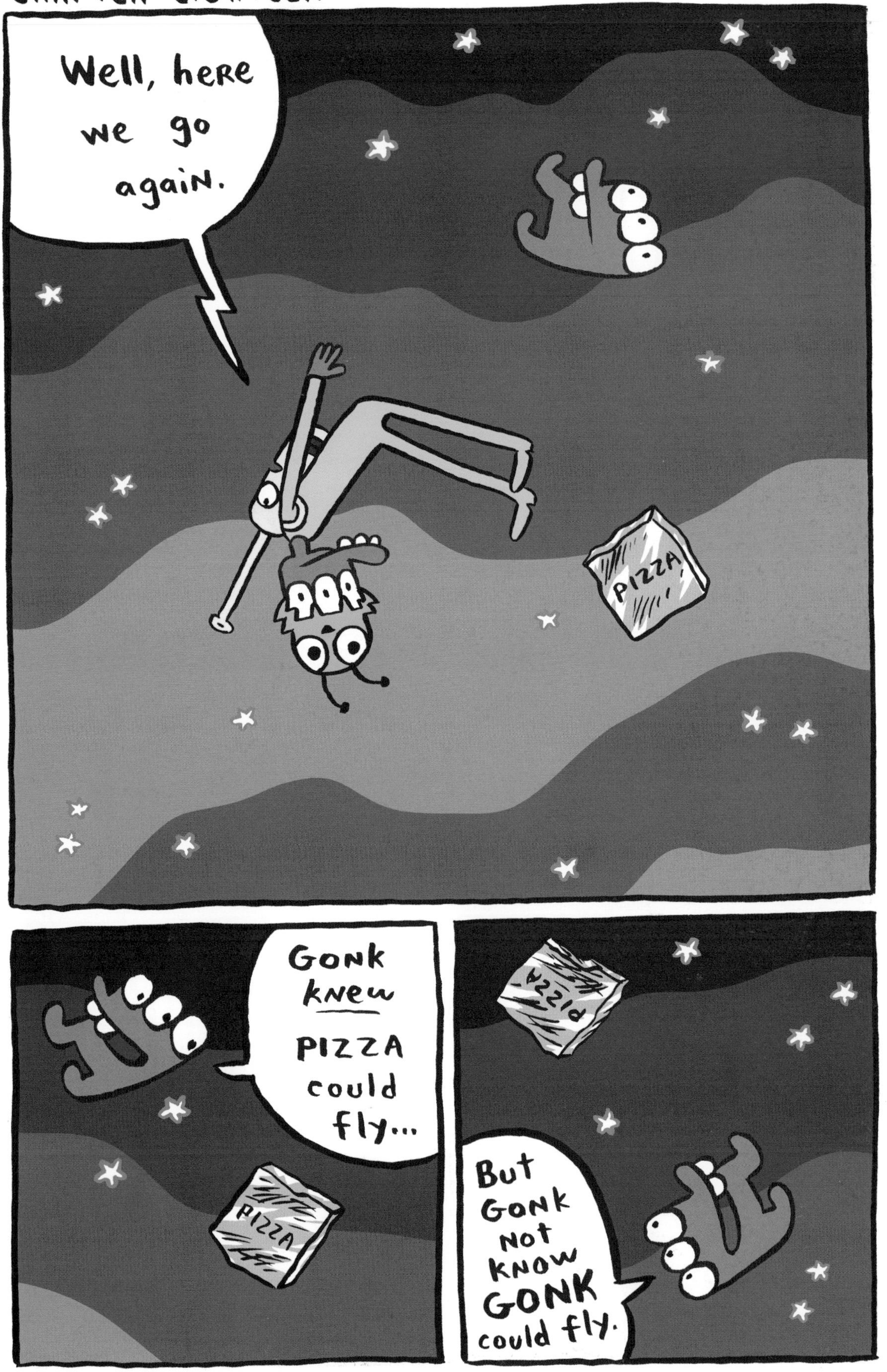
Well, here we go again.
PIZZA
Gonk knew PIZZA could fly...
PIZZA
PIZZA
But Gonk not know GONK could fly.

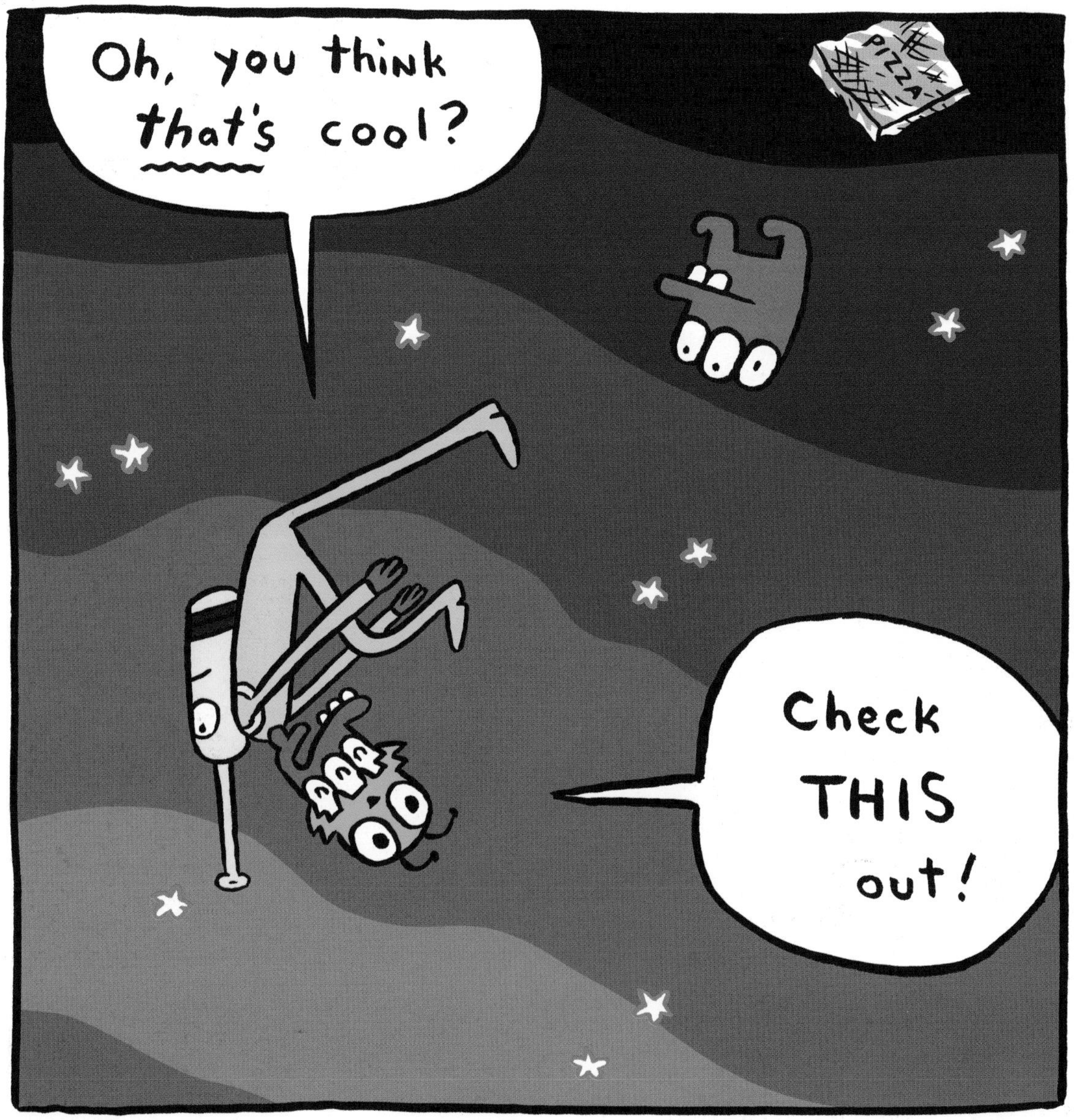
Oh, you think that's cool?
PIZZA
Check THIS out!

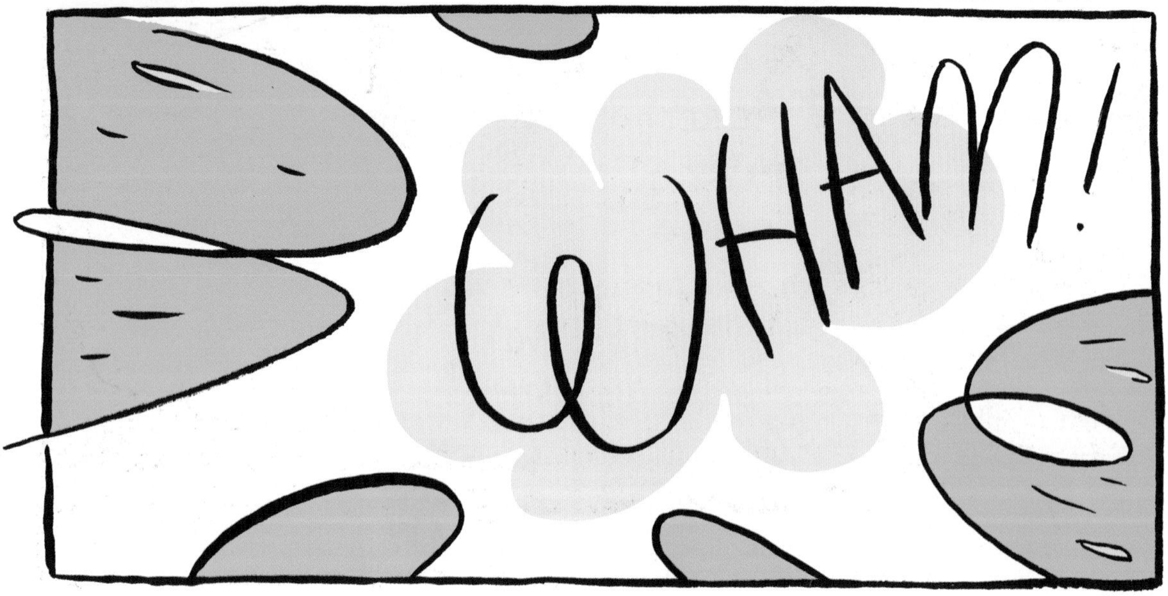
WHAM!

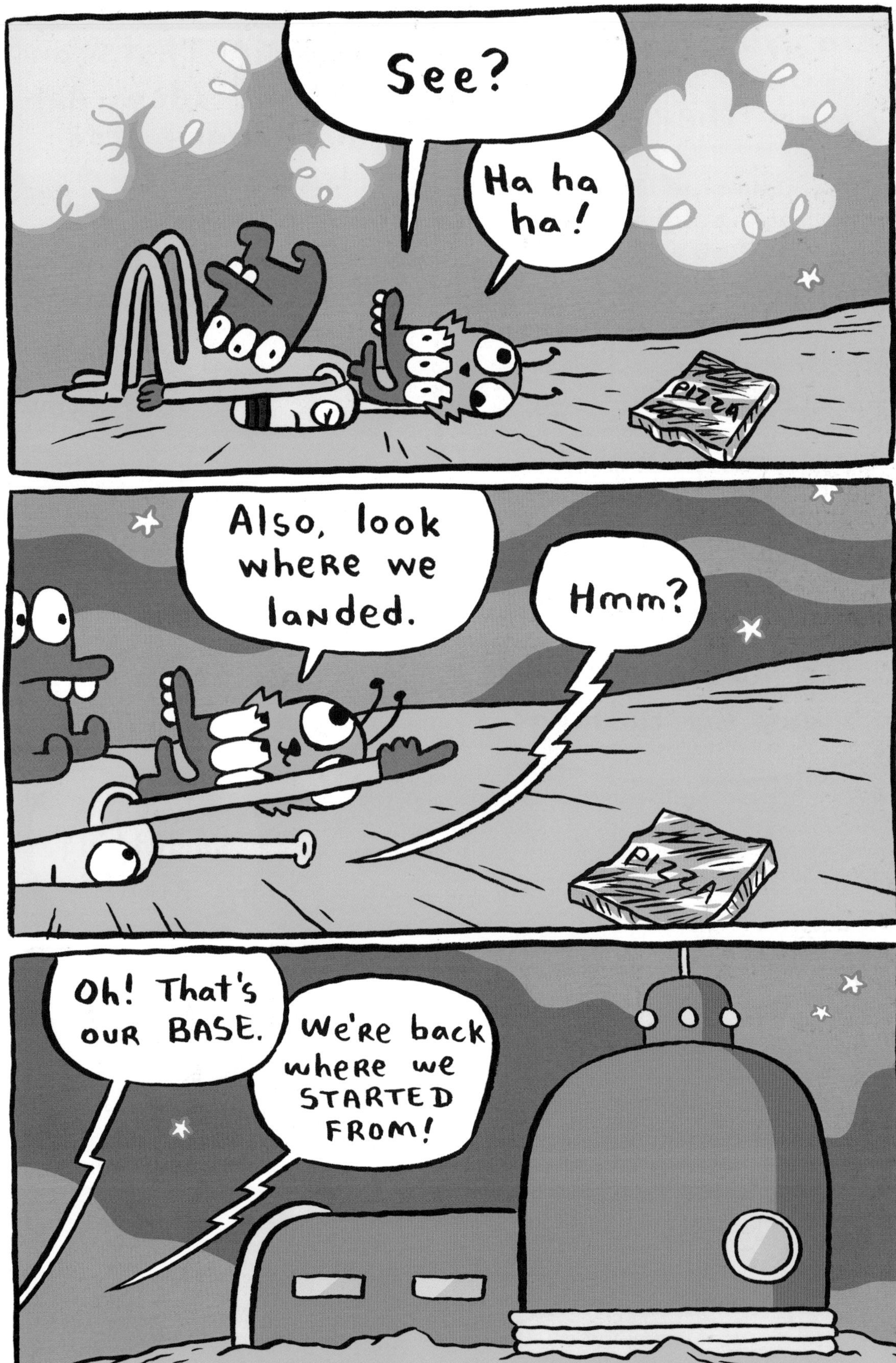
See?
Ha ha ha!
PIZZA
Also, look where we landed.
Hmm?
PIZZA
Oh! That's our BASE.
We're back where we STARTED FROM!

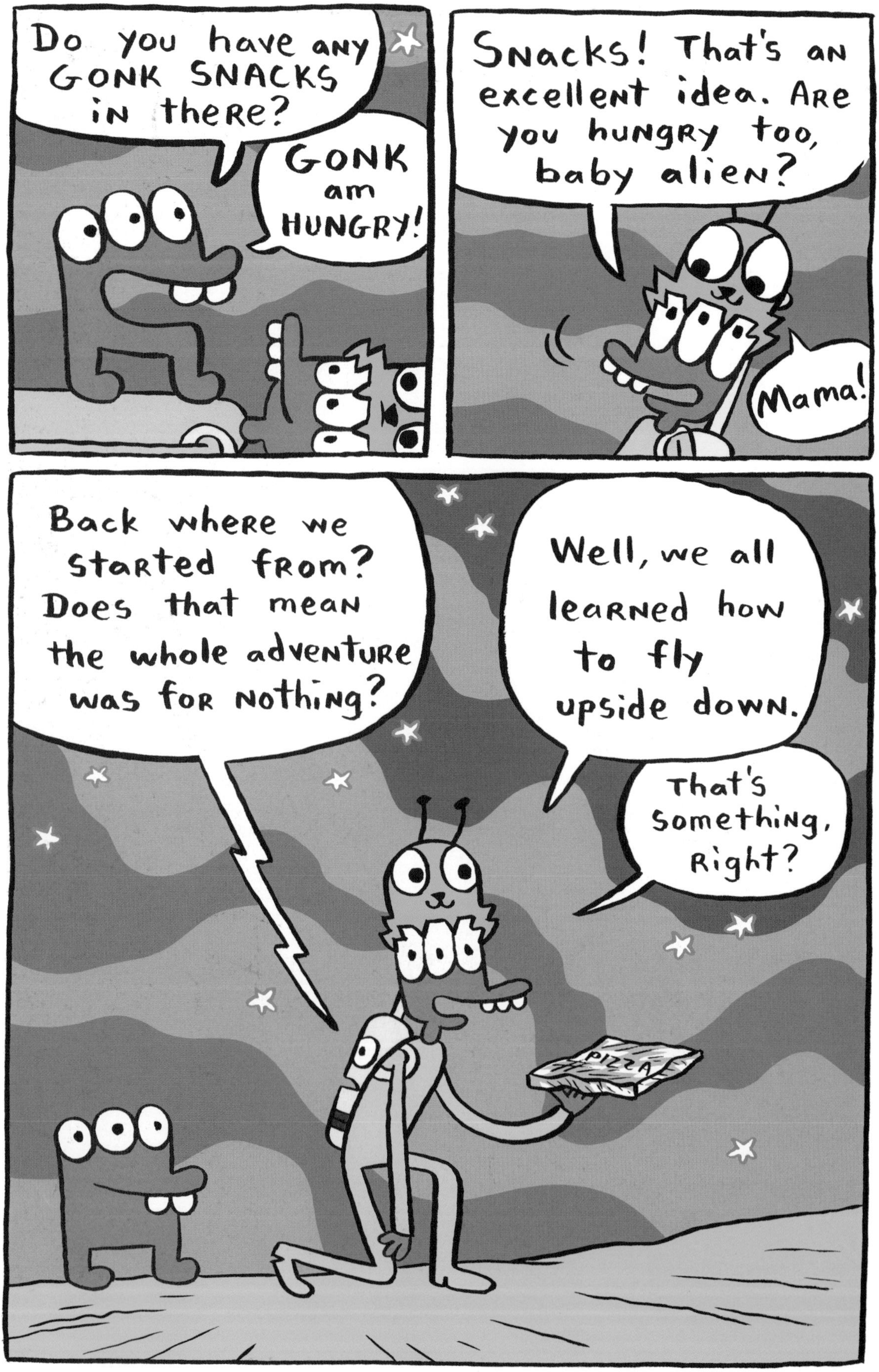

Do you have any GONK SNACKS in there?
GONK am HUNGRY!
SNACKS! That's an excellent idea. Are you hungry too, baby alien?
Mama!
Back where we started from? Does that mean the whole adventure was for nothing?
Well, we all learned how to fly upside down.
That's something, right?
PIZZA

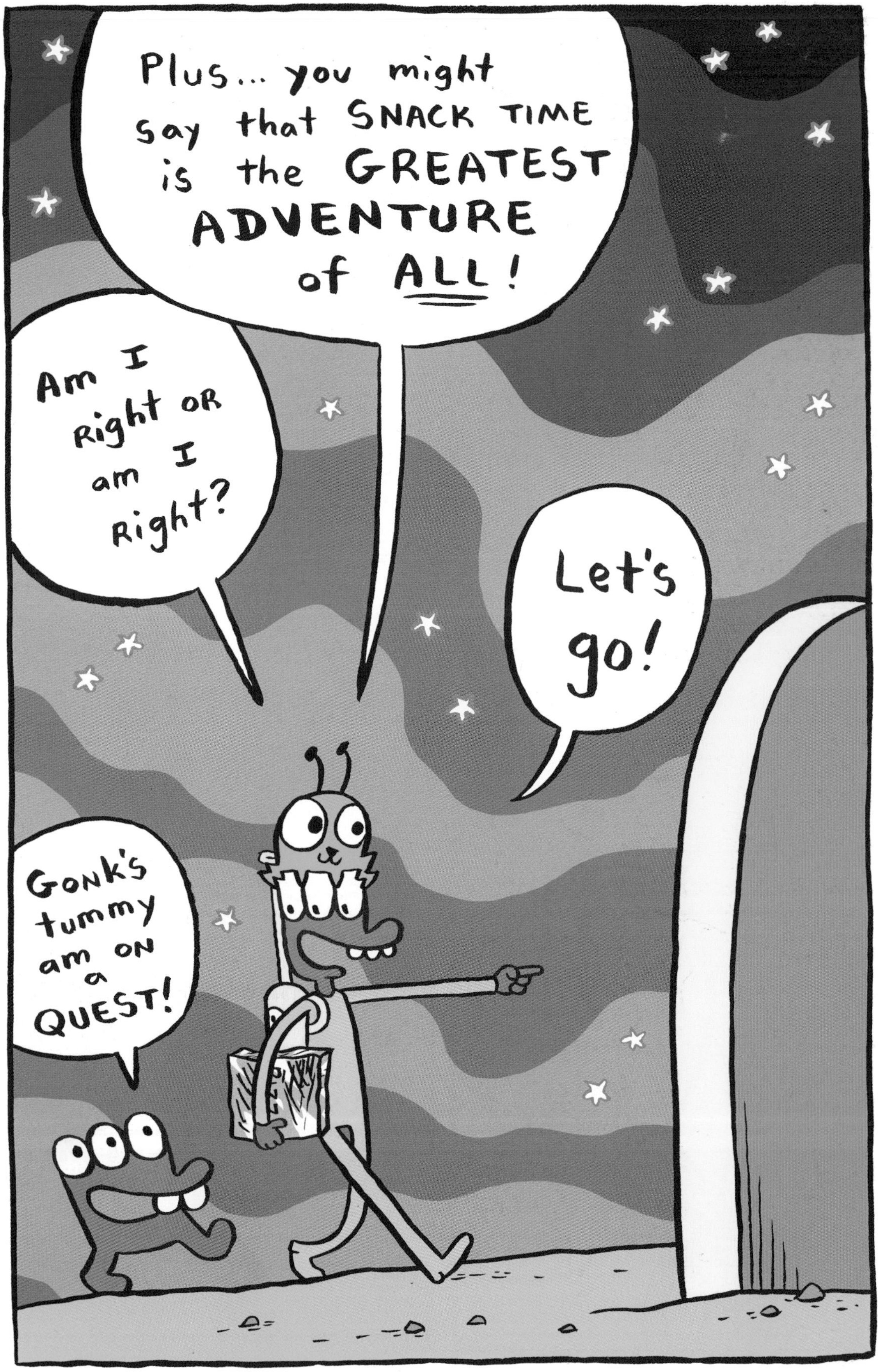
Plus... you might say that SNACK TIME is the GREATEST ADVENTURE of ALL!
Am I right OR am I right?
Let's go!
Gonk's tummy am ON a QUEST!

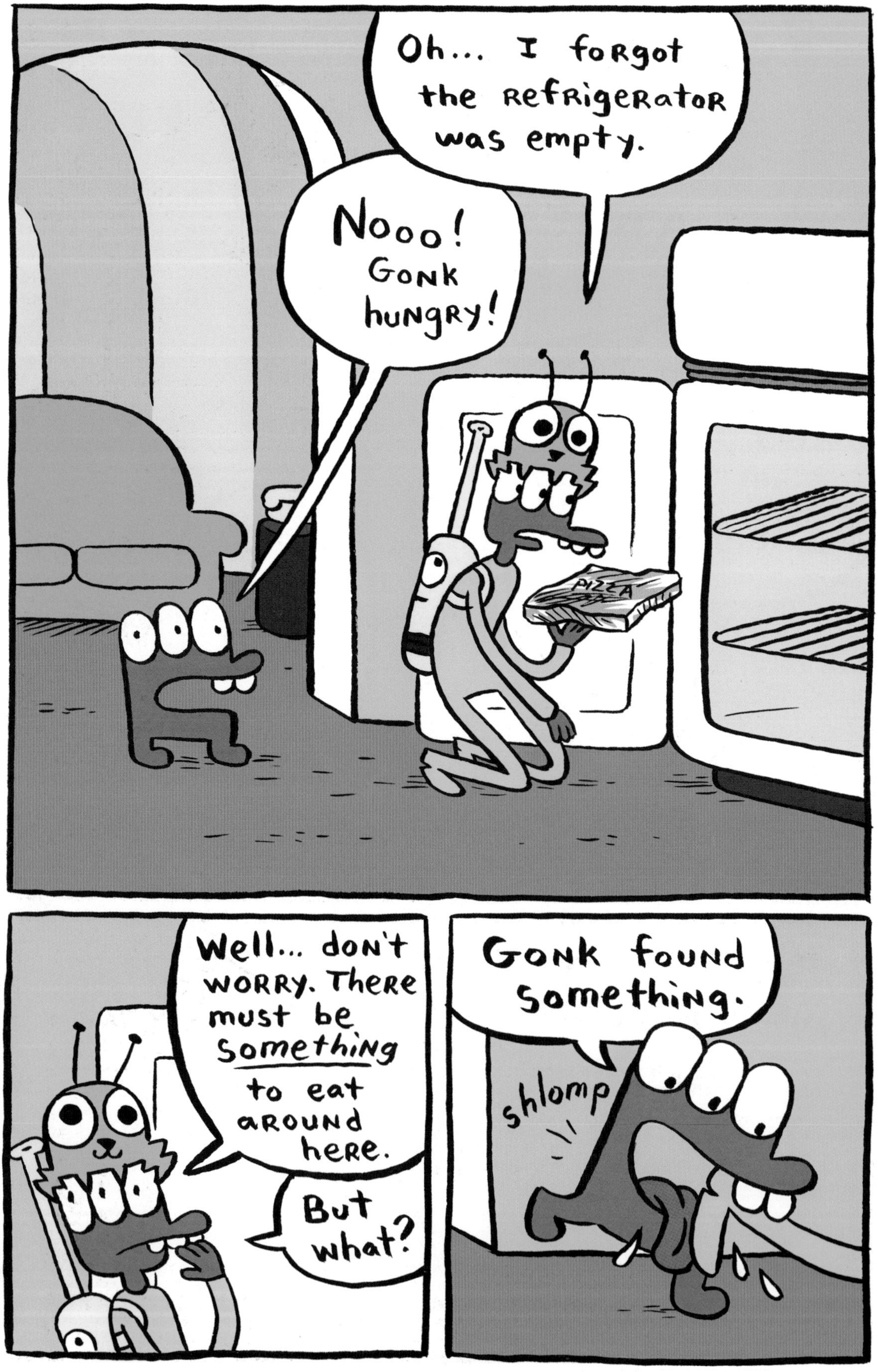
Oh... I forgot the refrigerator was empty.
Nooo! Gonk hungry!
PIZZA
Well... don't worry. There must be something to eat around here.
But what?
Gonk found something.
shlomp

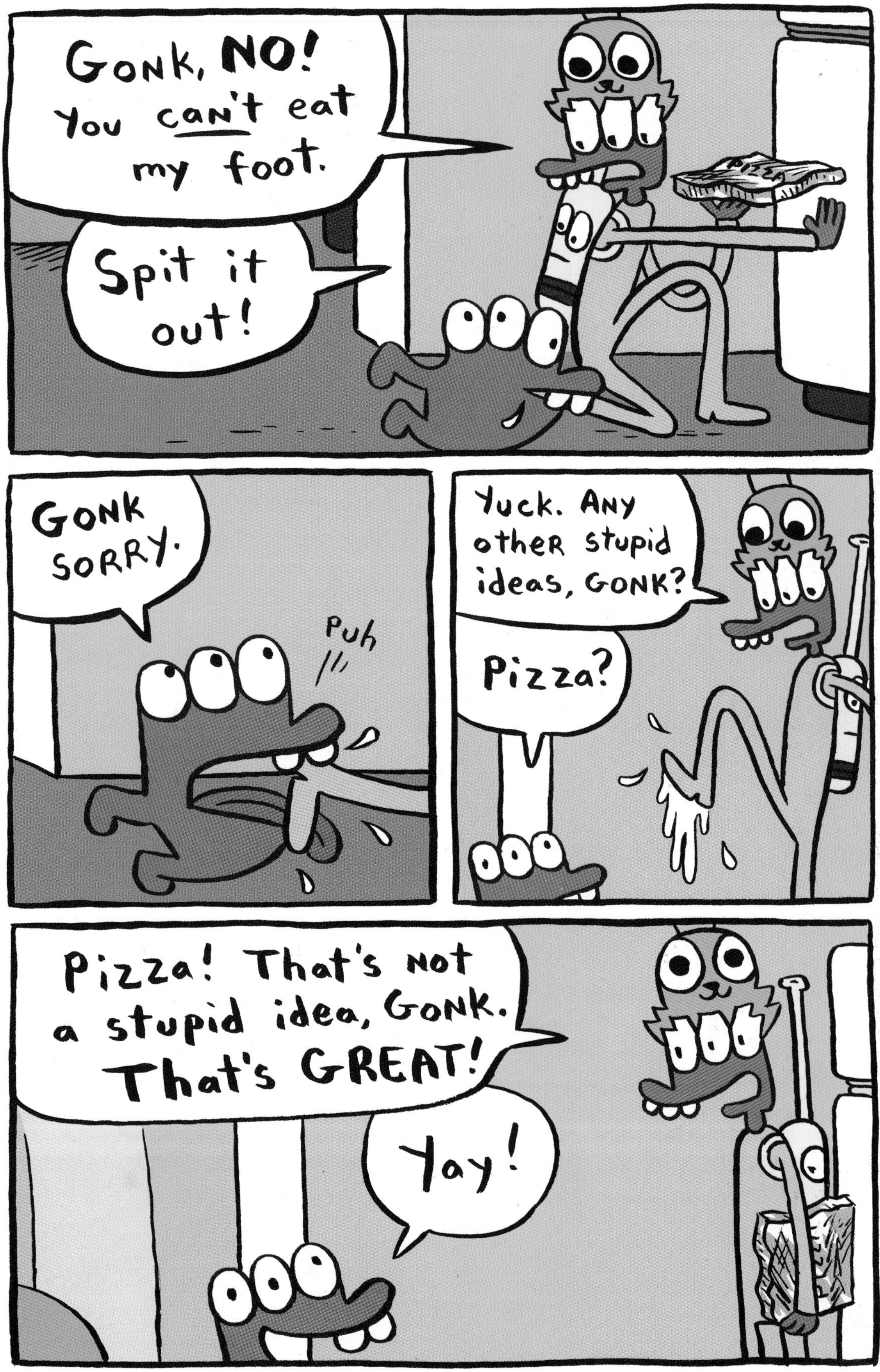

GONK, NO! You can't eat my foot.
Spit it out!
GONK SORRY.
Puh
Yuck. ANY other stupid ideas, GONK?
Pizza?
Pizza! That's not a stupid idea, GONK. That's GREAT!
Yay!

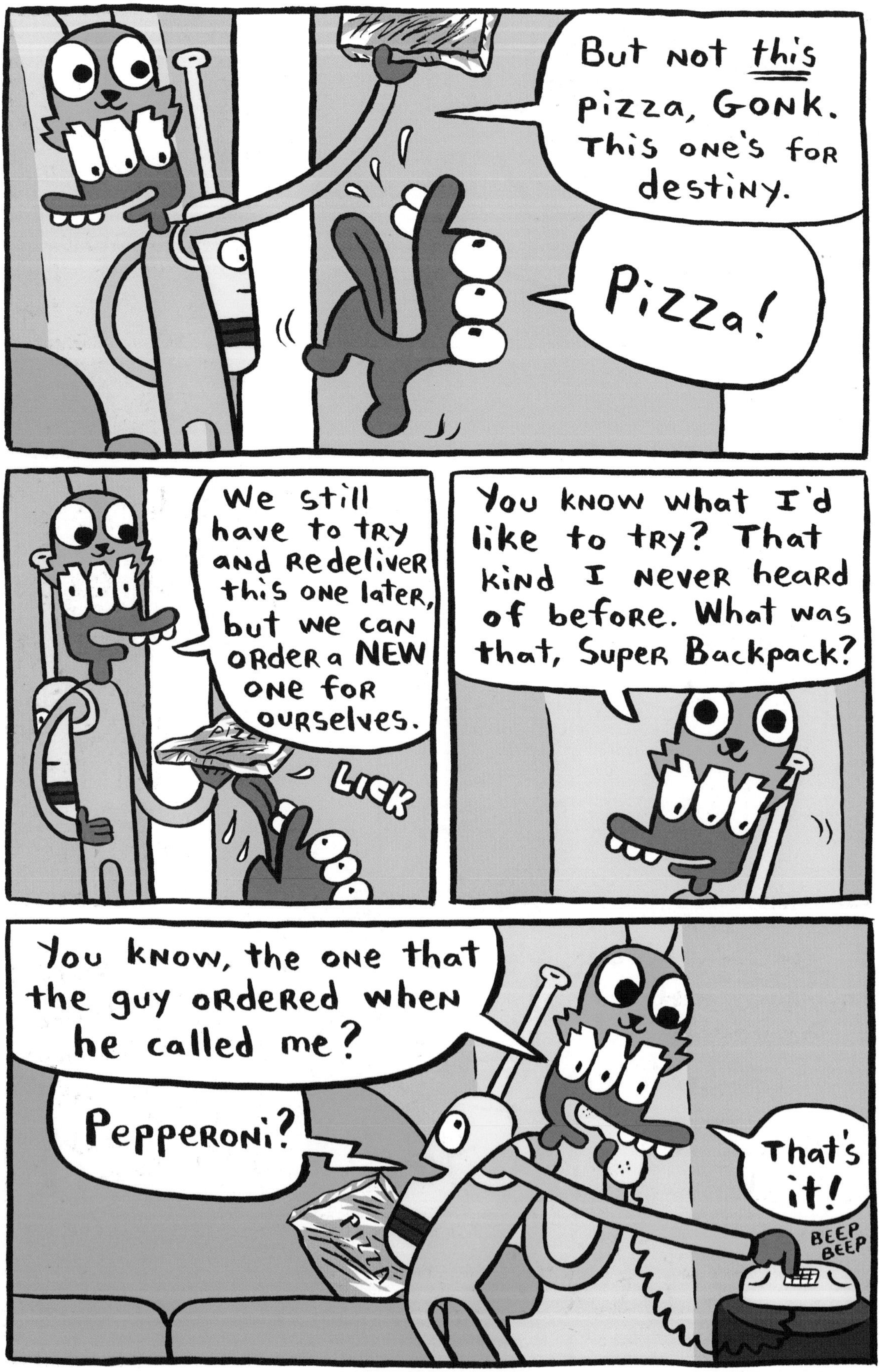

But not this pizza, GONK. This one's for destiny.
Pizza!
We still have to try and redeliver this one later, but we can order a NEW one for ourselves.
PIZZA
LICK
You know what I'd like to try? That kind I never heard of before. What was that, Super Backpack?
You know, the one that the guy ordered when he called me?
Pepperoni?
That's it!
PIZZA
BEEP BEEP

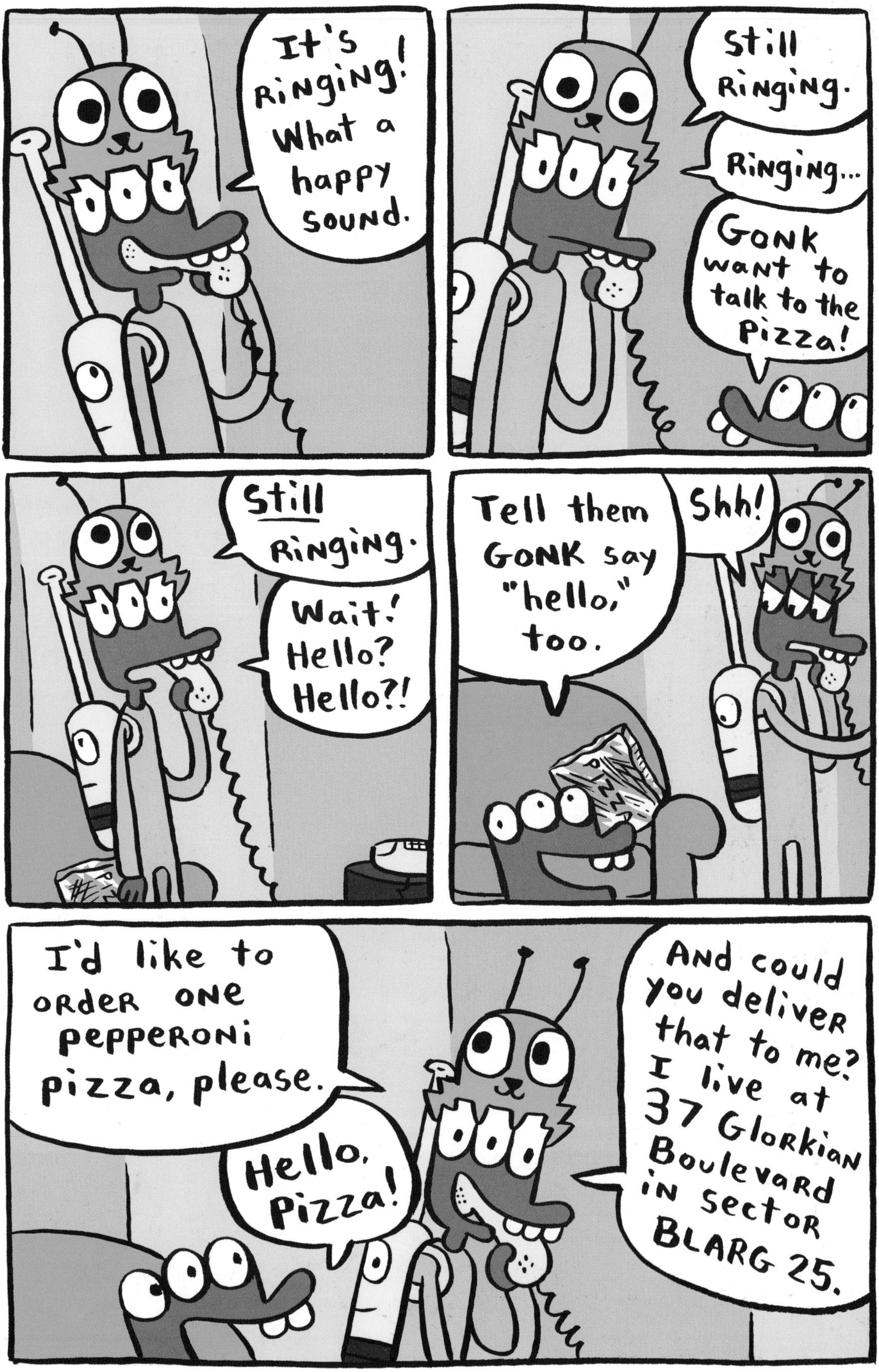

It's Ringing! What a happy sound.
Still Ringing.
Ringing...
GONK want to talk to the Pizza!
Still Ringing.
Wait! Hello? Hello?!
Tell them GONK say "hello," too.
Shh!
I'd like to order one pepperoni pizza, please.
Hello, Pizza!
AND could you deliver that to me? I live at 37 Glorkian Boulevard in Sector BLARG 25.

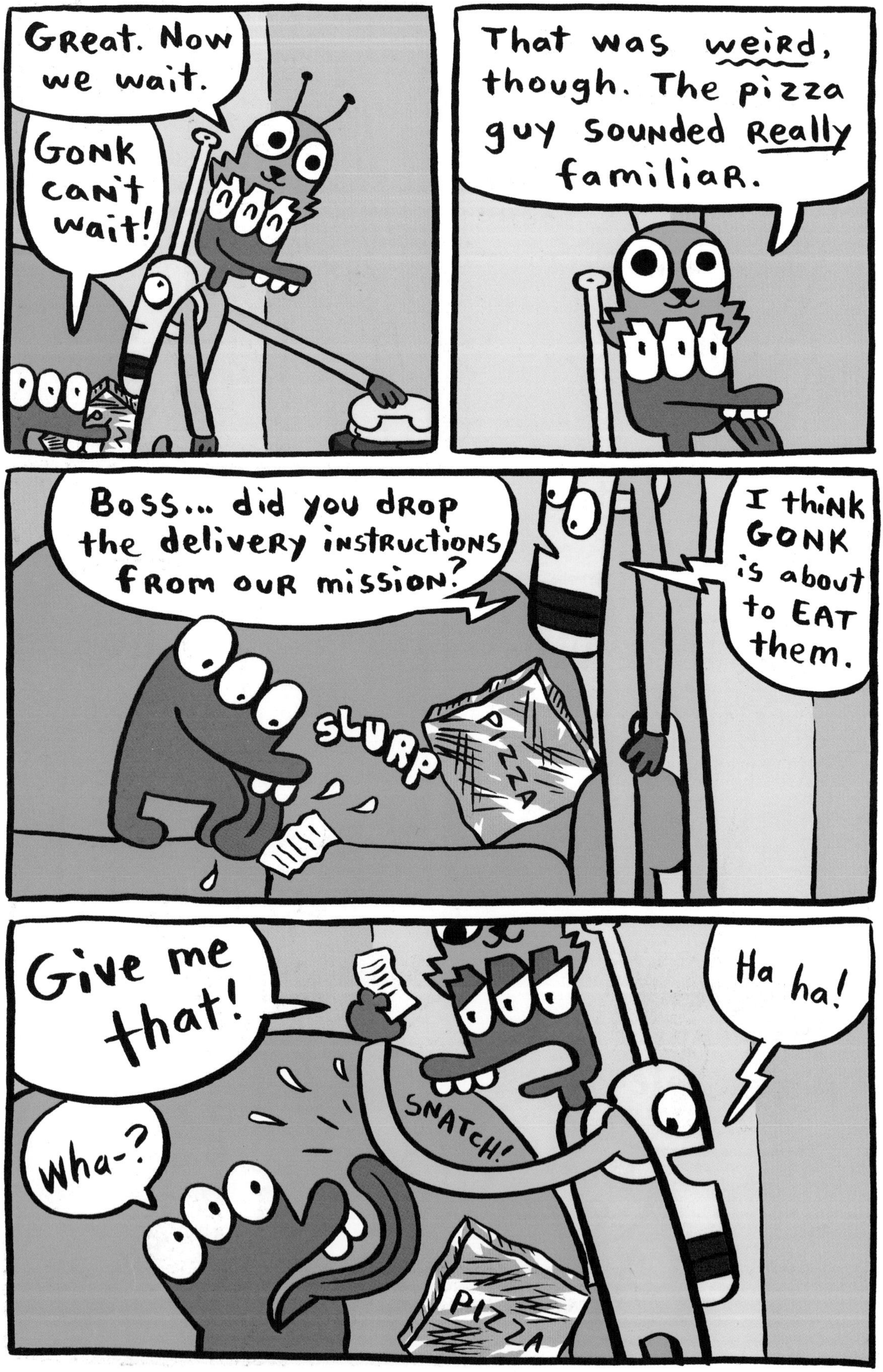

Great. Now we wait.
GONK can't wait!
That was weird, though. The pizza guy sounded Really familiar.
Boss... did you drop the delivery instructions from our mission?
I think GONK is about to EAT them.
SLURP
PIZZA
Give me that!
Ha ha!
Wha-?
SNATCH!
PIZZA

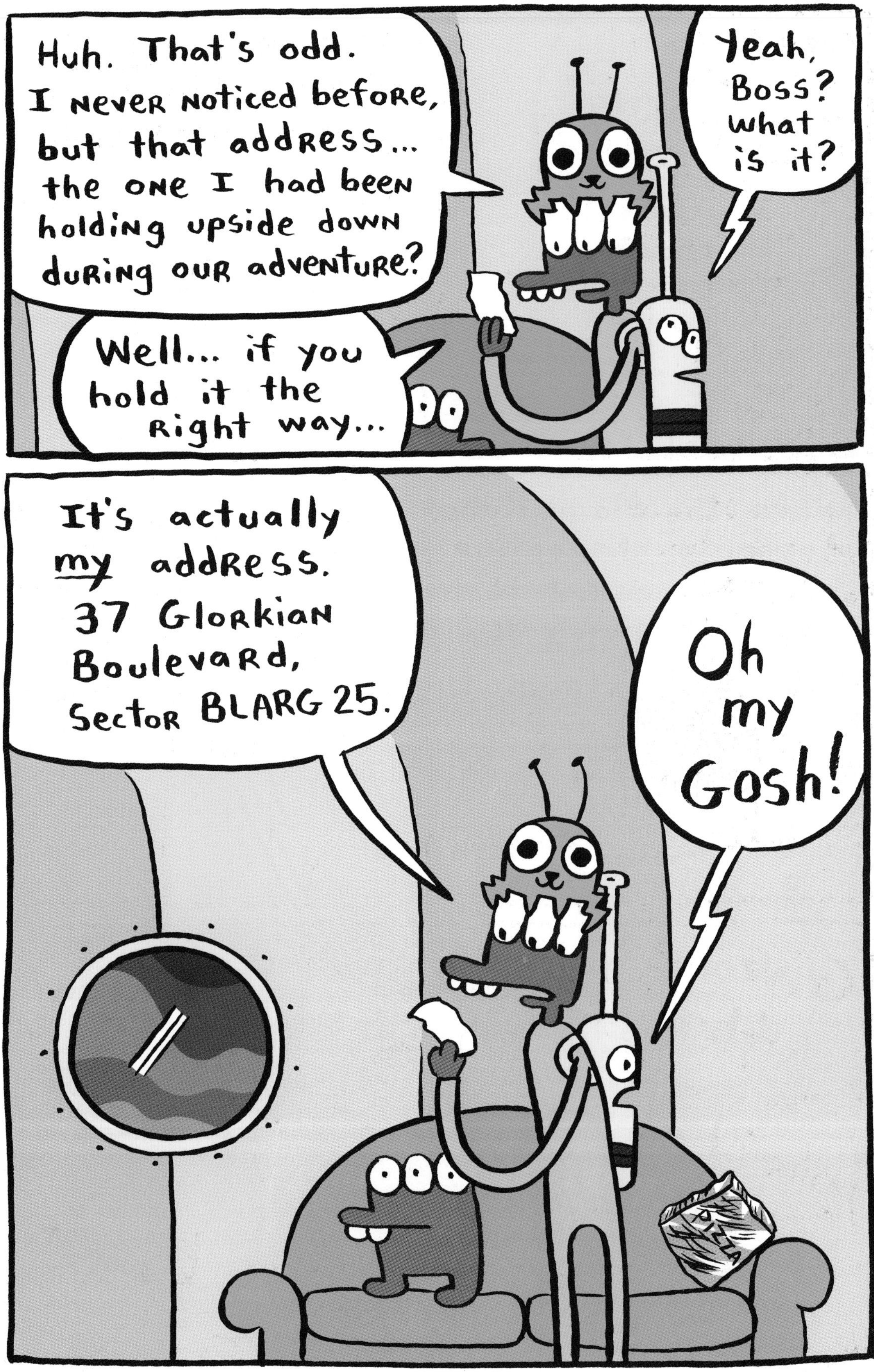
Huh. That's odd. I never noticed before, but that address... the one I had been holding upside down during our adventure?
Yeah, Boss? what is it?
Well... if you hold it the right way...
It's actually my address. 37 Glorkian Boulevard, Sector BLARG 25.
Oh my Gosh!

CHAPTER TWENTY:

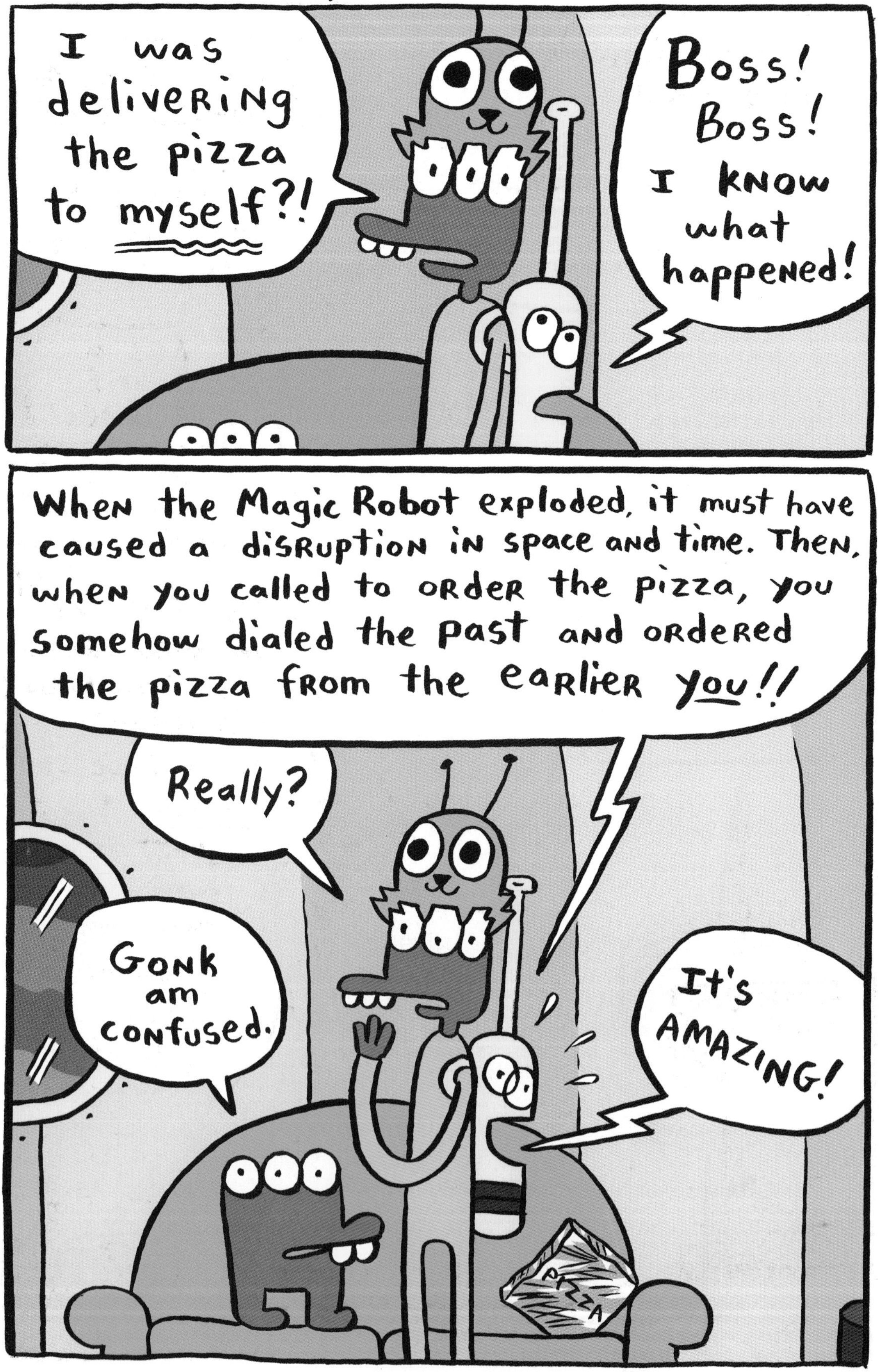
I was delivering the pizza to myself?!
Boss! Boss! I know what happened!
When the Magic Robot exploded, it must have caused a disruption in space and time. Then, when you called to order the pizza, you somehow dialed the past and ordered the pizza from the earlier you!!
Really?
Gonk am confused.
It's AMAZING!
PIZZA

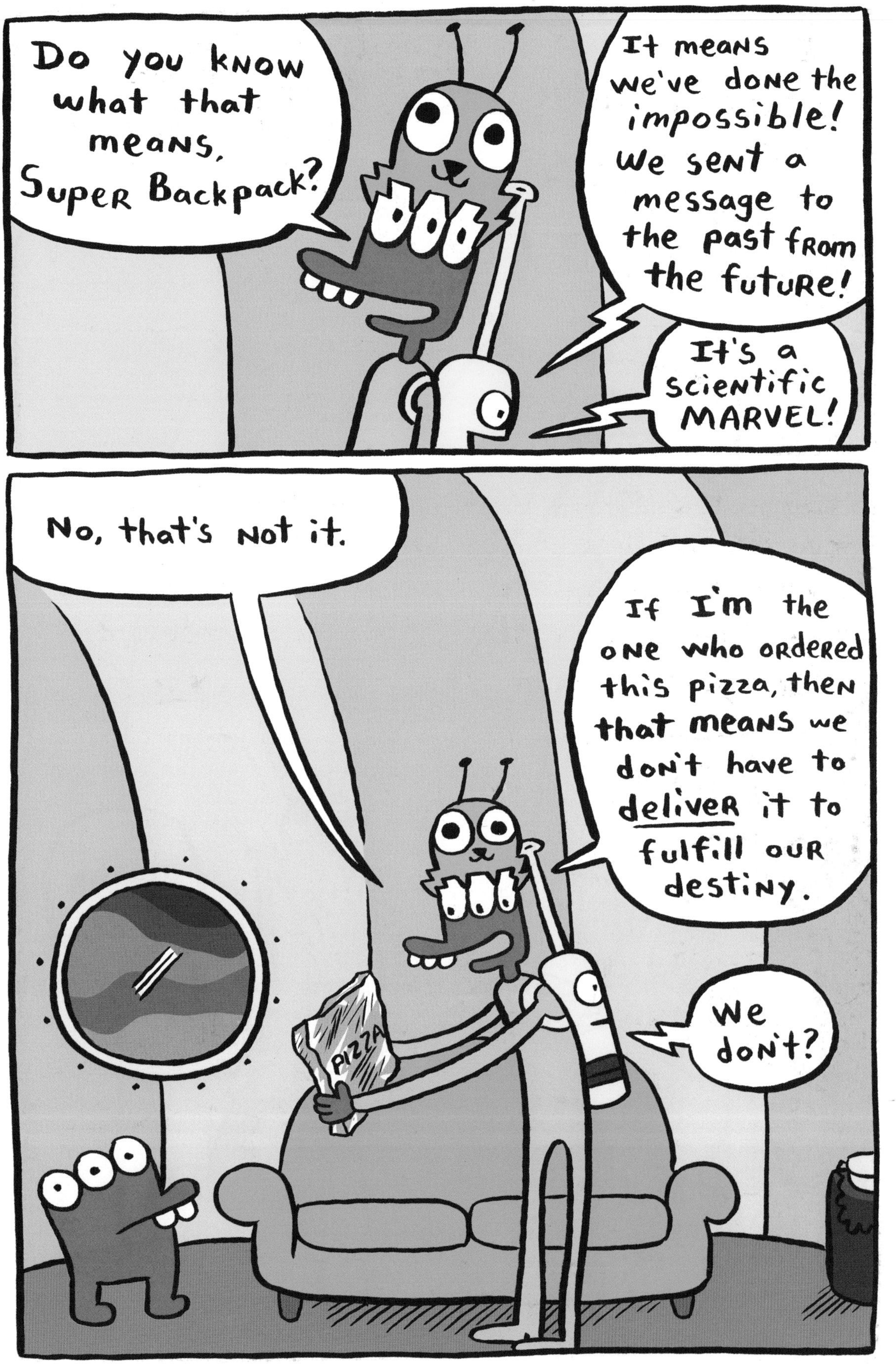
Do you know what that means, Super Backpack?
It means we've done the impossible! We sent a message to the past from the future!
It's a scientific MARVEL!
No, that's not it.
If I'm the one who ordered this pizza, then that means we don't have to deliver it to fulfill our destiny.
We don't?
PIZZA

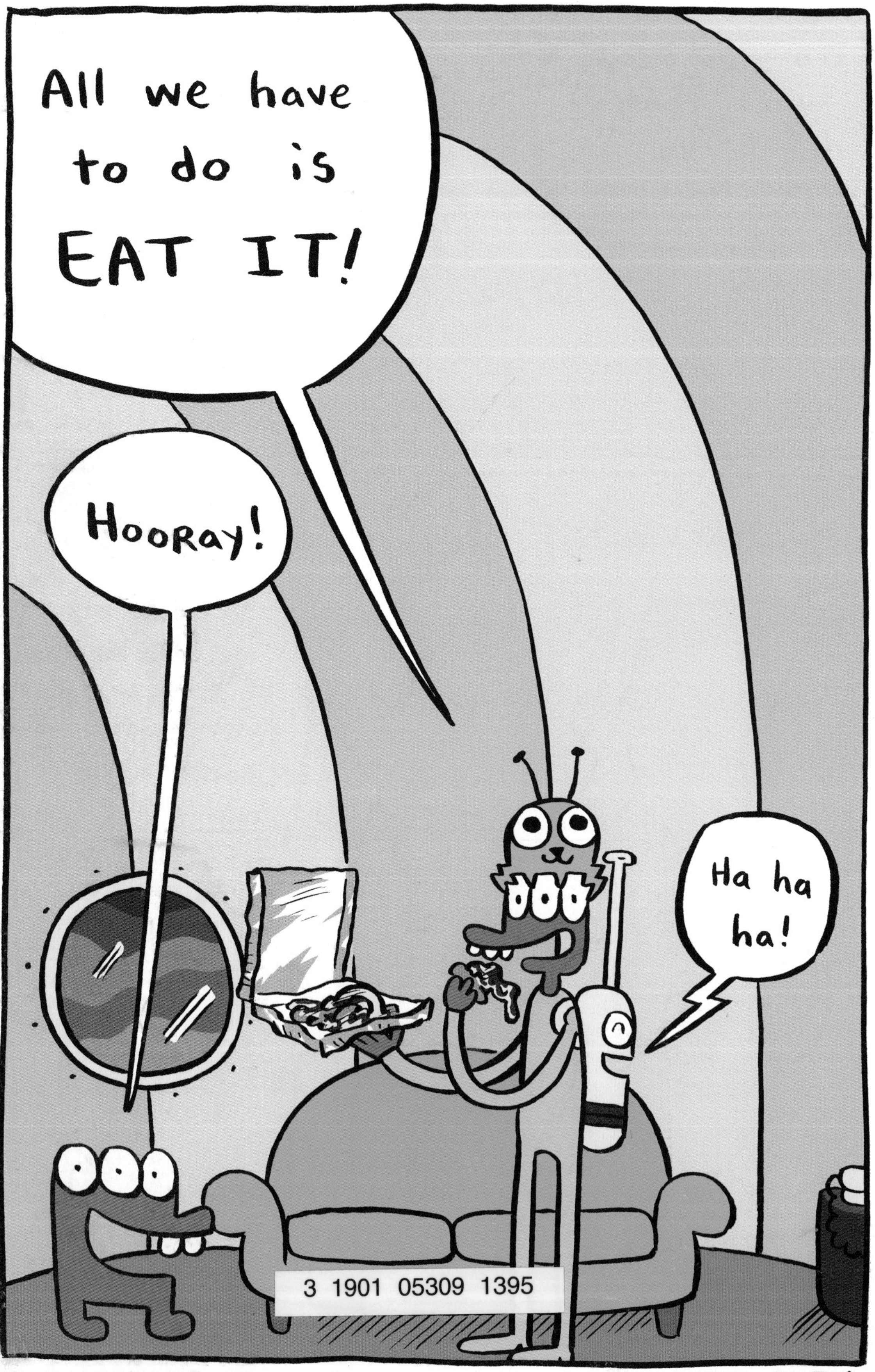
All we have to do is EAT IT!
Hooray!
Ha ha ha!

THE END!